I0746942

Alternative Energy II
Blow Me

By

Marc Gregory

Copyright © 2021 by Marc Gregory
First Edition - June 2021

ISBN
978-1-7776468-4-4 (Paperback)
978-1-7776468-5-1 (eBook)

All rights reserved.

The characters and events portrayed in this book are ficticious.
Any similarity to real persons, living or dead, is coincidental and not
intended by the author.

Published by:
Stand Publishing Inc.

www.facebook.com/mgregoryauth

Distributed to the trade by Ingram Book Company

Other books By Marc Gregory

Alternative Energy

Alternative Energy II - Blow Me

Price Per Barrel

Quantum Avidya

1

Where was I…?

I guess I dosed off. Too many beer, and too much having to dig way back in memory. Funny how the mind works. Such an incredible piece of my history that I thought would always just be there, everyday, as a constant reminder. Something that you would never-ever forget, now, all but forgotten.

I don't know if I want to do this anymore. Even as I try to lightly brush the thought, I get this shock of emotion. Like and electric fence… *stay away*.

But… I said I was going to tell you of the times from my past. This is definitely a time from my past. So, what the hell. Maybe I should go there? Maybe it will be good for me? Some type of emotional purging, or what's the fancy term… closure? Just give me a minute to crack a bottle of something stronger.

My sons, in my past lies one of the greatest love stories of all time.

But, before we get to that, I have to take you through this…

2

I jolted to partial consciousness.

Jesus Christ, it's hot! my parched brain screamed.

The atmosphere lay heavy on my body. My lungs heaved deeply, like the first breath of a newborn infant. My mind began to move—not too fast though. I'd been here before, and practised experience strongly advised I remain very still and search for the series of events that led to my current condition, so I'd know exactly what I was dealing with. Though my suspicions were strong.

My mouth was so dry and pasty and disgusting.

Why in the hell is it so fucking hot?

I really need some water… I'd kill for some water right now! Sonofabitch! Why do I do this to myself?

Everything attached to my stupidity hurt. Why I did what I always do seemed to be a question with no answer or ending. All I could do was muscle through it. I'd done it countless times before. They say perfection is achieved through practice… I'd mastered the art of the hangover, but being a genius gave me one hell of a headache.

At that point I customarily started jogging my memory, keeping it simple to start, name, birthday… But lately, after those two basics, any further recollection into where I was in my life no longer seemed to bring me any sanity.

Thoughts of my parents and home ran through my mind, of what I'd left behind to pursue special life achievements. Such as being broke and killing myself slowly with alcohol.

Of course I was mad. Who wouldn't be? The things that had happened back there were bullshit. I had every right to leave for a break. For those of you who wonder if I ever second-guessed my decision, my answer is, "every day." My self-doubt was undeniably a big factor in my excess indulgence.

I was a hero in my own mind. I'd spit in "The Man's" face. Held my middle finger up to the corporate world, then turned and walked away. Away to a beautiful Caribbean island. How many people are sitting in pubs around the world saying, "Fuck man, let's just do it. Get the hell out of here and start again on some tropical island."

Well, all you wonderers, I can tell you this: Islands get small really quick. Make sure to keep the booze stocked. Especially when your only real messages from home consist of sickening emails from your mother, describing how the banks and collection agencies are confiscating everything you'd worked for, and how truly disappointed she is in her son. Of course she'd never outright state it, but she leaves a lot of space between the lines.

It'd been just over a year to the day since I'd landed, which would put us at May-Juneish, and that's about as accurate as time gets when you're hiding out in the tropics. I'd mastered the sport of kiteboarding as much as I was interested in doing so. I'd ridden every bay and coast, in every condition the area offered. Then there's Aleida.

She's a great woman, don't get me wrong. The first few months were incredible. She's passionate like none I'd known before. But there's no man in this world who'll ever take first place away from those stinking, fucking turtles. Not in her heart.

I tried… I gave it an honest-to-God try. I even spent any money I had left to help fund some odds and ends for her. I replaced the tracking antennae.

I tried to settle into the supportive-man role. I was working odd jobs at various locations—taking care of equipment at the kite resort, bartending at various restaurants, and helping out with loading at the docks. There were less politics than in the oil industry, and less money. There was nothing for me to chew on there, to aspire to. So I joined in with my local friends and started drinking, usually about noon… usually.

Of course Aleida didn't approve of my behaviour, either, so that was us. She'd go do her thing in the morning, I'd go do mine. I'd stumble in the door sometime late in the night and we'd sleep with our backs to each other. The honeymoon had ended. I can't even tell you when, exactly.

That pretty much sums up how I ended up in my present predicament. But this hangover hurt a little extra; I must've really overachieved the previous night.

I knew what had to be done: I had to pull myself together enough to get my ass up and to the nearest source of freshwater ASAP, but I still hadn't found the courage to crack an eyelid. My head was pounding so fucking hard, and while my mind fought the battle on that front, it also had to hold the world from spinning out of control. In my head, a mob of angry protesters screamed for water while the powers-that-be in their suits and ties stood their ground, declaring that any form of movement right now would be a very bad idea.

Honestly, the only source of comfort I had at that moment was the bed. Gentle, rocking and sloshing, and the sound of... rushing... water?

Even without opening my eyes, I knew I'd never slept in that bed before, and I didn't know of any place nestled beside any sort of water feature that would emit a similar noise.

The previous night?... Ah yes. The pirates had come to town. We call them the pirates. Three guys I honestly didn't know much about.

There was the shaggy-haired blond Dutch boy, Adlar. And there was Dominic, a slender dark-haired, olive-skinned guy with some sort of Latin accent—maybe it had been told to me once, but for some reason I always placed him from Brazil. And finally, there was the one called Dong. I think that was a nickname, but I'm not a hundred percent sure on that. Dong was of Asian descent; Philippines I believe. He was about five feet tall, skinny as hell, had about three sporadically placed front teeth, and always wore a bandana.

There were some complications when we first met as I quickly defaulted to calling Dominic *Dom* for short, and, especially when all are pissed, *Dom* and *Dong* are way too similar. I struggled to convert to calling Dom *Nick*—problem solved.

They were all at some stage of their twenties, and their job was to deliver sailboats around the world. Picking them up in one location and delivering them to the next. I never even knew that was a job until I met them. Some of the nicest, most energetic guys I'd ever met. So full of life and always smiling. When these guys randomly showed up in the harbour, word would spread through privileged channles that the party was on, and myself and a group of locals would get together on their boat for a celebration. The previous night had only been my second encounter with them, but already we were good friends. I looked forward to their visits and the stories of their adventures.

That's where I'd been the previous night. Now, how had it ended? Drink, smoke some grass, laugh, party, more drink, more grass… How'd I get home? No, I wasn't home. It couldn't be home, none of the sensations were familiar…beyond the hangover.

The cobwebs were slowly clearing and it was time to make a move. My brain sent the signal down to twitch my finger; everything went off without a hitch. First move complete. I reached my hand straight up but didn't make it very far before I hit what felt very much like a canvas tarp. I pushed it up to have it gently resist and spring back.

I'd passed out in a sack? Slowly I cracked an eyelid. The room was filled with filtered, natural light. But it wasn't a traditional room; it was familiar as in I recognized what it was, but unfamiliar as in I'd never woken in it before.

As the pieces began to fall into place, concern began to grow. Some more dust cleared and instinct told me I should get my ass up and get this figured out. So, that's what I did. I pushed myself up fast and, forced to crawl around my containment, searched for an opening. Frantically pulling at ropes and knots and pushing at the tarp over me until finally I found a hole at its edge. I ripped it back and jumped to my feet, swaying and stumbling till I reached down and braced myself.

My lungs sucked in the fresh ocean breeze. The sun was bright and high in the sky. I blinked and rubbed at my eyes till I found focus. Something was really off.

I was in a rubber dinghy. A tender, I believe they're called. I did a slow three-sixty; there wasn't a sniff of land in sight, but off the front of my vessel was a rope that stretched about twenty feet to where it was tethered to a sailboat. A sailboat that could be the one I'd partied on the night before, though I'd never seen it from the back.

"Hey!" With my parched throat, my first attempt to call out was barely audible. I took a couple swallows and drummed up what saliva I could to grease the vocals.

"Hey! Hey, guys! You up there?" I scrambled to the front, grabbed the rope, and tried to pull myself toward the ship. "Hey! Guys! Nick! Dong! Adlar! *HEY*!"

I saw motion. It was Nick. As he noticed me, he hurried to the back of the boat, placing his hand over his eyes to block the sun.

"Hey! Who the…" He squinted. "Brando?"

Brandon actually; but the pirates called me *Brando*.

He started to wave and scream to his crewmates. "Hey, guys! Come fast, it Brando! Brando in our dinghy, here he is, quick, look!"

The other two rushed to join their friend, smiling and waving.

"Hey guys! Yeah, it's me! Can you pull me in? Please!"

Nick laughed and clapped. "Look at chu, motherfucker! Yes, we pull chu in!"

The guys pulled on the rope and I slowly inched forward. Saved, I took a seat and scanned the horizon again while the boys hauled me in. There really wasn't any land to be seen.

3

The guys greeted me with laughter as I reached the back of the boat.

Nick grabbed my hand and pulled me aboard. "Brando! My friend, look at chu!" His smile was as big as life could get. "You are here with us! Welcome to the ship my friend!"

I stepped past him and planted both feet on deck. Dong wrapped his arms around me in a tight embrace. "You motherfucker, ha! You come with us?" He raised his arms over his head, cheering. "It is good you come, now we are four pirates."

Adlar patted me on the back. "Yes, last night party fucking crazy Brando." He winked at me over his shoulder as he made his way back to man the wheel. He was ultimately the one in charge, but they all knew their roles and had much experience. "Fucking wasted you was man!" He laughed and shook his head.

"Come, our new comrade," Nick said. "Come, relax, like home."

"Uh, yeah… yeah. You have any water? I could really use some." I mussed my hair with both hands.

"Yes! Water! Of course we have thees. You must be thirsty, Brando, chu crazy motherfucker! Chu look like shit man!" He led me to a cooler by the helm, popped the top, and grabbed a cold bottle from the ice.

Everything else in life could just hold on for a second while I downed its contents in one session. "Ahhhhhhh." For once, the brain freeze was welcomed.

The guys all watched wide-eyed as I let the bottle drop empty from my lips.

"That's what I like 'bout this guy!" Dong said. "He do no fuck around with nothing, he just do it. Fuck ya Brando!"

The water was great, but health and sobriety were still a long way off. The sun was brutally hot, there wasn't a cloud to be seen, and the boat's motion wasn't helping. Best thing for me would be solid land, some water, and shade.

"Yeah, that was fucking crazy last night guys. I'm not going to bullshit you, I'm sick as fuck." I braced myself against the cabin wall. "So, when are we heading back?"

All three stopped what they were doing and looked at me.

"Go back? To go back where, Brando?" Adlar asked.

I wasn't sure why they were confused; I felt the answer should be pretty straightforward.

"Back to Bonaire," I clarified.

Adlar and Dong remained silent and looked to Nick.

Nick stepped before me. Then he placed his hands on my shoulders, looked me dead in the eye and smiled. "Brando, chu is my friend. Chu must to listen, okay? We can no go back to Bonaire. Is no possible."

The words he spoke rang true with everything that was happening around me. Boat under full sail, with not a speck of land anywhere. But things had changed now that they had found me on-board. Surely they knew they would have to turn around and take me back.

"Dom— I mean *Nick*. I can't go with you." I shook my head. "It's impossible for me to be going with you."

Keeping the smile on his face and his hands on my shoulders, he was quick to counter. "Brando, listen to what I say to chu. We sailing already, long time— five o'clock this morning. It is late, already past lunch. Is no possible to go back."

I looked at the sun with denial, but it honestly looked about right.

"Seven hours we go now. The wind and the... *agua*"—he made a paddling motion with his hand—"the... current, yes? The current is push us. We go long way. To turn, everything will be fight with us. Is no good my friend, it will make days for us. You know what I say chu?" He looked for confirmation.

Normally I'm a go-with-the-flow guy, pretty casual and laid back. But my hangover was super nasty and I just wasn't in the mood for that kind of shit. It had to be a bad dream, because... well, who in the fuck ever wakes up to that?

Doing my best to keep my cool, I raised my hands and shrugged. "So what,

Dom"—immediately Dong stopped swinging around the rope he was so fond of and looked at me—"I mean *Nick*... for fuck sake." I whispered, lowering my head for a minute to gather myself before looking back at him. "So what? I'm just supposed to, what?" I wiggled free from his grasp and began to pace the boat. "What! Huh? Guys? I got nothing, nothing with me at all. No wallet, no passport, nothing!" I reached in my pocket and produced what change I had, totalling about ten bucks. "Look! Here!" I held it up to them, my irritation growing. "This is what I got. How far will this get me? Huh?" I looked at them, and all were avoiding my questions; Nick was pacing his own line, head down with arms crossed and a hand stroking his chin.

"No one knows where I am. They sure as fuck would never suspect this! Guys, I know this situation sucks, and I really apologize for passing out on your boat. It was one hundred percent my fuck up. I get it, and I'm sorry. But we have to turn around, honestly." I'd given it to them straight and really felt like I'd gotten through. There was truly no other option.

"Brando, my friend, please," Nick said. "We must have the boat to this *hefe* on time. He has sell it to rich client. He very proud man, he do no want to be late. We lose our job, and what people thinking about us? I know chu do no like this. Is maybe very scared for chu now. But chu must know, we no going to turn around Brando. Is no happening. I am sorry."

So much for reasoning. It was completely absurd for me to listen to him talk about not turning the fucking boat around like it was a completely acceptable scenario. The only thing left for me to do was lose my mind.

"All right... All right." My pacing grew rabid. My head was pounding, but let's get crazy. "Well then, I'll take the little dinghy, right? How far out are we?"

"Brando, chu know chu can no do this," Nick said softly.

"Well, then, I'll just swim. How 'bout that, huh? I'll swim and I'll fucking die at sea and you guys can live with that shit on your conscience." I noticed some kiteboards tied to the side of the deck. "Or hey! You guys got some gear on here! I'll just do that!" I began untying one of the boards.

"Brando, chu be fucking crazy man. Please, chu must please stop this. Is no going to help nothing."

I leaned over the rail and shouted with all my might. "FUCK!... *FUCK!* There has to be... there has to be a boat heading back that way. We can contact it as it passes and then they can take me."

"Brando, please, is very possible we no see boat like this go to Bonaire Island. Is no very big, and is hard to contact ships we no know. Chu want how? Hmm? Send up smoke in the sky?"

"Well goddamnit Nick! What the fuck do you expect?" Exhausted, I took a seat on the cooler and buried my face in my hands.

Tentative on their approach, Dong and Nick sat cross-legged on the deck in front of me, twisting their heads to get a look at my face.

"Hey, Brando, man," Dong said. "You must chill man. Is nothing you do now. I know you mad, but look 'round. You on big beautiful sea man."

"Yes," Nick said. "We listen to chu all night. You drunk, but you speak from chu heart. The island is small chu say, is nothing new for chu. And the woman… Aleida? Chu say she no have passion with chu. She have passion only with turtle. This no normal in my country. For woman to have passion with turtle."

I laughed. It was really just a quick snort I then sucked back in. What they were saying was true. But true or not, there was no fucking way I should be on that boat.

"Yes, is right," Dong continued. "I know this story of her now, maybe she like one of these turtle guys? You know, the fight turtle from TV?" He laughed and slapped Nick, who burst out laughing with him.

Watching them roll on the deck lifted my spirits a bit, and lifting my spirits in that situation was not an easy feat.

I stood and turned to lean on the railing. It was bullshit. I looked back in the direction I guessed to be Bonaire. I kept trying to track the distance we travelled every minute the boat remained under sail, away from what had become my home for the last year.

What was happening was fucking ridiculous, but it was happening, and the fact I had no control to change it troubled me. The phrase *Going where the wind blows* came to my mind. I was literally doing that.

4

Words ceased as everyone took a moment to themselves. I listened to the wind stretching the sails, the soft creak of rope on wood, and the sloshing of the wake washing the hull. I needed time to accept the situation.

Only the unknown lay ahead. In my current state, I wasn't sure my mind could be trusted.

I was a poor example of a human. What I wanted was a warm shower, a clean towel, an endless supply of water, and the touch of my lover. I wanted home. Or the closest thing I'd known to it for some time.

What I had was dirty, stinkin' clothes. No toothbrush. That gritty, itchy feeling of sand and salt abrading my skin. The sensation a person gets when they pass out in a dinghy in the tropics. The reflection on the water was blinding, the sky spotless. I could feel my skin parching.

Just turn the fucking boat around.

It was a tough one for me to swallow.

I had a feeling they were waiting for me to ask the question, but I was stalling. I really didn't ever want to know. Somehow, I thought there was a chance they'd take pity on me and turn the boat around. How could they honestly not? It was the simple hope of a desperate man. But with every second I waited, the water rushed by, the same as it had the second before, and the farther we sailed away.

Leaning back against the cabin, I turned my head toward the front—or maybe it was the bow?—of the boat, toward the others. The attention flustered them; they lowered their heads and busied themselves. Reminding me of small fish in an aquarium that just noticed they'd been discovered.

I admit, I knew little about sailing, beyond a kiteboard. But I had a enough mental capability to figure out we were heading west. And the only thing west of Bonaire was the other side of the Atlantic.

I looked at Adlar, who was leaning casually on the wheel and whistling a soft tune I didn't know, as he gazed at the horizon.

My first shot at the question was inaudible because my throat was still scorched. I piled a ball of solidified saliva and choked it down for attempt number two.

"Where are we going?"

Adlar flinched, then looked over at me. His squint exaggerated, till he raised his hand to shield his eyes and pretended to finally see me.

"Brando, my friend. How is you?" He smiled ignorance.

I cleared my throat and repeated my question louder. "Where are we going?" I was doing my best to keep my tone non-threatening. It was just simple curiosity. I didn't even really care.

"Oh!" He nodded with a big ol' bullshit smile and pointed awkwardly to the front. "We going there… West."

I kept my eyes trained on him as my posture slumped. His mindless, smiling expression never wavered. Maybe it wasn't a façade?

"Yeah, I know we're heading west, Adlar. But where west? What's west, Adlar? How far west?... Where are we going, Adlar?" With the last question, I will admit, I was beginning to lose it a little.

"Amstertam." His mouth straightened and his jaw clenched. "We go to Amstertam."

Quietly, I accepted his answer and asked no more. I turned my head away from him— *Fuck me.*

My brain swelled, my breath laboured. Now I knew. Now there was something, a purpose, a destination. Shit just got real, Amsterdam was a really long way from any home I'd had… at least I was pretty sure it was. Geography was never a strength of mine.

Going to Amsterdam. No passport, no toothbrush, no fucking underwear.

The world blurred and my knees weakened as the bigness of it all began to sink in. Like concerns beyond a change of clothes and physical hygiene. Like my

Aleida back on the island. I missed her more than ever. And like my parents, my bed… my home. I was also about to cross the Atlantic ocean on a sailboat manned by three guys I'd met only twice before. Both times in a drunken stupor. There would be wind, waves, storms, triangles, and krakens as we drifted on fifty million leagues of certain death. Amsterdam, a place full of legal drugs, red lights, and… clocks?

The lack of solid support beneath my feet began to affect my mental being, chaos ringing in my head. I bowed forward, placing my hands on my knees and looking straight down at the deck. Bile formed in my dry mouth, trickling streams through the desert that precede the storm.

I can't…

My insides heaved and my body teetered, then tottered with the roll of the ship.

I can't fucking do this!

I stumbled to the railing, hung my torso over the side, and puked out all the filthy shit that had gotten me there. I blew chunks so hard it was like a complete exorcism of the devil from my soul. And I'm fine admitting to it because it was a situation that deserved such a salute. I give credit where due. Yes, I've been to sea Billy.

Dong and Nick rushed to my side, grabbing at me to make sure I didn't fall in. Dong doubled back to grab a bottle of water and then returned, patting my back and consoling me.

"Oh man, Brando. Is fucking disgusting, man!" The two men turned back around and pinched their noses. "I do no know what all is this, but you do no want it in chu. So is good, man."

When I'd finished, they rolled me onto the deck, where I sat with my back to the railing and my arms draped over my knees. Choking and gasping, I looked at Adlar. "I have to get a message to someone, somehow!" I pulled at the railing and the other two helped me to my feet. I walked toward Adlar, who looked absolutely repulsed at the sight of me. "I have to get a hold of someone, somehow! You have to have some way to get in contact with people on land. I have to get in touch with my parents or Aleida! Or the whole Canadian army will be out looking for me!"

Nick chimed in from behind. "Canada? It has army? I think only American has army?"

I turned back with a scowl. "Well, the Canadian army and the American army are very good friends, and I'm sure they'd be helping out!"

Focusing back on Adlar, I composed myself as well as possible. "Listen! I'm accepting the fact that I'm crossing the Atlantic with you guys. I'm not going to fight it anymore. But you have to let me get in contact with someone."

I watched his eyes turn from mine to the others'. Then he nodded.

"Yes, Brando, we have phone for satellite." He pointed to the sky. "Only to use for emergency. Our boss say it expensive and he not like when we use it. But we will let you. Please only one call and not too much." He waited for my assurance.

I nodded back and he reached into a cubby beneath the bench behind him.

I snatched the phone and made the call.

"Hello?"

A tear trickled from my eye at the sudden onslaught of emotion. It had been such a long time since I'd heard his voice, the voice of stability. Most of our correspondence had been through email. Any verbal chatter had been mostly with my mother. But there was no fucking way I could talk to her.

"Hey, Dad, how's it going?"

"Brandon? Hey buddy! How's it going with you? What a surprise. It's great to hear your voice."

"Yeah, it's really good to hear you too." I quickly wiped at the tear.

"You all right, son? Where are you? Sounds windy."

"Oh! Sorry." I reached up and cupped the receiver with my hand. "Is that better?"

"Yeah, it's fine. You all right, kiddo?"

"Yeah, I'm fine. Really good, actually." I sprinkled on some cheer. "I'm on a boat with some friends. We're, uh, going… on a trip."

"Oh! Well, that sounds great son." He laughed. "Where you guys taking off to now?"

I didn't want to tell him. How do you tell your father something like this? "We're going to, to Europe, actually. To Amsterdam." I slurred the last part.

"You're… Did you say you're sailing to Amsterdam?" The laughter faded. "That sounds like a long trip Brandon. That's across the Atlantic. You guys know what you're doing?"

"Yeah, of course. These guys do it all the time. It was just kind of an impulse thing. They were passing through and offered. I couldn't turn it down, right? Sail across the Atlantic, see Europe. Not too many people get that chance."

"Sure, I… I guess so."

"So, could you please let Mom know? You know how she is with these things. I can't call you again till I get there. We have a satellite phone for emergencies, but it's a good time to sail here, so everything'll be fine. I'll call you as soon as we get there."

"Okay, okay, as long as you're sure you're all right. How long is it going take for you to get there?"

Shit! I winced. I had no clue. Three or four days at least, I reckoned. I turned to the guys. "Oh, how long?" I raised my voice and motioned for help. "Well, you know…" I watched Nick mouth the words, with gestures. Frustrated after two seconds, I waved it off and made a writing motion in the air.

He managed to find a marker in a cubby and wrote it on his hand.

30 DEYS

My eyes questioned, *Are you fucking kidding me?*

"Brandon," I heard my dad say.

"Yeah, it's going to be three… ty." I cleared my throat. "Thirty, thirty days."

Nick tapped me hard on the shoulder. He was tilting his hand from side to side in a "give or take" motion.

"Thirty days, Brandon! Are you sure you guys are all right?"

"Yes. Yes, Dad, we're great." I injected some enthusiasm. "I'm really excited." I had to put his mind at peace, as much as one could in this situation. "I'm learning how to sail my own ship! These guys are great! I'm going to see Europe!"

"Sure. Sounds like it's going to be quite the adventure for you. As long as you're happy and safe. I'm excited for you. I'm not excited to explain this to your mother though. Thanks for that." It was good to hear his sarcastic humour again.

"I know. Thanks Dad, I gotta get going though. This is an expensive call. When you get a chance, can you send an email to Aleida and let her know too?"

"Do wha'?.. Aleida doesn't know about th—"

"I gotta go Dad. I love you! I'll call you as soon as I get there. Miss you!"

I hung up, set the phone on the bench and then turned back to the guys somewhat slowly and dramatically. "Thirty fucking days! Thirty fucking days and you can't take one fucking day to sail me back!"

"No, Brando," Dong said. "Our boss, he no nice if we is late. It take more time if weather no good. We can no take you back."

I turned and paced across the deck. I passed the wheel, then kicked an empty plastic bucket, sending it spinning over the side and into the great blue. "*FUCK!*"

I remained with my back to them. Hands on my hips, I bowed my head and took a few deep breaths. Then I looked up and faced my reality. I didn't like this. I wasn't excited about any of it. There wasn't a sniff of land anywhere and I suspected there wouldn't be any time soon. The best thing for me to do was…

I turned back to the boys and clapped my hands. "All right! What do I gotta do? Let's get this fucking mess across the ocean."

5

I stood straight and proud, using body language to declare that I was going to take no shit from anyone. I just wanted something to do to aide our progress. Pull a rope, steer a wheel, swab the deck, or give me a fucking paddle.

But we were up and going and apparently that was about as far as we could push it. We were at the mercy of the wind and the sea.

My spirit slumped, but it was going to be what it was, so I looked for a place where I could lock the door and pass out. The boat was decent. Not too old from what I knew, which was nothing, really. It was wooden, painted white, the cabin stuck up about waist high in the centre with windows lining the perimeter. Two big sails arched high overhead. Seemed a good size, I'd guess sixty feet.

I went down below. The cabin was more spacious than I'd ever pictured on a sailboat. A healthy-sized kitchen to the right and a living space to the left, along with a large table and a wraparound bench. A television was mounted to the wall beside the booth; I couldn't imagine what channels were available in the middle of nowhere. I continued through to a narrow hallway. Off to the first left was the bathroom. It was the average size in a camping trailer back home. Past that there was a room to the right, with two single beds on either side. Both were piled with someone's gear. To the left was another room, with a double bed and a small nightstand crammed in. At the end of the hall was what I would call the master suite. The bed was an odd shape, fitting into the front peak of the hull. It was spacious, with lots of storage and a small half bath ensuite. From the mess in all the rooms, I guessed they were all spoken for. Remember how I was complaining earlier about how small the island had become? I'd just downgraded. All I really wanted was some space to be alone in for a while. I wouldn't get that here, and I didn't know what would become of me when we landed. I might not have my own space for a very long time. For a young man who grew up in a country where everyone could have their own five square miles, that was a big deal.

Maybe it's time? Maybe this is it.

If I survived this crazy fucking ride, then maybe it was time to go home. Throw in the towel. Aleida and I were over. She'd never want to speak to me again, so that was dealt with, as shitty as it was.

I thought of my old bedroom at Dad's. The clean smell. The fresh, cool crispness of the pillow as I'd lay my head down. *Fuck, I could use some of that right now.* Alone in the depths of the boat, I wrapped my arms around myself, and tears began to swell.

At the sound of heavy footsteps coming down the stairs, I turned my back and did what I could to straighten myself up.

Dong approached and put his hand on my shoulder. I turned to him.

"Brando, you have my room, yes." His eyes showed genuine sympathy.

I moved to let him pass and watched as he entered the room with the double bed. A minute passed before he crossed the hall to the room with two single beds and tossed a duffel bag in the door. Then he faced me, clapped his hands together, and motioned to the now-empty room.

"We sorry this happen for you Brando. We do good for you, we like for you to be here. This room for you now."

Lost for words at his display of decency, I nodded. These guys were human, not just soulless party vagrants.

He slapped me on the shoulder as he passed by and headed back up the stairs.

I felt a little better. I had a spot. Somewhere in the whole universe I had a spot that was mine. And that made a difference.

I sniffled and wiped my hands down my T-shirt and shorts as if to straighten them out, then stepped into my room and closed the door softly. I eased myself down on the bed. Tears fought their way back, but I managed to hold them off. It felt like the initial shock of storm had passed, and things were maybe beginning to settle.

I inhaled deeply through my nose and tilted my head back, wiping my hands across my face. *Thirty fucking days at sea.* I noticed a perfect rectangular beam of light disturb the surface of the sheets, filtered red through the curtained window.

What I'd thought I wanted to do was pass out and wake up somewhere more realistic. But I was where I was. I was on a boat in the middle of the Atlantic, on my way to Amsterdam. I had no change of clothes, no toiletries, no money, cards, or passport. But in attempt to keep it positive, I tried to view the whole mess as an opportunity I would never have considered, ever.

And slowly, I didn't want to hide in my room anymore. I decided to stop being a bitch and start appreciating it for what it was. Because it wasn't going to change.

I sat for a minute longer. My pulse calmed, my body relaxed and my vision focused. I pushed from the bed and walked out the door.

Back on deck, the wind stirred my hair and filled my lungs. I found Nick sitting on the rail at the front of the boat, looking laid-back as he held a rope attached to the mast. He seemed to be entranced by a sight to the west. I followed his gaze and saw it in the distance. A storm on the horizon.

I fell into the same unblinking stupor as I slowly rested my weight on the railing span behind him. We sat silently watching the sharp bolts of lighting and listening to the faint rumble carried across the water's surface.

"Are we going to hit that?" I whispered.

"No." Nick smirked unconsciously, his eyes focused. "No my friend. This one is no for us… But we will have challenge. Many times. Chu should be ready."

His hand stretched out from his pocket, and his palm rolled over and opened. In it I saw what looked like a plain white cube of sugar.

"What is it?"

He paused as if he'd drifted away, then he returned. "Is LSD, acid. We all take this now. Take it Brando, my friend." He looked me in the eye.

I don't know where he was, only that it was a different place from where I was. I looked at the others; they were all in the same state. As if waiting for the storm, the storm on the horizon in their minds.

Acid had never been my thing. It was a line I'd never crossed, or even considered. But a lot of new lines had been crossed that day. And I had thirty to go.

What happened on the ship, stayed on the ship.

AE II - Blow Me

I retrieved the sweet cube from his hand and popped it in my mouth.
I returned to my perch to watch, and to wait.

6

The second I placed the cube in my mouth, I questioned my decision. I wasn't confident I'd allowed the proper amount of time for consideration. The problem with a drugs is, there's no refunds. Once you pop, you can't stop. It's like that moment after you hop on the super-insane roller coaster, the big plastic shoulder harness locks into place, and the cart takes that first lurch forward. That moment when you panic, knowing if you could make the decision again, you'd get the fuck off.

It was silent, but for the sound of the steady breeze, the soft creak of the rigging, and the gentle rocking and bobbing of the boat. By then, the sun had started its descent and the shadows were growing long. All scallywags had found their roost and a handhold, all eyes focused on the dark storm in the distance.

Nick was confident we weren't going to hit it; I couldn't see how we weren't. From my perspective, we were about to cut it off at the pass.

How it raged. A sinister shadow in an otherwise spotless, blue sky. Claws of lightning bared violently in all directions. Lost souls in search of ground. Salvation from eternal madness.

The closer we got, the stronger the wind blew. I turned to Adlar, who remained intensely focused on tweaking the boat harder in the wind. Like surfing the crest of a titanic wave. A practised surgeon of the sea lining up his scalpel for the cut. Using its strength to our favour.

My breathing grew slow, deep, and controlled as the wind pushed harder.

My entire being reclined to a tranquil state of confidence. I was young, wild, and free in every sense. Free to live and free to die. In the end, nothing out there gave a shit about us. 9-1-1 was a myth; no one would answer, no one would come. The ship to sink in the ocean as the tree falls in the forest.

The sound of my breath and the steady pace of my heart slowly blocked all else but the distant boom of thunder.

It didn't matter what challenges came forth. The general aura of the boat was a silent strength. I grew faith in my crew. They weren't bullshit, and neither was I.

Whatever lay ahead—demon storms, calm seas, or monsters of lore. We were not in for bargaining. We were our own force among them.

A cocky grin grew on my face and I turned to Nick. "It looks hungry, like it's hunting."

He turned his head toward me and I noticed something different, something peculiar that I couldn't quite put my finger on. After a few further seconds of observation, I realized Nick's face had developed circular black spots, reminiscent of a brook trout. He'd also grown a set of gills on either side of his neck that fanned in and out with the calm manner of his breathing.

Gills were a bit of a surprise, but it made sense for a man who spent so much time at sea. Gills seemed a sensible option.

"Yes, it hunt for us, is test. Now is only us and the gods. We fight now, for respect." As he spoke, a small bubble would randomly float from his mouth.

Having a genuine fish-man on-board really buoyed my ego. How could it not? Now these gods could do whatever they wanted. Sink the boat? Hell, I'd jump in right then. We had a certified fish-man on-board.

I looked over at Dong. He was standing on the corner of the cabin, a swinging rope in his hand, and he'd also transformed some. He'd grown hair all over his body, but his ratty beige shorts remained in place. Bigfoot was the first description that came to mind, but he hadn't grown to any size. Perhaps he fit more snuggly into the chimpanzee category.

Being part of the ape family had it advantages out here, make no mistake. Being able to scale and swing surely from tall, tree-like structures would be a useful talent as long as we stayed afloat.

I looked back at Adlar, at the helm. He'd taken on a most eccentric form of a centaur with a brilliant plumage of peacock feathers protruding from his back, shimmering high in the air. He could guide the boat just as well as any, and I knew each of them would play a vital part, but I decided to invest a little more energy on maintaining good relations with fish-man. 'Cause if shit goes down and drags the boat with it, you want to be close to fish-man.

I turned back to my aquatic friend, feeling the need to raise my voice as the sea intensified. "She have a name?"

He looked at me, disconnected, and failed to answer.

"The boat. Does it have a name? Isn't it good luck for it to have a name or something?"

He nodded slowly and a grin peeled open his lips. "Yes, my Brando, my friend. She name Miss Betany, Betany Bartolomew."

The name wasn't what I expected. I wasn't sure what I expected. Consideration demanded a moment of pause.

It lacked sex appeal. But would it be wise to name a boat *Elle* or *Heidi*? These are ladies needing to expel a mass of energy to displace water and stay afloat.

"Miss Bethany Bartholomew." She was a floatin' lass. She was all about water displacement. Forcing fluid to carry her weight was her sole reason for existence.

As time sank and dragged my conscious mind with it, I became very aware of specific things and completely unaware of obviosities. The motion beneath, a continual surge of microscopic gaseous bubbles racing passed the hull, white noise in my feet. The slappy clop of waves on the side resonating to my knees, and the slow undulation between swells bringing a next-level challenge to my vertigo.

The silence was a bitch. With lack of distraction, my mind spun its own dimension. Every clue acquired by combined senses analyzed and moulded to its own conclusion. Each void of simple common sense.

My soul begged to vomit, to purge the spinning delusions, but my political mind denied the request, calculating higher priorities. I needed to move, and fast. I took a breath, studied the required motion and all the potential hazards, then turned to the cooler. A couple steps and I lifted the lid, grabbed a bottle of water and cracked the cap and chugged it back. Eyes closed to the sky, I steadied my pace as I felt the cold fluid flood my cells. I lowered the bottle to my side and opened my eyes slowly, tipping my head forward.

Directly off the starboard side came a violent burst from the ocean. A massive plume of bats exploded from the water and flew up to create a giant dark cloud in the sky, casting Bethany in shadow.

The bottle dropped from my hand and my brain sucked required air through my eyeballs, pushing my eyelids back into my skull. My processor buzzed from extreme overload.

To the distance the bats flocked, swooping and diving to take another shape. Then, with great clarity, the form of a colossal Mickey Mouse head sporting a sailor hat leaned in with a devilish grin and an "atta-boy" wink. I gasped softly, a tremor rippling through my body as my every orifice clenched simultaneously.

It was a lot for one day, to be honest. Admittedly, a great story to tell. But I suffered permanent damage during the production.

My brain slammed the gearshift to neutral and took its foot off the gas. Everything toppled to auxiliary numbness. My skeleton slumped and my head dropped. Swerving and weaving, I turned and managed my path to the cabin stairwell, and with firm, four-point contact, I descended. Down the hall, into my room, I slammed the door closed behind me. I tapped out and fell to the bed. Slumbering before hitting the pillow.

7

My eyes jerked open. I was suspended in a sea of clear blue water, heavy. No sky above and no floor below. I could breathe, it seemed, which was strange, but it wasn't a time to question abnormalities. I paddled my arms to twirl around, looking for any danger and searching for direction. With no clues, I started to swim. *What in the fuck happened and where's the boat? The guys?* As scary as the situation begged to be, I was really very relaxed. The temperature was fine, and I could breathe, so all was good. I just floated around. I'd eventually run into something, someone, somewhere.

Time passed and nothing changed. I started to grow uneasy. My mind continued to run the formula for the sum of my new surroundings, and things weren't adding up.

Something finally changed and I stopped. It was slight and took some time for me to process. I realized the sleeves on my shirt were trailing behind me, even though I was stagnant. A breeze, or a current.

Trying to swim upstream is normally thought to be a needless waste of energy. But instinct suggested I start resisting and put some effort into it. A loud yawn came from behind and reverberated through the emptiness. A sound cartoonish in nature, like Homer Simpson relaxing in his armchair. But Homer and his recliner didn't belong down there… and neither did I.

I didn't look back. My plan was to just swim the fuck out of the thing's way. That noise didn't just happen by fluke.

My uneasiness grew as fatigue and frustration put me on a spitroast. Then another sound, the sound of something or someone taking a breath. A deep draw. Almost seductive. And the current increased.

I looked back because I couldn't ignore it anymore. In the deep-blue depth, a dark shadow grew. Oval in shape, it drew closer, then it changed, opening wide into the giant mouth of a whale. So big was it, that to swim around it would take time I didn't have. The only escape was forward, and fast.

I turned back and kicked into high gear. But I immediately knew that good enough was a target beyond my reach. I stroked and kicked with all I had, but the current continued to increase and pull till I was certain no matter my effort, I was being sucked in. My heart pounded, I screamed for salvation. There was nothing anywhere. Nothing to grab, nothing to rest on, no stillness of sanity. Why couldn't it all just stop? I struggled and gasped, stretching out with the very tip of my fingers for anything. *God… Help!*

The current drew so violently that it suddenly sucked even my reaching arms back, and all chance of hope with them. I tumbled backward into the unknown, into the abyss. Screaming silence…

I startled and sat up on my elbows, my chest heaved in air to feed my racing heart. It was pitch black but I could feel a soft mattress below. Faint starlight shone through the window, but the darkness of the room swallowed every glimmer, lending no hint to my surroundings. I started to piece things together—the boat and the sequence leading to it. Maybe I was inside the whale?

I felt for the edge of the mattress, then flopped my legs over its side till they found purchase on the floor, suspended over millions of fathoms. Bethany wasn't terra firma, but she was the most support I'd have till we reached the other side, or fell to the bottom. She may be my last fling.

I sat quietly, rubbing my arms and legs, twisting every joint. Everything seemed intact. The feel of my own touch was the only soothing familiarity I had, my own rock. I leaned over and put my head in my hands, taking time to calm and breathe. How long had I been out? It was either nighttime, or we were on the bottom. Nothing would surprise me at that point.

A juicy drop hit my shoulder and splashed onto my cheek. Another fell and then another, till it turned to a genuine drizzle. The water washed through my hair and began to pool on the floor. It felt good, refreshing. It slowly increased to a shower and the pool grew beneath my feet. I stood and navigated my path to the door as I remembered it. The rain fell steadily. Possibilities were either a heavy storm, or sinking. But in my mind I somehow knew the rain was acidic.

Twisting the doorknob, I pushed my way from the room. All was dry and silent beyond. Still dark, other than a couple blinking lights on a panel I knew nothing about. I meandered my way down the hall and up the stairway leading to the deck. All was dark and quiet, the sails were still up and lightly filled. The list to the boat almost undetectable. The sea air refreshed my spirit, and I stood for a period with my eyes closed to soak it in and dry my rain-drenched clothes.

Exhaling slowly, I relaxed and opened my eyes. The night was thick and empty. The sails ruffled softly, whispering something, words with no translation cast by an eternal sigh. The masts creaked like an old woman resting quietly in her rocking chair. The full moon was partially covered by wisps of cloud that trailed off like spilt ink to a constellation of an old feathered quill.

Was I messed up? Or was this just nighttime on a boat in the middle of the sea? The whole environment was alien to me. How does one question what is reality without a solid baseline?

No mammal moved on deck. The wheel sat steadied by a thick white rope, as if the rest had abandoned ship. Or maybe they were never there… Maybe I wasn't there? A swell of emotion heaved my chest and pooled in my eyes. A guy could buckle then. Why not? I guarantee most would, maybe all? But this was only day two, and I didn't have the energy to waste on falling apart.

I stepped quietly to the cooler and grabbed another bottle of water. I drank a quarter down and screwed the cap back on.

"Brando…," came a whisper from the front of the boat.

I looked and saw a faint arm illuminated by moonlight, begging me forward.

I took a cautioned step.

"Brando…"

Nick.

The sound of his voice sent my mind slobbering for human interaction, and I hurried over to rid my sense of isolation.

As I drew closer, I realized he was lounging in a rope hammock stretched between railing posts.

"Brando, my friend, come… Come sit with me." His face was dressed with a casual smile as he turned to me.

I sat on the chest beside him, bringing my head down to his level.

"Nick!" I softly greeted him, my lighthouse in my demented haze. "I'm really happy to see you man! What's happening? Where is everyone? Where the fuck are we?"

He let go a dopey snort. "Brando, we on this boat. We sail to Amsterdam."

"Yes…" My hope withered at his fuzzy logic. What answer could I honestly expect? Accuracy was limited to a few thousand miles. "I don't think I can make it Nick."

He chuckled again. "My friend, chu stop fight it." He found some life, lifting himself to sit across from me. He gave me a friendly pat on the shoulder. "It is okay now, yes?"

I breathed in, took a swig of my water, looked around a little, then turned back to him. My light bulb switched on and I studied his face closely. He was no longer fish-man. "Yeah. Seems good."

"Yes? Good. Now chu have rest. So relax." He looked around with narrowed eyes before producing a joint from a pack of cigarettes in his pocket. He placed it in his mouth, pulled a lighter from his pocket, sheltered the end, and set fire to it. The dancing reflection of light glowed from his cupped hand and shone on his face. A colour of life, my pupils expanded to soak in the beauty.

He took a deep pull and then handed it to me. "Here, have this. It help. But do no tell guys. I do no have much." He winked. "This acid is nice, but is very crazy sometimes!" He shook his hands on either side of his head. " But do no try to fight with it. It come and go like the wave. Chu find it out." He slapped me on the shoulder.

I took a drag and held it deep. Good old… marijuana? At least that's what I was banking on. But I should've asked the question.

It was good, the talking. It was settling my mind, giving me something to focus on. I exhaled and slouched in my seat. "Bats flew out of the ocean, then turned into Mickey Mouse and winked at me."

Nick paused in mid-drag. I'm sure the translation was a challenge. The concept was challenging if you spoke fluent English.

"Yes?" he said in a choked voice before evacuating his lungs. "The Mickey Mouse?" His face contorted, seeking confirmation that our pages were synced.

I nodded.

"He was… bats? And he wink to chu?"

At that time it was the most fucked-up thing a grown man ever repeated back to me.

"Mickey Mouse? Like draw on TV, uh, Disney mouse?" He rolled his hand over in front of his face, pulling words from his gut like a clown would scarves from his mouth.

"Yes, the Disney mouse."

He laughed and his eyes brightened. "Is fucking awesome man!" He raise his hand for a high-five.

I wasn't sure what the cause for celebration was, but I obliged him anyway.

"I do no get this like chu! I am getting fucked, yes?"

We let the excitement die, and the stillness of our environment set the mood.

"What's it like Nick?"

"Hey? What is what like? Disneyland? I do no know this, I never be to it. This place too expens—"

I chuckled. All those long-lost muscles working together in unison eased me further. I could laugh again. I had forgotten. "Amsterdam. What's Amsterdam like?"

"Ah!" His smile reflected to a place far from there, but dead ahead on the compass… I hoped.

"There, this is good, chu think about it? This now some excite for chu?"

He stood from his roost and paced out a circle to shake his legs out. With no warning, he made an explosive leap to the railing, which bobbed and weaved beneath his feet as his hand found support on a neighbouring rope. "Ha ha!" he cheered, looking back to me with boyish enthusiasm.

"Whoo-hoo!" came a distant cry of support.

I spun and froze, combing the faintly luminescent deck of the boat with my eyes. Nick's hand tapped my shoulder from behind.

As I turned, he raised his hand to the sky and pointed up the mast. Near the very top I detected some motion. I focused on the shape of a man sitting on a perch of sorts, just large enough to accommodate a single person on either side.

"Look at the motherfucker, huh!" Nick laughed. "He is fucking crazy, this Dong man."

I stared with disbelief. "How in the hell did he get up there?"

"Look at you Nick!" Dong yelled from his perch. "You motherfucker! You a fucking pirate, bra!"

"I am a pirate?" Nick shouted back. "No, chu a fucking pirate. Pirate

Captain Dong." He laughed. "We is all fucking pirates! HA!" He slapped me on the shoulder, then pumped his fist in the air to his comrade.

"Yes!" Dong said. "Brando is back? He still alive? I luv this fucking guy!"

Nick jumped down from the rail to stand beside me. "He climbs up there. He is part monkey this guy. Chu no fucking believe it."

"What's he doing up there?"

"He like it up there. Maybe he like to be high?"

"I'm sure he likes to be high."

"Yes!" He slapped me in the shoulder, his smile as bright as the stars. "He like to be high all time, huh!"

With the disruption, it was apparent my question needed repeating. "So what's it like? Amsterdam?"

"Yes! Amsterdam!" We turned to each other. "Is a great fucking place my friend. Is so nice. All water and flower and green grass, the buildings, is a beautiful place. The girls!" He winked. "We be there for summer. Many festival and chu smoke weed wherever you want. Is no problem."

"Yeah, I've heard that."

"Is fucking party there." He held up his arms and shook his hips. "Girls be dancing."

I'd heard this somewhere before, I was sure. Amsterdam women were hot and easy. They loved Canadians. As I searched back through time for the credible source, I came up with a zero. What did materialize was a list of every town or country my friends and I had bullshitted about. Apparently they'd all had girls that were hot and easy. Seemed legend of the beer commercial started just outside city limits.

"What about the police and the military? Are they walking around a lot? Will they arrest me when we get there?"

"Wha'? " Nick looked alarmed. "What is anyone go to do this for? No one to put chu in jail. Chu do nothing. We go to centre and smoke big fatty, yes! We get drunk, find girls, and have party."

I was pretty much partied out at the time, but Nick had a damn good sales pitch. If I ever had my feet on dry land again, I was sure gonna do me some celebrating. Hot, easy girls and legal drugs sounded like a pretty good start. His hand scrambled to his pocket and produced the little baggie of white cubes, then he bent to the cooler. "Here!"

"Nope!" I held my hands up and took a step back. "I… I'm good Nick." I shook my head. "Really."

He pulled a forty-ounce bottle from the cooler, then stood to look at me. "What? Brando, chu say no? Why?"

"I… I'm just, I'm down. It was fun and all, but I'm—"

"Brando!" He shrugged and lifted his hands to the side. A plastic baggie of drugs in one, and a forty-pounder of something that wouldn't help in the other.

"What? Why chu say no? What chu go to do?" He snorted. "We on here for a long time, this boat is very small in all this time. Hmm?"

I kept my hands up, continuing protest. "I just… I'm good Nick. Really."

"Hey, Dong! Chu hear Brando? He say he do no want more!"

"What!" came the response. "What he go to do?"

"Listen, Brando." Nick sidled up to me and put his arms around my shoulders. "Chu is here. Chu go to do this again? Sail boat around the world?"

I shrugged.

"Maybe? Chu think maybe chu do again? But maybe no? Maybe this be last time for chu? I think maybe chu never do again. Chu go to Amsterdam and get a plane to go home. This is more possible, yes?"

I dropped my head to avoid his eyes and shrugged again.

He reached across and slapped my face lightly, knocking it toward him, where I met his convincing gaze. What he said then came directly from his heart, from his belief.

"Then do this! Do this right. This one time chu must to do this!" He shoved the bottle to my chest.

I grabbed the bottle, looked at him one more time and hesitated, then tipped it back for a healthy swallow. Immediately he handed me a sugar cube, which I placed in my mouth, where it quickly dissolved. Then the bottle was pushed to my chest again, and I took another swig.

Coughing and sputtering, he patted me on the back. "Good for chu, Captain Brando!"

"Hey Brando! I luv this motherfucker!"So it was done… again. He was right, or so I convinced myself. This was only one time. Sink or float, I would do it for everything that it was.

Nick returned to his hammock and I perched on the storage box beside him.

I asked more about Amsterdam and their travels. He had so many fascinating stories to tell. Those guys, that crew. They reminded me of the Peter Pan's Lost Boys . They were so young and had lived so much, were so free and full of life, seemingly untouchable by time. I wondered if they'd ever get off this boat. Or maybe they were infinite and would exist through time to ferry young men across oceans. The Lost Boys' passage to manhood.

The more of my mind I lost, the more I understood. I'd never been in control, none of us ever were. Life was a pair of dice, constantly tumbling out random numbers. There was a time back then, back there, when I believed in control…

A whistle came from above. We both looked in unison to the scout.

"It is there!"

I looked back to Nick, who was now sitting upright in his seat.

"It is here…" Dong's voice trailed off in tracers, and a doorway to that other dimension opened once again. "The wave… it is back." He lifted his hand in slow motion to point behind the boat. "The wave is come back. It follow us."

My heart sped. *What now?*

Nick nudged me with his hand. "Do no be scared Brando. Go… See… Look at what chu see."

I swallowed, took a breath, and slowly moved in the direction Dong had pointed. Ducking beneath the sail, I straightened on the other side and saw what all the commotion was about. The wave, it was following us.

In the dark distance a crest of white-water appeared high on a bank of swollen water. A rogue in the night. My heart beat strongly. It was coming. So massive, it would surely be the end of us. The low roar grew threatening in my mind. But no one was stirring; there was no sense of urgency. Was it for real, or was it real only in my mind? I stepped toward it. Reaching the railing, I leaned over toward it.

"C'mon! You want this? Come and get it, you fucker!!" I challenged.

As my heart beat with every passing second, the wave never grew closer, it never changed in size, it just rolled continuously. Looking into it, I could see the past it had swallowed. Ships and debris rolled around in its turbulent stomach. Memories, my big truck, furnishings from my condo, the rig I'd left behind. Cold northern mornings, and the warmth of her in my arms.

On a boat, in the middle of the night and the middle of nowhere.

8

I sat on the deck for what seemed hours, watching the wave roll. The stories it revealed were as random as spinning spools in a slot machine. The brighter the eastern sky grew, the more the wave diminished, until it was little more than a ripple. As the tip of the morning sun reached the line of the horizon, it disappeared completely.

I huffed a breath, wondering how long it had been since I'd made any motion at all. I blinked a few times, then turned my head around, looking for the next distraction. It had occurred to me while watching the wave, that it wasn't all scary and negative. It really was about your reaction. A choose-your-own-adventure story. A scenario was introduced and you decided which path. The trick was, there was only a split second to choose, and once you'd decided, you were there until the end.

There was a jolt of commotion behind me, and I turned to the next scene.

Adlar stood atop the staired entrance to the living quarters with a blanket around his shoulders. His cheeks were streaked with tears. His body quivered and his expression was that of a man who'd climbed up from the pits of hell.

Nick rushed to his side and wrapped his arm tight around his shoulders. "Careful my friend." He coached Adlar onto to the storage bench, resting slowly beside him and continuing the consoling. "What is happen? Where is chu be, huh?"

Dong took a long slide down from his perch and stood beside me, looking down on his distressed friend.

Adlar was the one we all looked upon as our true captain. What in the hell could've happed to him? Was there a wild beast down there? It was my first glimpse into the truth of the Lost Boys' world, the flaw in the armour. Some of their times weren't happy. Sometimes they cared.

Adlar broke down, holding himself tight and sobbing into his blanket.

Nick rubbed his shoulders and whispered soothingly. "Shhh Adlar. Is okay. Chu here now, chu safe, is okay. The sun is up, look."

Adlar sniffled, then lifted his head. His eyes acknowledged our attention.

Nick grabbed a bottle of tequila from a bucket beside the bench and handed it to Adlar. "Chu must drink some of this."

I found it a completely inappropriate suggestion, but Adlar grabbed it as if it were a lifeline, tipping it back as though his sanity depended on it. He lowered the bottle with cheeks bulging and remnants running over his chin, then he forced the liquid down with a laboured gulp.

"*Good*. Now breathe. Breathe Adlar, take big breath in and hold. Like this…" Nick went through the motion, breathing in and expanding his lungs, then holding and nodding before the slow exhale.

It took Adlar a couple of attempts, but then he got control and began to calm, till he collapsed heavily into Nick's arms.

Finally, he lifted his head, turned to each one of us, and spoke. "I didn't think here I would be again. I think I lost in dark, always. In my head things go very bad, I put rope on wheel and go down to my room. A long time I'm there." A grin grew on his face, a sense of relief. "I still alive now. The sun is up, the wind is blow, my friends are here. It is good."

"Yes!" Dong slapped him on the shoulder and went in for a hug. "We is here for you. Do no fucking do it again! What you think, huh? You know we always here for you, we here for all!"

We took a bit of time to share some brotherly love. I realized I was not the only one who would face challenges during this journey. None were immune. As divided as I'd felt from the others previously, it was obvious we all needed to stick together to make it through. Although I was probably the only Canadian kid back home to never play hockey, to never be on a team, I could feel the blood growing thick between us. But this wasn't ice time, and the deeper I got into the journey, the more I saw danger from every direction.

Dong cracked open a large jug of wine they'd been saving for a special occasion. I was no wine connoisseur, but after my turn, I concluded that there was no event special enough. It was like no wine I'd tasted before. The closest reference I could muster was rocket fuel, with a twist of berry.

The celebration ended early as Adlar fully returned from whatever horror story he'd been living. He stood and looked at each of us, then marched attentively back to the wheel, where he began checking instruments and glancing at the sun and the horizon. He moved the wheel a quarter to his right and watched the nose turn. The sail fluttered and he yelled instructions to the guys.

Nick punched my shoulder and gestured for me to follow. He took off to the rigging of the main sail out front and showed me what needed to be done, having me assist him with some adjustments. For the first time since the trip started, I witnessed the band of misfits work together as a team. They had some real hustle when called upon and were very competent in their abilities. In that moment, I didn't feel like we were so helpless. It was nice to have an honest boost of confidence. One that didn't come in the form of a sugar cube or a bottle.

We busied ourselves by cleaning and straightening, checking gear, and sailing that fucking boat.

By midday the wind had increased and the chop was a steady, random drum on the hull. Nicked waved us all down into the cabin. Three of us took seats at the wraparound booth while Nick busied himself in the kitchen. He delivered a tray of fruit, nuts, bread, sliced meat, and cheese. Then set out a round of water for each of us. It was a flavour explosion. Pineapple and mango and grapes so crisp and fresh and juicy. I savoured them like never before, or ever since. As the nutrients flushed through my body, I felt like a juice-sucking vampire.

After scarfing a few mouthfuls of food, I rinsed it all down with a swig of water and then broke the carnivorous silence. "I gotta admit, you guys really got this shit figured out. I was starting to wonder if you knew how to run this thing. You really move when shit has to get done." I grabbed a grape from the platter and tossed it into my mouth, the crisp skin popping with a cool, juicy explosion. "This food is fucking perfect Nick, thanks."

"Is between waves," he slurred back to me through a mouthful.

I paused at the odd relation. "What? I think the translation…"

He looked up from his plate and swallowed. "We have to do it fast… between the waves." He made an undulating motion with his hand.

"The waves? I don't understand. You do things between the waves, the ocean? How does that— it doesn't make sense." I shrugged.

He laughed casually and shook his finger as if I were being a smartass. "Is no the water."

He continued to chuckle as the others sputtered laughter without missing a bite.

"The waves!" He made the undulating motion again, more exaggerated this time. His eyes wide with emphasis. "The waves"—he pointed his finger straight to his temple—"in chu brain."

Another short burst of laughter rounded the table.

"Chu go up," he sailed his hand upward, "then go down,"his hand dived. "Now we is down. Now we get this finish. Next wave come, hooo, fuck!" His hand blasted into the atmosphere. "We be to fucked up, uh!" He nodded, his eyebrows bouncing.

My frame sulked. We were down, so down I'd forgotten. It was in me, it was in all of us. The ticking clock to madness. I examined the others, heads down, gobbling up whatever they could, while they could. I couldn't quite fathom how we could all take different quantities at scattered intervals and still be on the same schedule.

Happy time had settled, anxiety scattered hope, and I wondered when it would come? What would it be? How would it start? How violent?

Was this it now?

My mind was turning. Control, I had to get control. Or was it already too late?

This time, these down waves, these moments of normalcy, in the flip-side dimension. This was the hallucination.

I grabbed a piece of bread, tore it in two and shoved a piece into my mouth. A sweat shivered through my body.

"Brando," Adlar said from my right. "You okay? You not look so good."

Nick jumped up and headed back to the kitchen. "*Yes*, he is fine, Brando. He just need some medicine."

I heard a loud clinking and he returned to the table again with a round of glasses and the same bottle of far-from-fine wine. He filled them all to the brim and slid one to each of us. Then he took his seat and pulled a fat joint from behind his ear and lit it. Taking the first hit, he coughed and sputtered, then passed it across to me.

I held up my hand and shook my head. "No, thank you."

"Yes," he said loudly. "Let us have adventure Brando! We here together! Come." He pushed it on me again.

"Yes!" Dong slammed his hand down on the table. "We must do together! Get fucking crazy!" He drummed violently on the table.

The other two joined, then the whole boat erupted into chant.

"BRANDO! BRANDO! BRANDO!"

I grabbed the joint and put it to my lips. I took the biggest drag I could, then coughed out a huge cloud of smoke, bathing the whole table. Maybe that would shut them the fuck up.

"Yeah!" they erupted.

"Now Brando, this!" Dong stood and stretched himself across the table to me, picking up my glass and holding it out to me. "Quick! You do it, yes!"

"Yes, Brando motherfucker! Do it!"

They cheered and clapped. Adlar was already pulling hard on the smoke, so I grabbed the glass and shot back the moonshine. Everyone went wild, more drinks were poured, and the joint was passed till fully ingested.

Then it all stopped. We sat, breathing heavily from the overload.

The next wave slapped Dong first, right in the face. He bent over the table, his arms wrapped around his gut, and it was hard to determine whether he was laughing or crying as his eyes poured a torrent of tears. "The fucking!" He could barely lift his hand to point in my direction, his laughter intensifying until it was a barely audible wheeze.

This was the next wave. Instead of burying and thrashing us in its turbulence, it picked us up. Like surfing life in all its glory. A euphoric feeling magnified by the group as a whole. We all joined Dong, laughing uncontrollably.

During the chaos Nick managed to muster up enough motor skills to fill another round, splashing most of it on the table.

"Fuck *yeeaaahhh*!" he screamed. His eyes bulged and his face turned beet red with effort as he held his glass in the air.

"Fuck *yeeaaahhh*!" we all repeated, then smashed our glasses together and tipped them back.

Dong pulled another plastic baggy from his pocket and spilled the contents onto the table. Little white cubes tumbled everywhere.

"*Yeeaaahhh!*" we all cheered again. I watched as Dong and Adlar each threw two into their mouths and Nick took three. I grabbed the last one and tossed it down the hatch. I was all in. That evening was a feast for the kings. For the rest of the trip, I can't remember ever sitting down together as a group.

The laughter continued, my head went sideways, and the whole scene slowed and distorted. I rocked back and forth in my seat, trying to focus. Everyone had fallen into the same stupor.

Forever seemed to pass with no one moving from their spot. There were random, incoherent ramblings. Tension built with the silence. I could feel the eruption coming. We all could.

"Oh… Oh, my fuck." Dong's voice resonated as if we were all submerged.

I teetered from one side, then overcorrected to the other. "God, oh shit…" The prayer lapsed in my mind.

Nick looked across the table at me. "What, Brando?" His whole faced sagged and was drenched in perspiration. "What is chu say?"

"Oh Jesus." I clenched at my gut, though it was my mind that churned. *Oh shit, Brandon. This is the guy you're sailing with. You don't even know who he is. He took too much. He's gonna die for fuck sake. They're all gonna die. They took too much. Then what? Then what the fuck are you gonna do! You're gonna fucking die out on the ocean, in the middle of nowhere.* Pictures of the future unfolded in my mind.

I stared blankly back at him. Had I said something? What did I say to him? *Shit, Brandon, what did you say to him!*

We sat there awkwardly for a time. His expression suggested concern for what I'd said. I shared his concern.

"No!" Adlar shouted. We all looked at him slumped in his chair. "Get up! We must go… the boat. We must go!"

He breathed deeply through his nostrils. Strong and full, flooding dementia with a haze of pot.

Breathing seemed like a good idea. I followed suit. Sucking deep for any wisp of something helpful. The rest joined in.

Adlar moved and all eyes shot back in his direction. A miracle unfolding before our eyes. A man standing again, for the very first time. Then he walked toward the stairs, grabbing any handhold he could to pull his way down the garbled corridor.

"Come!" he shouted. "We have the boat! Come!"

One by one, we started to find our footing. Once the first motion was completed, we remembered that movement came naturally for us. My mind could function, but nothing was real. I was locked in a tunnel of my own wild creation, searching for the light at the end. If there would ever be an end. Up the stairs we climbed. Stepping to the top, the walls fell open to darkness. I breathed again, the air so cool and rich with nutrients. Night had fallen on the day, the wind had ceased completely, and the sky was flawless. The moon hung in quartered state. Stars so bright and brilliant, found themselves looking back from the glass surface. We had become pirates of the galaxy, adrift in space. The sails hung lifeless and the silence was complete.

We stood still, bunched together.

Dong leaned forward and released a primal cry, holding it till his lungs emptied to the last whisper. "AHHHhhh!"

The sound shot down the water and rippled through the heavens, out to the Milky Way.

Maybe they'll come? I thought.

Turning from the group, I slid my way back over to the roof of the cabin. The surface was cool to the touch. It felt so nice. I boosted myself up and lay my body out along the smooth platform. My cheek rested and the support cooled and soothed.

I looked out into the starlit emptiness and fell to dream.

… Or maybe not?

9

"Brando!"

I began to swim back to consciousness. Someone was summoning me from above.

"*Pfft!*"

A heavy blob of something warm buried itself in my hair at terminal velocity. I startled, and shooed at it frantically.

I sat up and draped my legs over the edge of the cabin's roof. Our vessel was still floating through space. Floating stars, blinking satellites, and shooting comets surrounded us. We seemed to have gotten off course, floating somewhere inside the constellations. The deck of the boat was completely still.

"Brando!" came a whisper again, from above.

I looked up at the top of the mast, where Dong sat upon his perch.

"Yes! Brando!" He waved.

"Come, come look! She come to us!" He pointed out into space.

"She?... What in the hell are you talking about? What 'she'?" I was certain it was bullshit. There was no "she" within a few hundred miles of us, perhaps even light years. But I still felt a hope, a temptation. Having any type of "she" around would be a very nice change. No offence to Miss Bethany. The words *she's coming* were as enticing to me at that point as someone yelling, *Land ho!*

I looked yonder, with his direction, but saw nothing but stars. Sailing on acid with three guys with limited English ability was a challenge I never would've chosen. I ran words of things that might be in the ocean through my head. Thinking Dong may have misused the word *she*:… *fish*… *boat*… nothing else aquatic came to mind. Of course, on land, we would have *tree, flea, referee*, and multiple other options. "Brando! Come!" He waved me up.

"Huh? Not a fucking chance Dong. You're fucked if you think there's a hope in hell I'm going up there."

"She is coming!" he insisted. "There! You must come, fucking Brando! It is no hard."

He was so completely convinced there was a she out there, somewhere, that maybe there actually was a she out there? Maybe in a boat, drifting helplessly?… Maybe she had a friend with her? Under normal circumstances I'd never think this could be possible. But when you're sailing a boat through outer space, you may as well toss the rules out the window.

He was really up there…. *High* up there. It didn't even look architecturally possible. But if a young man is doing something incredibly stupid, there is usually a she nearby.

"How? How do I get up there?"

He pointed to the base. "Use this"—he shook his finger—"this rope."

Around the base of the mast was a heavy brown rope, knotted in a large loop. I picked up one side.

"Yes!" echoed a cheer.

I pondered the rope for a moment. I pulled it hard at different angles, hung from it, then tried sliding it up, looking for something that it perhaps hooked to.

"No!" Dong slapped himself in the forehead. "In! Get in on rope." He motioned putting on a pair of pants.

I stepped inside the rope and lifted it to my waist. Then things began to come together. I'd seen this done before, on lumberjack television.

I understood the concept. But how was I supposed to go from standing flat-footed on the deck to flat-footed on the side of a pole? I messed around a bit, raising the weight of the rope to my waist level around the pole and trying to place one foot at a time, from different angles. No matter what, I could never get it to feel right. Climbing vertically up the side of a ship mast with nothing more than bare feet and a ratty old rope didn't feel right.

"Up!"

"I'm trying 'up'!" I shook my head.

"No, Brando. The rope. Up, high!"

After a couple of attempts, I was able to secure the rope by positioning it higher on the pole and resting my weight back into it. I set one foot on the side of the mast and then bounced a couple times on the other, before pushing off and planting. My first step up a pole, and Mom wasn't there to take pictures or tell me to get down before I killed myself.

Didn't seem so bad, really. I shifted my weight around a bit in an attempt to unseat the rope, but everything seemed sturdy enough. My confidence boosted from none to a little.

"Yes! Come, my friend! She here, she watching!"

Well if she was watching, I'd best not bitch out. I needed to get the correct order of events down. I took one step, then with a quick jerk, I released my weight from the rope and slid it higher before resting again. I'd moved a total of six inches, give or take three—more likely take. But I was on the move, and things felt legitimate, whirling on a boat through space while climbing the mast.

Step by step, I took my time. The bristly rope chafed my back and the mast was cool and sometimes slippery, but it was nice to have that something to focus on. I'd forgotten about Dong and she. What I had was my breath, my body, and a small fragment of my mind. No matter how much substance we'd inhaled, my body and mind had to come together for the greater good. To see a chick, maybe. To fail would mean certain death. I stalled for a second to look back. I was up about four feet… Well, if not certain death, at least a nasty bruise on my ass.

Up I went, bit by bit. Suspended in a space odyssey, silent and eternal.

Dong continued encouragement.

"Yes Brando, you do it! You do it man!"

Things changed as I got higher. The mast was tapered, of course; a factor I hadn't calculated for. As it grew smaller, the loop of rope grew longer. The longer it got, the less effective was the geometry. I consistently had to stretch my legs longer and adjust the pressure, no longer able to rely solely on my weight for anchoring.

Extended to the balls of my feet, my steps grew even smaller, till I was forced to stop on fear of losing grip.

My legs began to tremble. I stumbled slowly. I was hit with a sense of urgency to descend, quickly descend. Which triggered my cursed reflex to look down. Urgency grew to panic. My focus shifted from climb to fall, and the odds of my survival were tipping heavily to splat. I was frozen stiff, other than my jitter legs, and so the endurance test had begun.

"Dong! Oh fuck! Oh fuck man!"

He was there, about four feet overhead.

"Brando! Two more! You can do this!"

"Dong! Shit! Reach down! Give me your hand!"

"No! Is bad idea. I can no hold you. You must to push on rope. If you stop, you go down! Step little bit down Brando. Lift rope up you back! Is make it better."

My energy was fading really fast. My legs were on the verge of failure. It was fight or fly time. Sweat began to drip from every pore on my body as toxins strummed notes of extreme paranoia. I played his instructions over in my mind till I could feel myself taking the step down and the burn of the rope scraping up my back.

It happened just as I envisioned. The rope slid to my mid-back, the angle changed in my favour, and my legs squatted farther, allowing for more muscles to interact. I took a big breath, and it never had felt as sweet.

My heart took its foot off the accelerator, and the gates to the dam of adrenaline closed. I managed a chuckle; a chuckle for still being alive, on the side of a pole.

"Brando! Yes! You do this! Thank you, fuck, so much, you make this! Now come! Step two more."

I gathered myself for the last push, then took the remaining two steps into a cut-out in the platform. As soon as I felt the time to be right, I slapped my arms down on the deck and hoisted myself up. A second after, I heard the thud of the rope on the deck below.

I rolled my body over, sat on my butt, and wrapped my arms and legs around the pole. Keeping my eyes closed tight, I thanked everything in the universe.

Then it hit me and I gasped. "The rope! How the fuck do we get down?"

"Oh, is okay, we do no need this to go down. We slide."

"Yeah, sure," I replied between tensed breaths. "Sliding sounds like a good idea." That was sarcasm.

I took the time to just sit, breathe, and not look. I hated that pole right then, but it also felt so good in my arms. I was safe. No matter how high, or how slender, it was sturdily attached to the ship. As long as I stayed exactly where I was, I'd be fine. If I kept my eyes closed long enough, I'd hopefully wake up in bed, back home in Canada.

"Yes!" Dong said and patted me on the shoulder. "You fucking do it man. You is real shit. Nobody come here with me. You badass guy Brando. Ha. Motherfucker!"

He shook me lightly, then stood. "Look, my friend! Look! She is there! She watch us." His voice trailed to a soft, spooked whisper.

Oh shut the fuck up Dong. She. Fuck she and her bullshit. Tell her to come slide down the fucking pole!

"She is be shy, I think. She *so* beautiful."

Whatever she was, he was strangely infatuated. Love at first hallucination.

He began to rub my shoulders soothingly. It was a little more seductive than I was looking for, but exactly what I needed. I felt my tension ease and accepted that keeping my eyes closed while hugging a big wooden pole wasn't going to magically transport me back to my childhood home. I wasn't Dorothy. We weren't in Kansas. And if you all think the land of Oz was a trip…

"Stand please, Brando. You no fall here." He shuffled around behind me. "I is here, in back of you. You have pole there." He rapped on the solid post. "Slide you up to stand, Brando. Please… come."

I slowly loosened my legs from their death grip, stretching them out in front of me till my feet found purchase on the deck. Pushing up and holding tight with my arms, I stepped back and slid up to stand.

"Yes, my friend. Now, open you eyes," Dong whispered in my ear. "She watch us."

Steadying my breathing, I prepared my mind as best I could for what it was about to see. A chunk of seaweed maybe? Some garbage? Slowly my eyelids loosened, then lifted to a vision no imagination could create… not without some form of accelerant.

We were floating, floating silently among the stars, our only anchor the centre post and deck below our feet. It felt so intimate. I could faintly see the rings of Saturn and the moons orbiting Jupiter. Comets shot past so close I could hear them hiss and crackle. I couldn't help reaching out because, just maybe…

Surrounded by miraculous beauty. Tumbling through the galaxy. Spit-roasted by a giant post in my front and a Dong in my back.

Another whisper swam around my head. "Do you see now?"

"Yes…"

"Good, my friend." He patted my shoulder and moved in front of me. One hand hung around the mast as he stretched himself out over the deck and pointed below.

I'd heard stories of the dead calm experienced in the ocean, but until then, I didn't understand how true it was. Not a flaw as far as one could see. I began to doubt its existence and ours. Then I looked where Dong pointed, hoping for a glance at she. Just a look, if only for a moment. What I saw was a sea of stars divided by rivers of glowing phytoplankton.

Almost too much beauty for the human mind to process. But she... I couldn't see she. A myth.

Then, as I stared unblinkingly, there was movement... Then another. Lights swirled to patterns, forming shapes that slowly came to focus, first as two giant eyes. Beautiful, seductive, they blinked gracefully, curiously. My heart fluttered. She was real, and she was watching.

"You see?' Dong swung around to me. I could see his mind spinning dizzily. "She there now, you see?"

"Yes. I see her. She's very beautiful Dong. You were right." I was happy for him. Happy he'd found her. The eye was the gateway to the soul, and her soul was of immeasurable beauty. We stood motionless. Watching those big beautiful eyes stare at us, then blink innocently. The rivers flowed again, stirring the stars and taking another form. The eyes shrank in size and the outline of her began to take shape as she reduced to human size. She swam playfully in the heavens, her breasts covered teasingly below the surface, her smooth buttocks emerging as she turned to dive. Resurfacing, she looked up at us, brushed the wet hair from her face, and smiled. Then she curled a finger to us, beckoning for some company.

"Yes, Brando!" Dong whispered back to me. "I want to have her! She is wanting me!"

"I... I don't know Dong." I was trying to take hold of everything that was happening. Somewhere among the spinning chaos, warning lights were flashing. "Are you sure this is real?"

"*Yes*. She is real. Look to her Brando. She so, so sexy woman."

"Yes, she is that."

We watched as she continued her frolicking.

Then faintly, deep below, another silhouette slowly took form. Gigantic, it floated casually toward the surface, multiple arms floating just below her—a terrible legend from the deep.

"No!" Dong shouted to she.

She startled and looked up at us.

Dong pointed frantically. "Look, my luv."

She treaded water, confused by his warning. A tentacle reached up and caressed her side. She splashed at the water, spooked by what she could only sense below. She looked back at us; a teardrop streamed from her eye.

"I must go to her!" Dong said.

"No, Dong." I reached for his hand.

He shook loose from my grip. "Yes, she is mine! I must be man for her!"

I watched him let go of the post and step to the edge.

"Dong! What the fuck!"

"I must go my friend."

He stretched himself tall, prepping. Then his foot slipped and he tumbled over the edge, falling, twirling weightless through space till he struck the surface full on his stomach. The sound reminded me of slapping the soles of two shoes together.

"Dong! What the?... What the fuck! Oh shit!"

The wound to the flawless surface quickly swirled back to a cluster of stars and bacteria. Swallowing him.

"DONG! Oh fuck, man! I'm coming!... I'm coming!" I was in complete hysterics.

I needed time for calculation, but it was not the time for thinking, there was only time for doing.

I went back to the gap in the platform and got down on my hands and knees. Carefully but quickly, I lowered myself through, dangling my legs to search for the mast. I wrapped them tightly around it, then dropped through the whole and wrapped one arm at a time around it. I began to slide, slowly at first. Urgency my driver, I soon sped up, throttling my descent by adjusting my grip. Dry skin screeched, then whistled as my speed increased beyond control. The burning quickly grew intense and I screamed out in pain. The pole grew larger as I descended, making it harder to maintain grip, till I could hold no longer and my body slammed upon the deck.

Moaning, I rolled back and forth, my arms and legs burnt and bloody.

I crawled and pushed my way to my feet. Holding my arms away from the sides of my body, I scurried, bowlegged, across the deck to the side where I'd seen Dong fall.

There was nothing. No Dong, no commotion in the water, no girl, and no monster.

"Dong!" I yelled into the emptiness. "DONG!" Still nothing. After a moment, his haunting voice surrounded me from every direction. "Brando… Help me my friend!"

I was desperate. What to do? Scared as I was, I couldn't just let him die.

"Brando! Please!"

Unbelievable to myself, and fuelled by nothing more than instinct, I climbed the railing, took a deep breath, and dived headfirst into the unknown.

With every stroke, the ghostly murk swirled and neon green threads spun from my limbs, floating weightless in the translucent dimension, untethered, drifting into space. I swam my way to where I calculated Dong had made contact with the surface. Although the salt water seared my many wounds, I couldn't stop.

But there was nothing.

I stopped and treaded water, searching for any sign of where he may be. Then the wisps of green drew my attention as they began to move, tendrils in the water gathering around me.

"Dong!" I yelled desperately. "Dong! Where the fuck!"

"Brando!" he shouted back.

I twisted left, then right, paddling a full three-sixty before locating him. He was standing on the deck of the boat, leaning over the railing and looking at me.

"Dong?"

"Brando! What in fuck you do out there?"

"Wha'? I, I'm out here for you. Looking for you! How the fuck did you get back to the boat?"

"Brando! Do no move! We come help you!" He turned and yelled to the others, who quickly appeared beside him.

"Brando!" Nick yelled. "What the fuck man!"

My body and mind suddenly grew very tired. I felt an eerie presence building below me. The water began to rise as if something was charging from the depths.

I began to bob with every stroke, my mouth sinking just enough to take on water with every breath. I forced it out in a heavy mist every time I pushed myself up.

"Guys!" My voice grew weak. "I don't think I can make it back."

"Brando! Stay there! We come to chu!"

I watched them scramble around the deck. The water around me grew suddenly warm and full, until the energy beneath burst the water into a turbulent fizz.

I flapped my limbs as frantically as I could muster, but the water became so thin, it could no longer support my weight. Too exhausted to speak, I stretched my arm toward my friends one last time, then sank below the surface.

"Brando! NOooo!..."

10

I woke on the deck, covered loosely by a bright-yellow raincoat and my head resting on a life jacket. The sun was high in the sky and my skin was dry and parched, sensitive to even the slightest of movements. A layer of salt had adhered and crusted to an abrasive film.

How much time had passed would never be anything more than a guess. I rolled to my side, coughing and sputtering.

"Brando!" I heard Nick's voice and the sound of rushed footsteps along the deck. I felt his hand upon my forehead, relaxing me back to rest. "Chu's alive! Is a miracle! Fuck man, we think chu died."

Cradling my head in his lap, he tipped a bottle of water to my lips, which I gratefully accepted.

My throat was raw when I spoke. "What happened, where the hell's Dong? Is he all right?"

He looked puzzled. "Dong? Yes, he is fine. He down have a sleep in room."

"He fell into the water last night." I made a weak attempt to point at his perch. "From up top. He was going to jump, but he fell. He— we saw a woman in the water."

"Yes? A woman?" He just about dropped my head as he looked out to sea. "There is woman? Out in the water? She is sexy? I like to see sexy woman." He looked down at me and winked.

"Dong, he fall? From here?" He pointed up the mast. "This no possible, he be died if he fall from here. Dong was no in water. Chu was in water. Chu *way* gone. Crazy motherfucker! Why chu go out so much? There is sharks in there."

"Dong." I tried to remember the happenings and explain to Nick. "He called me up there. He said she was watching us. So I used the rope and I climbed up with him. I did just about die. When I got to the top, there was a woman swimming. Her eyes were so nice. Dong was nuts about her, then a giant squid or something was coming up to the surface. So he was going to jump in and save her, but he slipped and fell."

"Brando"—he slapped me lightly on the cheek—"listen what I say. Dong can no fall from here, he can no jump. Dong be gong." He laughed.

I admit it was pretty good.

"Dong no in water Brando. Chu in water. Chu climb up to there? I do no think chu can do this. No one has do this but Dong. Dong, he fucking crazy man, chu no this crazy Brando. Chu see woman way up there, at night, she swim in water?" His face scrunched, then he looked out and waved his hand across the horizon. "Look! What woman? We is gone, there no woman here forever. She swim here? Brando, my friend, if there is woman swim in water here, chu leave her in water. She crazy bitch, yes?" He laughed and removed himself from beneath me, letting my head fall to the deck with a thud.

I stared blankly up to the tip of the mast. The sails were full again, and we were making some ground. I realized no one would survive a fall from that height—water landing or not, it was impossible. But if it didn't happen, then what did? Why in the hell would I be way out in the ocean? What about the girl, her eyes, her beauty, the giant sea monster? It sounded ridiculous now. It had seemed so real. If there was any one thing I'd been schooled on during our voyage, it was the insane power of the human mind.

I rolled over to watch Nick, who was crouched over and digging through the cooler.

"What day is it?" I asked. "How long have we been out here? How much longer till we get there?"

He stood with bottle in hand and let the cooler lid fall shut, then made his way back to me, fishing in his pocket. He sat cross-legged beside me, cracked the bottle's cap, and took a swig, then looked at the horizon. "I do no know Brando. Why it matter? We set boat in the way, straight to Amsterdam. We no see anything until we is there." He handed the bottle to me. "It only be what it is.

Just keep sail going."

I tipped the bottle back; maybe it would help to numb everything. Adrift at sea with no reference of any kind. No land, no time. Just the sun, the moon, and the wind; endless water and endless waves.

"Open," Nick said, pointing to his mouth.

With no real thought, I followed orders and opened my mouth. He tossed another white cube into it, causing me to just about choke.

"Today is good day, my friend." He smiled and nodded. "We have some fun today, I think, hey? The wind is good, waves is good… you sit here." He patted me on the shoulder, then stood. "I go find guys."

I shielded my eyes from the sun and watched as he disappeared down into the cabin. I sucked on my cube till it dissolved to a coarse stream that trickled down my throat. Quite the fucking adventure this was. I supposed it was time get to my feet. As I slowly stood, I felt irritating burns on the inside of my arms and legs and in a line across my back, dried and crinkled. *What in the fuck!* I looked up the mast.

"Hey! Brando! You alive, huh!" Dong laughed as he topped the stairs.

Adlar popped up behind him. "You look like shit, Brando, the fuck you think last night?"

A part of me felt like opening the discussion again, but I decided it best not to. I'd developed an understanding that not all things had an answer on that boat.

Adlar took his spot at the helm as the other two worked the rigging and dropped the sails. The boat instantly slowed and straightened.

"What the fuck, guys?" I raised my arms. "We're doing good. Why the fuck are we wasting this wind? We should keep that shit going!"

"Hey, Brando!" Adlar slapped my shoulder as he walked by. "We have to stop for fun."

All the guys went to the two storage benches at the front of the boat and began rifling. Dong threw boards out onto the deck and the others started to untangle a mess of kites.

"What the? You guys fucking kidding me? You're doing this now?" I marched toward them.

Adlar turned to me. "We? Yes, we go for this now. You also."

"Guys! We gotta quit fucking around! The wind is perfect…"

"Fuck yeah!" Dong cheered. "Is fucking perfect!"

"But… We have to keep going! While we can…. What if the wind dies down again?"

"Yes, Brando!" Nick said. "If the wind is finish, then we can no do this!"

"Yeah!" they all laughed.

It was clear we were taking a timeout to go kiteboarding. The conditions were perfect, I had to admit. But they were also perfect for making some distance toward getting the fuck off the boat. No matter the argument, they were going kiteboarding.

It didn't take them long to get one rig together. I'd never launched off of a boat before, so I stood clear and reluctant, watching the potential disaster. Dong was the first to slip his feet into the straps of his board, then swing his feet over the side. Adlar launched his kite, and as it took off into the sky, Dong leapt off the boat and splashed to a full plane on the water.

"Yeah, motherfucker!" He pumped his fist in the air.

Next up was Nick, and then myself, with Adlar finishing up by throwing himself and all of his gear over the side for a water launch.

The kites were older models that had seen their fair share of abuse. I noticed the blue sky shone through a couple tears in mine, and the handling left much to be desired. But the wind itself was flawless. I fidgeted with my lines some, found the sweet spot, parked it at three o'clock, and leaned in. And… it was a great day for a kiting. I tipped my head back and let the waves splash through my hair. "Wooohooo!" I screamed, and responses of sort came from all around.

I made several passes. Short ones at first, keeping close to the boat, but as my confidence grew, constantly turning back and forth seemed like an unnecessary nuisance. The others were taking longer runs, so I followed. Allowing time to really stretch out and enjoy it until I was a fair distance out.

We stayed out for what seemed the whole day. Carving it up in the middle of the ocean. Breaking free from the constraints of the thin silver railing that fenced us in, till the sun stalled high in the sky. Where any of us got the energy was beyond me, considering our diet of laced sugar cubes and the bottle closest to us at the time. But we were young men. When we played, we played hard.

It started on my way back to the boat. The skies remained clear and the wind never fluttered, yet the swells increased in size. At times, they blocked my line of sight to the boat and I'd have to adjust my kite for power in order to climb up the steep face of the wave. When I did catch sight of the boat, I found it odd that there were no swells surrounding it. I looked around for the other kites, but could see none.

I turned my head and noticed a cloud forming in the distance behind me. No immediate threat, but when I got back to the boat, I planned to shut 'er down.

But there was something else… I just couldn't quite get a grip on. A random gulping sound. I dismissed it as waves, or my board slapping across them. I was having to work considerably hard to get through the swells, though the boat somehow kept its distance.

I looked back again to see what was transpiring weather-wise. To my surprise, the cloud had grown closer and considerably larger, and it seemed to be rolling across the water's surface while boiling mountainous in the sky.

Then I heard the sound again.

"*Guuulp*."

I looked down. Approximately four feet behind my board, I saw something with a sizeable tail diving into the water. That was definitely the sound I'd been hearing, so I trained my eyes on the spot. Then it bobbed up again.

"*Guuulp*."

It could've been a catfish, or maybe a grouper. I won't lie; I failed the "Atlantic Fish Species" test in biology. Whatever it was, it was a flat oval with whiskers and bulging eyes. It's mouth was wide enough to swallow me, board and all.

But I didn't get the sense that I was on its menu.

I looked at the waves behind me and saw more… many, many more.

Bobbing up and diving down in no particular pattern, *gulps* and *glonks* were punctuating through the wind and chop.

I'm not sure if one can distinguish a look of fear in a fish's eyes, but I was sure they were in no way pursuing me… They were escaping.

In the not-too-far distance behind them, the cloud was bearing down. It was likely still a hundred miles away, but it was so utterly massive, it felt like I could reach out and touch it.

I paid what attention I could to it between flying the kite, riding my board, and avoiding strange fish. I'd reached some sort of conclusion, which made less sense than having none at all. We were being chased by a sandstorm.

Understanding sent a couple drops of crisis serum into my bloodstream. It was time to kick it into high gear and get back to the boat.

It's in your head Brandon. It's just the fucking acid. Just the acid. You're fine, it can't touch you, it's all an illusion.

I looked back in hopes it had disappeared with my enlightenment of it's non-existence. But it was there. More there than before. And such a really, very, so-good, detailed illusion.

I sheeted in and pushed hard for the boat. There's a betting chance I may have pissed my shorts then, but I'd never admit to it.

Time seemed to stand still, and I took a moment to really study the details of what was maybe taking place. I was on a kiteboard, surrounded by a flock of gulping Glonker fish, while being chased across the ocean by a sandstorm. Could a person's brain ever truly return to its original form after such an experience? There's gotta be a mandatory period of PTSD after something like that.

I'd be that guy of legend in town. Fifty years old, out for a walk to collect bottles, sporting a Sesame Street T-shirt that could no longer stretch over my belly, with a pinwheel on top of my beanie hat and training wheels on my sneakers that squeaked like a chew toy every time I stepped. The housewives would point me out to their children as they drove by in their SUVs: *"See Tommy, that's what happens when you do drugs."*

The boat was right there, maybe a football field away, but it just wouldn't come any closer. The swells were still heaving, and as I raced down the backside of one, I noticed three bodies appear on deck, jumping and waving to me and faintly yelling, "Brando! Come *fast*!"

"Guys! I'm coming! I'm fucking coming! Help me!"

They continued their encouragement by repeatedly telling me to go faster.

Why in the hell is this fucking boat not getting any closer? What the fuck!

The wind increased significantly and salt spray rolled off the crest of the waves. I looked back again to see the storm right upon me. So close I could see the fish being swallowed and tumbling around in the wash of the all-consuming cloud.

So close, I could feel the gravity of it pulling me in.

Then something snapped and let me loose. I was suddenly gaining on the boat very quickly. I had to decide how I was going to get on-board before the sandblaster of death ripped me to shreds. I didn't have time for the traditional dismount.

I was going to have to go in Kamikaze-style, and get it figured out in about three seconds.

With sand lightly combing through my hair and on the verge of running smack dab into the hull, I sheeted in hard and launched myself into the air. Taking into consideration direction, height, and speed, I released the bar from my grip, sailed clear over the guys, and crashed violently to the deck, sliding at high speed till my chest landed hard against the mast, causing my body to wrap around it like a watch band.

My lungs coughed and sputtered for air like a stalled engine as the storm instantly engulfed us, displacing all and any air. I felt the coarse grains tear at my skin and burn through my throat and sinuses, filling my chest.

Then it stopped.

My breath returned and slowly steadied. I carefully opened my eyes. I was curled on the ground, surrounded by straw-coloured blades of prairie grass. Confused, I did a system check of all my equipment, then raised myself on one elbow and looked over the tips of straw swaying gently in the breeze. It was an endless field of prairie grass. The sun was high and bright, the sky was blue—blue like I remembered—and the scent on the breeze was a memory long forgotten… I was home.

"Brandon…"

That voice… I knew that voice.

"Brandon."

That voice. I know it… How can it be?

I scrambled onto my feet, then lifted a hand to shield my eyes and scanned the horizon. She was not there. But when I looked back, she appeared.

"There you are." She giggled, then twirled happily in a light-blue summer dress.

How was it possible for her to be there? How was it possible for me to be there? I reached down and brushed the dirt from clothes I'd apparently changed into somewhere along the way, and straightened myself.

I stopped questioning why. Strange though, was the realization that I couldn't remember the last time I'd thought of her.

Distance closed between us till she was in my arms, spinning me around. She brushed the hair from my eyes and looked up at me. Her beautiful smile glowing, so peaceful.

"Silly boy. Where'd you go? I've been looking for you."

She felt so good in my arms. Warm and soft, the smell of her perfume.

"Katy? How?... Where?" I shook my head with disbelief. Then I stopped with the questions and simply took in the moment for everything that it was. Solid earth beneath my feet, forgotten love in my arms. What was my rush to question it from being?

She took my hand in hers and we walked side by side through the field, enjoying the silence. I wasn't sure how far we travelled, for how long. But it was serene, and I was happy. Like I hadn't been since... since her.

She lowered her head. I sensed she didn't know where to begin.

"I... I know I really messed up with us Brandon. I shouldn't have done what... what I did." She nodded confession, and a weight seemed to lift from her shoulders.

She stopped and turned to face me. Grabbing my other hand, she looked up, a lonely tear streaking down her cheek.

She was so beautiful.

"I want to try again Brandon. Give me a chance. A chance to make it right." Her hands squeezed mine tighter and she drew herself closer. "I was stupid. I know that now. I should've been there to support you. Come back to me Brandon. Come back..."

I stood motionless. I had no response. I just looked at her, so beautiful. I never realized how much I missed her until then. More tears fell from her eyes. I wanted to help. I really didn't want her to be sad. Not then, on such a perfect day. But how did I explain what I didn't understand myself?

"I..."

She clutched me tighter and pulled her face dangerously close to mine, anxious for the response.

"Katy, I... I don't know how."

"What?" Her voice broke and she began to sob. "What do you mean Brandon? Come back. Just, come back to me."

I could feel her heart breaking. I wanted to fix it, but how? As I reached for her cheek, my own eyes grew flush.

Could I really have her again? Could we go back? I caressed her cheek, so innocent and tender.

Then she was gone. As quickly as she'd arrived, she turned to a statue of sand and fell to the earth. To nothingness.

"*CH-CH-CH-TS-sssss!*"

I froze. That sound… I carefully scoured the ground for any sign of what I knew it to be. In the place where Katy had stood was a coiled snake, rattling its tail in wicked warning. My skin crawled and I jumped back, watching as it tensed, tongue flailing. We looked deep into each other's eyes.

11

My body recoiled as I lay flat on the deck, loosely formed around the base of the mast. Sand scraped beneath me and showered down off my clothes.

I sat up, coughing hoarsely. I did my best to take some breaths without inhaling sand as I slapped it from my face and hair.

I knew I was snapping, that I was honestly losing my mind. I lay back on the boat deck. Covered in fucking sand. *Sand? What!* I sat up, shaking my legs madly, shaking my head side to side, brushing at my torn, stained shirt. I sputtered, working what saliva I had left through the small crack in my mouth in an attempt to rinse away the sand.

What the fuck! You fuck!... This is real? This fucking part is real? Gotta be fucking kidding me!

A couple feet off to the right of my foot, a lumped mass of sand moved slightly, then two beady eyes opened and a buried fish arced its body. The flaps on the side of its head flexed slowly and sand fell from its face as its mouth opened for dying breath.

Spooked, I scrambled back, only to run into another behind me. "What the fu—" I looked around the deck of the boat for the first time. Everything was covered in a layer of sand deep enough to bury a foot. Small fishy bodies struggled everywhere.

The three randomly scattered shapes of the pirates moved from beneath the beach.

I stood and shook my whole body like a wet dog, sending sand flying in every direction.

The sea was calm, the sky a blank canvas of blue. I looked down at the mess. Everything was so fucked up. None of it made sense. But there it was: sand and fish that I could see, touch, smell. Not even my brain on acid could do this. *How in the fuck could this be real? This! Out of the shit that could be real, why this? If this is real, what was false? Katy!... Why could that not be real?*

My body shook and I sobbed. I lifted a hand to cover my eyes and kept as quiet as I could manage.

How much longer before we got to Amsterdam? None of them had an answer, we were just pointed in a direction they may or may not have a fucking clue about. We could be sailing in circles for all I knew. Was the boat real? How 'bout the sails? Nick? Dong? The water? Or was I lying in bed back at Dad's? Was everything, all of it, life, just a bad fucking dream? Or maybe I was back in our condo, back in Calgary? Maybe she was sleeping in my arms right then and none of it ever happened?

Please let it be that.

Looking toward the distant horizon, I walked through the sand. Weaving between the dying fish, toward the front of the boat till I hit the railing.

That fucking railing.

I looked down at it, then slowly clasped both hands around it. It was real. *Why is this real!* Anger began to boil and I gritted my teeth. *I want it gone! Why can't I make this go away? Why can't I make this all go away!* I was caged, held captive. Maybe it wasn't a dream. Maybe it was hell.

Maybe I should've been more accepting of the turtles.

I yanked at the railing, but it wouldn't come free. Then I pushed against it, but it held strong. In this life of illusions, why could I not bend this one to my will? I closed my eyes and thought back to the field with Katy. *Why can I not be back there? It was just as plausible as this fucking place!*

"No!" I screamed. Incredibly pissed off, I was ready to get the hell off the boat. I let go of the rail and waded through the sand, looking for something, anything. I grabbed a fish by the tail and lifted it. It wriggled weakly in my hands. It was a lot heavier than it looked, so I had to spin around to get momentum up for the toss.

"Ahhhh!" I screamed as I released it.

The fish flapped and twisted through the air till it splashed down about ten feet into the water.

For the record, I was not throwing a fish in anger. I was setting it free… in anger.

"Wha' da?" A voice came from my left. I looked to see Nick shaking off the sand. He started to chuckle, pointing at me and looking back to the others.

I was bent over at the waist, hands on my knees and gasping for air. A string of spit dangled from my lips.

"That Brando! Look at how fucking crazy he is! He throw that fish! It is flop around like, Ag, yay a!" He motioned a flopping fish with his arms.

"Ah, haha! I see he throw that fish!" Dong replied. "I think I do much farther." He looked around, found a candidate close by, grabbed it by the tail, spun around, and released.

That, ladies and gentlemen, was the first annual Trans-Atlantic Fish Toss. There were probably better sports, but it was good for cleaning off the boat and releasing some stress. I'm sure some of the fish survived it. Their chances were better than if we'd let them bake in the sun. Though I did see Adlar tuck a couple back in a cooler.

Fish after fish, I began to develop an actual technique. While my distance increased, my anger grew at the sheer ridiculousness of being there. Tossing fish off a boat that had just been bombarded by a sandstorm.

"Ahhh!" I shouted, releasing one of the heavier ones I'd found. I turned back for another, but contestants were growing short, which didn't help my mood. "Ah fuck!" I picked up a handful of sand instead and threw it over, but all it did was dissipate in the breeze and blow back in my face. "Sonofa! Fucking shit!" I grabbed onto the railing and shook it like a maniac. "Get me the fuck off of here! AHHH! Why the fuck can't I just get off this piece-of-shit boat!"

"Look at Brando," Dong laughed. "He is fucking doing it! He go fucking crazy, yes! You fucking go Brando!! You tell it to them!" He kicked a pile of sand into the water, then grabbed the railing and shook it violently. "Ahhh, motherfucker!"

The boat erupted into fish-tossing, sand-kicking, rail-shaking, screaming madness.

Nick slowly made his way up beside me, leaned over the rail, and shouted, "Yes Brando!" He smiled at me. "It feel good, yes? Chu go my friend, scream to whole world!" He pounded on his chest. "Get this out! Get all of it out, my friend.

This life. It shit on chu! Chu must shit back to it!" He curled his arm, clenching a fist in front of his gritted teeth.

I turned to him, desperate, and put my hands on his shoulders. I'd had enough of his psychedelic philosophy shit. "Nick! You gotta fucking tell me! Where are we? How much longer have we got?"

"Brando." He placed his hands on my shoulders. "I do no know where is this? I do no know this questions. I know we go that way." he pointed off the nose of the boat. "To Amsterdam."

I stared blankly at him. It was like interrogating one of the fish. I let go of his shoulders, then I really went off.

I screamed and yelled at the top of my lungs, shook ropes, kicked sand, stomped my feet. Anything I could do to express my most extreme of frustrations.

All other parties on-board followed suit. Marching, stomping, shaking, and screaming, all together as one. No one to hear, no one to care. A tree falling in the forest. A Glonker fish plopping into the water. Four boys lost ay sea and losing their minds.

12

As time passed, I battled through my ups and downs—more downs than ups it seemed, or perhaps they were the most memorable? The moon chased the sun overhead, or maybe it was the sun chasing the moon? What did it matter? What did anything matter? What does a young man do when trapped for a month or so on a boat loaded with booze and drugs? He loads himself with booze and drugs. And the more time that elapses and the more booze and drugs he does, the farther reality slips. I can't explain enough the number of times I looked beyond the rail at the endless nothingness that never changed over countless sunrise and sets, and honestly questioned if I was still alive.

There were no more fancy round-table meals. We were down to canned goods, crackers, and noodles. One morning I emerged from a bunk, a blanket wrapped loosely over my shoulder and passed a mirror in the galley. I must've passed by it a hundred times before, but this was the first time I took any kind of notice.

My skin was dark and weathered; I swore I'd dropped ten pounds. My facial hair, which had always been stunted, had reached its fullest potential; and I'd aged fifteen years or more. It had me questioning again how long we'd been adrift. I'd given up hope of ever reaching land. I found it impossible that we had been out there so long and had yet to spot a single sandbar.

I was simply running on basic motor functions. Sometime ago, the rest of my support had left on strike. I wasn't really sure when.

There were days when I was reminded of life, of its wonders, beauty, and innocence. Like when riding alongside a pack of dolphins, or the time the wind died and the boat was swarmed by a flock of manta rays. Animals in the sea were busy with their days, their lives, like so many billions of people somewhere out there. People like me, non-boat people. Able to run free, shop, sit down for dinner or a cold pint of beer, change clothes daily. I longed to change my clothes. Everything was stiff, salted, and burnt. And when the breeze stopped, there was a deal-breaking odour.

Those thoughts placed over a background of complete madness drove me to the edge of delirium… many times. *How in the fuck did I get here?*

I couldn't remember the last time I'd brushed my teeth. It was part of a routine I'd once had, when I walked among the existing.

I would sometimes notice signs, though, between the waves. The sky had changed, and so had the water. The blue was deeper. The sun and the air had somehow grown lighter. There were a few mornings when I could actually see my breath in the air, and a few nights when I had to retreat below deck due to chill.

With the change came some hope. Maybe, by the slightest of chances, we were getting somewhere? Maybe, just maybe, it wasn't all bullshit?

The sea also seemed more temperamental the farther we got along in our quest. Riding the churning edge of the battle between hot and cold, north versus south, I'd have been sick for sure, if there'd been anything in my stomach.

Everyone's spirits had diminished. We hardly talked anymore. A crew of walking zombies. Apparently it didn't matter how many times you had made the trip before. It was always a test of one's endurance, body and mind. Especially with the twists they liked to put on things.

I lay on the deck one evening, watching the final sliver of daytime surrender to the nighttime sea of stars, when Nick quietly sat down beside me.

He lit a cigarette. "What chu think? Huh?"

"What do I think? About what?"

"What chu think 'bout this, huh?" He slapped my leg. "When we go there? What chu go to do?"

It was a question that should probably be paid some attention. What was I going to do when I got there? Assuming we had a destination. First thing that came to mind was a shower and change of clothes, but I had no other clothes and I had no money. Without a passport, I didn't even exist on paper.

"I don't know," I responded sourly.

"I know what I go to do," he continued cheekily. "I go to party, and find some fucking *chicas*, yes man!"

"Where? What in the hell do you guys do when you're there? Where do you stay? Do you live there? You have an apartment or something?"

"I live in all this world, my Brando." He leaned back with a cocky grin and raised his hands to the beauty of the setting sun. "I am children in this world. All of this." He stretched his hands into the night sky, then spread them wide.

"Yes, I know Nick. Master of the universe."

"*Yeah*, I like this!" He patted me on the shoulder. "I is master in all this uni… firs." He spread his hands again.

"I don't know what the hell I'm gonna do. I just want a shower and some clothes. Then I gotta somehow get a passport or something. Find an embassy. Maybe they can help, if they even have one there? I'll probably just head home."

"Home? Wha' home? To Bonaire? Chu go back to small island? *Pfft*." He spit out a cloud of smoke. "Why chu do this?"

"No, not Bonaire. Back to Canada." I rubbed my face in my hands.

"Ah, Canada. Yeah, is a good country, I think? Why chu to go back there? What is there for chu?"

"Family, my friends. A warm bed."

"Friends?" Nick sounded offended. "What for us? We are no chu friends?" He slapped my arm. "Huh? We cross fucking ocean together. Chu do with you friends in Canada? Huh? Where the friends, huh? They in Bonaire? They go to small island with chu? Chu is only man from Canada I see there, huh? We is friends, fucking Brando. We is pirates, is like more than friend. We being brothers."

"Nick, I didn't mean it like that. Of course we're friends. It's just… I'm not thinking straight right now."

"C'mon, do this." He held his pendant toward me.

Not really understanding what he was on about, I held mine up. He leaned in till our bodies touched awkwardly, and he tapped his tooth to mine. "See, we brothers, always."

Brothers… friends. If it wasn't for them I wouldn't be there. But… they weren't the ones who passed out in a stranger's dinghy. I admitted to myself, finally, that I was still pissed they wouldn't take me back. But there was a growing part of me that understood if they had taken me back, I would still be there.

"Yes Brando, I know this time is crazy fucking time. But we get too close. We be there soon, I know. Chu see, and all will be okay." He gave me a friendly pat on the back.

It was nice to hear someone talking about the journey coming to an end.

"Hey!" Nick sat up. "Look now, Brando."

I looked ahead. The sky had been cut in two by a dense white wall.

"Oh shit!" My stomach clenched. I feared that the sandstorm of hell had returned. But it didn't have the same threatening feel.

"Wha'? Is okay Brando." Nick steadied my arm. "Is good!" he exclaimed. He jumped to his feet and pointed off the bow. "I, uh"—he rolled his hand around the way he always did when he was looking for a word—"uh… *niebla.*" He looked down to me for confirmation, and received none. "Fas, fut…"

"Fog?"

"Yes! Yes, the fog." He smiled and placed his hands on his hips. Proud man. "The fog, is good. It mean we no far. Amsterdam has this fog. Much fog."

"Sounds like fun."

His face went blank as his eyes darted around in thought. Then he simply looked down and smiled in a somewhat forced fashion. He had no verbal response. English sarcasm was still a little beyond him.

Fog is good?

The wind was light that night. The water, barely a ripple.

There was really no drama in the approach. It got closer until we slid beneath its cover with no impact, not even a *swoosh.* We simply and silently vanished.

Just when you thought things couldn't get any more spooky, they got so overwhelmingly spooky that I had to think of another word. Say, like *eerie.* Except, instead of two *e*'s, I'd use three: *eeerie.*

"Now what?" I asked.

"What, now what? We is in fog, we go."

Sounded overly simple. "Where's Adlar? Or Dong? Should we go get them?"

"Wha'? Why? No, it is fine. They soon come see. I thinking they sleep now. Is good, let them rest."

Everything within a few feet became veiled. I waved my hand and watched the mist swirl with the movement, like the wash of a jet. I couldn't recall fog ever acting in such a manner before—*eeerie.*

"Brando, look!"

Off the front of the boat was a shape forming in the cloud.

We both walked slowly forward, entranced by the spectacle. Gradually, the form gained clarity. A shark cruising the night. Then, appearing just behind the dorsal fin, sat a man. Wielding a knife over his head. He sat tall, holding onto the fin, legs wrapped tightly around its body. His long beard and hair flowed back.

The nose of the shark slammed into the tip of the boat, and the phantom extinguished.

Nick gasped.

"It's not real. This fog is haunted. Just like everything else on this fucking trip." I placed a calming hand on his shoulder.

We stood on the spot, all senses on high alert. Watching, listening.

Faintly, from all directions, more boats appeared. Large pirate galleons of old, flanking each side. For the most part, they were very faint and distant, easily dismissed as tricks of the mind. Others came so close we could look way up to the decks and see others peering over the rails at us. Some wore bandanas or hats associated with rapscallions of the sea. Others appeared as generals or soldiers from a battle long past. As real as they seemed with their intricate detail, nothing stirred fear or promoted panic. Just a brilliant feast for the senses, floating through a museum of lost history.

Fog is good and we are getting closer. I replayed the statement over and over again in my head. There was an end, apparently. It lent me a second wind. The changes in environment were undeniable. How much longer? A week? Day? What would it feel like to return to civilization? Would I be accepted after everything that had happened, the person I'd become? Would I be able to cope after having been removed for so long? Dumped in a foreign land, where little would work the same as I'd known. Could I still stand on solid ground?

I took a seat and relaxed. For the first time in a long time, I smiled, sincerely. The fact that it was just a boat ride across the ocean with a beginning and an end. I thought I might actually survive.

A dolphin leapt suddenly from below the rail, arcing athletically over the ship to disappear over the opposite side. Then another, and another, the population growing as the size diminished till it was a spinning film wrapping around the whole ship. Then it faded back to nothingness.

I heard her voice again, calling sweetly. Looking around, I spotted a point where the soup stirred. Then she appeared. Twirling through the field in her summer dress. Maybe soon I would have the chance to return and find her. Find her twirling in the sea of gold, so beautiful. I'd run to her and take her in my arms, then steal a kiss. An injection of innocence to my world. I missed it. I missed her. Seeing her then, I promised myself that I would be on the next plane home to grab her and hold on. Never let her go, ever again. I'd never leave or neglect her ever again.

My love for her felt so overpowering. But I'd also been on a boat with three other guys for a *long* time.

I smiled and waved. She turned and blew a kiss, then laughed merrily before she circled away, back behind the veil.

It seemed everyone took their turn floating by.

My father sitting quietly at the table, stirring a cup of coffee and looking off into the distance. Lost in thought. He looked concerned, and lonely.

A soft bout of sobbing circled the boat, then my mother stood alone, holding a tissue to her eyes. She wiped at her nose and sniffled, then her eyes peered over the Kleenex. So scared, so empty. Crying because that was all she could do. As the image turned I did a double-take; her face had transformed into Aleida's.

I'd always known it. It had always picked away at the back of my mind. Until then, I guess I never considered ever getting the chance to make it right. What would I do if that time was granted?

I began to tear up. Not out of fear, but out of sadness, and it felt so good for these worries of everyday life to return.

I relaxed back, pulling a jacket over me and creating a bed for myself. The boat continued silently and the spirits circled 'round.

With the excitement of the end nearing, there also rose a concern of fucking it up. Through the night, I hoped that morning would bring more clarity for us to confirm direction. We were close… *Fog is good.*

13

Night slowly turned to day. I may have dozed off a couple of times, but not enough to feel rested; mind you, I hadn't felt rested since we left. Maybe since I left Canada, even.

Most of the night was spent sipping out of a bottle with Nick, watching in marvel. The biggest event of the night I could remember was the epic pirate versus dragon battle. It lasted for what must've been hours. A dragon fearsome enough to contend with the great and powerful Smaug circled overhead, then dived below. In and around the ship, and then high into the sky, pursued relentlessly by a masterfully crafted pirate ship. Fire was breathed and cannons blasted.

It was like watching a movie in 3-D, without need for glasses. It reminded me of sitting beneath the stars at the old drive-in theatre back when I was a kid. Mom would make up a bed in the back of Dad's pickup truck, and I'd lay down there, then wake up in my bed. Good times.

That old drive-in had closed long ago, been torn down since. A bulk fuel station now, I recalled. I'd forgotten all about it.

The morning sun had slowly chewed away at the fog till the day opened to a partly clouded sky. The ocean was choppy, with a modest swell. Good weather for bringing her home.

Slowly, the crew began to emerge from their hiding spots. They took a moment to clear the cobwebs, then they found their bearings and we all got busy with adjusting the rigging to correct the course. All agreed on one thing: we were getting close.

The others gathered around Adlar as he did what he could to locate our position on the map. It seemed I wasn't the only one growing anxious.

I heard them mumbling softly through the wind. It sounded like another day or two. I wasn't sure whether I wanted to hear any attempt at a calculated guess, for fear of being let down.

On we surged, munching down on whatever reserves remained, each carrying a half-empty bottle of liqueur in our hand. Preparing for the final push. Dong was out front, drinking from his bottle and shouting challenges to the gods as the cold water heaved.

Sails stiff in the wind, we rode hard up the side of a swell, then plunged suddenly off the back, like falling blindly off the side of a cliff. Even after so much time on the water, my stomach churned. But Dong rode that bronc like a purebred cowboy, sometimes getting thrashed by surf cascading over the bow.

Nick and Adlar cheered him on. No one was roaming free at that point—conditions were too sketchy, we all had our anchor points. With all the various nautical powers at play, it was hard to determine how much distance we were actually gaining, if any. The wind pushed us forward, and the waves washed us back. A roller coaster that played havoc with my guts. The sensation topped any of the fiercest rides at any amusement park, and there was no getting off.

As sick as I was, I sensed that we all felt at the same time that the end was near, possibly on the other side of the next wave.

A dark cloudbank was growing nastier by the minute. It looked pissed, the leading edge taking on the shape of a massive sinister face contorting in pain and anger. Twisting side to side and bearing its teeth in rage. None shall pass.

I tapped Nick on the shoulder, then pointed to the storm. "That!" I screamed through the crashing turbulence. "Are we going to ride the front of that?"

He shook his head as a large wave slapped against the side of the boat and drenched us. "No! We can no get to go in front of this. We must go through!"

I stared at the monster bearing down upon us. Holding to my rope, I felt massive undulations beneath as the angry wind pulled at my hair and salt spray washed over my feet and battered my face.

The violence grew—on the wind and in the water, in my stomach and in my mind.

The perfect storm.

The next wave came and the ship thrust upward at an angle I'd yet to experience on land or water. I watched over the front of the bow as the mighty surge disappeared completely and the boat went into a free fall, for what seemed a lifetime, before burying its nose into the valley, almost washing Dong from its back.

I could hold it no longer. I leaned over the side and puked out whatever contents remained, then returned immediately to my position as if it were a simple step in the process.

Ahead, the storm curled in front of us, blocking our path. Its angry face snarled and spat. Lightning shot down in bolts, fingers of electrified energy escaping to the water beneath us. We were still only on the edge; what lay in wait for us in the heart of the beast?

I tapped my friend on the shoulder again. He turned his ear back to me.

I paused, I wanted to ask the question, but I was scared for the response. Emotionally, I needed all the confidence I could muster.

"Are… Are we going to make it?" I yelled.

He released one hand from the rope to turn and face me. The boyish charm once in his eyes had vanished. In its place, I saw a man uncertain.

"If chu wish to!"

14

Nick's response left me unsatisfied. Again, I wondered if this was a translation error. Did he understand what he'd just said to me? If he did, what in the fuck did he mean by it? *If I wish to? Of course I fucking wish to! Doesn't he wish to? Do we have individual options for this? What if I want to but the others don't? Then who gets to take the boat? By rights, the guys who want to make it should get the boat, and the guys who don't might as well grab a lifesaver and get the hell off.* Mentally, that's about where I was at.

The waves increased in size and the wash over the deck was rolling from front to back, creating the feeling that we were on a sinking boat.

Nick made his way carefully to the cabin stairwell, where he shut and locked everything up tight—which I took as a no-go for crawling down and hiding under my bunk.

The next wave hit, and as we crawled to its peak, the boat tilted so far to the side that the boat's railing drug in the water. I was convinced we were going over when the boat righted and crashed down the other side. From the helm, Adlar yelled something about the sails, pointing upward and making a slashing motion across his throat.

Dong and Nick sprang into action, tugging on select ropes till the sails released and fell to the bottom of the mast.

"What are you doing?!" I grabbed Nick by the shoulder, shaking him madly.

He turned, his wet hair pasted across his face. "What!"

"How in the hell are we supposed to get through this with the sails down?"

"We can no Brando! The storm, wind! It is too much! It push boat down."

"How the fuck are we ever going to get through this if we're not moving?"

"We can no do the sails! We must wait!"

"Wait for what? I don't understand!"

With everything going on around us, and the fact we had to scream every word while holding on for life, he was done with communication. All he had left for me was a shrug of the shoulders.

That was it. We were at the mercy of the storm… A storm with no mercy.

Dong and Nick flanked me and dragged me back to the helm with Adlar.

It was an appropriate time for a group hug, apparently. Dong bowed his head and whispered a prayer I would never understand, and then they all gave a final squeeze and patted each other on the back. All I really wanted was some assurance that we were going to be all right, but I knew none could offer it to me. I would've never bought it anyway.

As a wave washed over the deck, it sent us all stumbling. We grabbed each other for support and quickly reassembled. Adlar went to the bin behind him and passed out life jackets as Dong lifted a bottle to his mouth, pulled the cork out with his teeth and held it up.

He screamed to the rain pounding down. The others joined in. The bottle made its rounds, and they all reached into their plastic baggies and emptied them, dividing the cubes up between us. With no time for discussion and feeling I had nothing to lose, I dropped several pieces into my mouth, then drowned them with a mouthful from the bottle. Arms laced around each other in a circle, we screamed in unison to the sky.

I screamed out my madness, only to have the storm thunder back its intense annoyance at my pathetic stance by sending a furiously bright bolt of lightning diving to the sea right before us. Tears streamed from my eyes and the rain pounded them away. Nature was flexing its muscle in a completely fluid environment. I wasn't raised to deal with any of it. I could be the first Medicine Hat local to be lost at sea. Booze, drugs, and a high dose of adrenaline coursed through me. Time to die, or live… *If I wish to.*

A massive wave tilted the ship again and sent a heavy wash across the deck, knocking us from our feet. I managed to grab a handle on the side of the cabin, then pulled myself to my feet after the swell had passed. Though they were coughing and sputtering, everyone had made it fine.

I shouted to them, "So now what? What do we do?"

Adlar looked at me, leaning heavy on the wheel, and yelled, "Hold on!"

Hold on? I was hoping for something like, *If we pull down on the primary jib and rotate the keel clockwise, we'll make it.* I knew to hold on, I *was* fucking holding on.

The wind and spray pounded on, and I looked up to the sky just in time to see the mouth of the storm move above us. A line of shadow consumed us. Instant night, the clouds so dense they blocked out every grain of light beyond the intermittent blinding, violent flashes of lighting stabbing down to the ocean around us.

The wind was relentless, salt spray ripped at my flesh like shards of ice, and above all were the waves. You could hear them, feel them, building, growing. But the only time you could see them was during the strikes of lightning.

In one flash I was in the mountain valley, surrounded by Jurassic white-crested peaks. Then the lights extinguished. My stomach flipped upside over, the hair on the back of my entire body stood on end. Another blinding flash and we were on the peak, looking across a meadow of other jagged, knife-edged points. Then the lights shut off and all hell broke loose.

I latched every limb around the railing. So many deadly forces working together to take us down, once and for all. My shivers turned to convulsions. One moment I was being torn by the relentless, icy windblown water. In the next, I was completely submerged, floating weightless, waiting for a breath of air, wondering if it would ever return or if my rail was anchoring me to the final descent to the bottom. Screams from all around, the guys shouting to each other in phrases I couldn't decipher. The ascension up the swells would tip the boat so we were literally hanging from the side, then send us tumbling down the back. So complete was the darkness that it all could've existed only in my mind, if it wasn't for the sickening trauma in my guts.

At the base of the last cliff, we surfaced once again. As I gasped for air, another thick blast of water came crashing over the deck and filled my lungs completely. I choked, then coughed and sputtered, using what precious time I had before the next deluge to purge the fluid and consume oxygen.

The cold, the lack of air, the complete exhaustion had become overwhelming. I felt myself weaken.

The boat climbed again, then tossed and tumbled, rolling over and over. My body was thrashed repeatedly against the side, beating me like a filthy rug. Physically and mentally numb, I was reaching the point where I was ready to let go. What would be the big difference? I was clinging to something, hoping for her to save me, and all she was doing was abusing the shit out of me.

Another burst of torrential water pushed its way into my body and slammed my leg so hard against a post that I was certain it had broken. I wanted to scream, but my lungs were waterlogged and my spirit drained. The storm never let up. Not for a second. There was no break in between the rounds, where you could take a seat and get a pep talk from your coach. It was huge and all-powerful and we were small and wasted.

My limbs, one by one, unravelled from their branch, till all that was left holding on was one hand. One hope.

Slowly, one, by one, my fingers slipped and my grip loosened. Until finally, with one last violent jerk, Mother Nature pulled me free.

15

The darkness ended and the cold wind and rain all disappeared like a switch had been flicked. A strong ray of sun shone down and massaged my back like the hand of a loved one.

I lifted my head, put some weight with my arms, and vomited seawater like I was twisting it from a sponge.

Then I rolled over and the door to heaven opened before me. A hole of light surrounded by a circle of darkness brought calm to everything around us. My breathing was heavy and wheezing.

A vision of my father and I appeared before me. I was sitting on my bike at the top of Kin Coulee hill. My father knelt in front of me holding the handlebars, talking me through it.

"What do you mean you're scared?" my father said.

"I'm scared!" I replied. *"What if I go too fast and crash?"*

It was the most dangerous hill known to kids from our area. I'd been riding on my own for some time by then. But I'd never even considered attempting something so massive, so legendary. This was a task for big kids with much bigger bikes and muscles. Someone with a mustache and leg hair.

"It's all in your head kiddo." He winked at me, then reached up and mussed my hair. *"You control the bike, remember that. You have your brakes; they'll stop you from going too fast. What isn't going to stop you?"* He waited for me to repeat the answer he had drilled into me.

"Dragging my feet?"

"Yes!" He smiled proudly. *"Dragging your feet is not going to help you"*

"Brando!"

A shadow blocked the view to heaven, then began snapping its fingers.

I wheezed and coughed, then turned my head to the side and puked out some more water.

"Brando! Chu good?"

I realized it was Nick as my senses became restored.

"The eye Brando!"

I reached up weakly to feel around my eyes, thinking maybe one had fallen out.

"No, Brando!" He was pointing excitedly to the circle of clear sky. "The eye! Is eye in storm!"

As he moved from my line of vision, I began to understand what he was talking about. I'd heard of such things before, the eye of storms.

It was a hard tale to swallow on land. Being there in it, it made even less sense.

I found energy to pull myself to a sitting position and looked around. The boat was a wreck—ropes and sails hung everywhere, ripped and torn. Surprisingly, we still had a mast. Surprisingly, we were all still alive.

It was completely calm, the water even smoother than glass. The sun felt so good, melting away the stiff ice from my veins.

But all around us, a wall of black swirled and twirled, slowly sliding its way toward our oasis.

With renewed vigour, I began to panic. "Can we lift the sails? Can we row? Can we move to stay under the eye?"

"No, no Brando." Nick shook his head. "This is no work."

"What! What do you mean it won't work? It *is* working. Look—we're under it right now and it's beautiful! We can just stay with it until the storm finishes."

"Brando, please, is move too fast. But we have to be done now."

I looked off the side of the boat and saw the curtain drawing near to begin the second half of the show. I was totally on board with skipping out at intermission.

Fear possessed me and I grabbed Nick and began pleading. "We can't go back in there! We're not going to make it! We're fucking lucky to make it here!"

He handed me a bottle of water. "Here, Brando, chu have this. Then we go the other side, then we be finish."

"How do you not see? Are you fucking stupid? We're going to die!"

I stopped with him to survey our position. The wall was only minutes, maybe seconds away. The others were stumbling around the boat, looking at the eye in the sky, then to the storm bearing down upon us. Shouts started to come, warnings for preparation.

Tears of insanity rolled down my face. I stepped slowly over to the side of the ship and faced the storm. I couldn't believe we'd survived it once. I couldn't believe we were going back in. That we were throwing away the opportunity blessed upon us. I watched it draw closer, inch by inch, growling and snarling. We were handing it a second chance, and not one seemed concerned besides myself.

The madness behind the veil was hard to grasp, drifting there in the eye. Surely the instant shock of the transition from the light of heaven to the darkness of hell would rip us to shreds.

"AAAH!" I gritted my teeth as it bared down upon us, the final inches, till it tickled the tip of my nose. "NNNEEEAAAAAHHH!" I pulled and shook at the railing, trying to match it's fury.

It hit with instant, full-throttle power. Thrashing spray knocked me from my feet. Sliding across the deck, I dug my nails in deep, choking and gargling the saline current. Bethany twisted and groaned like a naughty girl suffering a dirty hangover. She was coming apart. I dragged myself back to the rail and pulled up to my feet. I could hear faint cries from the others as we climbed up, up, shooting into space. I had no doubt it would be the finishing blow. As we passed over the crest, I felt the floor fall away from my feet. I fell through eternity, the only tether to life a thin piece of piping in my hand. We crashed and rolled over and over. Then all stabilized and my feet found purchase again. I wasted no time raising my fist to the storm as shrill cries came from the others. Wondering if they had been carried away to their deaths, I turned to look… just in time to see a heavy wooden beam speed toward my face.

16

Cue the lonely guitar solo.

"He said I'm fabulously rich!... C'mon just let's go!"

I stirred from my slumber to the familiar lyrics from back home—home-home, in Alberta. Gord Downie's sweet voice felt like kicking back and cracking a beer and lighting a joint on a clear and sunny Canadian day. There's no way I'd be hearing that music anywhere but under the good ol' maple leaf. It had all just been a bad dream.

People were singing along and it was nice to hear, but none of it made any sense. The music resonated through my left ear, which felt well planted against a solid surface. I was lying on my stomach, somewhere.

My face felt… different. There was some pain, throbbing, maybe burning. I attempted to raise my right hand to investigate, but I felt the chaffing of a rope bound around my wrist. I quickly discovered the same scenario for my right leg.

I opened my eyes, and the pain in my head throbbed. I quickly discovered that only the left eye was functioning, and its vision was blurry at best. I wanted to rub at it, but there was the stupid binding again. I could've used my left hand, but that would've required either some form of contortionism or just simply turning my head to the other side, but I didn't have the energy. I felt completely spent.

I attempted a hefty breath and ended up sputtering and gurgling out a lungful of sea water. The warm fluid spilt from my slack jaw and pooled under my cheek. I really didn't care.

"Hey!... Hey!"

The shout came from somewhere near.

"Turn down! Turn music down!"

Footsteps drummed till a familiar shadow of a face loomed over me. Nick leaned down to my face, trying to see into my eye with his.

"Guys!" He sat up. "Guys! Hey! Fuck, look! Is Brando! He is live! He make it! Motherfucker, he do it!"

Cheers responded all around, confirming the continued existence of all parties.

Nick moved quickly, working the rope from my wrist. He grew impatient with the knot and pulled a knife from his pocket, sawing frantically at the tether till it fell free, and then he moved on to my ankle.

"Man, chu go smashed so fucking hard in chu face man!" Nick explained as shadows of other bodies joined us.

"We do no know if you die or what in Fuck!" Dong said. "So we grab you, we tie you to boat. We save you Brando!"

Although my body and mind were limp, I felt I could've responded, I just didn't want to. All I wanted to do was lie on the deck, lifeless. It did feel good to have the bindings loose and blood flowing back to my fingers and toes.

I then remembered the boom crashing into my face, and nothing after. It explained the numb throbbing. There had to be some brokenness.

The boys moved around, talking among themselves, shaking me softly, searching my eyes and checking for breath of life. All the confirmation was there, but my absence of verbal acknowledgement seemed to spook them.

They continued to pour water over my lips, and I managed to slurp in some.

"I think Brando is no well. We must hurry to land," Dong said.

"Yes, to land!" Nick responded. He leaned down until his head was close to my mine again and pointed a finger to the distance. "Look, my friend, Brando. Land… Is there."

Land?… Did he say land?" I blinked several times to clear the salt from my eyes, straining to see into the distance. There, very faintly—very, very far away, was a sliver of shadow. A hint of a cusp dividing water from sky. It could be land, I supposed. But even if it were land, how in the hell would we get there? The boat was in shambles.

"Adlar!" Nick yelled behind him. "Chu have the motor to go now?"

Shouts responded, bodies scrambled.

Motor? The boat has a motor? Interesting how they'd never mentioned that. So many days wasted in stagnation, for the wind to blow.

Grinding, cranking sputters transmitted through the deck to my ear. Several attempts were made, then, with a pop and cough, it burbled to life.

"Yes! Yes, my Brando! Now the engine is working, we can make to land now. Please be okay." He raced around, then came back and gently placed a life jacket under my head and a tarp over my body and shoved a bottle of water under my arm.

And so we made way for land. There was a gentle chop to the water, and a cool breeze soothed my battered face and burnt lungs.

I lay still and watched the minutes tick to hours and the cusp grow slowly and steadily thicker.

As much as I yearned to trust what I was seeing, over time on the journey, my mind had developed a heavy mistrust of any information downloaded from my eyes. *Assume it's all bullshit till proven otherwise.*

So close, swirling pinwheels glistened in the sun. Windmills of lands distant from my home, foreign idealism to civilization. My eyes traced the shore from a distance till two slivers of geometrical stone blocks jutted out to the depths, and we made a hard bank to split the difference between them. Down the channel, I remained lifeless. The low thrum of the engine calmed my anxiousness.

Towering smoke stacks of industry reached skyward, and pedestrian walkways lined the canal. People, other people, walked hand in hand. Happy dogs on leashes tugged at their masters.

It was hard to have it all right there and feel so alien.

Whistles and bird calls erupted from the crew at the sight of some scantily clothed girls walking on the land. At the sounds, the girls stopped and placed their hands over their mouths in fits of giggles before waving their hands high in the air and then turning and shaking their asses in our direction.

Girls… clean and dressed so nice, their hair so silken. I could smell their fragrance on the breeze.

Industry turned to office and apartment buildings. Marinas moored various shapes and sizes of boats, from small tugs to million-dollar yachts. The noise of traffic carried from the city. People talked and laughed, music played.

I felt my heart beat again, and a swell of tears rolled down my face. Had we really made it? Was it possible?

Why were we continuing to let it float by? *Please, just find the nearest point of anchor and dock this bitch!*

Then things began to happen. The engine slowed and the boat cranked hard to the right.

"Brando, my friend. We is come to Amsterdam." A hand shook my corpse.

Still I didn't stir.

Voices yelled, ones I didn't recognize.

The forward motion had stalled and the engine throttled up and down. Commotion on-board as the guys ran around, shouting to others. Others on the land.

I sensed our craft had found footing. Then the engine ceased.

It was the trigger. It was instinct I'd never tapped before. I sprang to my feet, snorting and grunting as the animal I'd become. Hungry, growling, nothing could stop the primal need.

"Hey, Brando! You fucking!..." Shouts from the boat chased me down the wooden pier. A heavy-set man was walking toward the boat, partially blocking my passage, and he shook his fist at the crew.

"You! You motherfuckers! What you do to boat? Assho—"

His eyes bulged as his attention turned to the skinny, torn, busted-up mess of a savage running toward him with a busted face heavy with tears. I let a guttural roar go and he began to backpedal, looking for escape.

"Whaaa! Fuck me!"

I tried my best to run around him, but he was too large and I clipped him on the side, sending me spiralling around him, and I skidded to my knees. Flesh ripped and splinters dug, but I never missed a beat, pushing back to my feet and charging. Onlookers took shelter, some looked as though they considered jumping off the side, to the safety of the water.

I could see it, it was right there. Step by step, closer. I leapt over the final few feet and skidded to the grass. Burying my face, I clutched clumps of it in my hands so tightly that it juiced between my fingers.

So fresh, so cool, so solid and confident, I broke down in sobs of finality. Give me the grass stains, filthy knees, and dirt beneath my nails! I was back! Nurtured in the arms of my mother. Nestled in her bosom. I beat at the earth with fists and kicked it with my feet, confirmation of its reality.

Then I calmed, my breathing steadied as I lay face down in the very small patch of lawn. Everything—the madness, the white noise in my mind, the weakness in my limbs was sucked from my body into the earth. I was grounded again. Clarity began to seep back to me. Clarity I had forgotten.

I had survived the impossible, I was alive.

Alive, like never before.

17

Amsterdam… More significantly, land.

So much peace had been delivered to me with the arrival. I felt a smile return to my face and happiness to my soul. At that moment, I realized the significance of having positive contact with land. It's where we're born; it's what we're designed for.

I took my time bonding with Mother Earth again, I'd missed her so-so much. I understood the importance of certainty in life, the certainty that solid land provided.

With the madness in my head cleared and the smell of moist soil and greenery in my lungs, I rolled over to feel the beautiful sun on my face and smell the fresh breeze.

"Hey!" Nick called.

I heard the building march of footsteps down wooden planks.

"Brando! Chu fucking go crazy man?"

The troops approached. One by one, their shadowed figures appeared, partially blocking the sun as they looked down at me.

"Hey, look, guys! Brando, he has shit!" Dong pointed down at me.

"Yes." I smiled. "I know I look like shit, but I feel absolutely fantastic!" I exhaled a breath of relief. A breath I'd been holding way too tight, for way too long. I did a glorious angel spread on the grass.

"No, Brando, you have shit. It is there, this dog, you roll in shit."

I raised myself up on my elbows and saw dog shit smeared in various blobs around my shorts, but it hadn't the slightest effect on my mood. Squinting in the sun, I looked at our surroundings; there were some people nearby, taking notice. Spectators-spectating—quite a few honestly. Despite what thoughts of "freak show" must've been rolling through their minds, I felt love for every one of them.

"Hey! You! Guys!" I vaguely recognized the gruff voice of the man I'd collided with on the dock and watched as he waddled hastily toward us. His shaking finger was raised high above his portly figure and mostly bald head, which twinkled in the summer sun.

The guys moaned in unison. Breaking from the huddle, they turned, lowered their heads and scuffed their feet in the dirt like children preparing for a scolding. I guessed the man to be the owner of Miss Bartholomew.

"You! You guys!" His speech had a heavy Dutch accent, making him sound even more pissed off than he was… maybe.

I looked back to our girl sitting peaceful in the harbour. She sure looked rough. Ropes and gear hung from every possible point; sails lifeless and tattered.

He budged his way into the group and was quick to get up in Adlar's face, holding his finger mere inches from his nose. "You! You do this! I give you this job! What did you? Look!" He pointed back to her. "She is destroyed! How much money you know it take now to fix? *And!* The motor you run! You know this cost money!" He planted his hands on his hips.

Adlar held his hands up in a calming gesture. "Faas, please, we have big storm at night. We lucky to still be in live. We must use this motor, or we can no come here. The sails is shit now."

Faas slapped both his hands against his forehead. "The sails? They are shit! You know how much to cost for this? How to make money now!" He raised his hands up in a choking fashion and lunged toward Adlar, who took a step back.

"Faas!" The even more menacing voice of a scolding woman came from a short distance away. "Not touch poor boys! Huh! You lucky they are here and the stupit boat. You know of the storm! The poor boys! Look at them!"

The woman approached. I couldn't tell if she was his wife or mother or sister. They were roughly the same build. But she had long hair streaked with equal parts of grey, and she was much prettier, in a motherly way.

Faas growled at the unwelcomed interruption. "Helen! You cannot!" He threw his hands into the air. "I having discussion wit these boys!... We must!"

"You not discussing wit them, you should thanks to them. They are heroes!" She placed herself between Adlar and Faas, getting all up in Faas's face and shaking her finger at him. "Huh? Who you think you are? These boys maybe could die out in the stupit boat!"

"But Helen! How?... Ugh!" He stomped around, pulling at what hair remained on his head. "How we make money now? On this!"

"OH!" Helen's hand shot to her mouth and her eyes jutted from her skull as she took notice of me on the ground. Torn and tattered, likely looking worse than Bethany with my face busted and swollen, and a side of dog shit all over my shorts.

"Oh! Who? What? Who is poor boy? Did he come wit boys?"

"He is Brando," Nick stated simply.

"Yes!" Faas butted back in. "Yes! This boy! He stowaway! Huh? Free ride to here he has?" He looked at me and shouted, "Not free boy! You will pay for this!"

"Oh hush Faas!" Helen swatted at him and reached down for my hand. "You poor boy. So awful has happen to you? Come, please, sweetheart!"

She motioned for help from the others. Dong grabbed my hand and they pulled me gently to my feet.

Helen immediately leaned in to inspect the busted side of my face. "*Tsk, tsk.* Oh, you poor boy, let us help you. You must be in so much pain. How skinny you look, hmm? You need some food?" She pulled a cloth from her pocket, licked it, and dabbed tenderly at the dried blood on my cheek, then flapped it out and swatted at my shorts. "Look at this, it is gross! Stupit people wit dogs. Why they not responsible for this, huh? Come, poor boy, Brando? This is your name?"

"Brandon, ma'am." "Bran-ton? Yes? It is a nice name, such a sweet boy. Where you from?"

"Canada, ma'am."

"Canata! My gootness, you are so far from home, huh? How you get so far? Come, we will get you cleaned up. Dong, help us to the house."

Dong gladly took the opportunity to escape the wrath of Faas, who shouted at our backs as we walked away.

"You not let them play games wit you Helen. They are not goot boys. They are on drugs, I know! All of them!"

"Yes, of course they are on drugs!" she snapped back over her shoulder. "They have to be wit you. Maybe I will have to get drugs also!"

We heard Faas's rant continue with the guys left behind as we walked into the shade of the surrounding buildings, toward a white-sided, two-storey boathouse.

Welcome to Amsterdam.

18

The boathouse was decorated with a large collection of maritime paraphernalia. Walls littered with framed pictures of seaworthy craft, mounted trophy fish, and old-school fishing poles with various monster-fighting tackle. Shelves lined with model schooners in glass bottles and decorative sculptures from all over the world. Everything was frosted in a fine layer of dust.

"Please, boys, not mind mess here. Is Faas office, he not let me clean, ever. But he also not clean." She led us to a weathered set of rickety stairs against the far wall, which creaked and groaned under our weight as we tipsily ascended.

The upper level proved to be the living quarters. The size of a small apartment, the modest dwelling was neatly kept and functional. A large window against the north wall captured a view over the bay and surrounding harbours that made up for any lack in luxury.

As the cool air of the house washed over me, my legs began to tremble and my body felt increasingly burdened by my weight. My mind took it as a signal that the time had finally arrived for me to have a peaceful, much-earned rest.

"Poor dear," Helen said. Her soothing voice was sweetness to my soul. She directed Dong to help me around to a plush recliner, which looked as though it had survived multiple generations, as did the handmade quilts that covered it. "Here, Branton from Canata, you will be goot here wit us."

I plunked down with finality. Normally it would be hard for me to find such comfort in the home of a stranger, but I needed it so very badly. The chair, with its softness and warmth, sucked me back and cradled me still. I squeezed the armrests between my fingers. The smell of family gatherings, of grandparents bouncing children on their knees and sharing stories of past wonders while holiday treats baked in the oven brought calm to my mind, and I drifted into a peaceful, catatonic state.

Dong found a spot on the adjacent loveseat and let out a puff as he sat down. Helen clunked and clanked around the kitchen till she returned to us with a pitcher of iced lemonade and a bowl of steaming water. She poured two glasses of lemonade and handed one to each of us.

Tipping it to my mouth, homemade sweetness kissed my lips and the cool, sugary blend trickled down my throat and busied itself replenishing the scorched desert.

Quivering, I set my glass down on the coffee table, then leaned back, took a sleepy breath, and softly closed my eyes.

I flinched. Pressure was being applied to my battered cheek, just below my eye.

"Hush," a caring whisper breezed into my ear. "Poor boy." Helen dabbed at my wounds with a cloth soaked in boiled water. "I have to check, make sure not is broken, hmm."

It hurt like hell. But after the initial sting, the gentleness of her heart was reviving, and very much welcomed.

Such fortune. During our time on the boat, I dreaded the uncertainty. Attempting to imagine what would happen when we landed, anticipating being tossed aside to try to survive in the cold gutters of a foreign country.

To be there, in the boathouse with this lady, so beautiful and so loving. A better reward for survival I could not dream of. For her to instantly take my hand and take me in made me realize there really are good people everywhere in the world. I could feel in her touch that she craved the time as much as I. It's just who she was.

I watched my blood consume the cloth each time she dabbed at my cheek and pulled it away. She rinsed it in the bowl and let it float while she returned to my face with pressing thumbs.

I winced in pain, it was so tender. Funny thing was, I'd forgotten all about it till she started tending it.

"Shshh now." She squinted and moved her head at different angles, surveying the damage. "I think you is lucky boy. I not think is broke. But is very bat for the… broos?" She puffed out her cheeks and raised a hand to the side of her face, cupping it to mimic a large swelling.

"Bruise."

"Yes, this is bruise. It looks not nice, but I think you will be goot. You must rest."

She left me for a moment to return to the kitchen. My face felt refreshed, but I had been reunited with the throbbing in my cheek and I was well aware of a large swollen mass below my eye.

She came back to butter my face will a foul-smelling salve. She then surprised me again by firmly pressing a cold compress to the spot, instructing me to hold it in place. I took control and she ran her fingers reassuringly through my hair. "It will only take time, boy." Then she let me be.

Silence settled in the room, but for the ticking of a heavy-handed clock somewhere beyond my line of sight. And an occasional snort from Dong, who had sprawled out on the loveseat as best he could and passed out.

The compress soothed my pain and my eyes became heavy, my mind and body exhausted. I turned slightly in my chair and looked out the bay window to the sunlit channel, where the chop of small waves slopped the surface. The fluidity taunted me into a trance, forming a vision of mystery and romance at a time not so long ago. Then, all I saw was turbulence and chaos. I suppose I was seeing it for what it really was, a powerful and tempting force of nature. The shimmering of sunlight on its surface detailed every crest and valley, so cunning was it. Lovers held hands while they walked down the boardwalk, smiling and laughing, falling in love on its shores. Dreaming of a life on the breeze, beyond walls of society… if only they knew.

A large yacht passed by, its hull carving through the light, playful spray. People clad in light summer wear and bikinis walked around on the deck with cocktail-laden glasses, waving to onlookers on shore. The "haves," wealthier and wiser, waving to the "have nots." The water carried them smoothly, baiting them away from civilization and prying eyes, leading them out to the hunting ground.

Fools.

A door slammed and I stirred in my chair, waking from a brief but welcome slumber.

Helen shouted down the stairs in her native language. Her tone relayed annoyance and was met with an equal response from Faas.

Dong twitched in the commotion and fell from the loveseat, slamming a hand hard on the coffee table during his unexpected descent.

Finding our wits, we both straightened ourselves and sat properly while waiting for what was sure to be the end of the party.

"Those boys! You have them?" His voice grew louder as we heard him start purposefully up the stairs.

"Yes, the boys are here, not be stupit! They need care and rest!"

Faas reached the top of the stairs and, surprisingly, Adlar and Nick poked their heads through the railing just below him, smiling innocently.

Faas shook an angry finger toward us. "They not in my home! They get out!"

Helen snatched the dishtowel draped over her shoulder and swatted her husband across his head, then shook her finger at him. "You! You stop! These boys! Poor boys! Look!" She waved a hand at us. "They hurt and so skinny, all this so you can have you boat. They need foot and some rest! You leave them alone Faas!"

He held his tongue, though his face was a shade that could be labelled "fuming-pissed-off red."

Helen reached around and beckoned the others up. "Come, boys. My God, yes, poor boys, such mess. Come have some drink." She ushered them through to a seat in the living room.

Faas leaned against the railing, arms very tightly crossed, and tapped his foot madly on the floorboard.

"Oh, thank chu much, Miss Helen," Nick said sweetly. "Chu look nice, pretty. Is it new, this dress?" He gently fingered the material.

She giggled and blushed. "You are such sweet-mouth boy. It is olt, this old dress. He not buy new dress for me. He is cheap." She scoffed at her husband.

Faas grunted from his spot, though his head dropped a little guiltily.

Helen shuffled back into the kitchen and returned with a dish of baked cookies, which we wasted no time digging into. Tasting the firm, buttery, melt-in-my-mouth crunchiness of it. I tried to recall the last time I'd had solid food. One bite led to a feeding frenzy and we scrambled to claim our share of the bounty. Every bite of yummy and sip of sweet drink drove Faas one step closer to the edge.

"Okay!" He moved toward us with more menacing finger-shaking. "This all! No more! These boys, they is no goot! They make mess of this boat. We cannot have money for this!"

"Ah, Faas!" Dong whined. "What you want from this? Is crazy storm! We almost dead. Look, look Brando face! Is fuck— I sorry, excuse, Miss Heren." He looked to her for pardon, holding a hand over his heart. "He smashed man, his face! Look!"

"Bah! Storm! Boat is goot for all storm. It is storm in you boys' stupit head. Drink the booze and the drugs. You party too much! And him!" He pointed directly at me, staring me down.

I did my best to hide at least one of my eyes behind my cold compress, wanting to disappear into the recliner. I hoped the question of how I arrived to their land and their boat would magically get swept under the rug. Because I hadn't come up with any respectable explanation, besides what actually happened. That truth would do no good to anyone.

"This guy?" Nick took centre stage, and then I had two fingers pointing at me. "We find him. He was at the sea. Not far off the Bonaire island. We see, he do the kite… board"—he raised his arms in front of him, manipulating an imaginary kite bar up and down. "He kite is so many colours there, so we find him and we go to him. He is died we think, yes. We bring him to boat, we see he alive. We know we can no take him back, we be late for chu. He beg us take him back, he have no money, no paper. He begging! But we say *no*!" He shook his finger back and forth dramatically, looking around to his captivated audience. "We say we can no. Our boss, he be pissed to us, we can no be late!

"So he ride on the boat with us, all way to here. He go through all the shit and storm. He get smash in his face, so hard, with the big… sail… wood! It smash so hard we think he died… more. So, we tie him to boat. Now he here!... He do no want be here!"

All parties off the SS *Bullshit* shook our heads.

Faas took it all in. Fists clenched by his side, left eyebrow raised high, tilting forward slightly. Listening, waiting for a chance to pounce on a flaw in the story. "You!" He pointed two fingers, one to Adlar and the other to Dong. "What colour is the kite?"

They answered simultaneously.

"Yellow," Dong said.

"Blue" was Adlars choice.

"Hah!" A single finger shot to the air. "Is shit! All this is shit!"

Nick countered by saying, "It is blue and yellow and many colours."

"Bah! It is shit, you all shit! You wreck the boat. And him!" Back to me. "You use the phone! Huh? It is you! You have to pay!"

"Oh, Faas!" Helen said, blocking the assault. "You are shit! These boys lucky to be safe! They help this boy! You know there is storm! I know you watch every minute, the weather!" She paused in the middle of the room, hands planted on her hips, dishtowel dangling from one. She looked around at the lot of us, considering options. "You need help. Help wit the boat. It is right, you cannot sell it like this. So boys will stay here for some time and they help with fix. Then they can go and everybody be goot!"

The whole room paused…

I surveyed the guys. They held subtle expressions on their faces. But I thought it sounded like a good deal for us. Like we would be put up there, somewhere, for the time it took to make the repairs. And I suspected Helen wood spoil the shit out of us with meals and pampering. A scarce luxury with life on the road… water.

Faas spit and sputtered for a moment. The fact that the situation had potential to reach a respectable compromise drove him nuts, that was obvious. But he was a man of business, and having to do the work himself or contract it out made no financial sense.

"Yes?" She looked around to all parties.

All on our side nodded with polite smiles. Faas… he took a moment to look down and drag his foot around the floor. Then he huffed, rolled his eyes, and nodded.

"Goot, then is done!" She nodded and made her way to the kitchen.

As she passed by Faas, he shook his finger at us again. "There is no drugs and no booze when you stay my house!"

We nodded again.

Dust settled, Helen returned with an armful of towels. She led us downstairs and through a door to a back area with a small corridor opening on the left to a bathroom and on the right to a room with two stacks of bunk beds.

I raced to claim one of the bottom bunks, feeling a fall from heights was the last thing I needed, and then I headed to the bathroom. The shower's stream was full and strong, covering my whole body. Lukewarm was as warm as it would get, but it was fresh and unsalted. It blasted away at the crusted grime, blood, scale, booze, acid, fear, and uncertainty. The soapy lather stung my many wounds, but the pain was welcomed and I scrubbed harder, looking for a fresh new start.

I was there, two feet planted, hope for life restored and the healing process underway.

I turned the water off and felt the drizzle escape my hair and wash down my skin to the drain. I could use a word like *euphoric*, or maybe *super-duper*, but I don't think there's honestly a word for how I felt. If you really want to know, drop a bucket of acid and sail across the Atlantic. It's the only way you'll really understand. And for that moment, standing in the shower with that feeling, I'd almost say it was worth it.

After we'd all taken our turn cleaning up, Adlar lent me a clean pair of clothes he'd had on the boat. He was a bit larger framed than myself so everything hung loose. I still had no change of underwear. Something I'd have to get resolved at the next opportune moment.

We followed each other back up the stairs to the suite, where the most beautiful smell greeted my nose. Helen hummed pleasantly and stirred a giant pot of stew while Faas sat in the recliner, watching some form of news broadcast, his head tipsy with sleep.

"Come, please," Helen said when she took notice of us. She dealt each of us simple chores to get the table prepared. It was not suited for so many, and some odd stools were robbed from other areas to allow seating for everyone. It would be cramped, but us boys didn't care. All our mouths were watering at the delicious aroma.

Finally, we all found a seat. I had no desire to sit beside Faas, and Adlar and Nick wound up flanking his either side. But it seemed peace had settled for dinnertime. All were respectfully quiet, bowls were filled, fresh bread passed around, and we all enjoyed.

The bread was perfect. When ripped apart, large crusted flakes fell to the table and the inside was moist and fresh. The stew concoction was hearty and delicious. I'd been known to be a picky eater at times, but that evening I threw caution to the wind and dove in headfirst.

Helen had trouble settling down to eat. She was constantly fussing. Monitoring everyone's supply, topping up glasses, exchanging dropped cutlery, and replenishing the bread plate. There was no lack of hungry mouths to feed. We ate like soldiers home from battle.

I watched the way she took so much pride in her service, smiling and humming along as she watched us enjoy her hard work. I wondered if she and Faas were parents. I hadn't noticed any family portraits in the place, but I also hadn't been looking for them. If they weren't parents, I was certain there was a legitimate reason; but what a shame, if it were to be the case. She was a wonderful woman, and her love and caring was evident in everything around us. It wasn't the nutrients in the food but her in heart that nourished most of all.

There was nothing left, not a crumb big enough for an ant, by the time we were done. I was fuller than I'd felt in memory. We helped with the cleaning, which took little time with so many hands. Then one by one, we said our thank-yous and Miss Helen escorted us downstairs and actually tucked us into our beds.

The pillow was feather soft and the bedding was fresh to the touch. Helen did a final inspection of my cheek and applied another layer of the stinking salve while I lay, but I didn't complain in the least.

As she wished us pleasant dreams, turned off the lights, and shut the door behind her, the room fell to exhausted silence. I was thankful for it. But in my pre-slumber, thoughts of new issues to address spun in my head. Real-world concerns, like money and identification were allowed to raise their hands to be heard. Technically, I was an outlaw. Where to begin piecing things back together was something I'd had no time or reason to consider before then.

But I pushed those thoughts aside. No more questions, not for that night. It was time for peace and thanks.

Then the unexpected happened.

At first, I mistook it for someone upstairs walking to the bathroom or kitchen for a glass of water. But as the creaking found a steady rhythm, it became very obvious what was taking place. Helen let go a pleasured moan, to which Faas responded with one of his own.

There was a sense of everyone in the bunkroom holding their breath.

Then Nick let out a snicker. "*Pfft!* Chu know this? Faas! He do it to Miss Helen!"

We all giggled.

Apparently having the house full of young boys to complete a family environment stirred mating instincts. They were not shy with their feelings. As things upstairs heated up, they got louder. To the point where it felt as though we were invading their privacy.

"Good for Miss Helen! Chu go Faas. He a big man, yes? Motherfucker!"
We chuckled ourselves into slumber.

19

"*Good* morning Miss Helen," the boys said with a teasing tone. "Have sleep good at night?"

She blushed, then brought down the trusty dishtowel to swat them out of the room and get them on their way. "You boys. You get! Get and go to help Faas on the boat."

I smiled politely as I went to pass by her and out the door. She stopped me, placing a finger to my chest. "Not you, you come with me today. Get clean and upstairs, we will have breakfast. Then we will go."

Puzzled, I looked at her. "Wh-where are we going?"

"To Canata," she stated as she left the backroom.

I considered the odd statement while I got prepared.

To Canada? Is she for real? Is she shipping me off on a plane? I hope to fuck it's not another boat. If it's a boat, I'm out!

We all gathered for a hardy home-cooked breakfast. Afterwards, we all cleaned up, then the guys and Faas began to head down the stairs.

"Brando? You no come with?" Dong asked as he noticed I didn't fall into line.

Helen shooed with her hand. "You! Mind you business! Brandon come with me today."

She disappeared into her room, and I stood in the living room, watching the crew make their way down the dock to the boat. Then she reappeared, wearing a very motherly, floral-print sundress, with a sweet little sun hat to complement. Down the stairs, through the door, and out to the street, we made our way. I followed behind Helen with my head down, not looking for any attention at the time.

It was my first step out into the general Netherland population. I would've preferred to make a more grand entrance, rather than in weathered hand-me-down clothes and a cheek swollen to a full crescent rainbow.

I pulled up beside my companion. "Miss Helen, I'm not really sure what you mean when you say that we are going to Canada? Are you taking me to the airport? I… I don't have any money, or a passport. So I'm not—"

"No!" She turned to me. "Not to Canata, the country. To Canata… Uh?… The Canata, the building, here."

A light bulb flickered. "Oh!" Even I was having trouble finding the right word. "The… the, uh, Canada building! The Embassy!"

"Yes!" She raised her hands in the air and smiled. "This, the Embassy. We need to get you to this. You must get everything to be goot here?"

"Yes!… Yes, this is a great idea Miss Helen! I didn't even think to do it. I've never had to visit a Canadian Embassy before. Thank you so much!" Acting on grateful instinct, I embraced her tightly. "Thank you!"

She wrapped her arms around me and patted me sweetly on the back. "All will be okay, Brandon. You are a goot boy. We will get you to Canata building and you will be goot." She held me back and smiled at me with motherly eyes. "Come now. We will go."

Turns out the boathouse was right around the corner from the train station. Rounding the corner from the marina, the area opened to a bustling city centre. It was the first city I'd visited where you could reach the centre by boat.

The sun was rising, but an evasive mist still hung in the lower lying areas of the bustling, foreign metropolis.

People of all races, with attire ranging from rags to suit and tie passed by on bicycles, in trams, and on boats in intercity canals. So many faces, from so many places I'd never guessed existed. A rainbow of flesh tones. They flowed around one another, one bending and turning instinctively to the other, an unspoken telepathy among the populous.

The environment stirred my curiosity enough that I'd abandoned my insecurities. Under the new sun of yet another chapter of my life, I felt displaced in public. Like a deep sea diver taking a moment of decompression, I needed time to reclaim my land legs and accept a social environment.

… Amsterdam is fucking cool.

Inside the main station, Miss Helen stood in line at the ticket window till her turn. After speaking our intentions in her native tongue, she led me through a turnstile and down a set of stairs to a busy corridor. Referencing the tickets as we walked, she counted off the adjacent wings till we found what she wanted. Down to the left, we ascended another broad stairwell to a massive covered platform, where we waited for our train.

Similar platforms, spaced evenly apart, lay under the massive roof. People waited, drinking their coffees, reading books, and tapping on computers, among vagrants who walked with overburdened packs or instruments slung from their shoulders.

Public transit of such scale was a thing strange to me. I'd been exposed to the smaller scale inner city trains in Calgary, but this was completely different. I looked down the multiple veins of tracks stretching beyond sight in either direction. Where did they go? What was at the end? How many borders would be crossed?

Helen stood beside me and mothered me. Smiling and rubbing my back or holding my hand. A few minutes passed and a long train glided before us, slowing to a final stop.

We stepped onto a sparsely populated car and had our pick of seats. Helen offered me the window. It was a comfortable, pleasant way to get around. As we started down the track, I watched the passing scenery. The trip was short lived as Miss Helen patted my leg when the train came to a stop at the next station, signalling our time to depart.

The rest of the trip covered pretty much every type of public transit available to Amsterdammers. Buses, trams, and two feet.

"Hansel and Gretel"… You know the story. If I had to give a single phrase to describe Amsterdam, it would be that. Many of the buildings were of the quaint Old World design. The roads were narrow and seemed more inviting to bike traffic. Cars were compact, but the majority of the people I noticed seemed most comfortable with a self-propelled or public transit option. I'd had yet to see one jacked-up diesel truck, barking black smoke through performance exhaust.

The air was thick and sweet, with a soupy essence of dewy flowers and freshly baked goodies.

People appeared happy, pleasant, and helpful. The women… there were many. I wasn't at my best, but there was no harm in scouting future prospects if my face ever returned to anything inside normal standards.

The final walk to the Canadian Embassy passed us by other embassies. It was an interesting area made up mostly of two- or three-storey apartment-style buildings. Some commercial, some office, and some residential. The sun had risen and the warmth kissed my face. I smiled. The closer we got to the Embassy, the better I felt. It'd been a long time since I'd met with someone from home.

Finally, we stood before it. And it was like no building I'd seen back home. It reminded me of a small replica of the White House.

I looked at Helen as she patted my hand and smiled up at me.

"Canata." She winked, then waved me on ahead of her.

Inside, the place was tastefully decorated with tapestries, hanging flags, and pictures of several Canadian representatives I didn't recognize. First up was the security-*slash*-information desk.

A uniformed guard at the desk greeted us. "Bonjour, hello."

"Ah, hell—" My voice cracked. I cleared my throat and tried again. "Excuse me." I grew suddenly nervous at the unknown of what they would actually do with a man in my situation. Would I be arrested? "I'm Brandon Baker and I'm a Canadian citizen. But I've lost all my identification and, well, everything."

The guard raised an eyebrow and remained silent.

"So… I thought… I… Can you help me?"

He finally smiled. "Yes, of course." He waved us around the side of the desk to a security scanner, where we removed suspect objects from our pockets and passed through. Poor Helen had to be scanned several times due to her jewellery.

After collecting our things, the guard directed us to an office on the left at the end of the wide corridor. Helen took a seat in the vacant waiting area as I approached a woman sitting behind a counter.

She smiled. "Bonjour, hello."

"Uh, yes, hello."

"Hello, sir, how may I help you today?"

"Well, my name's Brandon Baker and I'm a Canadian citizen, but I've lost my passport."

"Okay, we can help you with this Mr. Baker," she said with a very pleasant and reassuring smile. "Don't worry, you are not the first person to have this happen. We just need to fill out some papers and confirm your identity. Then we can get you a temporary passport so you can return home if you like. Or we can file for a full replacement, which usually takes one to two weeks."

She went to a filing cabinet, rummaged for a short time, then returned with a not-too-intimidating stack of papers. "So, do you have any other form of identification with you?"

"Well, no, actually."

"No? You lost your whole wallet? You don't have even a bank card or anything?"

"No, no bank card."

"Okay. What is your name please?"

"Brandon. Brandon Baker."

She busied herself, filing in information. "That's *k-e-r*?"

"Yes, that's correct."

"When did you arrive and what airline did you fly with?"

"Ummm." The sweating began. "I arrived yesterday, but... I didn't fly."

She stopped scribbling and looked up, her smile replaced with curiosity.

"You didn't fly? So how did you come to Amsterdam Mr. Baker?"

"Welllll, it's kind of a... different story."

"Okay. We will need to know how you arrived here. We need a timeline to file for a passport."

"I came by boat."

"By boat?" She smiled and returned to her scribbling. "Can you tell me what cruise line?"

"Not a cruise ship, actually." If there was ever a time for a simple white lie, It would've been then. But I couldn't handle the pressure of being under such scrutiny in an embassy. Sweat stains began to soak through my shirt, which only added to my anxiety. I was certain I was going down.

"No? Not a cruise line?" She looked up again, and this time her curious stare was accompanied by the rapid clicking of her pen. "I really just need an explanation Mr. Baker. So, why don't you just tell me the story so I can quit playing guessing games."

"Yes, okay. Well, I was down in Bonaire—"

"Bonaire?" Her interest piqued. "The island in the Caribbean?"

"Yes, that Bonaire."

"Okay." She returned to the paper. "How long were you down in Bonaire?"

"About a year."

"A year? So you had a visa?"

"A visa? Well, yes, I had a visa."

"How long was the visa good for? Did it expire? Is that why you left?"

"Well, no. I think it was good for another three years."

She looked up with a raised eyebrow. "Three years? A work visa for three years?"

"Work? No, just my personal visa—credit card. Sorry." I shook my head, placed my elbows on the counter, and rubbed my hands through my hair. I was failing miserably. "I think, maybe, I'm not sure what you mean."

She inhaled deeply and did her best to be civil. "Normally, when you travel out of country for an extended amount of time, you need to apply for a visa. I'm guessing you didn't do this?"

"No. No ma'am. I was unaware of this, thing."

"Well, you were lucky you were down in Bonaire. I think they probably don't keep track of these things as thoroughly. So, then, let's continue. You were down in Bonaire, then how did you come here?"

The pressure was on and I was cracking like an amateur. I looked back at Helen, sitting so obediently in her chair. Her hefty purse resting in her lap.

I leaned over the counter, causing the attendant to lean back, and lowered my voice. "There's these guys I kind of know. They deliver sailboats, and they came by the island. So we got partying on the boat and I… I passed out on their boat. And when I woke up, we were already out to sea and they wouldn't take me back."

She blinked her wide eyes several times, then clicked her pen and sighed.

"That lady that came with me, she's the wife of the owner of the company that owns the boat. We kind of told her and her husband a different story."

I could tell by the look on her face that my circumstance was a first.

"So I have nothing. No passport, no credit card, no licence, no money!" I stared back at her pleadingly.

It was she, then, who rubbed her hands through her hair. "Well, this is an exceptional case. Do you have family? Do they know where you are?"

"Yes! Yes, I have family back in Medicine Hat, Alberta. That's where I'm from. They know that I was on my way to Amsterdam. I contacted them on a satellite phone on the boat. That was, like, a month ago."

"A month ago! Really?" She blew out through her lips, letting them vibrate, and tapped her pen on the counter. "All right." She grabbed the phone in front of her and set it up on the counter beside me. "First thing is to contact your family. See if they can get you some money. We have an account they can transfer to. Then I'll do what I can to get you a temp passport. We'll need to get some pictures and maybe some fingerprints. I'm going to write this down as you sailed here from Bonaire with some friends. If anyone asks, that's how it went. Got it?"

"Yes! Yes, thank you so, really, very much!"

"I'll do what I can to get a permanent passport for you, but it'll likely take a little longer than standard as this is obviously an exceptional case. After you speak to your parents, I also strongly suggest you call your banks and cancel whatever cards you may have floating around."

I nodded and called my father. He thankfully picked up on the third ring.

"Dad!"

"Son? Brandon!"

Emotion flooded at the sound of his voice. A reminder of how far gone I'd become. I turned and raised a hand to shield my eyes from the attendant. "Yeah, it's me."

A heavy sigh bled through the receiver.

"Thank fuck you're all right. Your mother's worried to death. She's been calling me every hour. It's been a month Brandon! Where the hell are you?"

"I'm fine Dad. I'm safe, in Amsterdam. I lost my passport and everything. I'm at the Canadian Embassy."

"Okay. I'm so relieved to hear your voice and that you're safe."

"Yeah, I'm really sorry Dad, really… so sorry. But everything's okay."

"It's okay son. It's been a tough go, waiting for some word that you're all right. I know you said you were going to be about a month, so against every instinct I had, I gave you that. It's so good to hear your voice." I heard him choke back a sniffle, which was immediately contagious. "You gotta call your mom, Brandon. She's so worried. She had her finger on the button to call the police, the coast guard. She even asked if there was an emergency contact number for NATO. It was hard enough for me to accept the situation as it was, let alone with her yelling shit about you being dead in my ear."

"I know Dad. I'll call her, but I can't do it right now. I'm standing at the desk in the Embassy."

"Okay, but get on it as soon as you can, please. So, now what? When are you coming home?"

"I don't know. The lady here is gonna work on getting me another passport. Could take a few weeks she said. I'm staying with a nice couple, the ones who own the boat we sailed on. I'm working at their dock for the time being, helping fix boats. So, I'm not out on the street. I can survive until things are straightened out. Then I'm on the first plane home." Another swell of emotion breached the gate and I shuddered. "I'm coming home! I'm done!"

"Okay. Okay son. You don't know how happy I am to hear you say that! It's been too long. We've been so worried. Everyone misses you so much."

"I know… I know Dad. I'm sorry, for everything… I'm coming home."

After the emotional ride, we got down to business. Dad passed his credit card number to the lady to get me some cash to last, hopefully till I could get the hell out of there.

"All right Mr. Baker. I think I have enough information to get the ball rolling on this. You have a safe place to stay? Somewhere we can get hold of you?"

I waved Helen over.

The two ladies spoke to each other in Dutch. There was a lot of nodding and Helen patting my hand. Then she wrote down contact information on a paper for the lady. We smiled, said our goodbyes, and left.

It was a big day. Legal wheels were rolling to reclaim my identity, my family knew I was alive and surviving, and I had some money in my pocket. Walking out of the Embassy, my feet were a bit more planted, my head a little higher.

On our way back, I managed to communicate to Helen that I'd like to stop by a store and get some toiletries and some clean underwear.

She nodded and found a convenient spot along the way. Then we returned to the boathouse, my home for the time being. And I was very thankful for everything. You can bet Miss Helen got a big ol' Canadian bear hug when we got back… And I got a cookie.

20

Helen woke us early again the next morning. There would be no more special treatment for me. Well, maybe a little when no one was looking. But I was thrust back in with the others to repair the boat.

It was the first time since we landed that I would step foot on Miss Bethany Bartholomew. She looked different. Safely moored to the dock and through a sober mind. We shared a history now, she and I. I'd compare our one-month journey crossing the Atlantic together equivalent to at least ten years of marriage.

The day was warm, muggy. A thick overcast sky shielded the sun, and a silken fog hung light in the air.

On-board we went to work, scraping and painting, removing pieces of damaged trim, and identifying all things in need of repair. The booms needed to be refinished or replaced and the sails were a complete writeoff.

It was hard, demanding work. We went head down, ass up from sunrise to sunset. Helen made sure our meals were ready on time and our beds were always clean and made when night fell.

Days rolled on till a week had passed us by. Day by day Faas began to develop a new respect for us. Of course he'd never admit it, but as things started to come together, his mood lightened. To the point where he complimented some of the effort, and even cracked the odd joke. We'd laugh—sometimes before the punchline, as much of the time we never understood what the hell he was saying. He'd talk for brief periods and then break out into weighted laughter, slapping his belly or the back of the nearest man to him. So we tried to at least humour him.

For the first week, none of us left the compound. Knowing Faas's strict rules against booze and drugs, no one seemed willing to risk losing the sweet setup we had. Apparently, usually the guys either stayed on the couch or floor of some friends' places. Or paid to stay in a hostel. Though I was the one who'd likely had the hardest time with the crossing, I think we were all a little spent, and proper accommodations and home cooking were much needed.

At times, Dong would run around the corner to a café to get some grass. I'd had yet to go anywhere other than the Embassy. But the thought that one could just walk into a café and get marijuana whenever they wanted was something I was interested in experiencing before I left.

Leaving... The thought rolled over in my mind repeatedly as I performed mundane tasks on the ship. Sanding the deck, I thought of my parents, home, my friends. I shouldn't have a problem getting another job on the rigs. If not with Big Johnson, there were many others. I had the experience. I'd be right back in the money. Mind you, there was that thing where I just walked away from all financial obligations. The repo men had come and taken back anything I owned. It could take time to build up any level of trust credit-wise. So, there was some amount of damage dealt.

All the old gang were either married or in strongly committed relationships. Aaron's girl was expecting, I guess... *Holy shit...*

At night I'd lie awake, staring at the top bunk and replaying the past in my mind. The events that led me to a small bunkroom on the other side of the world with these people. These strangers I hadn't known for more than a month. But as strange as they were, they all helped me turn to the next page in the chapter. So far from home, I could sleep knowing that they had my back. They were weird to me. I was the same to them. But they lived in the weird... Then again, so did I. We were all accepted for who we were, and our contribution.

Every morning my body felt stronger, my mind more settled, and my confidence steadier. My cheek was still smashed up. The swelling had diminished for the most part. But the area had turned a deeper purple, which was more attention-grabbing than the rainbow it had been.

Another week passed in what felt a day's time, and the boat was all but complete. We stood on shore at the end of the day and took her in. She had her sexy back. And she'd earned it.

We shared a laugh and passed around a set of backslaps and high-fives. Nothing was said, but I could feel a true sense of pride. No matter how many times one had crossed the ocean, each path was different, and we'd gone through some serious shit out there. Acquaintances at the start and brothers by the end. Bethany had brought us together. We owed it to her to help her get dressed up. She was our girl, and to see her smile again made it all worth it.

That night around the dinner table, the announcement came. The boat was complete and our debt to Faas was paid. He passed out envelopes to each one of us. The other three guys got their full wage for delivery, plus a small amount per day for labour. Minus, of course, what he felt to be a fair charge for room and board.

I even got an envelope, minus the boat-delivery wage. After looking inside, I raised my head to suggest a mistake when Helen caught my attention with a sly wink and smile that warmed my heart. It wasn't much money, but I was surprised to get anything at all.

"So," Faas began his speech, "I like to say that is nice for help on the boat. It look very nice." He smiled with pride and nodded around the table. "You boys, nice job. So I think, now there is not hard feeling wit us. I will still like to use for more boats deliver, if you like?"

The others nodded their heads and raised their glasses, toasting to Faas.

"Goot! I is maybe having something come after the summertime. We will see. So, it is all finish for now, and you cannot stay here anymore, so tonigh—"

I noticed a shuffle beneath the table. Faas flinched, then glared at Helen briefly before looking down. "I, I mean tomorrow. You must all find other place to stay. Except this Brandon. He must stay wit here till he passport is arrive. But the rest must leave tomorrow. This is not a hotel, and we not need young boys running around causing trouble."

We all nodded.

"Then you are goot. Please enjoy food."

And we did. The last supper, so to speak. The next day, things would change, so we shovelled food into our mouths and passed around plates.

Nick nudged me with a mischievous grin, then leaned in to whisper. "Now, tonight, we go fucking party!" He chuckled and little bits of food jumped from his mouth. His hand shot up to cover his lips.

After cleaning up dinner, we all headed down to the bunkroom and took our time in the shower. I didn't have anything fancy to wear. The best I could do was a plain blue T-shirt and a tan pair of cargo shorts.

Awkward as it was, Helen had come down with us and was mussing around, ironing wrinkled clothes and straightening hair, making sure we all looked to our full potential. Against my subtle protests, she slathered her stinky salve all over my still slightly swollen face. As soon as she turned, I was in the bathroom scrubbing it off with a heavy lather of soap. Finally, dodging and deeking around her motherly intentions, we fell out into the dusked street, untucking our shirts and mussing our hair to suit our personal statements. The night felt warm, inviting, free, and wild.

The guys knew exactly where we were headed. They trotted swiftly, and I had to work to keep up. No time to absorb the sights, we had some apparent mission I was not informed of—but had a good idea what could be so highly prioritized.

Dodging rivers of foot traffic, bikes, and buses, we scrambled to the far side of Central Station and around a canal where tour boats passed beneath. We followed a bustling crosswalk to a little hole-in-the-wall shop on the corner of an apartment-style complex. The green and red letters above the door read CENTRAL COFFEE SHOP. We weren't there for coffee.

It was my first experience inside any type of cannabis café, legit or not. This particular shop was quite small. Dark, rough-finished wood lined the walls and floor. Half a dozen small tables flanked the aisle down the middle, leading to the counter and display case. Baggies, joints, baked goods, a candy store for cannabis connoisseurs. My eyes were as wide as my smile.

Adlar and the guys high-fived and shook hands with the guys behind the counter.

"Hey, look at this shit! These guys are back. How long has it been? We thought maybe you sink." The main guy behind the counter laughed. He was a husky man with short dirty-blond hair, wearing an AMSTERDAM CANNABIS CUP T-shirt.

"Stephi!" Adlar shook the man's hand heartily, the way old friends do. The two rattled to each other in Dutch for a while. Judging by the hand gestures, I guessed Adlar was explaining our harrowing journey.

While story time passed, the rest of us browsed the showcase, pointing and putting together our wish list.

After a few minutes, Stephi planted his hands down on the counter. "All right, all of you trouble guys get a joint for free. It has been hard times for us here since you leave." He winked, then reached below the counter and produced a notebook and pen. "What else you want?"

He wrote down names and orders, then came to me. "Hey, this guy"—he pointed the tip of his pen to me. "He wit you? I know this guy?"

Adlar spoke up. "Oh yes. This is Brando! Our friend." He snorted and leaned one elbow on the counter to begin my story in English. "Brando is badass. He get shit-drunk on boat in Bonaire. We were party. Then he pass out, we not know he there till morning. He wake up in dinghy boat, he wave, 'Hey, guys! Help, help.' So, he come wit us. He badass, from Canata."

"Brando!" Stephi offered his hand to me in the non-traditional style used between brothers of type. "You friend to these guys, you always welcome here. Except that guy!" He pointed to Dong, who was over on the side, staring down into the glass display case. Nose inches from the surface.

He raised his head. "Wha'?... Huh?" He shrugged.

Stephi turned back to me and winked, then chuckled and waved off Dong. He started scratching down my name in his book. "Bra-a-ando. All right man, what will it be?"

I ordered a pre-rolled joint on top of my freebie, a little baggie of White Widow, and a brownie. I'd never sampled edibles before but had heard they can really kick a guy's ass.

Wish lists filled, we spilled out onto the street. The sun had sunk lower and a deep rosy pigment painted the western sky, highlighting the towering structures of square blocks, domes, and steep peaks. The streetlights flickered on and the city came alive with Old World charm. People had arrived home from work, changed out of their formal attire, and re-emerged to the splendor of Amsterdam nightlife.

We each dug into our supplies and pulled out our freebies. The joints were immaculately rolled and bigger than any I'd seen before. Tapered like baseball bats, with the end to be lit as big and round as an index finger, then slimming to the size of a pen tip.

I'll admit, even in Amsterdam I was a little hesitant about whipping out big, home-run slugger fatties on the street with a heavy stream of people passing by. But not one person seemed at all bothered by our shenanigans. Nick passed around a lighter and we lit them up.

Dong raised his above his head. "Fucking pirates!" he shouted, causing some "*whoots*" from the public.

We all followed suit, raising joints in the air and all calling together, "FUCKING PIRATES!"

Joints clashed overhead in the night like a Jedi battle, sending sparks raining down. I was alive again, my spirit returned. I placed the blunt to my lips and took a deep draw, pulling in the sweet night air of Amsterdam, filtered through tangy kush. Exhaling in unison, we watched the large psychedelic plume curl off into the night sky.

After we'd smoked them complete, end to tip, we headed out. Young men with some money burning holes in our pockets, loose on the streets.

We cruised, turning our heads as pretty ladies passed in their form-accentuating attire. Apparently bras were less of a mandate in Europe than back home. At first, I felt as though looking was a violation. But I assumed, after number ten walked by that they were fully aware they'd left them hanging in the closet.

The first stretch of sidewalk sidled a canal, and when I wasn't looking at boobs, I was watching the wide variety of watercraft passing by. Lovers rowing; a man in his fishing apparel with a cigarette hanging out of his mouth; an old motorized woody boat, nicely restored, with a small flag billowing softly off the back. Two young bucks dressed in khakis and polo shirts manned the captain's chairs of that boat while two ladies in flirty evening wear sat on the rear bench. They held up their cocktail glasses as they passed and called out to us. I waved as Dong jumped up on the edge of the cement barrier and called to them.

"Yeah, sexy ladies! You like pirate? Come get some Dong baby!"

They laughed and *whoo*ed back to his bold advances.

The canal opened to a wide, main reservoir, where most tour boats lay moored for the night while a few others puttered on an evening excursion. The waterway was surrounded by the streets and boutique shops of all imagination. Pedal bikes parked in racks were absolutely everywhere. It was just like vehicle parking in downtown Calgary, but with bicycles by the thousands.

People strolled by or lounged on patios that extended out to the cobblestone street, sipping alcohol and smoking marijuana in merriment. The buzz of communication and laughter filled the air; the night was alive and so were we. Hansel and Gretel after dark.

"This place is amazing!" I remarked to Nick as we waited in the square for

Adlar, who stepped into one of the local pubs.

"Yes, my friend Brando." He patted me on the shoulder, smiling from ear to ear. "This Amsterdam. Is fun! Better than Bonaire, yes?"

"Yes!" I replied.

Senses heightened, I looked up to the shining lights of the surrounding buildings. Buildings that had survived multiple wars of the world. Tall and narrow with peaked roofs and clay shingles. It was a place of fairytales, as well as some of the darkest hours of mankind.

Adlar returned from the pub, arms stuffed with bottles of beer. We cheered at the surprise as he passed them around.

I looked around. "Wha'… can we… do this?"

"Do what?" Nick asked. "This?" He tipped the beer to his lips.

"Well… yeah."

"Yes, Brando!" He put his arm around me. "Look, is everybody doing this! We are here in Amsterdam. It is good. No problem. Fucking pirates!"

All the others raised their bottles.

We stood in the night, in the middle of the passing crowd, drinking our beer, chatting, and people-watching.

I passed around the brownie I'd bought and we gobbled it up like drug addicts with a pot brownie. We washed it down with a swig of beer, then Dong left the group to casually chase down groups of passing women.

"Hey, beautiful ladies!" he would say each time. He walked slightly bowlegged, with his arms arched to the side and swinging with emphasis, like some gangsta gorilla. "Where is the pretty girls like you go?" They would giggle at his antics, picking up on his innocent inexperience. "Hey ladies! I'm the Dong… You like the Dong?... The Dong likes you." That last bit of poetic seduction always sent the girls into hysterics.

Watching the performance, I'd lost control to fits of laughter. The bent-over, gut-clenching, tear-streaked-face, stoned-in-the-middle-of-Amsterdam-with-a-guy-named-Dong kind of laughter. I realized at the same exact moment as the ladies that Dong didn't really understand the slang definition of the word "dong" in the English. He was making an honest attempt at introducing himself, with a sexy edge.

Nick and Adlar joined in the laughter simply because they couldn't control themselves.

Dong stood in between the two groups, turning in circles with his hands up to the side, repeating, "Wha'?... Wha'!"

I turned to the others and placed a hand on each a shoulder. "Did…" It was a challenge to maintain myself long enough to speak a word, let alone a whole question. "Didn't you… you guys tell him?"

Nick calmed some, I think more from curiosity about what he was laughing at. "Tell? To him?" He nodded his bottle toward Dong.

"Yes! To him!" My stomach was seriously sore, but I couldn't stop.

"'Bout!... 'Bout!... *d-dong*!"

He had stopped laughing completely by that point and stood straight. He placed one hand in his pocket and put the bottle casually to his mouth. He tilted his head back slightly, but I noticed his eyes remained trained on me as if he still wasn't quite sure.

"Oh!" He turned his head to the side slightly and waved his bottle. "*Pfft*. Yeah… Fuck, man, the Dong, he is do this all time." He rocked up and down on the balls of his feet, continually sipping from his beer, as if buying time.

Adlar had also tamed his laughter to little more than a chuckle to listen in on the conversation.

Mine only grew as the story progressed.

"He do it when we go… to be like this. He go to sexy ladies, 'Hey, sexy ladies.'" He strutted around mockingly. "Chu know I'm Dong? Chu like Dong!" When I meet him, once time, he always like, 'Dong on this, I'm Dong, yeah-yeah.'"

He stopped the teasing march and placed his hand back in his pocket. "So, I think, *Fuck man, this guy is Dong?* He is there, look, fucking Dong, man. Fucking pirate." He raised his beer and voice to his friend. "Chu go Dong! Fucking pirate man!"

"*Yeah*!" I heard Dong cry from behind me.

"Chu get one those girls. They like Dong! Chu keep going man, my friend. Chu watch. Ladies, they go have some drinks, then get Dong when finish some drinks! Hey!" He raised his beer again. "Fucking pirate."

"*Yeeeahhh*! I Dong!"

I was practically on my knees by then. Snot ran from my nose and spit flew from my mouth. I wanted to cheer Dong's name as well, but all I could manage from my crunched position was to steady my bottle.

When the laughter had halted around me, I eventually began to gain control, till I was finally able to straighten myself, still yielding to bursts of giggles. I turned to look at our friend and raised my bottle. "He is the fucking Dong."

21

"Does he ever pick up girls?" I asked the others. "Like this?"

"*Pfft.*" Adlar waved his hand. "Dong, doing like this? No. He is never get girls like this. He like try. We let him. Sometimes he get some girls for us. But there is no worry for girls here, Brando, we go to get girls when we like."

His confidence was inspiring, but a little far-fetched. "Huh? Really?"

"*Yes!*" Nick said with a clever smirk. He patted me on the back. "There is ladies for us when we like." He pointed down a side street to some of the lights on the buildings. "Is like this."

When I focused, I noticed that many of the lights on the buildings were red. Odd it seemed at first. Then something slowly started to dawn, just before Nick started his explanation.

"The lights. The red. This place. Chu know? This"—he waved his hands around his head, looking in all directions—"place?" He snapped his fingers.

"Ah! This… Is this the… red-light—"

"Yes! *Yes!*" Nick's eyes widened.

"—district?" I finished, looking through the neighborhood with renewed interest.

The red-light district of Amsterdam. Legendary. I'd always pictured it to be a lot more… back alleyish. I'd envisioned shady men in darkened clothing, heads down to conceal their identities and jumping from one shadow to the next. Knocking on random doors, with small neon lights flickering above.

But we were there, right in the middle of it. The reality was something else entirely. As darkness settled and the brownie kicked in, the streets exploded with people in open celebration, men and women alike. None shy of their freedom. Most were just everyday-looking people, and many were couples holding hands and strolling along with no mind that they were in the middle of a sexual amusement park.

We regrouped and the guys took me to experience the new world I'd risked my life to reach. A long way from home, where being sexually perverse was as acceptable as smoking drugs on the street.

The ambiance had changed, as if simply being told that we were in the red-light district had pulled back the red veil and the hidden became visible. Between coffee shops were oddly named boutiques to feed the sexually curious. Check out a boutique condom shop, buy some sex toys, then grab a chunk of hash and a bong on your way to the next.

The streets were a maze. Intersecting, meandering, and bridging the canals.

"Look! See!" Adlar nudged my shoulder as we passed by what was, exactly, a urinal in the street. Men stood in line for their turn at the Tupperware stand: a circular plot of plastic with three modest dividers. As if privacy were a concern. I admitted to myself that I wasn't quite there yet. Some guys were just letting it rip right off the edge of a canal. The waterways instantly lost some of their romance.

The time came when the guys decided they were done with the finger foods and it was time to head inside.

Cover charges were paid and doors opened to fantasies of curious men... and women.

Plays were being performed in theatres where drinks were served and daring audience members were invited to participate. At first, they appeared to be raunchy versions of Broadway classics, with scantily clad performers. Then the sex began, right there, on stage, right in front of us.

At one such show, the ladies were holding various foods in their... use your imagination. Viewers could pay a price to go and take a bite or a lick, whichever was appropriate per supplied edible.

Sinking deeper into the backstreets, the buildings closed in around us. Ladies appeared from the doorways of their lairs to entice men who may be looking for their particular menu options. There was no end to what one could order. Shocking delicacies whispered in my ear, caused me to recoil as if a gun had been pulled. I heard fetishes I didn't even realize were a thing. *Something for everyone* was not just a marketing tactic.

Dong convinced me to try out some peep shows; he was pretty excited. For a small fee you can enter a small, dingy room and watch whatever surprise was happening, through a window in the wall. I won't even speak of it because I didn't understand exactly what was happening. Plus, the smell inside curiously reminded me of the portable outhouse on a jobsite.

Continuing on, the streets opened up and the windows for the girls became larger and more attention-grabbing. Like a window display at the mall, they danced and gyrated beneath the red lights.

After a moment of observation, Adlar approached a door to a larger room occupied by four women rubbing each other down and toying with their panties.

A brief conversation later, he smiled and waved the rest of us in. Once we were all inside, one of the ladies secured the door behind us while another drew the curtains and yet another prodded us up a short flight of stairs. The room was tasteful. Well, it was decorated in someone's taste. Each one of the ladies grabbed a guy and led us to a chair in a separate corner of the room. The one who'd let us in hit the Play button on a stereo to set whatever mood they were shooting for. A Gwen Stefani ambiance.

My date fit the stereotype of every man's fantasy. With her imitation-blonde shoulder-length hair and boobs for days, which were lifted to her chin by a white push-up bra. A little white hat sat on her head and a matching thong left little to the imagination.

She bent at the waist and ran a finger teasingly around my lips and giggled at my line of sight. She straightened and danced around slowly on six-inch heels, shaking what her momma gave her. Each article of her outfit displayed the universal red cross symbol. Maybe it wasn't her real job? Maybe she was a doctor by day and gave herself to men for money as an after-hours hobby.

But I didn't buy it.

The ladies gathered in the center of the room to dance with each other. They rubbed each other down, pulled teasingly at their garments, and spanked each other's asses playfully while the guys cheered them on.

As I sat back in my chair, everything began to settle in—the booze, the drugs. Until that point, I'd been able to ignore just how fucked up I was. I became muted, my eyes maintained simple communication with my brain to accomplish little more than acknowledge the spectacle of seduction beneath the veil of dim red light.

As the Cowboy Junkies sang "Sweet Jane," my mistress stepped up the level of intimacy. Placing a hand on either armrest, she leaned forward with an alluring look, enticing me with her full-lashes, pouty lips, and lifted breasts. I felt her breath on my eyes as she passed by like a shark, circling silkily through the deep.

Climbing up, she straddled my lap and formed her body perfectly to mine. She was warm and firm as she slid herself slowly up and down, her hands cupping my cheeks, commanding eye contact at all times like a charmed cobra. She was there, on top of me, in my hands—every man's fantasy. But there was no beat in her heart. One of those things money can't buy.

She pressed her breasts hard to my chest while she reached behind herself and unclasped her bra. She leaned back and slowly the bra pulled away as she slid her arm in its place. She giggled and lightly bit her lip before sliding her hand from her breasts. They were perfect, they were real, she was physically flawless. I wondered why she didn't choose to be married to a Wall Street millionaire, instead of living beneath the glow of rose-colored spotlights.

She leaned forward again, then, with nothing between us, she continued gliding around, pausing for moments to bounce her tits around my face. The song switched and she changed positions, climbing from my lap and turning around so I faced her backside.

She spread her legs and slowly bent forward till both hands touched the floor. She looked back at me between her legs, followed by the trademark giggle and lip bite.

Straightening to a ninety-degree angle, she reached up and looped a finger around the string of her thong on either hip. She twerked her cheeks a little between long sways of her hips, in time with the music. She teased, pulling her panties down over her curves just enough to tease. She left them partially down, then backed up the caboose to extend over my seated legs, until she tickled my nose. Then she placed her hands on the chair's armrests once more and pressed her ass to my groin, reverse cowgirl-style.

The song ended and she stood up, turned around, and pulled me to my feet. Leading the way in her stilted footwear, she kept one hand draped behind her and locked in mine. I noticed the others were at the same point, and my friends and I all disappeared with our separate ladies behind individual doors. Almost as if it had all been choreographed.

She pulled me past the threshold and closed the door softly behind us. We stood in a small room with a double bed and a simple chair beside a nightstand. There was a window with a thin, semi-transparent curtain drawn.

The music was still audible, though muffled, and she slid herself around me again to its rhythm. She grabbed the bottom of my shirt and pulled it up and over my head. Taking a moment, she purred as she ran her hands over my chest and greeted each of my nipples with a light suckle of her lips.

She pushed me back, step by step, toward the bed, till my legs touched its edge. She reached down and unbuttoned my cargo shorts and let them fall to the ground. Then she pushed, and I fell to a cushioned landing.

Mounting me, she ran her tongue along my neck, then wiggled it down my chest and stomach to the band on my boxers.

She began to inch down the fabric with gentle kisses, then abandoned the task to mouth me through the material, while she slid her hands up my torso. She lifted her head and our eyes connected. Mine glazed and bloodshot, hers reflecting tiny clocks with ticking hands and fifteen-minute increments highlighted with green dollar signs.

Slowly, she traced her fingers down my belly to my waist and tugged down my boxers. I lay my head back and looked at the ceiling, to the red light, and I felt that I should be more excited than I was.

My mouth was dry and funked with grass and stale beer. While I worked on building enough spit to have a swallow, my body grew numb to whatever else was taking place. I realized something about myself right around then. As exotic and appealing as the legend of Amsterdam's red-light district was, it just simply wasn't my scene.

I wanted to smell the scent of her skin, feel the beat of her heart, see the love in her eyes.

No matter the male stereotype, I could never be the man this sexy nurse needed me to be.

I felt her weight lift and looked down to see her pulling down what string remained on her body.

I lay my head back again and recounted all the events of the evening. Separated from my comrades, I wondered if or when we'd meet up again, and where we'd stay that evening.

As my eyes grew heavy, the room slowly began to spin. I could feel the cool touch of my pillow and the fresh scent of clean sheets. It was the first time since I'd left that I had imagined my bed back home so vividly.

I was really missing my home.

22

My body was cold. My brain sent demand for air to my lungs and they sucked in a giant, heaving breath. The air was stale, perfumed with "Naughty Hottie" personal lubricant.

One thing I can say about my life to that point is that opening my eyes in the morning was always exciting. I know many of you wake up in the morning, go to your same bathroom and brush your same teeth, then put your socks on one at a time. Then you walk to the window, crack open the blinds to the same landscape you looked upon the day before and the week before that and the year before that.

When I opened my eyes that morning, I found I'd passed out in the bed of a prostitute in Amsterdam's red-light district, with my legs draped over the side and my boxer shorts around my ankles.

Normally I'd be somewhat self-conscious about how many people happened in the door as I enjoyed a nap in such stunning form. But I knew it was likely the most boring door they'd walked through that evening.

My naughty nurse had managed to find enough room on the bed to lay down perpendicular to myself, and she appeared to be sound asleep.

I didn't know exactly where I was or how to get back to the boathouse. I didn't know where the others had ended up or if it were proper for me to be bothering them. What I really, really wanted was to get out of there and take in some fresh air. Clear the cobwebs, soothe my aching head, and get the recovery process under way.

So, with little consideration for an exit plan, I slowly and gently raised my body from the bed. Pushing off with only as much pressure as absolutely necessary, so as not to wake the very nice and accommodating host.

Next, I secured my underwear and pants back into position, then I quietly opened the door, just enough for me to slip out into the main room.

Things looked different in the morning. Sun washed through the windows and cleansed the sin from beneath the red light. All was quiet as the wolves lay in dens, waiting for the day to pass and night to fall once again.

The guys had either left or were still in the rooms with their girls. I'd like to think that they wouldn't leave me there alone, but I'd crossed the Atlantic, so I was certain I could find my way back to Central Station.

If they had not left me, then it was time for me to leave them. I exited the door that opened to the staircase. As I descended, the ancient wooden planks held no secret of my departure. Reaching the bottom, I grabbed the door and was about to push my way out to freedom when one last unsuspected obstacle appeared on the opposite side of the glass pane.

Why not? A young man with innocent curiosity, on his very first visit to an area such as this, where nothing had even really happened. I came, I saw, I learned a valuable lesson, and I was about to return stronger and filled with priceless knowledge and warnings for other young men. Then, God threw the hottest woman I had ever seen right smack dab in the way of my secret escape.

Her hair had such a perfect sheen. Blonde and silken, that must've been brushed a thousand strokes every day. She had the most beautiful blue eyes and such a sweet smile. Truly natural beauty. This could be the woman I was meant to marry. We could've made a life together, with white picket fences.

But we would never be, because I stood as a partied-out mess with a busted face. And for the nail in the coffin, I was walking out of a hooker nest. *Thanks big guy!*

She knocked firmly on the door.

I stood frozen like a deer in headlights. I was looking right at her, and she was looking directly at me. The gig was up.

I placed my hand on the doorknob to signal my exit, but the young lady didn't budge. I carefully opened the door a crack on a squeaking hinge.

"Hello?" she called with a sexy accent.

Speaking with her was something I really would've liked to avoid. The ideal play would be to slide past her, with my head as far down as physically possible and get on my way out of there.

"Hello," I responded. I nodded for her to move and tried to push open the door a little more, but the door resisted.

I was beginning to get a little annoyed. No matter how hot she was, I really just wanted to get the whole awkward standoff over with and never see her again. I couldn't understand why she wouldn't get the hell out of the way. I pushed my head against the window to see just exactly what was blocking the door. It was a dog. Golden retriever was my best guess. Sitting primly on its leash, long tongue flapping from its mouth as if quite content.

What the fuck! Why won't this woman move her fucking dog? Just move and I'll go my way and she can go hers.

"Hello!" I called again.

"Hello!" she responded.

"I'd… I'd really like to just come out now if… if you could just move your dog back away from the door, please?"

"Oh! Pardon, excuse me." She stepped back cautiously and instructed her companion to come as she gave the leash a light tug. The dog moved beside her.

I didn't place her accent as Dutch or anything familiar. Her voice was as beautiful and as properly postured as herself.

I stepped out, my first in a long walk of shame. As the door pulled itself closed behind me, she said, "Please, excuse me." She looked up at me with her beautiful eyes, and I noticed the cutest dimples in her cheeks. "Is this— how you say in English? Um, pharmacy?"

"Oh. Um…" My confusion grew. Obviously this young lady wasn't just new to the area, but also to life in general. There was nothing on the outside of the building that suggested it was anything remotely like a pharmacy. I suspected there were several pharmacies in the area, considering the local industry, but that place was beyond a doubt not the place she was looking for. I raised my eyebrows and held my breath through my quick response. "Nope, not a pharmacy."

"Oh? Oh dear." She tugged lightly on the leash again. Her eyes remained forward and she reached down to the dog, who happily moved in for her caress. "Sasha," she laughed, "where you take us? Huh?" The dog lifted its head and pushed harder against her hand. "Pardon myself. My dog, she is new, maybe is not prepare for trip to pharmacy. She has maybe got lost?"

My light bulb flickered, not a red one. Taking her in, I noticed that her hand opposite the leash had a long slender cane tethered to her wrist. It was black except for the tip, which was painted red.

"I, I'm really very sorry. I just noticed that, uh…"

"I'm blind," she finished my sentence.

"Yes! I see that now." The pause was uncomfortable for myself, but she seemed at ease. "I'm Brandon. I'm from Canada." I reached out my hand before realizing my mistake.

"Hello Brandon. Is nice meet you. My name is Tatiana. This, my puppy, is Sasha."

"It's nice to meet you both." We stood on spot for a moment longer. Looking into her big blue eyes, I found it hard to believe she couldn't see.

It became obvious that she was waiting for something from me. "Sooo… you're lost?"

"I think we may be little lost. I know area okay, but Sasha took many turns to here. So, I do not know she can get back. Is first time I let her do on herself. She still being trained."

"Well, I've only been here for a little while. I'm a little lost myself."

She nodded with her cute smile.

"Maybe if we work together, we can find our way out of here? I have to go back to the train station. Central Station. Do you know that area?"

She beamed. "Yes! I know this. Is where I must go also."

"Well, would you be comfortable walking with me? Is it all right?"

"Yes. I like this, please. Thank you."

"Okay. How do I…?"

"Yes! Just walk and Sasha follow to you."

"All right. I can do that." I took a few slow steps past them and called back softly to the dog. "Sasha! Come on."

Tatiana shook the leash and the dog followed, happy and obedient.

"What this place?" she asked as we began our journey together.

"Oh, it's… books! A bookstore."

"Book? Really? *Tsk*. Sasha, silly girl."

23

As we our way out from between the buildings to the main streets, I found the innocence and beauty had returned to the city. The sun was only beginning to poke between the peaking rooftops, and a heavy dew glistened in the morning light. Shopkeepers were putting out tables and sweeping walks, while small street cleaners made their rounds. Daytime traffic had returned, with people walking and riding their bikes.

My day had started in a way I could've never imagined after the night I had experienced. Leading a beautiful, young blind woman and her dog back to Central Station.

The dog remained close to my heels and Tatiana trailed at the end of its leash, tapping her cane lightly ahead of her feet. The system limited conversation. Although the going was slow, my pace still proved a little too challenging for her. As the dog pulled on her to keep up with me, I would hear random chaos from behind as she did what she could to avoid the patio arrangements, and other obstacles.

"Oh, please!" she called.

I stopped immediately and waited for our group to assemble.

"Please," she said as she caught up, "is okay?" She tucked her cane beneath her arm and reached out her hand. "Can we please?"

I resisted at first. I couldn't understand my hesitance to contact with this woman, or the opportunity to learn more about her. I think if she had caught me at a different time, when I wasn't saturated in such filth, I would've been more approachable.

"Please… You move fast. Is easy if we do this way."

I reached for her slowly and touched my hand to hers. And it was her hand that steadied mine. Skin soft and warm. A tender confidence in her nature. A blind woman trusting in me so completely, a stranger she had picked up at a… bookstore.

"Okay," I said as our hands cupped together.

She moved even closer and dropped my hand to wrap her arm around mine. "There! This best, yes?"

"Uh, yeah! If, if you're all right with it?"

She giggled. "What! You think I strange woman? I hear this in you words."

Her joking caused me to chuff out a snicker. "Well, Tatiana, we just met. You don't know who I am. I'm just a little surprised that—"

"Yes, I just meet you and now I hold you arm?"

"Um, yeah."

Then she turned her face up to me. "You not know much of blind women." She smiled slyly. "I blind, I no can see you. But I tell much from you. You voice, the way you speak to me."

"Really?"

"Yes, of course. The bookstore you come from, is open very early. And you like much booze and drugs when you read." She slapped me on the chest… almost. "I know enough about you, Mr. Brandon from Canada. Much of my life, I learn who can trust. I must know this by other sense, not my eyes. Also, my Sasha very good dog. She tell me if you are not good."

"Ah, but she can't find the pharmacy."

She laughed and slapped my chest again… kinda. "She no can find pharmacy, I smell the alcohol and the drugs on you and maybe… Naughty Hottie?" She laughed.

I couldn't help smiling at her investigative talent. It seemed I was the naïve one in our trio.

"But if I no can trust a man with this… he smell of this. Then I have much trouble in Amsterdam."

It was my turn to bust into laughter. "I suppose you're right about that. I guess it's probably better that you can't see me right now 'cause it's worse than the smell."

"Oh yes?" She smiled again. Then she let the cane and leash fall to the tethers around her wrists and began feeling her way around my arms and up to my head.

It was definitely beyond my comfort zone, especially in my present state. But there was no stopping her. She started with my hair, mussing it worse than it had already been. "Ah yes! This mess! You brush for this."

"Yeah, I'm aware."

Her hands slid down my forehead and across to my ears. She was incredibly thorough, her fingertips like a laser scanner. I had little doubt that she was drawing a very accurate description in her mind.

"What? Oh! This!"

She had paused at the lump on my cheek, which surprised me because by that point, the swelling was minimal, though the discoloration was still visible.

"You have fight? Huh? This hurt? It hurts you? How you get this?" Her fingers ran up and down the lump softly.

"No, it's not from a fight. It's… It happened on a boat."

"On boat, yes?"

"Yes, that's how I got to Amsterdam. I was on a boat and there was a big storm."

"You come here on boat?"

Her hands stopped their exploration and she folded up her cane neatly and stuffed it in one of her jacket pockets. Then she secured Sasha's leash around her wrist and wrapped her arm around mine again, and we walked as I poured out my story. From Canada, to Bonaire, to my eventual and unexpected arrival in Amsterdam.

I found it nice to have someone I could tell my whole story to. I don't understand what enabled her to be this person for me. As if someone as beautiful as her would never be interested in me anyway, and she was blind, sooo…

"Where you live? Now… here?" she asked.

"Oh, well, at the place of the people who own the boat. An older couple, husband and wife. They're really nice. I'm staying with them until my new passport is ready."

"And? After you have this passport?"

I shrugged. "I'm gonna go home. It's time for me to go. Go and get back to life, reality."

"*Pfft!*" She snickered. "I think maybe you like back to where you must stop drugs and booze."

I laughed and nodded. "So, I've been talking all this time. You know way too much about me already. What about you?"

She smirked and let her head drop slightly. "Me? What you like know 'bout me?"

"Well, like, where are you from? And how are you, I mean, have you always been…?"

"Blind?"

"Yes, blind." I didn't understand why I was so uncomfortable with the subject. After all, she knew she was blind.

"I am from Ukraine."

"Ukraine? Really? I didn't expect that. I haven't travelled to Europe before and I really don't know much about… anything"

"Yes, Ukraine is my country. I love it. Is only small country and have much problem, for many years." She stopped, thinking back to somewhere only in her mind. "I am blind since I born. I never see the world, but I hear and smell, and I know is much beauty in this."

"Wow!" Was the best response I could come up with.

"So… you came here with your family?"

"No. My family in Ukraine. When I grow up. I want go to school, be teacher. So, I do this. It not easy, take me long time. Then I think I want help others. Maybe children with this blind, like me."

I could tell emotion grew behind her story, but she remained very composed.

"My family, they help so much for me do this. Then I have offer for this teacher job here, in Amsterdam. They have many children in orphanage for blind children. So, I come here only for one month to see is good for me, and is now two years."

I raised my face to the rising sun as it began to crest over the buildings. Rays twinkled off the golden, dew-covered surfaces and spread warmth over two people from very opposite ends of life's spectrum, as they helped each other through the streets.

"Ah, our stories are very similar, really. Did you also get drunk and pass out on a boat to get here?"

She sputtered and a smile returned to her face. She slapped my arm… kinda.

"No! I not get drunk on boat. I take trains, I not drink alcohol. I think my life not so exciting as you life."

I stopped walking and she turned her face up to a little off to mine. "I don't know. I guess when you look at it from your point, it seems exciting. But from my point… My face hurts, my head hurts, I have no job, I'm years behind my friends back home as far as getting my life together. I guess the story's exciting to hear, but sometimes I think I'm just… stupid. I can tell you that I definitely don't feel like I'm good enough to walk down the street with you on my arm."

She had no comment; she just stood there, looking up and listening.

"I think navigating my way from Ukraine to Amsterdam by train would be exciting enough on its own. If someone were to dress me up like a beautiful young woman and put a blindfold on me… I think I'd be safer back on that boat. So, your life may not seem that exciting to you, but I think you're a really strong and very beautiful young woman. You're beautiful on the inside and… and this is coming from a guy who can see. You are the most beautiful woman I've seen since… like, forever. And I mean that."

It happened sometime during my speech. I can't recall if it was me who moved to her or her to me. But our free hands were clasped together. "So, just… I don't know. I think you're really great and I don't want you to think you're not exciting 'cause… you are."

I felt kind of stupid, for a moment. I wasn't sure why I felt the need to say all of that to her. I was punched in the guts by the sense of coming on a little too strong. It was the negative reference of herself that set me off. Maybe because I was feeling really bad about myself, and she was just this beautiful person. Above all my shit, she was helping others and making the world a better place. I gave her hand a friendly shake.

Her eyes stared directly into my chin. Even though I knew she was blind, I wiped at it a couple times.

Through her smile, she inhaled deeply, then let the breath out slowly. "How long we walk for? I think maybe is being late. I go out quiet this morning. Take Sasha on test before children wake. They would like to come, if they up, but I like quiet for test."

"*And* she still didn't pass the test." I chuckled.

She laughed along with me. "No, she not pass this test."

"So, you got out of bed early for nothing."

"Is not for nothing. All good for practice." She shook my hand and laughed again. "But I must go. The children will wake soon. They will not be happy if I gone, also Sasha."

She offered Sasha's leash to me, then reached in her pocket to produce her cane once again. She let it extend to its full length and lightly tapped the ground around her, then she turned away from me.

"Can you see something? Any big... things? So maybe I know where are we?"

"Oh!" I snapped out of my lull. "Yes, actually. We're standing in this square? A big open space. There are bike racks and coffee shops and then a big statue thing in the middle.

"Ah yes! I maybe know this. Is straight ahead?"

"Yes, straight ahead."

And off she went, like nothing. The woman stepped with even more confidence than myself, especially in my current state. Then I wondered what the statistics were for blind people tripping versus the unblind. I'd tripped on more than several occasions. The surface we walked was not of smooth concrete construction. There was stone and brick, risers and shit everywhere, bikes and racks all over the place, and people sitting in random spots, reading and drinking their morning coffees.

She never ran into anything. Her path curling like a snake as she anticipated everything ahead of time and took an approach very similar to any person with sight. A few times I was tempted to jump to her aid, but the longer I watched her, the more I understood how little she needed. She didn't need a dog, and she sure as shit didn't need me.

Meandering her way around and up the risers, she found the giant sculpture in seconds. It consisted of a large white pillar that stretched up about five stories. Ten feet up was the bottom of a platform, a stage for stone carvings of ancient characters from maybe, Roman times.

She touched the base and smiled, then called for us.

"Brandon? Sasha?"

We went to her side.

"This the way." She pointed down a street to our left. "We go this street. We will be to train station. Is not far." She grinned.

I got the feeling she didn't get many opportunities to showcase her special abilities to new people.

"Okay then." I smiled and looked down at Sasha, her tongue flapped and her tail wagged with pleasure. We made quite the trio. "That way it is," I said and I held my arm out and placed her hand on it. She felt along to entwine hers again. "I'm glad I brought you. I was guessing the totally opposite direction." I patted her hand and she blushed.

Down the selected streets, she would call out obstacles and some key shops by name as we passed. Obviously we were in an area where she had spent some extended time.

"How do you do it?" I blurted out, unable to contain myself any longer. "I've lost count of how many times I've tripped over curbs or ran straight into, like, light posts, parked vehicles, or even whole buildings! What in the heck's in that cane? I literally could not tell you were blind when you walked up to the statue. If I didn't know you, I never would've guessed you were blind. Never."

"I do this!" She faced me and pointed to her mouth with open lips and clenched teeth; she clicked her tongue on the roof of her mouth. "*Tick, tick, tick.*"

"Uh…" I wasn't sure how to respond. "That's pretty cool?"

She laughed and slapped my shoulder… on her second attempt. "I do this"—she faced forward and made the noise again. "Then, the… sound?"—she made a fanning motion outward from her mouth, "it go through air. Then come back and I can see."

I felt my jaw clench at the bullshit she was shovelling on me. "Wha'…? Now you're just being funny. This is some kind of Ukrainian joke!"

"No!" She looked up to me. "I tell you, is no joke."

"Yeah, yeah." I waved her off. "Have you heard the one about the horse and the rabbi?"

"No!" She pawed at me. "Here." She struggled to free her arm, "let me go and I show to you."

I released her. "All right, you go girl."

Not that the last test had been novice in any way, but we were no longer in an open square. We were on a sidewalk on the side of the street. When I say *street*, I mean one bike lane immediately off the sidewalk and a single lane for vehicle traffic headed in our direction, then a train rail in the centre and another vehicle and bike lane on the far side, heading in the opposite direction. It was like Frogger, but this wasn't a video game, and the "frog" was blind.

There was a constant stream of pedestrian traffic passing by us in either direction, and at times, Tatiana would walk the edge next to the bike lane. How she never took even one step off that curb or clipped a passing biker absolutely astonished me.

I could hear it then, the clicking, very soft. I'd assumed she made the noise really loud to scare people out of the way, but it was imperceptible, unless you were listening for it specifically. And there was no bared-teeth expression; no one would suspect for a second that sound waves were being reflected off their bodies. She never touched a thing, and she shocked me again when she traversed the madness to the other side at the appropriate crossing. I wondered how much information she was receiving from her super-human skill.

She stopped and reached for me again, calling, "Brandon?"

I slid my arm out for her.

"You see?" I see this things!" She beamed.

"Yes! I do see that you can see everything Tatiana, very well. I'm very impressed."

"Yes!" She rocked up on her tiptoes, then slowly lowered herself back. "Is like dolphin, or bat!"

"Yeah!" I nodded. "That's exactly what it is. Like the dolphins, they click. It's amazing Tatiana, really! It's hard to believe this is even possible! How long have you been able to do it? How did you learn to do it?"

"Is just something. Because I am born with no eyes, doctor say I just learn to do it myself. Is something I teach also to children. Some that do not know how to do. They do not know… So I help."

"Oh, so you teach them how to be… bats? Or dolphins?"

She shook her head and grinned at my tease. "I teach them all things. I am teacher. I teach them all school, and I teach them have a good life with being blind."

"You live with the children? You're the only one there to look after them?"

"Yes, I live with children, in orphanage. I have my own apartment there. Is small, but is nice, I like. There is other ladies work at orphanage. They take care of all children. I teach blind children. There four blind children. Three girls and one boy." She stopped walking and looked up to me. "I think maybe we come to station?"

I looked around and saw we were standing right in front of Central Station.

Surprised, I could remember nothing of the journey. It seems I'd turned into the one being guided by Tatiana, and I felt strangely comfortable with it.

"I guess we are," I turned to face her. "I guess this was the deal, Central Station. Are… are you okay to go the rest of the way?"

"Yes, I am fine. I be fine since statue. I must get to going." Her fingers were like stalking spiders as they traced their path down to my hand, which held the leash. "Excuse…"

"*Oh*! Right. I'm sorry, I don't mean to hold you up." I raised my hand and slid the strap into hers. Then I bent over and scratched the top of Sasha's head. "Goodbye puppy."

Tatiana looked toward me. "Is funny, do you think? She was to take me pharmacy this morning." She smirked. "Goodbye Brandon. It was very nice to meet with you." She held her hand out to me.

I took her hand between both of mine, holding onto as much as she had offered. "It's very nice to meet you, Tatiana. You're a very special young lady. I wish you all the best."

"I wish you good luck too, Brandon. Thank you for you help. I hope you have safe travel to home."

Our hands slid apart as she smiled one last time, before turning to go to her children, who would be waking from their beds and missing her. Something I could understand, then, after having spent that time with her.

As she stepped away, her hand held firm to mine until the limit of our reach. I watched as she walked away, through the bustling crowd.

She never looked back… Why would she? Because she was blind, and I was…

24

Ms. Helen let me use her computer to log into my email, so I could message my mother. I also sent a message to Aleida. I was surprised to see nothing in my inbox from her. I shouldn't have been.

As sunset came, I walked out and had a seat on Bethany for a while. I really didn't care to see the guys. I could do with a moment of peace, but I was growing curious about where the hell they could be. There'd been no sign or word from them for two days. They'd just disappeared into the streets. I guessed they'd found a spot at one of the local hostels or at some friend's house. I wondered if they would come looking for me. I wondered if I would go looking for them before I left, to say goodbye… Or was that it?

Thinking of the uncertainty of such a lifestyle as theirs, I was thankful for what I had for the time being. I realized I was in a fantastic city on the other side of the world, a place many people back home talk about as a "bucket list" destination, but so very few would ever see. But I really didn't feel like heading out to explore on my own. All I really wanted was to get my papers and get home.

Then I remembered the coffee shop where the guys had introduced me to their friend. I knew it wasn't far away and I was due for some grass. So, after dinner, I walked over.

When I came through the door, I saw Stephi right away, counting some baggies with one eye squinted in concentration. I smiled and approached the counter.

He looked up. "Brrrrando, yes?"

"Yeah!" I chuckled. "I can't believe you remember me!"

"Yes!" He smiled and held up his hand to me. "It is what I am goot wit. Names and faces. So, how are you? I heard you and the guys had a fucking crazy night?" He laughed.

"Yeah, fucking nuts! How'd you know? Have you seen them?"

"Yes, yes, I see them all. They are not togeter though."

"Really? I didn't think they'd split up."

"Hah!" Stephi waved off the remark. "Who knows wit those fucking crazy guys! That is how they be when they come here. They have a big crazy night, then they split up. Some I think have girlfriends, or maybe they find girlfriends. They not talk much about where they are stay. So, I not ask. I think they spend much time togeter on boats. So maybe they need time that is not togeter?"

I nodded. "I'll take one of the joints," I slid some cash across the counter.

"If you need to get message to them, if maybe you go to stay in another place, or something. You need them to know, just tell me here. I will make sure they get the message. They know where to find you." He winked, then slid my order and my change across the glass top.

"Yeah, thanks man." As I slid the change into my pocket, a reflection in the small mirror behind the counter caught my attention and I quickly looked over my shoulder.

I was fast enough to just catch the latter half of her passing. Tatiana. To confirm my suspicion, following close behind her were four young children: three girls, one boy.

Never taking my eyes from the street, I took a step away from the counter. "Thanks, Stephi. Tell the guys I say hi."

Out on the street only seconds after they passed, I saw they were already a ways down the block.

There she was, Tatiana. Her trusty guide dog out front and three little ducklings in tow. All tapping their canes along the street.

I placed the joint in my mouth, pulled the lighter from my pocket and lit the end, then took a pull and slowly exhaled, forming a smoky haze between them and myself. I just watched. Then she stopped suddenly and turned back to look directly at me. Sasha also turned to me and perked her ears.

It was obviously just timing, but knowing Tatiana's uncanny abilities, I tucked my head, turned quickly, and walked away. *Fucking spooky.*

A couple more days went by with no more sign of the guys. I passed the time helping Helen and Faas with odds and ends. Then I would head out to Bethany to sit and watch people pass on the canal, smoking a joint and thinking… thinking about home and trying to remember the feel in the air and the smell. About what it would be like to drive a vehicle for the first time in over a year. I'd have to first get a job and buy a vehicle. I'd be starting over, completely. Living in Dad's basement.

Every day after lunch, I would walk around the corner and sit on a bench in front of Central Station until I grew tired. I watched for her… Tatiana, and her minions following. Stalking a blind woman was a lot easier than stalking one who could see. I shouldn't refer to it as stalking, really. I had no intention of approaching her, or communicating with her in any way. I was just bored, and I liked to watch her. She could walk through a crowd of hundreds and no one would take a second to understand how truly special she was, beyond her looks, of course.

It didn't matter either way 'cause she never came.

Then one morning, Helen busted into my room and gently shook me awake. "Brandon! Brandon!"

I rolled over in my bunk.

"Brandon! The Embassy, they call. The papers is done! You has a passport there for you!"

I sat up, careful not to bang my head on the bunk above. "Really!" I rubbed my eyes.

"Yes!" She patted my hand. "You have shower, then come up for breakfast. We will go."

"Okay," I said with a modest smile.

She looked at me a little quizzically, as if expecting something more. Then she grinned and patted me on the head before leaving the room.

I made my way to the bathroom and looked at myself in the mirror. Soon I'd be looking at my face in the mirror back home. In a day or two, I suspected. I supposed, if I really wanted, I could book the flight immediately. There could be something heading that way even that night. But I decided it was best to take one step at a time. I should get a legitimate passport in my hands first.

I showered and dressed, then went up for breakfast. I was the only one at the table as Helen finished up final details in the kitchen, before setting a plate of berry crepes in front of me. *Crepes… what a great thing for breakfast.* I'd heard of them, but had little understanding of what they were until Helen's kitchen. Everything breakfast was a crepe to her. Fruit with jams and chocolate and whipped cream, or bacon and cheese.

Soon I would return home. To getting up at 4:00 a.m. in the frozen white North. To washing down a truck-stop burger with a Styrofoam cup of an exceptionally special blend of coffee, before heading to work to freeze my ass off.

Even after a year on a tropical desert island, that chill still remained deep in my bones. Thinking about those times could still make me shiver.

Understanding that it may be my last Helen breakfast, I took a little longer with my food that morning. Swishing it around in my mouth so that each taste bud would have a turn sampling every flavour. I looked around the kitchen, across the living room, and out the big window to the marina. Knowing that I should take the time to appreciate where I was, for what it was, with the remaining time I had. Because I could realistically go straight to the airport from the Embassy, buy a standby ticket, then sit and wait patiently for my turn.

I dried dishes at the sink while Helen washed. I looked over at her and smiled. But she wouldn't lift her head to me. I could tell she was aware of my attention, as I could see her jaw clench and I noticed her scrubbing was overly focused. She was one of the best people I'd ever met, and I was so grateful for everything she'd done for me. I never really considered how hard that day would be, and not just for me.

When we'd finished tidying, she disappeared into her bedroom to get freshened up. As I waited, I stood in the living room and looked out over the early morning canal traffic.

She appeared again in her pretty sundress and hat and finally looked at me. I smiled at her.

Then the waterworks began and she sniffled and waved her hand at me. "Don't… please!" She reached into her purse for a tissue and dabbed carefully at her eyes, doing her best not to smear her makeup.

I wanted to give her a big hug. But I knew doing so would definitely fuck up her paint job. So, I abided by her instructions and did my best not to taunt her emotions.

Down the stairs, out the door, and into the crisp morning air we ventured.

As we came around the front of the train station, my eyes scanned the crowd for Tatiana. I knew the chances of seeing her again before I left were slim to none, but I couldn't help making a conscious effort to catch one last glimpse.

Helen was silent till we found a seat on the train. Then she reached her hand over to mine, stealing my attention away from the window. "So?" She smiled timidly. "Today is big day, huh? You get you passport. Then you can go… whatever you like? So, what is that you want? You can stay little more wit I and Faas. I will speak to him, it be no problem … if you like?"

I mustered a smile. But the answer she didn't want to hear must've been written across my face in a universal language. She looked away immediately to maintain, I assumed, her composure. But she kept her hand in mine.

"I… I really think it'd be best for me to go home Miss Helen." I patted her hand. "It's been a long time since I've seen my family. I think they're starting to get a little angry with me. Honestly, it's more than a little angry."

"Yes, I understand this. They miss this boy." She turned to me and placed her other hand on top of the pile of hands that had gathered between us. "You are goot young man. You mom and dad are proud. They miss you."

"Yeah." I looked up and chuckled. "They miss me, and I think they're getting pretty worried about what I'm doing with my life."

"What? Why they worry? You are very nice boy, they should not worry."

"Yeah, well, thank you. But all my friends back home, they all have jobs now, good jobs, for a lot of years. Some have bought houses and are starting families."

"Well, you have job! You sail boat and then you help Faas fix boat! This is job, goot job, for honest man."

"Yeah. It's not really the same…"

"Yes." She let go of my hand and searched through her purse for another tissue. "Of course, you family miss you. You should go home to be wit them."

"Yeah. Time to go back and face the music." I smirked.

"Music, you play this?"

"No, no, what I mean is it's time to go back and get on with life."

I could tell by the way she looked at me that she didn't quite understand that reference either. But she didn't ask for clarification and I wasn't sure I could provide it. I knew she didn't want me to go, just as she knew I had to.

So, we kept communication to basic small talk, but I was growing tired of constant translation. It had been a long time since I'd held any length of conversation with someone who could understand and explain. Maybe it wasn't so much that I was tired of it, maybe I'd just accepted that it wasn't worth the effort anymore. All that was left to say were sad goodbyes, that wouldn't matter as soon as I stepped on the plane.

Helen held my hand all the way to the Embassy, even through the extended silence. Strange how two people from opposite sides of the planet, could meet in such an uncommon manner, and mean so much to each other in such a short period of time.

As the time grew nearer to the moment when I would step on that plane, the more stressed I became.

When I'd left home over a year before, all I wanted, all I needed, was a break. I just needed to step out of the stream for a second, out of the stereotypical normalcy of then and there. But now that I was standing on the edge of that stream, watching everything rushing by at a pace that seemed unsustainable, I remembered it.

When we arrived at the Embassy, the same lady who had waited on us before was sitting behind the counter. She grinned as I approached.

"Your father," her eyes widened and rolled as she blew up at a strand of hair that hung in her eyes, "has been calling every day at 9 a.m.!" She had a light growl of tolerance in her tone.

I tried to make every part of my expression apologize to her. "I… Jesus! I'm really so sorry."

"It's all right," she said as she made her way over to the filing cabinet, "he was really polite every time, but I get the feeling he wants you to go home.

"Yeah, right."

"He said that I'm to get you to call him as soon as you came to pick it up." She returned and slid an official envelope across to me. When I tried to retrieve it, she held onto it till I met her eyes. "We've done our part, you have the passport, and I am not here to get in the middle of domestic issues. But he's already made his call this morning, and knows you've been notified. I have to insist you call him." She let the envelope go and lifted the phone and put it in front of me.

I smirked. "Okay." I tore open the end of the envelope and shook out the contents. A passport and driver's licence fell to the counter.

I looked over the identifications, ensuring the information was correct. Then I looked at the young man in the photo. Young… The passport photo had been taken only a couple months before he left Canada for the first time. That kid had been through more change and turmoil in the time since that photo than the many years before.

I stuffed the driver's licence in the passport. I looked up and nodded to the lady. "Thank you."

She pointed to the phone. "You're welcome. Call your father!"

I picked up the phone and dialled home.

"Hello?" Dad answered.

"Dad!"

"Son! You're at the Embassy? You got it?"

"Yeah, yeah, I got it. Checked it out and everything looks good."

"Okay! Stay on the phone. I'm going online right now and booking you a ticket."

"Well, I was thinking I could just go to the airport and get a standby ticket. Save some money, and it shouldn't take long to get a spot. I'll just crash there till they find me something."

"Nope. It's fine. I'm going to book you a flight, then I'll know where you are and when you'll be back, and I'll have some answers for your mother. She's driving me fucking crazy Brandon! You never called her."

"No. I mean, I don't want to use the phone at the place I'm staying. Don't want to run up the bill."

"Uh huh! And I guess they don't have a pay phone in Amsterdam? Prepaid phone cards?"

"Oh, uh, I guess I never really considered…"

"Yeah, sounds like chicken shit to me, but whatever. I found you a spot. It leaves Amsterdam at 7:00 a.m. their time, tomorrow morning. Which will put you back in Calgary at 8:00 a.m. our time? That's crazy!" He huffed. "So, you have your passport and I've booked you in, flight number 1460. Write it down!"

"Uh, yeah, right." I reached over the counter, swiped a pen and scribbled the number down on the envelope. "Done."

"Good. So, you're doing good in Amsterdam, you have your passport, and you'll be landing in Calgary at 8:00 a.m. Finally! It'll be good to have you back!"

"Yeah, it's good, I'm excited! Thanks for everything, Dad."

"Well, it's been a challenge. But, you had some fun, saw some stuff I've never seen before. So, even with all the shit I've been through here covering for you, I'm proud of you kid."

"Thanks. Thanks, Dad."

"Okay, go enjoy your last night in Amsterdam and we'll see each other in the morning."

"For sure. All right, I guess we'll see you in the morning. Bye."

That was it, written in stone.

I explained the plan to Helen on the way back. She seemed to have accepted what was happening and we were able to talk more on the return trip. She told me the airport was easy to access by train. She would check the schedule and get me a ticket, then make sure I was well prepared to get there on time the next morning.

We made a few stops at some markets. Helen wanted to explore while we were down in the area. When we finally got back to the station, it was late afternoon.

Helen made her way around inside the station. Checked the schedule, questioned the ticket agent some, then had instructions written down for me. She wrapped the instructions around the ticket and handed them to me.

"You put in this." She tugged at the envelope in my hand. "You put there, it is safe, then come."

She led me out to the front of the station and stood in front of a large-scale map of the building. I was doing my best to follow where she was pointing as she explained my morning route, when I felt a heavy nudge from behind.

"Oh! Please excuse me."

I turned around.

25

"Excuse me. I do not run—"

"Tatiana?"

She stood in front of me, her face red with embarrassment. Sasha sat nicely beside her and looked up to me with a steady, happy pant.

"I… huh?... How do you know…?"

"Tatiana."

She placed her hand to her mouth. "Br-Brandon, is this you? For really!"

"Yes!" I ran my hand down her arm. It's me Tatiana, it's okay."

The blush retreated from her face. "I no can believing this! Is you I run into? I do not crash to nothing for many years. Now I run into you, Brandon?"

"Yes, I know, this is crazy! I can't believe it either." I looked behind her and there stood her four ducklings. Dressed very nicely, clean and proper. "I see you've brought your shadows with you?"

She placed a hand to her chest. "I bring this? My shadow? What does this mean?"

"Ah, I'm sorry. I shouldn't have said, I mean the children. You've brought the children with you." I looked around her and waved to the kids, then remembered that they were blind, and I was stupid.

I'd forgotten about Miss Helen. But when she turned around from the map and absorbed what was happening, all hell broke loose.

"Brandon!" Her hand clamped heavy on my shoulder. "This?" She looked

Tatiana up and down, then turned her astonished eyes to me.

Tatiana's head snapped back, surprised at the sound of Helen's voice. "Brandon?"

I held my hands up for those who could see. "Yes, ladies, please. Just a second. Tatiana, this is Miss Helen, the lady I'm staying with, the one I told you about. Miss Helen, this is Tatiana. I met Tatiana the other morning. She helped me find my way back."

Tatiana nodded to me. "We help us both, Brandon."

"Uh, right. We helped each other back. Miss Helen, Tatiana works at the orphanage with the children. She is blind, she works with the blind children, these children."

The introduction was awkward for me. I really wasn't sure if I should've introduced Tatiana as being blind. Maybe it was obvious.

Either way, it was done, and Miss Helen was ecstatic.

"Oh dear, Tatiana? You so pretty young lady." She slid her hand down Tatiana's arm till it met her hand, which she held with no apparent intention of letting go. She looked around Tatiana to the children behind her and a motherly smile burst open on her face "Oh, the children! They so precious! Look to them, little darlings, oh! They are so pretty, and such a handsome young man!"

The children blushed and gripped each other's hands a little tighter.

"They is yous? The children?"

Tatiana giggled. "They is mine, from orphanage. I am teacher to them."

"Yes? You teach to them? Oh, ho, hooo!" Tears welled in her eyes as she went down the line, taking a moment to cup their little cheeks in her hands. "Yes, they is perfect angels! They cannot see?"

I laughed as she waved a hand in front of them.

"No, they can no see. They are blind, like me. So we, today, learning more, how to walk in city."

"Yes? They very goot!" Helen then looked down at Sasha. "And this? This you puppy, huh? What a beautiful puppy!" She scratched Sasha up good with both hands. The dog happily accepted, licking her hands enthusiastically. "Yes, goot puppy!"

"So, how is you day?" Tatiana asked me. "What do you and Miss Helen do today?"

"Oh…" I considered my response. For some reason, I was a little apprehensive about spilling the news that I would be leaving. "I-I-I-I…"

Helen butted in, taking Tatiana's hand in hers once more. "We went to the Canata. The place…" She waved to me for the word.

"Embassy," I said.

"Yes. Canata, the Em-bas-sy. Brandon, he's passport is finished. He has it now. So, he's father, he get him plane ticket to Canata, tomorrow."

"Oh!" Tatiana's interest piqued. "You leave? You wish to leave Amsterdam?"

"Um, yeah. My plane leaves tomorrow morning. Seven o'clock, going home."

"Oh. I see. Well, this is good. I happy for you, of course."

Happy was the word she used, but her expression seemed oddly disappointed.

"Ah, I…," Helen started. "You, you will all come to my house. You will come to dinner. I will make big dinner, and we can have some ice cream! Huh, yes?"

All the children smiled and squirmed in their spots. I'm not sure what languages they all spoke, but the phrase *ice cream* enticed smiles all around.

"Oh! Please, Miss Helen. Of course this is nice you to offer, but it is not… there are many people."

"Hush, Tatiana. I must have this! Brandon, he is leave. We must have party for him, yes." She took the young lady's hand. "Please come! It will be such nice, I will cook big food. You know this food, I not know English for this a-a-a…"

I'm not going to try to spell what she said because it's possible there is no spelling for it. But as soon as Miss Helen said it, Tatiana responded to her in Dutch, and that was it; there was no tearing the two apart from each other.

Tatiana brought all the children and the dog to attention, then Helen took the lead, holding Tatiana's arm while I followed in the back to make sure we didn't lose anyone. Even I couldn't resist the cuteness of all the children tapping their canes lightly on the ground. It was easy to see how tightly knit the little ducklings were, and how much they loved their teacher.

At the boathouse, I helped Helen get everyone up the stairs to the living area. Once there, Tatiana gathered the group and instructed that the stairway was strictly off limits. Then, with Helen's blessing, the children were given permission to explore the place freely.

I agreed to watch over them, which was more of a handful than I initially expected. They split up in all directions, and the little tykes were fast and armed with sticks and tiny probing fingers.

Helen helped Tatiana into the kitchen after Tatiana insisted on helping with dinner preparation. It was apparent that Faas was not yet home. I was curious to hear his reaction to what was sure to be a very unexpected welcome.

"Is this?" the children would ask of me as they encountered certain furnishings and structures.

"Table," I said to one little girl.

"Table? Huh." She continued on her way.

"Children!" Tatiana called from the kitchen. "You must find this bathroom."

The command set up a frenzy of tapping and feeling till they all eventually merged upon the bathroom door. As they felt their way around the room, I was thankful the toilet seat was down. But it was interesting to see them avoid that specific area. It wasn't their first bathroom adventure.

After receiving praise for their quick discovery, they all scattered in separate directions again. I eventually accepted there was no way for me to keep up with all of them, so I surrendered to standing guard at the stairway.

"Is this?" was continually shouted from different sources throughout the room, and I did my best to answer each.

"Chair!"

From my spot, I was able to clearly watch the ladies at work in the kitchen. Tatiana had insisted on cutting vegetables. Helen was hesitant at first, but in fear of insulting the lady, she stacked up the vegetables beside a cutting board and handed Tatiana her best knife.

With everything assembled, Helen stood back to watch with as much curiosity as myself.

Very quickly and studiously, Tatiana held the knife flat in both her hands and ran her finger down the length of the blade. She then grasped the handle and reached to the side and gently retrieved a potato. She turned it around in her hand, then lifted it close to her nose. Satisfied with her diagnosis, she identified the edge of the cutting board with her fingers, set her victim down in the centre, and diced the shit out of it.

It was so fast, I couldn't believe everyone had survived. Like nothing, she grabbed the next and did just the same. Then she picked up the board and used the knife to scrape the even cuttings into a strainer placed in the sink.

"Huh!" Helen responded. She looked over to me and nodded toward the young lady with a smile.

Then I heard the familiar slam of the door downstairs. Faas had returned.

Helen looked at me and her brow crunched, insinuating a battle was coming up the stairs. Faas thumped and grumped along as always, and I noticed all the children stopped on spot, along with Tatiana.

"Get away from stairs!" Faas growled to me as he reached the top and physically removed me from his path. His first hint that things were different that day was the strange young woman standing in the kitchen with his wife. Then, as he slowly turned around in the room, he noticed each child, one to four. Then the dog, who had taken up a spot on the couch and was in mid-belly rub from the little boy.

His eyes bulged. "Whu! What is this? All this? In my house!" He stomped his foot.

Tatiana immediately dropped what she was doing and was on her way to find the children.

"Faas!" Helen scolded from behind the counter. "You be nice Faas. This is our guest for dinner!"

"*What*! Guest? We cannot have guest for dinner. We not have food for all this!"

"Faas! Not be stupit!! We have food for all people." Helen grabbed Tatiana gently by the arm. "Not worry dear. He is nice man. He just asshole."

"Kits! Who is all these children? And dog! On my couch! They have sticks, they bang my chair wit sticks! All my stuff, they bang wit the sticks!"

"Oh, Faas! You such embarrass to me! The children is blind!"

"Uh? Blind?"

"Yes! They is blind. They cannot see you. Is goot for them, I think. Maybe I can be blind too?"

Faas took a step toward one of the little girls and bent over so his face was but a foot from her own. "Blind, huh?" He waved a hand in front of her face, which caused no reaction. But his nasal breaths gave away his position, and slowly and carefully, she reached her hand up. Softly, she felt her way around. Entertained by his big bushy eyebrows for a moment, she let go the cutest little smirk, then traced her fingers down to a gentle hold on the end of his big sausage nose.

No matter how tough a man was, none could withstand the power of that little lady. Though Faas did what he could to maintain his façade, I knew he'd been wrapped around her finger.

"And this!" He placed his hand on the top of her cane and gave it a little wiggle. "What you wit that, huh?"

The question was answered with an instant swat to his shin. Not hard enough to do any damage, but it took everything I had not to bust out laughing.

"Ah" is all he said.

"Is this?" the little girl inquired.

"Is this? This me, Faas."

"Faas... huh?"

Faas looked over his shoulder to Helen. "Okay, they stay." He took off into the bedroom to change and clean up for dinner.

I looked at Tatiana and could tell she was still a little on edge about what had just happened. It looked like no matter what the agreement was, she was ready to take the children and leave. So I felt I should go visit her.

I approached softly from the side. She was still leaning over the counter, but she had put down the knife and potato and had both hands planted. She tensed at first as I reached out and touched her softly on the shoulder, then she eased, realizing it was me. I moved behind her and placed my other hand on her other shoulder, then I slid one hand down to rest on hers and I whispered in her ear.

"Tatiana, it's okay, really. The children are fine. I'm here. Faas is a very good man, He's just... Faas. Everything's okay now."

Her breath steadied and she took hold of my hand, then turned into me and slid her other hand up my stomach to rest on my chest.

"Brandon," she whispered back, "thank you." Beside her hand, she found a spot to rest her head, and I instinctively wrapped my arms around her.

I realized then how scary a place the world could be if one couldn't see. I realized, also, how strong a woman she was to be out on her own, and to be taking on the additional responsibility of four of the sweetest kids I'd ever met. I held her close and felt her tremble ever so slightly, which unlocked something inside me. Something unknown and something I had yet to come to terms with.

Not surprisingly, I caught Helen out of the corner of my eye and turned my head to her. She had been watching everything, the whole time. There she stood with a towel in one hand, the other pressed over her heart, and a tear of joy in her eye as she smiled sweetly at me. And I smiled back.

Having settled Tatiana, I set the table and then returned to the living room to answer more "Is this's."

Faas returned from his room and approached the kitchen peninsula to feed his curiosity of the pretty young lady. He was as gentle about it as he could be. "Hello." He held out his hand, "I am Faas."

"Faas!" Helen barked. "I tell you now, she cannot see. She cannot see you hand."

"Huh, she cannot see? You say children cannot see. I not know she cannot see."

"Yes, she cannot see also. This is Tatiana, the children are for her."

"Uh? All the children?" He looked back around the room. "They are for her?"

"She is teacher, they are from orphanage. She teach the blind ones."

"Ah, okay, okay. Now maybe I know something. So, where is you from, Tatiana?"

"I am from Ukraine." She smiled.

"Ah yes, Ukraine. I have friends from this country. They are goot people. Hard-working, very goot."

"Yes," Helen cut in from the sink, "I have friends from Ukraine, they are goot women from this. Very strong women, very beautiful." She shot a look over to me.

Tatiana blushed as she wiped down the peninsula's counter. "Oh, I do not know this. I am just do what I can do. I am educated as teacher and I am blind. So, I teach blind children."

Then Faas revealed a soft side I'd never seen before. It took some blushing of his own to get the words out. "I say, it is goot for you to come to my house, uh, for dinner. Thank you. It is nice to see the children, and dog. Looks like nice dog."

Helen dropped what she was doing and shuffled around the counter. She rubbed his shoulders tenderly and gave him a kiss on the cheek.

It was too much praise for Faas. It caused his face to turn deep purple before he left the counter to gather himself with the children in the living room. His voice echoed through the room as he walked toward the couch. "Hey, you kids. Look at the dog, is this you dog?"

"Yeah!' shouted little voices.

"Yes? Is goot dog? What goot is this dog? All I see is dog on my couch."

"Sasha!" came the little cries again as the children made their way to the couch to meet Faas and the dog.

"Sasha? This is the dog? Is girl dog?" I watched as Faas knelt down beside

Sasha and the children crowded around them.

"Do this," the little boy said, and he felt his way to scratch Sasha's tummy.

"Yes? She like this?"

I smiled and turned back to Tatiana, who was still fussing with things on the other side of the counter."

"See, I told you everything'd be fine."

She smiled and put her hand out to pat my arm. "Thank you Brandon. You are a good friend."

The ladies had completed as much as they could till dinner was finished simmering. So, we all took a time out and assembled in the living room for some rest and proper introductions, while the children continued to busy themselves with satisfying their curiosity with the room. Helen insisted Tatiana and I sit together on the loveseat as she set a kitchen chair next to Faas's recliner for herself.

Tatiana smiled as she began the conversation. "I like to say thank you very much to you, Helen, and you, Faas. This very nice treat for children and me. We never have anything like this to happen before."

Helen smiled and patted her husband's arm lovingly. Faas reached over with his other hand to pat his wife's. The two sat like very happy and proud grandparents. Judging by the twinkle in their eyes, I'd say it was they who were most thankful for the gifts the day had brought.

Tatiana called for the children, and following the sound of her voice, they made their way to the loveseat, where she guided them all to sit on the floor in front of us.

She patted the first one on the head and the young lady stood with a practised curtsey. She was the tallest of the lot, and the oldest by my guess. Taking time to study the young girl raised my curiosity, as she looked very close to a mini-Tatiana.

"This is Anna." Tatiana smiled. "She is oldest of the children. She very good help to me. She say she will like to be teacher someday."

"Like Tatiana!" the little darling said.

Tatiana blushed. "Yes, like Teacher Tatiana." She touched the young girl on the shoulder and she returned to her spot on the floor.

Next to rise with the same curtsey was a little brunette girl, who introduced herself as Lilly. She loved to sing and was eager to perform a little ballad for her new audience. I didn't understand a word of it, but her voice was incredible and she, adorable.

Gaby was next up. The curly-haired redhead was the youngest of the pack at six—*and a half,* she made everyone take note. That girl could talk. She went off on a rant about something beyond my ability. Even those native to the language sat wide-eyed, doing their best to keep up. One word I caught was *Sasha,* and at the mention, the loyal friend stood and went to the little girl's side.

It took a while for Gaby to settle back in her seat. Then it was time for the one and only boy of the bunch. Good-looking kid, white-blond hair, beaming blue eyes. He came off as the shyest, and perhaps a little behind on culture. He was instructed by Tatiana to remove his hands from his pockets and speak clearly. I felt sorry for the youngster, surrounded by women all day. He didn't have much to say and wasn't as comfortable in the spotlight as the others. He blushed as he stood, introduced himself as Hans, said he was eight, and sat back down.

After some time spent watching the children display some of their special talents and share some interesting stories, I noticed Helen slip into the kitchen.

Not wanting to disturb teacher and students, I slid away myself to see if she needed help. I felt Tatiana's hand brush my side as my weight lifted from the seat. I reached back and squeezed her hand to let her know it was all right. There was no fooling that woman.

Helen looked up as I came into the kitchen. "Oh, Brandon, you not need be here. I am fine, you go, be wit them." She opened the oven and released the enticing smell of her freshly baked bread.

"It's fine Helen, I don't mind. Let the others have their fun. Faas seems like he's actually enjoying the company."

She transferred two warm loaves to the counter and closed the oven, then smiled at the warmth in the living room. "He is a goot man, my Faas. He is asshole sometimes, I know this, but he is goot. He has always been for me. Many not know him, they only know he is asshole. But I not see only this. We have been love since school. He is hard-working and has always give to us what we need."

I turned from watching the group and looked at Helen. "Do… do you and Faas… did you ever?"

She lowered her gaze to the bread. "No, we never have the children." She went to the drawer and selected a knife, then returned and began slicing. "We always want for this, but things was hard when we was young. There was no money, and we want many things. Then time pass, we get to a time when we think yes, is time to have this children. So, we try and… I not know. We cannot have.

Doctor says this, maybe we wait too long?"

It was easy for anyone to see that she was holding back emotion, holding her face stern as a statue. Practised perfection from years of being asked, and tired of breaking down every time.

She lifted her head and forced a smile. Then her expression took on a natural state again as she watched Faas interact with the children while scratching Sasha's head as she sat happily beside his chair.

"It is goot for us, to have children here. Is goot for heart." She returned to her slicing. "This home, most time is quiet. People think maybe we like this quiet. But we like this. Is like to have family. We like to have you here, Brandon. Now, this girl you meet?" She stopped for a second to lift her head and point the tip of her blade toward Tatiana. "She is goot girl, yes. She is strong woman, you see in her, huh? Time in life. There is many time… times. But there is only one time of this, one time. You understand?"

I nodded purely out of politeness.

She looked directly into my eyes and tried again. "This time! Now! Is only now, then it is gone. It is here only one time. Then is gone." She pointed her blade toward Tatiana again. "One time!" She then turned the tip of her blade toward me and regained deep focus. "One time. Then… is gone." She returned to her duties and I turned to look at the others in the living room, my gaze drawn to Tatiana.

The setting sun streamed through the window and illuminated her silken hair and her smile. A smile so bright, it displaced starlight.

I did understand.

26

Helen passed me all the fixin's over the counter. Once I had put them all on the table, she came over to make sure everything was in its proper place, then called everyone to dinner.

We had to scrounge up two more chairs. One from the bedroom and one from downstairs. Enough to let the women and children sit together at the dinner table.

They were such amazing kids. I'd never spent much time with children in my life. Never really felt I was missing out on anything. But at the sound of dinner, it was funny to see how they knew exactly where the table was, and how to get to it. Little feet padded and sticks clacked as they led the charge. Faas played a proud gentleman, following behind them with a beautiful young Tatiana on his arm.

I watched the kids walk by, one by one, each caning me in the shin as they passed, so prim and proper. On closer inspection of their garments, I noticed some stains within the floral prints and some patches in high-wear areas. But they didn't care; they probably weren't even aware, because it was all they'd ever known.

Then I looked at the young woman responsible for teaching them to be the exceptional people they were. I realized how big the powers were that had brought them all together, and I felt I was in the presence of something on a higher level. All the smiles on all the faces, a table stuffed with food. In a tiny boathouse, hidden in the shadow of Amsterdam's Central Station.

With everyone else seated, Faas and I stood back against the wall, while the others passed around the feast and dished up. Well, mostly Helen just ran around the table with every option and dished everyone up herself.

Tatiana said a prayer of thanks, then the kids began raising spoonful's to their noses and smiling before diving in.

With everyone at the table occupied by their dinners, Faas and I managed to tiptoe around and dish up our plates, then we retreated to the living room.

Faas chuckled as he pulled apart a piece of bread. I caught him looking at me from the corner of my eye and turned to match his smiling face.

"It's goot, huh?" He nodded to me. "The kids… is fun. And this woman, huh? This is so goot, this woman. If I were young man"—he elevated his eyebrows— "Hoh!" He reached down to the coffee table for his iced tea and lifted his glass to me. "Is goot, thank you, Brandon." He nodded to his glass.

Caught unsuspecting, I wiped the crumbs from my hands before reaching for my own glass and tapping the rim to his.

"*Hmh*," he acknowledged before taking a swig.

"It is really nice, Faas. I'm the one who has to thank you for everything, really. I can't believe how lucky I am to have you and Helen to help me. I'd be in the gutter otherwise, I'm sure."

Our eyes connected, and he paused with his chewing. He flinched slightly and I sensed he wasn't comfortable with my praise. Then he nodded with a soft grunt and quickly returned to his feast.

It took a while, but those kids finally filled up, and there was not a scrap left to claim. Tatiana and I made our way into the kitchen and caught the dishes and cutlery as Faas and Helen handed them over the counter to us.

Once everything was piled high, I filled one side of the sink with warm, soapy water. Tatiana slid up next to me, armed with a dishtowel. She instructed me to wash one round of every dish and utensil, so she could start a separate pile for each around the kitchen. I washed one of everything till we had covered the entire spectrum, and then she was more than fine on her own.

I can't ever recall a previous dish-cleaning adventure with so much hand groping. It got me hoping the pile would never run out. Twice she dipped her hand in the soapy water and slapped me playfully on the cheek. She was so fun and beautiful, and yet so humble. I guess because of her lack of that one big thing. But I thought the lack of that one big thing was what made her so perfect.

I started to seriously ask myself what a woman like her would look for in a man. Looks were probably not even a concern. Why would they be? I mean, she probably wouldn't date anyone really ugly. But, then again, why wouldn't she? If she did, he'd be the luckiest guy in the world by far, and all us other guys would watch in wonder.

"Okay!" Faas thundered from the dining room, causing everyone to jump. "Who is liking the ice cream? Huh?" He raised his arms as the children cheered.

He disappeared around the corner to the storage room, where the ice box sat, and brought out two 5-litre pails of ice cream, one chocolate and one vanilla. "Huh?" he shouted again as he passed the table, holding them high in the air.

Helen greeted him and took the pails, then she muscled her way between Tatiana and me to reach the counter.

Everyone was served with their choice of flavour, then Faas lifted Hans from his seat and sat down, placing Hans upon his knee. They both dug into their dishes.

I whispered to Tatiana as we stood in the kitchen. "Hans is sitting on Faas's lap. They're both shovelling down ice cream like it's a new invention."

"Oh yes?" She pawed at my arm. "This is very good for Hans. I worry for him. He has no man in his life."

"Oh?… Yeah, I guess."

"There is no man at orphanage. There is other boys. Boys who see, but is problem for Hans to be with these boys. They do not understand. But even this, they is only little boys. Little boys need to have time with man."

"Yeah, I get that. He seems to be having a good time. I can't believe how good Faas is with the children, and the dog! He even put down a little bowl of ice cream for Sasha."

"Sasha? No," she placed her hand to my chest. "Is no good. No good for Sasha have this."

I tensed. "Oh? She'll get sick?"

"No. She not be sick. But she stink, all night, she will be stinking."

I laughed. "Tatiana! You're not that mean. You won't take the ice cream away from Sasha. She's so good to you and the kids, she deserves her treat. Don't think I'm going to take it away. I'm not being the bad guy. You're just stuck with a stinky dog for the night," I chuckled.

She slapped at me and stuck her tongue out. It was the first real sign of feisty playfulness I'd seen in her, and it made her even hotter.

Ice cream completed, Faas went into the living room with the children. He sat in his recliner with one child on each lap and the other two sat right in front of him with the dog. He had the television on to a news program, and the children sat incredibly quiet and listened to the reporter, as Faas softly explained what was happening.

We finished the cleanup in the kitchen, then retreated to the living room to put up our feet with the others. Tatiana sat beside me on the loveseat again. She yawned and rested her head on my shoulder.

"Ah, I am tired. Is late."

I looked at the clock. "Yes, it's nine."

"Oh yes? I should get children back. They will start to worry already. I sure the children is tired too."

I looked over at the intent children resting around Faas. The dog was out completely, stretched long on the floor in front of the television. "Yeah. I guess you should get going." I looked out the window; the sun was all but down and the night was creeping in. "It's almost dark Tatiana. I'd like to walk you back. Please?"

She raised her head and placed her hand on my lap. "Yes, of course. We will like this, thank you."

The kids moaned a bit when she told them it was time to go. It was the first time they stepped even a hair out of place. But you could see they were sleepy, and the air in the house had grown heavy with nurturing comfort. I sensed there was still a lot of work for her to do to get them all to bed. Especially after the exciting night they'd had.

We gathered them up. Tatiana lifted the two off Faas's lap, to the disapproval of all parties. Then she leaned down, found Faas's cheek, and gave him a kiss.

Everyone filed down the stairs to the main level, then out onto the street.

Helen couldn't help shedding a few tears. "Tatiana! I know this, this orphanage close, down end of block? This is you?"

"Yes Miss Helen. This is the orphanage."

"Please let us come sometime. Faas me, to see you and children. You can come to us when you like. We will have food, and ice cream. Please!"

"Yes, of course! Please come to see us when you like. If we is not at orphanage, just tell to woman who open the door. She will know to tell to me."

Helen smiled, nodded, and sniffled, then pulled Tatiana into a big hug. Faas fell in behind her and they both did their rounds with Tatiana and the children.

Then Tatiana led her little ducks into the streetlights, their tapping and clicking echoing off the pavement as I followed behind.

I noticed Hans was in the rear, so I stepped up to keep pace with him. "Hey, Hans." I leaned down to his ear. "If you want, you can hold my hand and we can hang out together. You know, just the guys."

A little grin formed on his face and he shook loose from Lilly's grip to place his hand in mine.

At that point, I was enlightened on another fact that people who don't hang around blind people much should be aware of. When one member in a hand-hold chain suspiciously breaks away from the others, the one's attached to said member have been instructed to scream like a fucking emergency vehicle. At the snap of a finger, Tatiana turned around and snarled; her claws were bared and shit was about to get very real.

"Whoa! *Whoa*!" I yelled. "Hans is right here! We're just trying to have some guy time. Everything's fine, everyone's all right!

"Oh!" Tatiana placed her hand over her heart, her chest heaving with adrenaline-fuelled breaths. "You must say, when this…"

"I know! I know!… *Now* I get it, it's my bad! I just forget sometimes, I'm an idiot. I'm sorry."

The crowd's panic eased and Tatiana managed a small laugh. "Is… is okay. I am sorry to you for this, but we are not used to this… 'boy time.'" She smiled.

"Wha'! Boy time? I don't know about any boy time. I can't see any boys around here. Nope, just me and Hans hanging out back here. Where the *men* hang out, right, Hans?" I looked down at him and didn't have to wait long for a smile.

"Yeah!"

"Yes, I am sorry. This *man* time, but we still must follow rules, for now. We think about how to do man time at different time." She smirked.

"All right!" I said. "But I'm going to hold onto Lilly's hand and then Hans can hold onto my hand, 'cause there's been too much of Hans holding girl hands."

The little ladies lifted their hands to their mouths and snickered.

"So that's how we'll do it. I know how it works, and if anyone lets go of me, I'm gonna scream like a fire truck!"

All the children cheered and made their own emergency noises, drawing curious attention from others.

Tatiana smiled. "Yes, children, all very good noises for emergency. It work very nice."

The line formed again, and as promised, I took Hans's hand in mine and then held onto Lilly's.

The orphanage wasn't far. Down the block a ways and across the street. A modest building of brown brick, with a simple light fixture over the door. Tatiana tried the handle, but found it locked. She explained that it was late for them and the ladies who ran the orphanage had locked up. So she knocked loudly and waited only a few seconds before someone answered.

She was a heavy-set lady, whose grey hair was streaked with blonde. She wore a mauve, ankle-length dress and had a stern look to her at first. But a smile of relief popped as soon as she saw Tatiana and the children.

"Oh!" She placed a hand to her chest. "Oh, Tatiana and children! I am so worried for you! Where have you been?" She stepped down to the sidewalk and reached for Tatiana's hand.

"Oh Tessa!" The two shared a comforting embrace. "I know, I very sorry. We had invite for dinner." She waved her hand, signalling behind her. "This is my friend, Brandon."

Tessa looked around the crowd to me, holding hands with Hans. I smiled as politely as I could; I was never at my best with new introductions.

"This is him, the Brandon? The boy you meet in the morning, wit Sasha?" She looked me up and down, then smiled suspiciously.

I took note. Tatiana had mentioned me to her friend.

"Hmm, he is a very handsome young man. Hello Brandon, it is nice to meet wit you."

"Thank you… Tessa, is it? It's nice to meet you too."

Tatiana continued, "Yes, we find Brandon at train station. He is with Miss Helen, the lady he stay with. She invite us for tasty dinner. The children and Sasha, everyone have very much fun. We have ice cream for dessert."

"Ah! Ice cream." She looked at the smiling faces of the children. "This sound very nice for you. I am happy, but I also am very worried for you."

"Yes, I am very sorry. I did not mean for this. I forget how late time it is."

"It is all right, my dear. I am happy you and children have such nice time. Now, please, everyone, it is time to come in." Tessa stood aside as Tatiana handed Sasha's leash to little Gaby, and the children all carefully made their way inside.

Then Tessa smiled at me and followed them, leaving Tatiana and myself on the sidewalk, alone.

There was silence, then she reached her hand out and brushed my forearm before taking hold of my hand. Her mouth curled into an endearing smile, her eyes so deep and captivating in the streetlight.

I'd never been more torn in my life.

I'd only known her a total of maybe six hours. But she was the real deal, the best woman a guy would ever meet. The happiness I felt with her…But… she was blind. She had four kids. They may as well have been hers, the bond was unbreakable, and a dog. It was commitment, complete commitment. And I had nothing. No job, no money, no place to live.

It was time for me to go home. I had been too long in the uncertain and unfamiliar. Time to breathe that hometown air, to feel that hometown asphalt beneath my feet. To clean up my shit and get on some kind of track.

For a man to go after her, he'd have to step into the light. Step into the light and never look back. For a man to go after her, he'd have to be ready to leave the shadows, abandon all secrets and all dark curiosities. I wasn't there, yet.

"Would you like to come in?" she asked. "You can see inside. Maybe see children before their bed? They would like this." Her thumb tenderly massaged the back of my hand.

I grabbed hold of her other hand and stepped back, drawing a distinct line between us.

"Tatiana." I looked into her eyes. "I have to go. I have to go back home. Back to my family, my friends… my life. You're so beautiful and such a great woman. I really wish—"

The door to the orphanage made a light creak, and I watched it open a sliver. A little boy's head popped out.

Tatiana squeezed my hands. "What is it?"

I cleared my throat. "Hans! Hey, little buddy." I kept my voice to a loud whisper and leaned over to the door.

He opened it all the way and stood there in his Winnie the Pooh jammies. The cuffs on the ankles and wrists rode up far enough to regulate blood circulation. He tapped his stick to confirm his position, then smiled. "Brandon, you come see me to sleep?"

He was like the little kitten you find on the side of the street. I bent down to him and held his wrists gently. "He-e-ey, buddy! I… I can't. I have to get up really early. I have to get on a plane and go all the way back to Canada. You understand?"

His smile tightened and he nodded eagerly. Which I read to mean either he didn't understand, or was happy I was going.

"Okay, I'll tell you what. I'll show you how men say goodnight. Would you like that?"

He nodded again.

"Okay, can you make a fist?" I made one of my own and let him feel it. "Like this?"

He copied my action, and I straightened his arm out in front of him.

"Okay, just hold it there. Now I go like this!" I lightly bumped my fist to the end of his. "Fist bump! That's what we call it back home. You like it?"

He nodded again.

"Wanna do it again?"

He nodded and held his fist out once more.

After round three, I patted him on the head. "Can you find your way back to your room?"

He nodded and went inside.

I closed the door and returned to Tatiana. Tears streamed down my face, but I was able to control my voice.

"I really just have to go, Tatiana." I grabbed her and hugged her close while I whispered in her ear. "I wish you all the best."

Releasing my grip, I took one final look at her as tears welled in her eyes. I gave her arms one last squeeze, then turned and walked into the lonely night.

27

I didn't sleep that night.

When I got back to the boathouse, I went through the regular routine. Shower, brush the teeth, put on the sleepwear. There was literally nothing for me to pack. I just had to ensure I had my passport, ticket and the clothes on my back.

Miss Helen fussed over me for a bit, confirming I had what I needed and going through the instructions for my train ride. In order for me to be at the airport on time, it was best for me to wake at four in the morning, get ready, and make my way to the airport for my flight at seven.

But it wasn't the itinerary rolling through my mind that caused my restlessness. It was the visions of Tatiana and the kids. The time I'd been able to spend with them had released an urge to guard, provide, and shelter them. The traditional male instincts that had lain dormant inside me for so long. I'd had no idea they even existed, until then.

As I tossed and turned beneath the blankets, visions of her smile and caring nature flashed in my head. Along with thoughts of the precious children looking only for someone to care for and accept them.

But what could I even do? If I were a bigger man, a man with means, I'd take them all beneath my wing and be that man they needed and deserved. But on a global scale, I was just a snot-nosed little kid, with not one honest penny in my pocket.

So… roll around in bed, lose sleep over it, let it drive you mad, but get on the plane in the morning. Time and distance will cure it. I'd had success implementing the same prescription in the past. But it was never an easy pill to swallow.

By three in the morning, I still hadn't got a wink of sleep, and decided it was time to start putting it all behind me and look forward to the future.

I sat up in bed and threw my legs over the side. I took a little longer and moved a little slower, breathed a little deeper, listened closer and looked longer. I took my time to accept my finally leaving from the place that had welcomed me so openly after such a traumatic adventure. The floor creaked beneath my feet as I made my way to the bathroom. I quietly filled the sink with cold water, washed my face, and looked it over in the mirror. How it had changed over my time in exile.

After I brushed my teeth, I returned to my room, dressed, and gathered my things. I turned off the light and waited a moment for my eyes to adjust to the darkness, before walking out of the bunkroom and into the main area of the ground floor.

The twinkling lights that surrounded the canal glistened off the water and sparkled through the window. I opened the door and locked the knob. I paused for a moment to review my checklist, knowing, once the door was closed, there could be no return.

Slowly and softly, I pulled the door into the jamb till I heard the final click.

The air hung stagnant with a heavy stench of rain, moistening my skin. Bethany sat, peacefully tethered to her mooring. I smiled at her and silently sent her my thanks.

I turned away from the boathouse and never turned back, as I rounded the corner onto the street. There were others shuffling through the darkness, not one of us making eye contact, no one asking any questions or offering any explanation.

The fluorescent lights in the underground station flickered and hummed in eerie abandonment. Creating the perfect set for a variety of horror film plots.

I checked my ticket, found the right platform entrance, and ascended the stairs. The open air greeted my face as I climbed to the surface. The great expanse of the boarding area was populated by a select few individuals, from polar opposites of the life spectrum. Some were properly groomed and tidily dressed, while others slept on benches or rooted through trash containers.

I stood and did my routine of guessing each one's story. Then I wondered if they could guess mine. Predict the thoughts that ran through my mind.

I heard a train approach in the distance to my left and watched as the nose of a steel serpent poked its head from a black curtain, slinking silkily to a halt before me. A loud hiss and a screech burst from beneath it, and the mechanical doors popped open in a hollow clop.

I stepped on-board and had my pick of pretty much any seat I wished. So, I chose one overlooking the canal.

Some time passed before the doors closed, then the titan began to slither forward. Steel tracks sliding along its belly. I was able to catch sight of the boathouse on my way by, and then the train veered left and accelerated, seating my weight against the backrest. From that point on I kept my head facing forward, the only option I'd left myself. The rubber band stretched with time and distance and would continue till it broke and the weight released. And life would continue. That night I'd be sitting with Joey at the pub, and Amsterdam would exist as nothing more than a tall tale in my rear-view mirror.

Back home, steady job, money in my pocket, beers in a pub, with people who speak English. I wasn't meaning to shit on everywhere else. It was just time for a break. I would be able to return someday, if I wanted. After I got my feet under me.

The changing landscape sped by the window. I exhaled and let my head fall back. *It'll be like I never left.*

The airport was quiet. Just airline attendants, janitors, and security, for the most part. I approached the counter and got my ticket, then cleared through customs.

The band stretched further.

Isolated in confinement, I was in neutral territory, where nothing from either side could get to me. I walked to my gate, found a row of vacant seats and sprawled out. Two hours till my flight.

I was never skilled at sleeping in public. My body shifted down into auxiliary and let my mind drift off to the future. Call the guys together for a "welcome back" at the pub. Wings and beers at Roscoe's. *Fuck, it'll be good!*

I decided I'd get working on a new set of wheels first. I wondered what was new on the car market. Been so long since I'd cruised the lot. Driving a vehicle again was going to be an odd feeling.

There was just one more thing to suck up, a nine-hour ride in a flying sardine can. I vowed then to not get on any type of boat or plane for a couple years.

I watched the sunrise through the windows. Traffic increased on the runway and the airport began to bustle. *Next sunrise in Med Hat!*

I sat up in my seat to clear some room for the gathering passengers. I checked my ticket and boarding time to confirm once more. I also double-checked my window seat…maybe it was the triple-check.

I stood and paced the floor around the gate. Then the plane pulled up and the gangway maneuvered into position.

After a few minutes, people began to exit the hallway. Checking their watches, looking for gates, and digging through their carry-ons.

The time came to board and the gate attendants began to call out the boarding order, section by section. I found my place in line and, step by step, made my way to the counter. The pleasant stewardess checked my ticket and passport, then welcomed me aboard. I looked over my shoulder to take in what last piece of Amsterdam remained. Then I crossed the threshold to the jet way.

28

There's another side to that metaphor. The one with the rubber band stretching over time and distance. Sometimes the band doesn't break. Sometimes it holds tight and it pulls you back. It's usually very sudden and sometimes violent.

I made it to the door of the plane. The steward smiled at me and held out his hand for my ticket.

"I, uh… I forgot something." I pushed my way back through the gathered line. Quickly I walked down the plank to the terminal gate.

"Sir! Can I be of assistance?" The gate attendant smiled at me.

Anxious to get back to where I needed to be, I shook my head. "I… I just, can't." I pulled the ticket from inside my passport and handed it to her, then hurried on my way as fast as I could, without drawing attention.

First things first. If I was going to choose the path of irresponsibility, I would have to inform my parents. I found a payphone and called my father. *"Quick, like a Band-Aid"* was the only approach for such a case. They were going to be pissed, and rightfully so.

"Dad!"

"Brandon?" He sounded startled. "Son, it's midnight here. I'm trying to get some sleep. I'm leaving to pick you up in a few hours… Wait…"

I pictured him sitting up in bed and gathering his senses.

"Brandon, shouldn't you be on your plane?... Brandon?"

"I'm not coming."

Dad sighed heavily into the phone. I could feel the disappointment. "Bran… Son… FUCK!"

"I'm… I'm sorry Dad. I'm so sorry. It's nothing bad. I'm not in trouble or anything. I just want to stay a bit longer."

"Yeah?! I can only imagine why you want to stay longer, hmm. All right, it's your life, your choice. Stay out of trouble. I'm sure you'll call when you need something. But, kiddo?"

"Yeah, Dad?"

"Don't call me again till you call your mother. Got it?"

"Yeah, I got it."

"I love you kid. But I'm tired. And I'm tired of this shit, honestly."

"I know Dad. I love you. Everything's gonna be good."

"Be careful over there son."

The phone went dead.

Quick like a Band-Aid, I thought once more, then picked up the receiver again and dialled my mother. It was late and I'd be waking her up. Not ideal timing, I knew. But it was hanging over my head, and I needed to shake that monkey if I were going to have any chance at enjoying myself.

"Hello?" She sounded groggy.

"Mom."

"Brandon?" She had snapped to immediately.

"Yeah, Mom."

"Brandon! I'm so happy to hear from you! But… shouldn't you be on—"

"I'm not coming home Mom, not right now. I just talked to Dad. I just wanted to call and tell you."

"What do you mean, you're not coming?... Brandon?"

"Yeah, I'm here. I'm just not ready to come home. Not yet. I'm not in trouble or anything, everything's fine."

"No! No, son! Everything is not fine!" She was becoming unhinged. "You! Your life is not fine, Brandon! What are you doing with yourself over there? Huh? Drinking and drugs, huh? It's drugs, isn't it!"

"Mom! It's not drugs!... It's a girl."

"A girl? Really, Brandon? This is what you're willing to throw your future away on! Who is this girl? Some stripper? I know about Amsterdam and the… the girls over there!"

"No! Mom, it's not like that. She's not… She's blind."

"Blind?... Wha'?… Why would you find a blind girl sweetie? You're a good-looking boy, you're just as good as any other boy out there. You shouldn't be asha—"

"No! Mom!" I shook my head. Only my mother could twist something in such a fashion. "It's not that. She's a really good person, and she's really beautiful."

"But, Brandon, son, what's there for you? How can you afford a woman over there?"

"It's not like that Mom. But… I, I have to go. The phone is going to quit right away, I'm out of time. I just wanted to call you and tell you I'm fine, and I love you and I miss you so much!"

"Brand— But?"

"Love you Mom, bye!" I pressed my finger down on the lever.

It was bullshit, the time expiration. I had over fifteen minutes left. But I couldn't do fifteen minutes in the ring with her then. I just needed enough time to clear my conscious. As much as I could from an airport payphone.

It was a heavy weight lifted, and I was completely free to go where the band pulled me.

So, I ran. I ran through the terminal, following the signs, and managed to locate the escalator down to the train station.

"I need to get to Central Station!" I called out to random people till I found someone who understood English and was eager to help.

They helped me purchase a ticket at the automated terminal, then pointed me toward my platform.

Riding back on the train in daylight, I got to witness what I'd passed by only hours before. Doubt swirled in my mind. What exactly was I doing? She'd never given any official indication that she wanted anything further than my friendship. Who was I to assume she was romantically interested in me? The first time we met, she found me coming out of a hooker suite and I smelled like drugs and… lube.

I started to second-guess my decision to not get on the plane. *How can I be so stupid?*

The clouds had grown dark and heavy, engulfing the area. Juicy drops began to slap the window of the train, eventually bursting into a full-on downpour.

Stepping onto the platform at Central Station, I walked in a confused, depressive state of thought, with my eyes trained to the ground just before my feet like a mindless zombie.

Was I a fool? Had I been played by my own arrogance? *Quick like a Band-Aid,* I mentally repeated.

I climbed the stairs and exited through the turnstile. The sliding doors parted and I stepped outside, into the monsoon. Instantly soaked from head to toe, I walked between the morning rush of people huddling beneath umbrellas and running for cover from the torrent. Crossing the street, I continued down the block till I rounded the corner to where the orphanage sat.

Cold began to dig into my bones, so I hunched my shoulders and increased my pace, the rain pouring from my hair and over my face. Heavy thunder clapped waves through the air.

Half a block to go, the door in sight. I saw it open and the point of an umbrella poke out before expanding its shielding dome. There, she emerged, her blonde hair still managing to shimmer in the flat light, as it draped like a satin curtain over the collar of her black trench coat.

She closed the door behind her, extended her cane, and turned toward me. She raised her head and froze instantly, her jaw hanging open with a look of surprise.

I stopped a hundred feet out. Frozen, silent, in my tracks.

We stood there looking at each other. At least, I was looking at her. I have no clue what she was doing. But she knew. Somehow, she fucking knew.

In awe, I took a step forward, then another, and so on, till I stood right in front of her.

She smiled, the way she always smiled at me.

"How?... How do you know? How do you know it's me?" I waved my hand frantically in front of her face. "You can see! You have to be able to see! Look! You're looking right at me!... Kind of."

Her smile widened. "I do not know this, Brandon!" She raised her voice to be heard over the rain. "How do I tell you this? I do not know!" Excitement exploded in her. She fumbled around, reaching for my hand. "I know, Brandon. I know you sound. I feel you breathe. I feel you heart!" She placed her hand to my chest. "Oh! You are much wet with the rain!" She stepped closer to me, smacking me in the forehead with the rim of her umbrella before elevating it to shelter us both.

She placed a hand on my cheek. "I could no sleep in night. I think to you. I pray for you. I pray to us… Now you is here. I know you will not go. I know you will be here." She grinned smartly.

"How? How'd you know I'd come back?"

"I… I find to you two times. I am blind woman. So, I know now, it is you time to find me… You are here." A tear streamed down her face, tracing her smile.

I wiped the streak from her cheek and brushed the bangs from her eyes. "So, is this good? Was it good for me to come back here? Is there something here for me? For us? Do you understand what I'm saying?"

She smiled and bit down on her lip. Her hands felt their way around my chest, to my shoulders. "Yes, I understand. There is all, everything here for you, Brandon, and us." She lifted herself on the balls of her feet and puckered her lips, then paused.

She was a little off and she was insanely cute. I suppose, in that relationship, all kisses would be met halfway.

I placed one hand on her cheek and the other around her waist and guided her to me. Her lips were soft and gentle, tender and sweet. We kissed once and then again, and again, over and over, pulling each other tighter every time.

She broke from the passion. "You are very wet man. Very cold, huh?"

I nodded, and she reached up for another peck. "Come, please come, let us go. We will get you dry and warm. The children must to see you, they will be excited."

I smiled, kissed her again, then rubbed my hand up and down her back and guided her to the door.

She turned the knob and we rushed inside.

29

Tatiana closed the door and collapsed her umbrella.

She smiled. "Okay, follow, please." She found the stair railing and began her way up.

On the first floor, the stairwell opened to a spacious room with a kitchen and a large island, along with about half a dozen picnic tables.

Tessa stood behind the counter and looked at us a little confused. Then she covered her heart and a warm smile bloomed on her face. "Who is this I see, this handsome young man? He has come here, he no go home on the plane? I think he was to return to Canata?" She winked.

Tatiana's head dipped as she blushed. She felt around to find my hand. "He has decide to stay for more time. He is very wet and cold, you see. I am taking him upstairs. Maybe for shower, to warm, and dry clothes."

Tessa simply nodded, with a sparkle in her eye. "Yes dear, get him warm and come here. I make soup for him."

"Thank you Tessa," Tatiana pulled me around the corner to the next stairwell.

Up one more flight we went. The landing opened to one room on the left and a closed door off to the right.

Tatiana turned and whispered to me. "Be quiet here, please. Is children's room. I will wait to tell them when you shower and warm."

We crept softly around the banister, cringing with every creak in the floor. It was still early in the morning, but she said the children could awaken at any moment.

She felt for the knob on the closed door, then pushed it open, ever so softly. A tiny cough sounded from the children's quarters as we rushed passed the threshold and pulled the door gently shut behind us.

We giggled quietly as I leaned my back against the door and took a breath. She found my shoulders and then ran her hand through my sopping hair. She lifted herself again, her lips searching for mine. I wrapped my arms around her, then pressed my lips passionately to hers.

After a moment, she pushed away when she felt my body shiver.

"Oh, poor man. We must get you to warm." She slid her hand into mine as she turned and pulled me carefully behind her, toward a hallway across the room.

This was her own room, I concluded, as I looked around. It wasn't a five-star at the Ritz, but it was a lot more than I'd pictured. The colour theme was grey, but there were two beautiful, large-paned windows straddling either side of one corner. Grey light filtered in from the cloudy sky and rain spattered the glass in fat, lazy-morning drops. Her bed looked to be queen-sized and was nicely made with a puffy white comforter. A modest white wardrobe and a small dresser sat against the other wall. Beside one of the windows stood something I really never expected to see in Tatiana's room. An easel.

"Tatiana." I pulled on her hand, "you paint?"

"Yes! I really like to do this." She shook my hand and pulled me harder. "I show you when you is done shower. You must get warm, or you will be sick and then we all will be sick."

"Yes ma'am," I obeyed.

She giggled and shook my hand again. She felt her way down the short hallway and led me to a small bathroom with a sink, toilet, shower, and a small window high up the wall.

She pulled me past her, into the room.

"Okay." She placed her hands on her hips and smiled, giving me the feeling I was supposed to be doing something more than just standing there, dripping.

"Clothes!" She motioned. "Give me clothes. I get them clean for you. Clean and dry. I will find you more clothes for after."

"Oh, all right." I started by removing my T-shirt, then slowed down a little when I reached for the button on my shorts. She was blind, so really, what did it matter? Technically, I could walk around naked all day, except for her being so handsy. So, I dropped the shorts to the floor and kicked them off.

I handed them to her, and then I stood with my hands on my hips, waiting for her to leave.

She giggled again, found my stomach with her hand, and slid it down to the waistband of my briefs and snapped the elastic. "These also. I need."

"Oh. I guess…" I hesitated. "What? You want I turn around?" She laughed.

"*Pfft*, no. That wouldn't make any sense, I guess." I dug my thumbs in beneath the band. "Wait! Are you going to do that clicky thing?"

She burst out laughing. "No, I promise, I not do this."

"Yeah, 'cause I've been walking in the rain, I'm pretty cold. And remember, I came all this way for you, so I'd hate for this to go wrong over misrepresentation."

"You is silly man. Come, give to me!"

So, I went all the way. Dropped 'em down, spun them around on my finger, then handed them over. It wasn't that I wasn't ready for that step in our relationship, I really was. I mean, if she were going to take off her clothes, maybe we could crawl under that duvet together. That would be a good warm up too. But for the time, it was just me, naked in the bathroom.

She draped my clothes over one arm, then reached into the cupboard below the sink and fetched a towel. "You will know to work the shower?"

"Yeah, I'm sure I can figure it out."

"Okay, kiss to me." She leaned in.

I leaned in, and she kept her hands to herself. Then she felt her way back through the door and closed it behind her.

I didn't realize how cold I was until I stepped beneath the steaming spray. Tiny droplets pierced like needles, till my skin grew numb. Deep, to the bone, the cold was rooted, but I could feel the wave of warmth pushing it out. I didn't want to take too long. I didn't want to run them out of hot water. I pictured the orphan children standing alone and cold on the street. But I needed it… She was right, I must've been pushing hypothermia.

I cranked the temperature up to as hot as I could bear it, to minimize the time. When my insides reached their boiling point, I turned off the water and stood for a moment with my eyes closed, letting the water run down my body.

Stepping out from the stall, I found the steam to be suffocating. I grabbed my towel and dried myself, then wrapped it around my waist. Through the fog, I fumbled for the window clasp, flicked it unlocked, and pushed the pane till it tilted out. The steam rushed out in a poof, in exchange for a cool stream of fresh air which cascaded down, over my face. I sucked in the refreshment, taking a moment to let it pour down my body and to listen to the splash of the rain on the glass and the bustle of traffic below.

I'd made it back to her. My parents knew I was safe and sound, and I knew there was something for me in Amsterdam. Something worth turning back for. It was a day full of big steps. With the cold washed from my bones, I was ready to see what adventures lay ahead. All I had to do was twist the knob on that door, and find out.

So, I did…

I found her sitting on her bed. Then, one by one, four little pairs of eyes turned in my direction.

No one said anything, and it was awkward, so I took it as my cue.

"He-e-ey, all you guys!"

Five smiles popped, one after the other. The children blushed and played shy, holding onto Tatiana and each other.

"Children, do you know who is? You hear his voice?" Tatiana prodded.

"Is Brandon!" Hans led the charge and they all followed along with their little voices.

With the ball rolling, little Gaby came on full force. She crawled up on her teacher's knee and ran her fingers through her hair. "Brandon! You go to Canata and now you come here? You come back? You bring ice cream?"

I chuckled. "Ice cream from Canada? You like ice cream from Canada?"

"Yes, ice cream from Canada is best ice cream. Is snow all time there."

"Well, there is snow there sometimes, but—"

Hans had found a burst of courage and tapped his way across the floor and held his fist out with a proud smile.

"Oh? Hey, Hans, look at that, you remember the fist-bump?" I tapped the end of his fist with mine.

"Yes!" Tatiana said. "Hans, he make us stay awake late into night and always do fist bump, more and more. Is one thing I say, blind people no good with fist bump. There are much bruises for all of everyone."

"Really?" I looked down at Hans's guilty smirk and mussed his hair. "Well buddy, you think maybe it'd be good for me to spend some more time with you and all these crazy girls? So we can be the men of the group, together. What do you think about that?"

He nodded excitedly, then held his fist out again.

I smirked. "Yes, fist bumps all the time."

"I make clothes for you on this chair, come, please." Tatiana lifted the pile of children from around her and held out her hand.

I guided Hans back to the others and helped Tatiana to her feet.

She had me help her over to the chair where a pile of clothes rested. She unfolded them one at a time, holding them out for me to see, then draped them over her arm.

"Okay, this," she tugged lightly at my towel, "off."

"Hey!" I playfully resisted.

"Why?" She giggled and pulled harder. "You is still shy? You are warm now, yes?"

I lowered my voice. "What about the children?"

"They can no see, stop you be silly. I protect you from little children."

I did as instructed, but still did my best to shield my everything from everyone.

I slipped on a pair of boxer shorts and a pair of pants; both garments obviously belonged to a much taller and rounder man than myself. A dark-blue turtleneck sweater completed the ensemble, hanging loosely, almost to my knees. She had a belt, but it was too big to secure anything further, so I chose to just hold everything in place.

Warm, dry, and dressed, I sat next to Tatiana on the bed, with busy children buzzing all around. Then Tessa knocked on the door, before she poked her head inside with a pleasant smile.

"Okay, everybody, is time for breakfast."

The kids' voices raised with chitter-chatter and clickity-clack as they followed Tessa's voice, with Tatiana herding them along. I brought up the rear, holding up my pants to keep them from falling down and dragging on the floor. I was impressed that the little ones didn't seem to need much guidance down the flight of stairs; this was comfort for them. Their familiar, their family, their home.

Into the kitchen we piled, and much to my surprise, other children already occupied most of the tables. Passing through the door, the line ahead of me scattered into spots at the end picnic table.

"Where did all these children come from?" I whispered to Tatiana.

"They all the children, is not only for blind, is for all orphans. There is others, they stay on," she pointed down, "down floor?"

"Bottom?"

"Yes, this bottom floor is for them. Is much more big. But we all eat here, together."

The kids all had their preferred spots, and I was the odd one out, but they made room. Tatiana bumped Anna to the middle of the one bench so she could sit on the end, beside me.

Tessa delivered bowls of soup and large dishes of bread to each table with help from a few of the sighted children.

Nothing shut those kids up better than a meal, and all that could be heard was the soft chewing of bread and slurping of soup, for which each would get a mild scolding from Tatiana. I got my share of elbows to the ribs.

But the food hit the spot, the soup warm and nourishing, the bread fresh and fragrant. I remember looking around at everyone and thinking how they actually had it pretty good. Better than I'd pictured.

Finished our breakfast, I followed the others in a single line through the kitchen, to place our utensils and dishes in the appropriate bins for cleaning.

I smiled at Tessa, who stood at the end of the gauntlet, and thanked her earnestly.

"You very welcome, my boy. We all happy to have you here."

Back up the stairs we filed, little voices echoing.

"Teacher Tatiana, we go out today? We go, take Sasha out, Brandon will come?'

"Children, it raining outside, very cold. We stay inside now. We do school."

"Awwww!" they moaned altogether.

"Yes. I know this, *awwww*. We do it now, when is rain. When sun comes, we go outside."

At the top of the stairs, we took a left into the children's room.

A wall jutted out across the room, dividing it in half. On one side was a single bed for each child, as well as various wardrobes and cupboards for storage. On the opposite side of the wall sat a large, rectangular table full of craft supplies and shelves full of books. Placed against the far wall was a small piano. Scattered throughout the rest of the space was a couch, a recliner, and a rocking chair.

"Gaby, please go get a book and come to me in rocking chair. Anna, you make craft to show to Brandon. Hans, you go on piano, and Lilly, you can sing for us."

Without a word of resistance, they all scrambled to their stations.

Tatiana found her way over to the rocking chair and the little red-haired girl followed shortly after, crawling up on her teacher's lap and snuggling comfortably back into her.

I crouched beside the chair as Gaby opened the book so I could see exactly how it all worked. She flipped open the cover and began to run her fingers over little raised dots, reading a story in English, about a bear and a fox.

I was amazed at how fast she could develop words from what looked like ancient hieroglyphs. Tatiana held her tight in her arms and intervened when help was needed, which wasn't often.

Anna was busying herself at the table, digging through different supplies, when a powerful note was struck on the piano.

"Hans!" Tatiana said sternly. "There are many people in building, not so much loud."

The cord struck again with less emphasis, and I chuckled.

Lilly found her spot, just behind the piano and straightened her posture as the musical introduction wound up. I thought I recognized the rhythm, somehow, as Hans entered into the meat and potatoes of the tune, tickling his fingers across the keys. Then Lilly began. Her voice was strong, disciplined, and practised. Beautiful beyond my words.

My eyes popped immediately at the lyrics of "I Do It for You," by my home country's Bryan Adams. I wanted to interrupt, but I held back. The song's origin didn't matter; it belonged to them that morning. Being honest, I liked their version better.

Rain continued to pummel the windows, and the whole scene was very calming.

I placed my hand on Tatiana's shoulder. She placed her hand on top of mine, then slowly slid out from under Gaby.

I helped her over to the couch as she requested, and we settled in together. She lifted her feet onto the cushions and pressed back into me, as I wrapped myself snuggly around her.

I placed my lips close to her ear and ran my hands tenderly up and down her arm. "They're beautiful, Tatiana, you did this? You taught these children all of this? You're a really good teacher. You're an amazing woman."

She lifted my hand to her mouth and kissed it with her soft lips, then pulled my arms tighter around her.

"They is good children, smart. They do not need much teaching. Already, they speak more English than me, better. I only help to focus."

"I think you do a lot more than that. They love you. I know you can't see it, but I see it." I kissed her ear lightly.

"I is very happy you come back to us, Brandon. I know you will come. I know you is good man."

"I guess, when my clothes dry, I should go see Helen and Faas. Let them know I'm here and see if they'll let me stay with them for a bit longer. Until I figure out what I'm gonna do."

She squeezed my arm. "What? You do not like stay here? Stay with us?"

"W-well, I… Is it all right for me to stay here? Where would I sleep?"

She laughed, reaching up and over her head to pull my lips to hers. "You can sleep on floor, in kitchen." She nudged me with her elbow. "You stay with me, in my room, in my bed."

"Oh… Is Tessa okay with that?"

She laughed again. "I am grown woman. It is my room. I ask Tessa, she say is fine. She is happy you here, you welcome here."

So, it had been decided, and it didn't even require any convincing on my end. She was the one who orchestrated it all. It would be our first official night together, same bed. It wasn't the only reason I'd returned to her, but it was a definite perk I'd considered, over and over.

"I'm glad I came back to you, Tatiana. This week, I'll look for work. I don't know what I can get? I think I need a work visa. But maybe I'll go talk to Faas. He maybe has some boats I could help him with? It wouldn't be much, but I'd like to help with you and the children."

"There be something for you. I know, I help with this. We are strong together." She reached back and kissed me again.

There was something for me to return for. I had no idea how strong it would be.

30

Time passed slowly that day. Tessa brought my clothes when they were ready. Cleaned and ironed, better than I was used to.

The rain poured down… and poured… and poured. Coming from one of the sunniest cities in Canada, via the tropical island of Bonaire, it was somewhat of an adjustment.

"Does it always rain like this here?" I asked, looking at the dismal outdoors.

"No, is summer, is less rain now."

Anna had called the others over to her project; it was all very secretive, with much whispering. After a bit of time, the group delivered their present to me, a beaded, leather-strap necklace. They'd each taken their turn picking out their own garnishing for it, and the result was… interesting. No matter, I marvelled at its beauty and let them hang it over my neck, and they all burst with pride. Then they all crawled up on the couch and nestled into their own little pockets, between Tatiana and me.

"Wha'! Look at all of this!" I said, chuckling as we were swarmed with munchkins. "Yesterday I was just me, a pair of shorts, and a T-shirt. Now I have to share a couch with all of these crazy kids!"

"You stay wit us forever, Brandon?" Gaby blurted. "You love Teacher Tatiana? Is you going to be marry to her?"

Tatiana and I both blushed and I was at a loss for words.

"Gaby!" Tatiana said. "This no talk for now. Love is very big thing. Is not a light to switch. Is not you business now. We is all very happy to have Brandon with us. Now, all kids off. You must do thirty-minute read."

"Aww!"

"I know, is *awww*. But you know this is what has to do. Go to get book and go to you reading place."

The children dispersed and Tatiana sat up in her spot, holding my hand on her lap.

"Do you talk to you family? You family in Canada?"

"Yeah, I called my dad and then my mom."

"Yes?... And?"

"And?... They were mad, really mad. I don't blame them. It's been a long time since I've been home. I think that they think I'm in trouble. Maybe living on the street."

"Yes, they worry for you. Do you tell to them?"

"Tell them… about us?"

"Uh huh."

"Well, my dad just kind of assumed there was a woman involved. He was pretty mad, but it was late at night there, so he didn't feel like talking. Then I called my mom. I had to call her, 'cause I can't even remember the last time I spoke to her on the phone. I've just been emailing her, sometimes. She was driving my dad nuts with questions. I told her about you."

She smiled. "Yes? You Mom, she know of me?"

"Yes. Not very much about you. But I had to tell her, because she would've thought I was on heroin or something. She probably still thinks that, anyway."

"Well, we have busy day tomorrow. First to do, we will visit to Helen and Faas. We take children, you can see for work. Then when is time, when you parents are wake, we call them. We have telephone here. We will have to pay for call."

"Wait… you, you want to talk to my parents?"

"Yes, of course, we must call. They must know you okay. And, is good for me to talk and know you mom and dad."

This girl is mad! I thought, as I looked at her in shock. "Wha'? Bu— Are you sure? Do you think maybe… you're ready for that?" Truth was, I wasn't sure I was anywhere near that point yet.

"Yes, of course, I like this. Is good to know you family. They must know you is okay." She patted my hand reassuringly. "Maybe, also, we do pictures with children. We send to email, show them fun and happy time here? I think they like this, yes?"

"Uh, yeah, I guess. But, maybe we should give them some time to cool down. Like a year, or so?"

She slapped at me. "Do not be like that to you family. They love you, miss you. They like to know you okay."

"Okay, I'll give them a call tomorrow, kind of feel them out, see what kind of a mood they're in."

"Yes, I like, is good."

The rest of the day continued as such, spending time with the children. Tatiana turned on some soft music in the afternoon. We played some board games, ate our meals when they were ready, and watched the relentless rain pummel the streets below. I began to wonder if it would ever stop.

Nighttime came; children were dressed in their pajamas and settled in around the couch for story time. Tatiana volunteered me to read the evening story; it would be an exotic change for them, as I could read from a book on the dusty top shelf. The ones published for the sighted.

I wasn't a reader, and I'm fairly confident my explanation as such was not required. If I were to read, I think I'd like to do it in a quiet room, inside my head, to myself. But there I had landed, front and centre.

As I browsed through the selection, I looked for something short and simple. You know, light material, like maybe a local menu or something. But I saw a title that had been beaten into me somehow, subliminally, perhaps? It was one from the Harry Potter series, of course. I lifted the book from the shelf and checked to ensure it was the first in the series. *The Philosopher's Stone.* From what I could tell, it was the first. I walked back over to Tatiana on the couch and whispered the title. "Have they read this one before? Do you have it in the Braille version?"

"Yes!" Her expression glowed, as she rubbed my arm. "Please do this! The children will like this so much. I do not even know we have this! I can tell them this?" She patted my arm and I could very plainly see it was tearing her apart. "Okay, I tell!" She clapped her hands for attention from the sombre audience.

"Children, we have big surprise. Brandon has chose book! I do not know we have this. But he find, he read to us"—suspenseful pause—"Harry Potter book!"

The kids snapped to, and sat up. "YEAH!" The scream was deafening, and hands were thrown into the air.

Tatiana clapped excitedly, then grabbed my hand and pulled, sending me toppling over her, to the couch.

Little girls climbed on and very poorly aimed kisses came from all angles. Beneath the dog pile, I felt a little hand pulling and twisting mine just so, then a bumping of a little fist.

After a moment of letting the gang have their way with me, Tatiana instructed them to settle down and get back to their spots.

I righted myself in my chair, stunned from the onslaught. Then I looked down at all their smiling little faces. Each child held a stuffed animal of some type. Some with battle wounds and patches, but it made no difference to them.

The room was warm and quiet, dimly lit with the soft glow of a lamp in the corner. The sound of raindrops pattered the windows. I flipped to the first page and began.

I was rusty at the outset, I admit. But after the first-page warm-up... I crushed it. Once familiar with the story's ambiance, I began to alter my voice for characters and add sound effects where I felt they were needed. Sometimes I fucked it up. But no one caught on, and they were all highly involved. I'd never done anything like it before...I'd never read a book before. Suddenly, I was reading to orphaned blind children.

I managed through three chapters, then I nudged Tatiana. She was looking a little groggy herself. I whispered that it was late and some of the children were barely hanging on.

She yawned, then removed her legs from across my lap and righted herself in her seat. "Okay, children, is time to stop with book for bedtime."

"Awww!" They groaned, and pleaded for just one more chapter.

"No, Is good for now. Brandon will read more next night, if you is good children. Now, up to beds."

I followed her around to each of them, placing their stuffies just right and tucking the blankets in around them. There were many kisses and thank-yous, and of course the fist bump from Hans. But I got a hug out of him too.

That night I'd been elevated from weird Canadian guy who was trying to molest their teacher, to kickass *Harry Potter* champion. I'd cemented my position in their little hearts.

We reached the door and turned to say our final goodnights, to the responses of tired little voices. Tatiana closed the door until there was a slight crack. Then she slid her arms around my waist and tipped up for a kiss, before leading me into her room.

In the darkened space, she was an ace. Me, not so much. I tripped over the leg of a chair and almost took her down with me. Then she instructed me to a lamp in the corner. It was painful for me to locate, but life was better once I did.

Tessa had brought up some toiletries for me, and Tatiana kicked me to the bathroom to clean up before bed.

Duties completed, I entered back into the room. She greeted me with a kiss, as she passed by on her way to the washroom and told me to get comfortable in bed.

Comfortable… it was somewhat of a grey term for that first-time experience. There are multiple forms of comfortable, and I didn't know exactly what her expectations were. Surely, she wouldn't expect me to be in bed fully clothed? So, then, how much clothing removal would be appropriate? How much clothing would she be wearing when she came out? I should aim to match her level.

In the end, I stripped down to my boxer shorts and climbed beneath the covers. It was forward enough, without being overly presumptuous.

It was a little nerve-racking, lying in her bed for the first time. Waiting for her to appear from the bathroom. It seemed like she was taking an unreasonable amount of time. Would it be sweat pants or black lace… or maybe leather?

I really didn't know with her. On one hand, she was the sweetest, most grounded and responsible person I'd ever met. But on the other hand, she was moving things along really fast. There'd been lots of touching, kissing, and all-around affection since I returned. Like the switch was flipped to all green lights. She'd gotten me naked in the bathroom and invited me to stay with her, and she was planning on talking to both of my parents the next day. And here I was, mostly naked in her bed the first night. She didn't seem like that type of girl, but… she kinda seemed like that type of girl.

I heard the tap shut off in the bathroom and held my breath through the creak of the door.

There she emerged, wearing a very beautiful, baby-blue nightgown. She looked amazing. It was more of her than I'd seen any time previous, but there was still much to crave. It did nothing to clarify the direction of our first night together.

I could sense a hint of uncertainty in her. I was convinced, by then, that she knew how to dress herself, and so was conscious about what she was wearing. But still, there had to be only so much she could really know for sure.

She managed a vulnerable smile, and I sensed she was on the verge of retreating back into the bathroom.

I knew I had to say something immediately. "Tatiana, you look so incredible... So beautiful!"

Her smile lengthened and she relaxed. "Yes? You like this?"

"Yes, of course I like this. Come over here, sexy. Do you need help?"

"No, I do it."

She put a little more sway in her hips and a little more allure in her stride as she walked to the bed, but I could see she was also a little wary about bumping into things. She made it to the foot of the bed, then found my legs and crawled up, cat-like, onto me. Finding my lips with hers, she fell into me. My hands wandered freely down her back to rest on her sexy little bum. We stayed in that position for a while, both having problems resisting long enough to switch it up.

Then she placed a finger to my lips and rolled off, to her side of the bed. She lifted the covers and crawled beneath. I wasted no time invading her space.

We were engulfed, breathing through each other. She displayed no signs of letting up, so I pressed her on her back and reached my hand to her tummy. Up, beneath her gown, my hand slid to her breasts and she moaned with pleasure. She arched her head back as my lips trailed down her neck and my hand started down the path to her panties. I became more heated with every inch of the journey. My finger tickled the top of the lace, and—

She grabbed my wrist and yanked back on it as if it were the parking brake of a shitty old Honda.

"Brandon, please. We must not do it," she gasped between passionate breaths.

"Wha'? I... I'm sorry. I know it's our first night."

"It is just to... only for my husband."

Shock gripped me, my breath stalled. "You... you're married?"

She slapped my chest and laughed. "No, I not married! I would not have man in my bed if I married." She kissed me lightly and rolled away, pulling my arms around her and nestling her body into mine.

"So... you're saving... you, for your husband?"

"Yes, is only for him, never other man."

"So… you've never done… this, before? I mean… sex?"

She laughed again, then turned her face back for a kiss. "No, I have never do sex. I have never had man in my bed."

"So… you're… a…"

"Yes, there is the word you say to this in English, I have not done before. Is only for married and husband."

"Oh. Okay."

"Is not okay for you? You like other woman? One who do to all men?" Disapproval grew in her tone.

"No! No, no, it's fine. I understand."

"Is good, I like to have you with me." She turned for another kiss, then snuggled harder into me, and fell silent.

I was awake… really awake, staring past her to the streetlights through the window. And I was hard… really hard, and having her pressed so fully to me was not helping.

I respected her way, but I had a situation requiring tending to. I felt that a trip to the bathroom for approximately five minutes would be toward the "un" side of acceptable. So I held her tight in my arms and resorted to the breathing exercises I'd developed for just such an emergency, and counted sheep.

A lot of really unattractive sheep.

31

It was a long night. It was a great night, though, once the… swelling subsided. I really enjoyed spending the night with her in my arms. It felt strange in many ways—how it all happened so fast, how I was so suddenly there, and accepted by her and the children. But then again, how long is it supposed to take?

When I woke the next morning, our bodies were still entangled. Everything seemed to align so precisely, airtight, with a thin film of perspiration.

It may have taken some time and breathing to fall asleep, but the sleep I did end up getting was very refreshing, nourishing. Better than I'd had for longer than my memory reached.

I peered out the window and saw the sky was still overcast, but the rain had stopped.

I delicately slid my arm out from beneath her neck and kissed her shoulder tenderly, pulling the blanket over her as I slithered off the far side of the bed.

The air in the room was damp and cool. I hugged my arms across my bare chest and softly crossed the floor to the window.

The streets were sparsely populated. Few people trotted past, hunched over, hugging their raincoats tight to their bodies.

As I looked down the street, something enchanted caught the corner of my eye.

The easel.

The painting was indecipherable. I even tipped my head from one side to the other, but nothing familiar appeared, anywhere. It was just many colours of paint, brushed and spattered everywhere. I knew one fancy art term: *abstract*. Whether or not it was accurate for that work, that's what I decided to label it.

"Hmm."

I heard her stir from across the room. I peered around the piece and whispered, "Tatiana, I'm here."

She managed a smile, though her body still lay very heavy and lazy. She looked quite committed to staying in that exact spot for at least four more hours.

She raised a floppy arm in the air. "Come!" she blubbered, "you must come to bed. Is cold." Her lower lip jutted out. "Where you? I know you is here."

I smiled. "This painting… Do you paint?"

"You is not to see this yet! Yes, I paint."

"Really? Well this is *really* nice."

"*Pfft*! Is not nice. Is for clean the brush."

"Yeah! That's honestly what I thought. I didn't even know painters cleaned their brushes like that. I just guessed that's what it was."

Silence. And a growing feeling that maybe I'd said too much, too fast.

"What?" Her voice had dropped low and flat. "I am only joke about this. This is what I paint."

Oh fuck!

I was disgusted with myself as I watched her sit up and swing her legs off the side of the bed. She shivered and reached for the housecoat she had hanging from a hook on the headboard, then made her way over to me with surprising speed. She slapped lightly at my chest, then pushed me down on the stool and took a seat on my knee.

"I know it look like maybe I clean brush. But is story, you must know story." She rubbed my arms, which I had wrapped around her waist.

"The middle"—she waved her hand over the painting—"here, is road, or maybe tree. It is road of my life. In top, there is start. My life in Ukraine with family—my brother, sister, my parents, and my granny—is bright, and is very happy. Now, down the road, school and travel to here for work, and at bottom is Amsterdam and how I feel here. The paint colours and the lines and this shapes, are all very… bended?"

I nodded my head, rubbing it against her back.

"Because I am blind."

She was passionate in her explanation. I began to see the things she described, noticing how the scheme transitioned from light to dark as I followed the story. At first I'd thought it was referencing the night lights of the city, but then I wondered if she even knew the colours she used.

"I see it now." I lightly kissed her back.

"No." She smiled. "You never see with eyes." She lifted my hand in hers and brushed my fingertips lightly over the painting's surface. "Close eyes."

I did as she instructed.

"Paintings are different with you eyes closed."

At first, I was simply murmuring *uh huhs*. How do we see with our hands? Up until then, mine had been used to lift beer, make nachos, pull wrenches, and pick at stuff. I was capable of appreciating the softness of a pillow to the hardness of a brick, but what she was showing me was beyond my ability.

Paintings are different with your eyes closed.

Little ridges on the dried surface, peaks, valleys, sharp edges, and waves swooping to clouds. An intimate glimpse into her world, I could feel her sincerity.

"You are the most beautiful woman, Tatiana," I whispered before scooping her off my lap and into my arms. She let loose a shrill squeal. I carried her over to the bed and fell down on her, laughing as I smothered her with kisses.

"How did you like your first night with a man in your bed?"

"Is good." She kissed me on the lips, then yanked at the blankets till she found that spot she liked so much. She pulled me in behind her and wrapped the blankets around us. "Except man wake up too soon?"

After another hour of snuggling, the little clickety-clack of tapping canes echoed across the hall, and the door creaked open.

"Teacher Tatiana?" Lilly's sweet voice squeaked like a mouse.

Tatiana groaned. "*No, is too early.*"

I watched as little bodies piled inside, canes in one hand, stuffies in the other.

"Is time to wake up," Anna stated. Gaby took a step and the charge was on, sounding like a herd of tap dancers as they came to the foot of the bed. Then they crawled on up and sat on top of us, lending their early morning encouragement.

Void of options, we were forced to acknowledge the morning, and the little ones. Tatiana chased them all into the bathroom, one at a time, to get the morning rituals completed.

I never realized how involved with them she was. All those turkeys were a lot of work. Collecting towels, picking out clothes, and brushing the girls' hair.

She had the children, but she was also all alone. I thought I could see the reason for the dark descent to Amsterdam in her painting.

I watched and helped, fetching things when requested. I think the little things I did were a big help as zipping across and between rooms was a lot easier for me. Every time I had a moment, I would be by her side, rubbing her shoulders and stealing a kiss. Every time, she'd return the gesture with a smile.

We managed to get everyone decent just before Tessa entered the room to announce breakfast.

With all tummies filled, we returned to the upper floor to prepare for our adventures outside. The rain had let up, but the heavy overcast sky suggested it could return at any time, so everyone was to be dressed in rain boots and jackets. It was madness at the closets. The children needed assistance finding what was theirs and then putting it on. Most of their clothes were mismatched and some of the boots had duct tape wrapped over points of leakage.

Even though I said I didn't need anything as long as we had the umbrella, I finally gave in to Tatiana's insistence that I wear a bright-yellow, rubber rain slicker that just about burst at the seams when I put it on. And greatly constricted my movement.

Then, one by one, clickety-clack, we went out the front door to assemble on the sidewalk.

Tatiana guided everyone into place, so they could take hold of each other's hands. Hans was sure to remind me how I was to go between him and Lilly. Tatiana and I laughed and I did as instructed.

It may seem strange that in a train of blind people, the sighted member was placed toward the back. But I honestly felt more confident in our direction with Tatiana and Sasha leading, and I also think she preferred it that way.

Down the block and across the street we waddled. Then behind the train station to the marina. And without so much as a single stumble, we made it to the door of the boathouse.

Tatiana knocked, then waited a moment, and knocked once again. We heard footsteps coming down the stairwell and Miss Helen's voice calling out.

Her eyes bulged when she saw us through the window. Instant tears began to rain as she waved frantically and fumbled with the doorknob.

When she had pulled the door from between us, her hand shot up to cover her mouth, then down to her chest. "Oh! My gootness!" She grabbed Tatiana's hand and counted the children down, one by one, till she found me, smiling in the back.

Her smile intensified and her jaw quivered as she flapped her dishtowel toward me. "You! You is such a goot, goot man!" She parted the crowd, then threw her arms around me and sobbed on my shoulder. "You is a goot man," she whispered in my ear while patting my back. "You come back for her, for children. I know this. I see this in you eyes. You is a goot man, Brandon. Look at them, all so many smiling." She turned her head to the others, looked down the line, and sniffled.

"Well!" She placed her hands on her hips. "I think is too cold for ice cream today, yes?"

"NO!" little voices cried.

"No?" She smirked. "Well, we must ask Faas if he share wit you. I not know, you think he will share?"

The children remained quiet, hiding behind their shy smiles and rosy cheeks.

"Okay, come! Is cold out. Come inside and we can see what we find." She shooed everyone into the house.

Tatiana held the door open, guiding in the children till she felt my hand slide around her waist. Then she leaned back into me the way she always did.

Helen followed the others through the door, then took a second to caress Tatiana and I. Her face beaming with joy, "oh, such beautiful you are!"

I leaned down and gave my girl a kiss on the cheek before we stepped inside.

Up the stairs and into the kitchen we went. All the kids found a seat at the table, and Sasha sat in between two of them, tongue frolicking with excitement.

"Well, Faas is not here, he is to be here soon. It is Faas ice cream, maybe we wait?"

There was a polite silence again, but the tension in the air was as thick as double chocolate swirl.

"Ah! Why wait, is not our problem he is not here."

Voices erupted. "Yeahhhhh!"

When Helen went down the hall to fetch the goods, I found Tatiana and wrapped my arms around her. Forming addictions to the security I lent, and the feeling of pure beauty in my arms.

The crowd froze at the sound of a door closing, then the clomp of heavy feet up the stairs. I saw Faas breach the top and pause for a moment, taking in the cluster of little ones in his kitchen, and the tubs of ice cream sitting on the counter, in front of Helen.

"*What!*" he bellowed. "You let kids have ice cream one time, and now we cannot get them to stay away!" He smiled, then snuck up behind Gaby and slid his finger under her chin, catching her by surprise and causing her to flinch and giggle. The tension in the room eased.

"Huh! They come to steal my treat when I work!" He went around the table, sharing tickles with each one. "And this! Puppy dog!" He reached down and scratched Sasha behind the ears, laughing. As he rounded the end of the table, he looked up at me, holding Tatiana in my arms. "There, this boy, from Canata. He is still here. Maybe he is not so stupit as I think?" He leaned in and placed his hands on Tatiana's shoulders and kissed her cheek. "Such a beauty, it is nice for you to be here again." He reached over and shook my hand. "You cannot leave? Huh? Ha ha ha, I know you could not leave this, huh!"

Tatiana went to help Helen make sandwiches for everyone, before dessert was served. Sasha and I followed Faas into the living room, where he took his usual spot in the recliner and I sat on the loveseat.

He grinned slyly at me. "I know why you stay. This"—he waved his hands to the kitchen, stuck for words—"it is goot, this. Very goot. I would not go. If I was you, man, I would not go."

"Yeah." I smiled and leaned my elbows on my knees, clasped my hands together and bowed my head. "It is good. I guess I had to stick around and see… see what happens, I guess."

"Yes, you were single man, all party all the time. Now you have all this, it is much for you, young man."

"Yeah, well, anyway, it looks like I'm going to be here for a while. I don't think I have all the paperwork to legally work here. I could go for it, I guess. But I really need to get working as soon as possible. I don't think my parents are going to offer me any help. They're pretty mad I didn't go back."

"Yes, I see they is mad at you. But they will be more better in time."

"Yeah, I think so… I hope. But anyway, Faas, I was wondering if you could maybe…" I rubbed my hands together nervously. Faas seemed like a good guy when the children were in the kitchen eating his ice cream, but I knew how unpredictable he could be. "Do you have any work for me? Anything? Helping on the boats maybe?"

His face contorted, as if trying to understand what I was asking. "Work, for you, here?" He leaned forward in his chair, and his expression turned to understanding. "Yes, of course there is work here for you. You can help with boats. If I not have work here, I have friends in marina, they have boats. I get you work, Brandon, yes, of course."

I breathed a sigh of relief. "Thank you Faas, thank you very much." I reached out and shook his hand. "Can I start tomorrow?"

"Yes, tomorrow, in morning, come to six thirty. Have breakfast wit us."

"Okay, six thirty, I'll be here." We sat for a second, watching the commotion in the kitchen, then I turned back to Faas. "You hear anything from the other guys? Adlar and them?"

"Huh?" He grimaced and waved the question off. "I not hear from these guys. They will come to here when they have no money, and girls kick them out. They should come soon, I think. I have sell more boat I think, maybe. They can take the boat to people, hope they not fuck it up."

My interest piqued. "Oh, another delivery?"

"Yes, I think. Is big boat, we work on tomorrow. It is maybe to go Peru."

"Peru... Really?"

He shrugged. "I think I sell this."

"When do you think they'll have to deliver it?"

"Who knows, there is much work needed, I think. They will say if they like to buy, then we will work on boat. Long time I think, many monts, maybe in spring. But the boys will be here for work when they need. They help work to get boat ready. By then, Amstertam will need rest from these boys." He smirked and winked. "Ha!"

32

We stayed for the afternoon, to let Faas and Helen have a visit with the children. At four o'clock, Tatiana announced it was time to return to the orphanage. The news was greeted with resistant groans.

Outside, we said our farewells to our friends and formed into our positions just as thunder clapped overhead and jellybean drops began to explode on everything. We pulled up our hoods and made our way across the street. I could've sprinted the distance in less than a minute, but we were all for one and one for all.

We rushed in the orphanage door and crowded the landing, struggling to get the rainwear off without creating too large of a mess. Then up the stairs we went to our floor.

Lightning flashed outside the window as we got the children into some dry clothes and wrapped them in blankets. Tatiana put on an audiobook for them and we escaped across the hall to her room. Once we had dried and warmed ourselves, she found a spot on the bed beside me.

"So?" she asked.

"So?... So, what?"

"Faas. Can he get work to you?"

"Oh, yes, he said there's lots of work in the marina. I can work for him, and if he's slow, he'll find me work at some of the other boat places."

She smiled and kissed me excitedly. "Oh good! This is good, yes?"

"Yes, it's good, really good." I rubbed frantically at her arms. "He said I can start tomorrow. I have to be there at six thirty, for breakfast."

"Oh! They is so nice people!" She kissed me again, then ran a hand down the side of my face.

As her touch lingered around my cheek, I realized she was checking for a smile. I was catching on to her little techniques.

"He said there's a big boat for us to get ready. He thinks he's sold it to someone in Peru. He said it'll be ready for delivery in the spring, maybe."

"Yes, to deliver? Take to Peru? This is long ways. How long you think for this, to Peru?"

"Oh, I don't know—three, maybe four months by the time they got back. I don't even know if they'd come back. I'm not really sure how it all works. I think they'd have to have a boat to bring back."

"You… You want go this? With boat?" Her voice heightened curiously.

"No! No, I don't want to do that." I smiled and kissed her on the lips several times. "I've done it once already. That's enough for me. I think it pays decent money though."

"What we need more money? We is happy."

I looked into her eyes, which were staring just past me. "Yes honey, we're happy."

She smiled and blushed. "Honey?" she said, gently caressing my leg. "You call this to me?"

I smirked as she caught my slip. "Yes, honey. Is it all right?"

"Yes, I like this. I like this very much." She pushed me onto my back and fell on top of me, kissing me passionately.

After a minute she pushed herself up. "Okay, we get you work. Now we must do other."

"Other… what?"

"Come, we must do all things today. You remember?"

"What are you talking about?"

She navigated her way to the dresser across the room, where I'd failed to notice a phone resting.

Then it came back to me. "Oh, uh, I mean, we've had a busy day, and we found work for me. Things are good, can we just wait till later in the week, maybe on the weekend?"

"No, Brandon… Honey!" She shot a coy smile over her shoulder. "We must do now. You mom and dad, they worry for you. We must do this."

"But, Tatiana…"

"Huh? Is this? I no do answer for this name anymore." She laughed.

"Honey, please!" I begged.

"Come! Come and call to you mom."

"Uh, my mom, really? That's like, the hardest one to do." As I took a moment to consider, I really didn't think either were going to be easy. I was really happy with the progress we'd made that day, and I just wanted to snuggle up for the rest of the evening. I was never really the type to rush my new girlfriends on my family.

"Brandon!"

"What happened to *honey?*"

"No! Is *Brandon*, to come call you mom."

I took a moment to beat my face with a pillow.

"Stop this! Act like children… Come!"

My mind raced with the possible outcomes of the actions. A foreign woman speaking broken English to my mother from across the ocean. She would call out the military, and then have a heart attack.

It was still early in the morning there, so about a fifty-fifty chance we'd miss her. I sulked my way over to the phone and punched in the number.

Just as my luck would have it, she answered on the second ring.

Shit!

"Hello?" Her lonely voice transmitted through the receiver. She sounded like she hadn't been sleeping. I knew it was because of me. She probably hadn't had a decent sleep since I'd left. Maybe that's why I had such a hard time facing her.

"Hello, Mom."

I felt Tatiana's tender touch on my shoulder and it gave me strength.

"Brandon! I… Sweetie? Thank God!" She gasped and I heard her sinuses begin to plug. "Are you all right? Where are you?"

"I'm great Mom. Really good. I just… We just wanted to call, make sure you're okay."

I heard the shuffling of little feet behind me, and noticed that Tatiana had disappeared to collect the children.

"I'm in Amsterdam, Mom, at the orphanage."

"The what? Orphanage? Brandon, why are you at an orphanage? Oh God, you're on drugs, aren't you!"

"No, Mom, it's just… that girl I met. The one I told you about, Tatiana."

"Tati— who? I don't understand, Brandon, what's happening? Why are you at an orphanage? Do you need help? Should I call someone?" Her speech was growing frantic.

I was getting frustrated. I inhaled deeply and ran my hand through my hair. Tatiana was quickly by my side, rubbing my shoulders, then she tapped and I turned.

She was smiling and reaching for the phone.

It was against my better judgment, but I didn't have the answers for my mother, and I didn't have the patience to try to explain. So… *What the fuck?*

"Mom, she wants to talk to you."

"What? Who wants to talk to me? Are you in troub—"

Tatiana's hand had found the receiver, and she pulled it from my ear while rubbing my back reassuringly.

I managed to squeeze in a few words before the phone was pulled from my grasp. "No, no trouble. It's Tatiana, the girl I told you about…"

Tatiana gave my back one last rub. I held my breath as I watched her place the phone to her ear.

"Hello, Miss Brandon? I am Tatiana."

I waited for the shrill scream from the receiver, but it never came. I waited for the choppers to start circling overhead, but it never happened.

"Yes, we are in orphanage. Is where I live. Brandon is here, he stay with us." She giggled into the phone. "No, Miss Brandon Mom. Is good, is nice, is warm. I is no orphan. I is teacher to children, to orphan children. I am blind… Yes, blind. I teach to blind children… Yes."

The tension seemed to relax, and the two women fell into conversation. So, they talked… and talked… and talked. Until I began to wonder what long-distance charges to Canada were like.

Tatiana's laughter grew and then she started putting the children on the phone. One by one, they introduced themselves, and I eventually lay down on the bed.

I'm not sure if it was an hour. It felt like at least an hour—before I heard Tatiana start to wrap things up. Then she took her mouth away from the phone and called for me.

I went to her as she said her goodbyes and handed me back the phone.

I placed it to my ear, not knowing what to expect. "H-Hello?"

"Brandon!" She sounded absolutely delighted. Ten years younger.

"Yeah."

"Oh, honey! She sounds so wonderful! And the children, they're so adorable!"

"Oh… yeah, they're really great." I couldn't believe how she had turned around.

"So, you're there? You're living with them?"

"Yeah, I'm here, with them. It's honestly really nice, warm, and comfortable. It's really good here Mom."

"And she—Tatiana—she said you found work?"

"Oh, right. Yeah, I'm working down at the marina, fixing boats. I start tomorrow."

"Oh! She sounds like such a beautiful young lady, Brandon! And you're helping her with the children? She said you help."

"Yeah, I'm helping Mom. I help them get dressed, and with their school stuff, a little. I'm reading them *Harry Potter* at night."

Little cheers erupted around me.

"You're such a good man. My son… I love you, Brandon. I miss you, and I love you and… I'm so very happy. Thank you so much for the call. Tatiana said she'd email me some pictures of everyone."

"Oh, she did?" I looked over at her mischievous smirk. "Uh, okay."

"I'm so excited to see everyone. I can't wait!"

"Yeah, it'll be great. Listen, Mom, could you maybe call Dad and tell him I'm all right? We were going to call him too, but I think we should maybe wait to see how much these calls are going to cost. We'll call him as soon as we can."

"Yes, of course dear. I'll call him right away."

"Okay. Thanks, Mom. I should let you go now. I love you."

"I love you too sweetie. Bye-bye!"

I was in awe. Again, another very large, very heavy weight had been lifted from me. I put down the receiver and walked over to the woman sitting on the edge of the bed.

I looked at her… Then I looked at her some more, to the point where she became flustered.

"What!" she finally blurted. "I know you is right here, you act strange. What is it?"

"How?"

"How? What *how*? What is this?"

"How did you do that, with my mother?"

She grinned. "She is you mom. She must know you okay. She think maybe you sleep in street, in cold, maybe you is hurt. Now she know you good. With nice lady, help with children." She reached for my hand. "Now she know. She is you mom. She must know. Now her heart have rest."

"*Hmph*." I squeezed her hand gently.

"Now we must have photo of all, everybody."

The girls clapped and cheered. Hans and I did not.

"Come, is everybody!"

So, we spent some time taking photographs of everyone. Some with everyone making their most-silliest of faces, others with us sitting together as a happy… family, I suppose. Sasha too. Then the girls got carried away and wanted to dress up and have some action shots of them displaying their talents. I was lucky enough to be the only one qualified to run the camera, and Hans was made to fill in where required. We even had Tessa come join for a few before dinner.

After dinner, Tatiana and I sat in the dining hall, where I helped her download the pictures to the computer and send them off, to both my parents.

Back in our quarters, we bribed the children to get ready for bed quickly, in return for spending the rest of the evening in Harry Potter land.

The children sat on the floor around the couch with their pillows and blankets, while Sasha sprawled out in the middle, available for anyone feeling the need to pet something furry. I sat at one end of the couch and Tatiana lay with her legs curled up and her head in my lap.

I completed five chapters, till little eyelids drooped heavy.

I tapped Tatiana lightly on the shoulder and whispered, "I think they're ready for bed."

She didn't move a wink.

So, as gently as I could manage, I slipped from beneath her and began to round up our herd.

Gaby groaned at my disturbance. "Teacher?" she squeaked.

"No, Gaby, it's just me. Teacher is sleeping on the couch. It's time for bed."

She rolled over and wrapped her arms around my neck, and I hoisted her into my arms, while the others dragged themselves to their beds. Sasha did an amazing job of helping them along, like a sheep dog caring for her flock.

I set Gaby in her bed and tucked her in, and she gave me a big hug and a kiss, which was very unexpected, but very welcome. I followed up with a big hug, before tucking her stuffie into her arms and pulling the blankets up around her.

I stopped at each bed to make sure all were well. Hans was the last. He was pretty much out, but in his last waking moment, he decided on a hug instead of a fist bump.

"You the best Harry Potter," he mumbled, before falling back and curling into slumber.

I took a moment to sit on the bed and look around at all the children, safe and warm in their beds. Then I looked at my princess, sleeping soundly on the couch.

I smiled and stood slowly, then padded over to her. Doing my best to not disturb her, I squirmed my arms beneath her and lifted her up. She was surprisingly light. Light and warm and beautiful. She fit quite nicely.

I turned with her and made one last check on the kids, then navigated across the dark landing and pushed open the door to her room. A faint glow from the streetlights below her window shed enough light on my path to make it safely to the bed with my sleeping beauty. I placed her down softly and ran my hand gently through her hair, while admiring the beautiful contours of her face. I gave her lips a tender kiss, then pulled the covers over her feminine figure.

I turned my head to the room and listened to the nothingness. I realized then, that I had a moment to myself, a moment of silence. It had been a long time since my last; I couldn't recall it.

I stood and walked to the window. The streets below glistened from the deluge of rain, which had stopped for the time. I looked at the sky to see the clouds had parted some. And there the stars hung, as always. They followed me everywhere I went, coming to light a path. Were they watching? Little old me and my bizarre adventures. Should I be paying more attention? Was there honestly a path for each and all of us?

It wasn't long ago I was unconscious and tied to a broken boat in the Atlantic. Intoxicated to a point that would drive most to insanity.

I looked down beside me to Tatiana's painting. It looked different in the night, beautiful and haunting. How did two strangers from complete opposite lives end up in this little room together?

Visions of the children in their funny poses for the camera danced in my mind. The feeling of her in my arms warmed me somewhere that had been very cold, lifeless.

I really wasn't sure where I was, or how I came to be there. For all I knew, it could still be the acid. But wherever and whenever… I wanted to stay.

33

It was somewhat of a sleepless night. I really wanted to sleep, but as I snuggled into a sleeping Tatiana, I realized I had no means to alarm myself awake for work in the morning. One thing I was not interested in was being late and pissing Faas off on the first day. He wasn't a chipper morning guy to begin with. So, my sleep was very broken and unsatisfying. I would doze off for brief moments, then shudder awake, sometimes sitting up in bed. Horrified by the possibility I'd overslept.

I noticed there was a clock on the nightstand. But it was a special design for the blind, and even if I could figure out how to set an alarm with it, I would never trust it.

I spent the night holding Tatiana. Watching her, and pulling the blankets back over her whenever she kicked them off. I accepted, after a couple rounds, that maybe she was actually hot. So, I'd let her sit for a moment with the blankets off, then pull them back over.

My eyes closed for more than a moment and cracked open again to a natural morning hue. I checked the clock and it was six, I hoped. So, I slid off my side of the bed, drew on my clothes, and made my way to the bathroom.

After freshening up, I emerged to see her awake and sitting on the side of the bed. She yawned and called to me.

"Brandon, honey?" she said sleepily, her eyes facing the floor and her hand held out for me.

"Yes, sweetie, I'm here." I hurried to her, taking her hand and giving her a morning kiss on the cheek. "What are you doing up, silly girl? It's too early for you."

"Yes, is early. But I must know you is up. You must work today."

"I know, I'm up." I hugged her close. "I don't have an alarm clock, and was scared of missing work. So I couldn't sleep."

"Oh! I am sorry to this. I will fix today, for you. So you have good sleep tonight."

She lifted her hand to my face for a smile check.

"It's okay honey. I'll make it through today. I'm super tough."

She smiled. "Yes." Her hand slid to my chest. "You is my big, strong, tough man."

"Yes, I am." I kissed her again. "I have to go now, sweetie. Before I'm tempted back into that warm bed with you."

"Yes, come, I walk you to door."

The morning was brisk and damp. The rain had stopped and the clouds were scattered. It looked as if we would get to enjoy some sun.

The streets were lightly populated. Many men were sipping coffees as they headed toward the marina. I made my way to the boathouse and knocked on the door before entering.

"Hello?" I called.

"Yes!" Helen's voice echoed from upstairs. "Come, breakfast is ready now!"

It was quiet around the table. Faas had his head buried in a newspaper and Helen busied herself with serving the food.

"Goot morning, Brandon." She smiled as I pulled up a chair. "How are you? How was the sleep last night, hmm? You sleep nice with you beautiful lady?"

Faas paused and looked up at me with a grin.

I felt my cheeks grow hot. "Yeah, it was good."

Helen placed a plate in front of me and patted me softly on the shoulder. "So, today you work wit Faas. It is goot he has strong boy to help. I am tired of him growl about how much he work."

Faas sneered at her from across the table, then went back to reading and stuffing food in his mouth.

I chuckled. "Well, it's really nice of you to let me help. I can't thank you enough. I've never worked for a place that cooked me breakfast before."

Faas looked up from his business and dabbed at his mouth with a napkin as he finished chewing. "Today we must finish boat. This boat you come on. The people come to get this tomorrow. We must clean and finish little tings. Make nice."

"Oh, okay. So, Bethany will be gone tomorrow?"

"Yes, this boat, Betany, tomorrow. You work here, eight hours, Monday and to Friday. I will pay to you money, cash, on all Friday."

"Okay, thank you Faas, and Helen. Thank you very much."

Helen smiled. "Sooo, the lady. Tatiana and children, where they today?"

"Uh, I guess they'll probably do school work."

"Ah yes, the school is important. The lady, she smart. She have goot heart."

"She is, really. A really great woman. I've never met anyone like her before."

Helen grinned ferociously. "Yes, maybe some time, you and this girl, maybe you will be marry, hmm?"

I felt blood rush to my face again and I looked down at the table. "I don't know. That's a long time away, I think."

"Maybe you think this is long time. But you come back for her. You know her for only small time, and you come back. Maybe is not so long for time?"

I noticed Faas check the clock, and then he set his napkin down, folded his paper, and stood. "Is time, we must go, come." He motioned to me.

Happy to get out of Helen's spotlight, I stood up immediately, thanked her for the breakfast, and followed Faas down the stairs.

As we walked down the dock, a light breeze blew against my skin, embedding the cool moisture into my bones. The radiant heat of the sun promised warmth later in the day, but admittedly, I was underdressed for the climate. Something I would have to adapt to.

It had been a while since I'd seen her. Bethany sat there, sparkling in the morning sun. Her youthful beauty had returned, and she was a real looker when she was all dressed up.

Faas broke out a tub of wax and introduced me to a buffing wheel. "This is today. We must get her dry and wax. She must shine when people come tomorrow."

So, we went to work, waxing and mopping, dusting and polishing. I found that Faas was very skilled at staging the boat, organizing furniture and securing ropes in just such a fashion.

At noon, Helen ran sandwiches out to us. We ate on the go, as it all had to be completed by the end of the day. The sun was setting by the time Faas was satisfied.

We sat down on the bench at the edge of the boat. Faas reached into a cooler he had packed and grabbed a couple beer, passing one to me.

He smiled and patted me on the back. "Looks goot, yes?" He clinked his bottle to mine.

"Yeah, she looks really good, Faas." We sipped from our bottles. "So, what now? Bethany will be gone tomorrow. Then what?"

"Ah, yes, then we work on another boat, Peru boat. Is in the yard, not far, on land. We must take all paint off the bottom and put on new paint. Is much work for this boat."

"Yeah? Sounds good. Then it'll be delivered to Peru? You gonna get Adlar and the guys to take it down?"

"Huh? Oh. Yes, they will take this."

"So, how do they get back?"

He wiped sweat from his head. "I look for boat, maybe, to buy from there. They can bring back. Maybe I look for some people who like boat from there. I not know. Maybe they be there for some time."

"Really? You don't mind those guys sailing your boats?"

"I like to have someone better to sail. Some not crazy and all the crazy party. But is not easy to find this. Is not nice life for many people. You go, weather can be shit, you not know when is coming home. Is not for man wit family. Only crazy man."

"Must pay pretty good though?"

"Pay? Huh?" He scrunched his face. "Why you ask all the question of this? You think you like this? Why? You have goot here. Warm bed, beautiful young lady." He looked off to the horizon. "This woman, she like you. I know this. Is everything, in the way she be wit you. I know she like you very much. I know you like this lady very much."

"No— I mean, yeah, I know. But it'd still be nice to make some money."

"What? You make goot money here, work wit me. These crazy boys, they make money, then they go party, have crazy girls. Then one week, maybe two week, they have nothing. Why you want this?"

"I… I was just asking, just curious."

"I live like this one time. When I is young, like you. I sail, I travel, drugs, women, party all this time. Then I have nothing. Now"—he pointed his bottle toward the boathouse—"she give me all this, togeter we make this. I have warm bed, clothes is clean, goot food for belly." He smiled and rubbed his stomach. "If not for this woman, this beautiful woman in my life, I would have nothing."

We fell into silence again. Sipping our beers, we watched the sun set and the boats pass us by.

I considered his words of wisdom. But in the end, they seemed like simple ramblings from an old man. I don't think he quite understood my mindset. It wasn't that I was unhappy with Tatiana, or that I was wanting to leave her. I honestly had no desire to get back on a boat with that group of yahoos. But a man's gotta make some money… right?

Bottles empty, Faas packed up his cooler and slapped me on the back. "Is goot for today. Is late, yes. You should go, go to be wit family." He smiled with a wink.

I nodded and followed him to the ladder, where we descended to the dock and made our way back.

34

I stepped in the door to the orphanage and a barrage of footsteps pattered down the stairs to the landing above.

"Brandon?" Hans stood at the top of the landing with his blank stare, calling to me. The girls slowly came around the corner, one by one.

I smiled at the sight of them. "Yeah, it's me."

"It is late? How come you so late? We need *Harry Potter*!" He clutched the railing and descended, one stair at a time, till I picked him up in my arms.

"I know, *Harry Potter*." I poked him in his belly for a giggle. "How come you're not in your pajamas yet, huh?"

I looked up to see Tatiana had joined the others on the landing. Her beautiful smile was something special to come home to.

"Okay, children," she announced. "Please let us take Brandon to kitchen for food."

I walked up the first flight with Hans in my arms and then set him down on the landing. I leaned over to give Sasha a pet and then stood to meet my woman.

"Hi, honey." I kissed her lips.

"Oooh! You smell like this beer." She turned and led me to the kitchen, waving her hand in front of her mouth.

"Yes, I smell like beer. We had a long day. We're only supposed to work eight-hour days, but we had to get the boat ready for tomorrow. The new owners are coming to pick it up. So, we had a long day. Then we sat on the boat and had a beer to celebrate."

"The boys and the beer." She smiled and squeezed my hand. "Is good, yes? You have busy day?"

"Yes, very busy, and hot and sweaty."

The kitchen was empty of people. She took me to our table and sat me down, then stood before me, pulling my face to her stomach and massaging my scalp. "You are a good man. Hard-work man." She leaned down for a kiss. "Now stay, we have surprise for you."

"A surprise? Really?"

She rounded the kitchen counter and handed a plate of bread to Anna, then followed cautiously behind her with a bowl of soup. It was what we had pretty much every evening. Still, I did my best to sound shocked and awed.

"Bread! Soup! Oh, wow! How lucky am I!"

"Oh, hush!" Tatiana scolded, slapping me playfully after she'd put down the bowl.

The two girls hurried back around the counter, where I could see the tops of little heads waiting. Then there was a flicker of light, and Tatiana emerged once again with a tray of iced cupcakes. Each decorated with a lit candle.

I was a little apprehensive, watching her carry the tray across the room with kids in tow. But she was very graceful, so I let her go to it.

"Oh, wow!" I cheered and clapped from my seat.

The children's faces exploded with proud smiles. As Tatiana reached the table, I helped her gently set the tray down.

At first glance, the cupcakes looked like the icing machine had a catastrophic malfunction. I can only imagine what the kitchen looked like after such a creative adventure. But I could see they were made with love… and sugar, lots of sugar.

The children took their seats as instructed, although they were practically jumping out of their skin with excitement.

There were a dozen cupcakes total. Each one had toothpicks stuck along the edges. The number of picks ranged from one to five.

"Wow! They all look so awesome! Who wants to help blow out the candles?"

Their faces turned aghast, little eyes widened at the mere suggestion.

"We can blow on candles?" Gaby screamed.

Tatiana just stood confused.

"Well, yeah! Of course you can blow on the candles. I can't blow on them all by myself. Just move slow and feel around the table for the edge of the tray. Then feel for the bottom of a cupcake and blow at the top of it. Don't touch the fire though."

Tongues were hanging and faces were scrunched in concentration. But they all found their positions, hands on cake of choice.

"All right, one, two, three, Blow!"

The sound was like four little motorboats roaring through the kitchen. What the breeze failed to extinguish, the slobber clobbered. All except one. One I'd put aside for my lady.

I snuck around the table and put my arms around her and held the cake a safe distance from her face. Her hands quickly scrambled up my arm to search out what I was up to.

"Blow, but you have to make a wish first," I whispered. She smiled and blew a light wisp that turned the flame to a smouldering ember.

"You got it." I kissed her cheek.

I sat back down and the children quickly assembled around me. Anna took a seat on my left knee. She was getting so big, it was hardly sufficient for her. But she'd never really approached me before. She was a teacher's pet. So I enjoyed her acceptance.

And on the other knee was, of course, my man Hans.

They pulled at the cupcakes one by one, removing the spent candles and feeling for the toothpicks.

"We all have number for toothpicks," Anna explained, "so we know who decorate all of them. I is one, Gaby is two, Hans is three, Lilly is four, and Teacher Tatiana has five.

"This is Anna idea," Tatiana added. "She think this with toothpicks."

"You did, Anna? Wow! That's very smart. I wouldn't have been able to think of something like this. I would've just smashed my face in the icing."

Cheers echoed.

Gaby leaned over the table with one of her cupcakes in her hand. It could only be the work of a very passionate artist, as this cupcake was lopsided with its heavy burden of icing of all different colours.

"You know is this?"

"I-I-I-eee, ahhh... a rainbow mountain?"

"No, is not rainbow mountain, is castle!" She glared at me as if I were challenged.

"Ah, right, it is a castle. I see now."

"Yes! And see princess here, in very tall tower." Her fingers poked every nook and cranny.

"I see, very nice Gaby."

"This is a picture of Teacher Tatiana." Anna put her cupcake before me, running her finger around the edge. I was happy the cupcakes came with narration.

"This is Harry Potter!" Hans blurted.

"Ah, yeah! Harry Potter, that's super cool Hans. And what did you make Lilly?"

Lilly was off to the side and had remained silent. Her smile perked at my attention.

"This is my house, and is family. Family I have someday."

"Oh." I looked at her face for a moment. Her beautiful little smile and large blue eyes. I guess I'd never given much thought to what an orphanage really was, to that point. I just thought of it as an Amsterdam thing. But apparently some of these kids wanted to have a piece of normal. I really didn't know how to respond. "That's really beautiful, Lilly. You did really good with that."

Anna and Hans moved off my lap and I went to work on the soup, which had cooled to the perfect temperature. The first bite reminded me of how starved I was. The kids dug into their treats, sharing bits with Sasha, and Hans kept the Harry Potter cupcake for me as my special dessert.

We all helped with dishes afterward, and it was quite late by the time we got upstairs. I told everyone that if they were good and got ready for bed quickly, we could read some of the book.

After one chapter, they lobbied successfully for another. Then it was tuck-into-bed time and Tatiana and I retreated to her room.

After our preparations, we crawled into bed and snuggled together.

"That was really nice to come home to tonight. You and the children and the cupcakes. Thank you very much, for everything."

"Yes, but is not my thought, is children. All day they ask where you is, when you come back. They miss you."

"Really?"

"Yes, I think they like you. I am jealous maybe. They like you more than me."

"Ha, no way! I don't think there's anyone in the world those kids like more than their teacher."

She turned to me. Her lips searched for mine, kissing their way up from my chest.

"Hey, that cupcake, the one Lilly made, with the family. Is that real? I mean, is there a chance that these kids might get adopted?"

"Yes, Lilly, she want this very much."

"But does it actually happen? How?"

"Yes, of course. They have open doors to people, once in month. Every three Wednesday of month. People come if they like. Visit children."

"Oh?"

"Yes, this day is tomorrow. Lilly always get excite for this day. All children do, but Lilly the most."

"Have you ever had one of the children get adopted?"

"Yes, some of the children down the stairs. They get this sometime. But not many people come to visit here. I think people is scared the children is blind, maybe."

She pulled in closer, placed her head against my chest, and curled her leg over mine.

"I do not like to speak of this too much to children. Is not much possible for them. Anna, she maybe too old now. She will grow here, be teacher like me. Lilly, Gaby, Hans—it is possible for them, maybe, but not as possible as the others. So maybe I do not like them think too much of this."

I ran my fingers lightly up and down her back. The thought of one of the children leaving saddened me a little, and I hardly knew them.

"I think you'd miss them too much, if they left. And they'd miss you just as much. I think they should stay here with you."

"They stay here, with us." She grinned and ran a teasing finger down my face.

35

The next morning I went for breakfast at the boathouse again. The sun was out for the second day in a row. I felt like we were breaking records.

After breakfast, Faas took me down to a boatyard and introduced me to our next, very large project. The boat was on a trailer, towering into the air. He had a rolling scaffold platform and an extension ladder up the side, extending to the deck.

We walked around the vessel as he explained the first project, painting the hull. The hull was substantial, to say the least. The first step would be labour intensive, consisting of scraping, stripping, and sanding the old paint off. The response in my mind rhymed with *phit*. My best guess at the timeframe to finish was sometime after I was dead.

Faas brought out the tools and gave a thorough demonstration of how to use each, emphasizing the importance of taking time to do things in the correct manner. Then he got everything set up, and we climbed the scaffold to begin on the first section.

He stood by me till about nine, then took off back to the boathouse for a shower and change. Bethany's new owners were scheduled to arrive at ten.

I was already sweating my ass off. When the summer sun decides to shine in Amsterdam, it doesn't fuck around. My skin and hair were infested with paint chips, dust, and chemicals. As I rounded to the back on the first pass, I noticed the faded, pencilled inscription on her bumper: *Atta Gurl.* My new mistress.

Scrape on, scrape off. The Mr. Miyagi-esque chant played in my mind, till I found my zone, my mindless work zone. Then songs took over, along with questions of why I never applied myself more in school.

I stopped for a moment to wipe the sweat from my forehead. As I reached down to the platform for my water bottle, I caught her out of the corner of my eye. The great Bethany was sailing again.

Turned loose from her mooring, her masts gleamed in the morning sun like I never thought possible. Watching her then, floating away from my life, I regretted ever letting her go. She was beautiful in her way. A real man would've fought for her. But I was a fool. Too young and immature for her, a true woman of the world. I wasn't sure there was a man out there who could tame her.

I was sad to see her go. We'd been through a lot together. If only she could talk; I wonder if she had even more passionate secrets in her life than the time we shared.

As she passed by slowly, I saw a man, woman, and two children running around, looking at their new boat with wonderment. They were in good hands. I hoped they would treat her with the respect she deserved.

As she disappeared from sight, I settled back into my methodic rhythm, until Faas rounded the corner with a basket lunch.

"Ha! Did you see?" He pointed to the canal. "She sail again!"

"Yeah, I saw. They look like a nice family."

He climbed up the scaffold and stood beside me. "Yes, I think is nice family. They will all be goot togeter. They go now, to spent some time on her, in the ocean. Get to know the boat. Then they are plan to sail to Australia sometime, all the family."

"Australia?" My eyes bulged. "Really? That's a hell of a trip."

"Yes, is a long distance, but not so bad. There are times to cross oceans. Some in summer, some on other times. All will have bit of problem."

"Yeah, some problems all right. I know about those."

Faas reached into the basket and handed me a sandwich and a beer. "Here, take break, eat. Is hot today, yes? Is goot for us. When weather nice, we work outside; no nice, we work inside. Soon is summer no more. We must have finish paint before is cold. You no want this in winter."

Faas popped the cap from his beer, took a swig, and let go a satisfied gasp. Then he reached to his waist and pulled up on the bottom of his muscle shirt, lifting it over his head and letting it fall to the scaffold.

It became apparent that during some point in his life, the hair that once covered his head had run for cover, retreating beneath his clothing and onto his fur-cloaked midsection. Which draped over his impressive beltline. His hands slapped off his belly like a drum, as he turned his face to the sun and took a deep breath. "Ahhh!" He looked down at me and his eyebrows raised above the smirk on his face. "Is nice, yes?" He tipped the bottle to his lips.

The scaffold, which was small to begin with, shrunk a little more. I scooted over to the point where my safety was compromised. I'd developed respect for Faas over our time together. And I could say with confidence that I liked him, but liked him even more with his shirt on. It was an honest mystery how the removal of his shirt in public made me more uncomfortable than it did himself.

I took special precaution to not pay undue interest in his awkwardness, and he took notice of my abstinence.

"What?" he bellowed, reaching down to rub his girth. "You not like this?" He laughed, and it jiggled. "Is okay for me, I is this man. Is big man. You still young, you think you must have to be muscle and pretty boy. This no matter when you get too old. Maybe I no too much goot-looking. But I have life for me and my wife. We make good life togeter. We is happy people. My wife, she no mind this." He continued massaging himself and smirked. "She like this!"

He set his beer down beside him, then found a scraper and started to work. "I have my life, to me is all… everything. Today, I sell boat to nice family. It make them happy. Togeter, they will enjoy life. So today, I will enjoy the sun, is warm and feels nice."

He cleaned a patch in front of him with much more speed, precision, and accuracy than me.

"Maybe sometime you have luck like me. Find nice girl, who love you and be in life wit you. Then you know what I say."

"Yeah, maybe someday."

"Ha ha! Yes, if I was you, I take this girl now. I marry to her. She is beautiful, goot woman, we know she is goot mother to children. They no her children, still, she love them. This is goot woman."

I didn't like it. Right then, I got it. take her while I had the chance, or lose her and look like a fool. She was a great, gorgeous, foreign woman. Centrefold material, literally. But… marriage? I was in my mid-twenties, my prime. I had big adventures, more than anyone I grew up with. But was that it? Was I done?

I'll just throw it on the table. The no-sex thing was bugging me. I know, it shouldn't be that big of a deal. But it was as though she knew my weakness and was playing on it to get what she wanted. If what she wanted was a nice dinner, some flowers, that was a decent starting point. But she wanted it all, lock and key. First thing, no compromise.

As if it weren't already weighing on my mind enough, like, every second of the day. Where was I? What were my plans for the future... if any? What were my intentions with her and the kids? Add to that, Faas barking in my fucking ear every day that I should *Just do it, everything will be wonderful!*

I was beginning to feel that if I looked up the word *sucker* in the dictionary, there'd be a picture of me scraping the side of a fucking boat in the company of a plump, hairy, shirtless Dutchman.

Marriage!... They all took it so lightly. Like it was nothing. No big deal. Only the rest of my life. The rest of my life with a blind woman and four blind children, none of whom were biologically mine! The rest of my life, sitting there on a scaffold with paint flakes all over my body, down my shirt, in my eyes, and up my nose, irritating the shit out of me. For "chump change."

Everybody pressing, backing me into some corner. She was even talking to my parents, and they loved her, and the children. They'd probably be thrilled. Finally, someone decent had tied down their reckless son. Grounded him, given him focus and direction.

Not one of them had stopped to ask me what I want! The thing that really pissed me off, was that I didn't have an answer! I didn't fucking know what I wanted. But did the rest of my life have to be decided right then?

"Whoa!" Faas said, interrupting my internal rant and bringing to light my reckless scraping. I was scouring away like a man possessed, paint chips flying everywhere. "Slow! You must be slow, go wit care! You make scratch in boat. This no goot!" He looked at me. "What wrong wit you?"

I placed my hands on the deck beside me, leaned forward, closed my eyes, and took some breaths to calm my nerves.

"I... I'm sorry. I just got a little... excited."

"Excite? You go fucking crazy, I think. Look what you do!" He pointed to a couple considerable gouges in the hull. All was silent as he observed my state, reading me. He calmed some. "Just relax a bit, huh? Have some of beer, cool off."

I nodded and took a long drink.

We paused for a bit, in silence. Though he didn't say anything, I think—one man to another—he picked up on what had set me off. For the rest of the day, there was no more talk of a good woman, or marriage.

We worked till the sun sat just above the horizon, and then we said our goodbyes and I made my way home… to the orphanage. People dressed up in nice summer wear strolled down the sidewalks, clean and happy. My clothes and every inch of me beneath them was covered in flakes. My skin itched like mad, my back hurt, and my hands were parched and heavily blistered.

A word to describe my day: *honest*. A lot of soul-searching had been done. I was beginning to realize that maybe I wasn't the man for this. Not then, maybe not ever. They were good people, honest people, living a life where everything was good and pure. I definitely wasn't that. It was time I understood that, if I had no real intention of marrying this woman, then I should just get out of her way. She and the children. They were growing attached, hopeful. I'd already taken it too far. As upset as I was, I really didn't want anyone to get hurt, especially not Tatiana and the children. But the longer I stuck around, the more harm would be done.

I crossed the street to the door and stepped inside. There, at the top of the stairs, stood the troops, all of them smiling so sweetly.

They carefully patted down the stairs. Hans lifted his arms for me to pick him up. Lilly and Gaby clung to a leg. Anna stood a couple stairs up, like a proper lady, in a pretty yellow dress, with her teacher beside her. Like mother and daughter. So beautiful, so precious.

"How is work, Brandon?" Hans asked. "You work on big boat?" Excitement filled his voice.

"Yes buddy." I smiled and mussed his hair.

"We miss you, Brandon!" Gaby's voice filled the stairwell.

A silent tear rolled down my cheek. In all my short years, I'd never had anything like them to come home to.

I took a step up toward Tatiana. Putting my arm around her waist, I pulled her close.

"We missed you," she whispered to me, with her voice that could melt the coldest of hearts. She felt for my smile and I made sure it was there, as strong as ever.

"I missed you too, honey." I kissed her, deeply and longingly, as if surrendering an apology for a fight she played no part in. My heart beat, my body warmed, and my pain and doubt disappeared.

A warm shower soon rinsed the tension from my muscles. The soapy lather boiled deep into my pores to flush away the sweaty toxins.

Taps off, I towelled down and wrapped it snugly around my waste. I stepped out toward the vanity, the heavy saturation of fog layered in the air. I wiped away the dense film of sweat from the mirror and leaned in for a closer cheek examination. Back to normal size and shape, which was a relief to see. I was honestly expecting some permanent damage after such a hit. It had definitely felt more permanent.

I exited to the room in a poof of steam. The lamp glowed from the corner and Tatiana sat on the bed in a silken nightgown.

I took a spot on the edge of the bed. I rested my elbows on my knees and took a breath of the cool air. Her hands slid down my shoulders to my waist and she slid her warm body against my back, pressing her breasts into me as she spread her legs and wrapped them around me. Her hands dug into my chest, deep and firm as she began her massage.

I closed my eyes and exhaled as she melted everything bad from my world.

"Where are the kids?" I moaned.

She pressed her lips to my ear. "They is in they room. I tell them to clean, and to wait for us." Her lips began to caress my shoulder. "You have a hard day, I know this. I feel it in kiss when you come to home. Now, I take care this."

What she was giving to me then was in no way influenced by money. No amount could ever acquire the energy she was spending on me. Even without vision, she was a woman who could lift you to the heavens, or push you to your knees with only her passion. If she truly was a trap, you could call me sucker.

The smell of her skin, the warmth of her breath   it was more than I could resist, or wanted to. I rolled myself around in her embrace, pushed her back, and slid on top of her. She smiled and our lips locked.

She heated fast and blood pounded through my veins. One hand shot to the back of her neck, the other to her thigh, quickly moving to her ass and digging in. She moaned and I rounded third, pumping hard to take it all the way home.

Then…

"No, Brandon." She stopped my hand. "We must not do this."

I paused, panting heavily. "But…," I pleaded.

She smiled understandingly, but there was no give to the woman. Not with that. So, I collapsed on top of her.

She ran her hands lightly up and down my back, then up to massage my head, which did nothing to help my condition. "You hair is long, yes. We can cut this? You like?"

I huffed and puffed, head turned toward the wall, exhausted by rejection, again. "Yeah, we can cut it, if you want."

She kissed my neck, then pushed herself out from below me to lay beside me. She draped a leg over me and continued rubbing my back, then kissed my shoulder. "We should go now, go to children. They like for some *Harry Potter.*" She snickered.

"*Phooo*," I blew out, "right, *Harry Potter.* We should go." I shrugged it off. I knew the sacred rule. I really did want to respect it, but a bigger challenge I hadn't faced. Acid pirate was amateur.

I got dressed, and we went to see the children. We all gathered in our usual spots, like the night before, and the one before it. I sat on the edge of the sofa. My girl put her head in my lap. Our four children lay spread out around us, snuggling with their stuffies and our dog…

I felt strong, warm. My head was clear and tomorrow… who knew? Maybe things would work out for our happy family.

36

The rest of the week passed to Friday.

Faas had ceased asking questions about my future intentions and poking at me to make a move to secure things with Tatiana. So, for the most part, my mood remained positive. But when I was left to my work and thoughts, there were times I would begin to worry about my direction. There were many hearts' hopes and dreams weighing on my shoulders. It was heavy.

That evening, I returned home to an unexpected surprise. After my shower, Tatiana and the children were waiting in the room for me. They were smiling and snickering anxiously among themselves. I teased at them to tell me what they had planned, till they were almost bursting at the seams.

After I got dressed, they pulled my hands and led me across the landing to their room. In the middle sat a chair, which they sat me down in.

Tatiana gleamed. "Do you know yet?"

I admit to growing slightly uneasy, and it turned out I had reason to be.

Hans and Gaby appeared on either side of me, Hans holding a white sheet. They each took an end and felt their way up to my neck, which they then wrapped it around and tucked it into the collar of my shirt. The ritual stoked some sense of familiarity, and it dawned on me as soon as Anna came around with a pair of scissors and a comb in her hand.

"We give you haircut!" the children shouted.

My eyes bulged. "Oh… Heh, heh… Really?"

"Yes! Really!" Tatiana cheered from behind. "It is fun for us."

"Yes… fun… for us." I swallowed nervously. "You're going to give me a haircut? You? All of you? Isssss Tessa going to come help maybe?"

"No, is just us. We will all help." She rubbed my shoulders, then wrapped her arms around me and gave me a reassuring kiss on the cheek.

What could I say? They were all so excited. They'd likely been planning and waiting for it all day. Could I be the one to say no? Smash their little hearts? Should I point out the obvious lack of a specific perception involved with cutting hair? I pictured them swirling around my head with sharpened blades, and gulped.

"It is fine, do not be worry. We practise today, with Lilly doll."

At the announcement, Lilly held up her dolly to me, now sporting short hair jutting out in all directions at various lengths. A look of fear and helplessness in its eyes.

"Oh, ho, ho! I see. It looks very… nice," I responded through gritted teeth, my expression matching the doll's.

"Okay, everybody. Are we ready?"

"Yeah!" they cheered and circled in closer.

It was the longest and most suspenseful grooming adventure I'd taken part in. There was no mirror, so I did what I could to catch a reflection in the window, but the panes were distorted and the lighting uneven. So, I quit trying and hoped for the best.

They were very careful and attentive. Tatiana would assemble a tuft of hair and feel out the length, then each child would take a turn lining up the shears by feel and making a cut. Little hands giggled and patted around me.

Finally, after much examination, Tatiana announced the transformation complete.

They led me back across the landing to the bathroom to look upon the new me.

It wasn't bad, really. I could honestly say I'd had worse… maybe.

It was short—shorter than I'd seen it in years, shorter than I would've requested. But the length was surprisingly uniform. More so than the poor little dolly's. There were no lacerations and ears and eyebrows were unharmed. Impressive, all things considered. I would be fine with it in public. Preferably under a hat, but I wasn't sure a hat would be an option. Not without exciting some little insecurities.

It wasn't a performance I wanted to overly praise, because next round I wanted the option of sourcing out my own barber, but you gotta support the family. "Oh, wow! Look at this! It's awesome! This is the best haircut I've ever had!" I looked around at all the contented smiles.

"You like this, Brandon?" Hans shouted. "We do goot?"

"You sure did, little man! Gimme knuckles!"

We bumped fists, then I gave a round of hugs to the ladies and a special squeeze and a kiss to Tatiana.

We'd been burning through *Harry Potter* pretty quickly. I wasn't much of a reader before then, but I was enjoying myself along with everyone else.

Maybe that was something I could go track down on the weekend with my new-found wealth. Faas had handed me some cash at the end of the day. A few hundred bucks for the week wasn't much, but there was nothing to tax, and free room and board meant maybe we could have some fun. The weather was supposed to be good.

As we settled in for the read, I asked, "Are we doing something tomorrow? Do you have anything planned?"

"Oh!" Tatiana clapped her hands together, looking excitedly toward the children. "Children! Brandon ask what we do tomorrow!"

They sucked in their breath in quick anticipation, holding onto it through airtight lips.

"We go to park! Is tomorrow, is people playing music!"

"Oh? Like a festival?"

"Yes! A festival. Like this. The children, we never do this before."

"Oh?" *Can we stop at the hat store on the way?*

It was Friday night. Party night. Ain't goin' down till the sun comes up! I read till everyone was passed right out, about nine thirtyish. I was all right with it. I was beat and looking forward to sleeping in some.

With heavy eyes, I smirked at the scene. Then, one by one, I carried the children to their beds and tucked them in good and tight, stuffies secured.

Sasha was close on my heels with every step; head and tail drooping. I could see the night was late for her as well. We stopped by the couch to pick up Teacher. I carried her across to her bed and lay her down sweetly, then crawled up snug beside her and wrapped my arms around her. Sasha jumped onto the foot of the bed and curled up.

Marc Gregory

I slept in the next day.

37

Sun poked through the window, bringing that early-Saturday-morning glow. I stretched out and smiled. It was the weekend, my head was on straight, and all wounds were healed. I started that day snuggled in bed with my beautiful lady, and I had some honest cash in my pocket. Been a long, long time since things had been that good.

My hands and lips wandered lightly over Tatiana, till she stirred and rolled into me with a good-morning kiss.

She buried her head in my chest and wrapped herself around me. "You up too early, my silly, handsome man," she groaned.

"I know." I smiled and kissed the top of her head. "I didn't mean to wake you up."

"Yes. I think you do mean to do it." She kissed my chest. "We must wake now. I know children is wait for us. They so excite for this park and music."

"Hmm." I kissed her again. "I think it sounds like a perfect way to spend the day. The sun is out."

"Yes, I like it be gone for one more hour. Maybe two."

"Ha ha, sexy girl. We should go get ready."

"NO! Do not go, is nice, warm here."

"I'm not going. You have to go first. You take the longest to get ready."

"Mmm." She wrapped herself tighter.

I wrestled with her for a bit and finally broke loose from her clutch. I scooted out my side and walked around to hers. The air was cool, but the sunbeams were summertime warm.

"C'mon, lazy teacher." It took some prodding, but she finally sat up and let me lift her to her feet and guide her to the bathroom.

I offered to help, if she needed. She smiled and kissed me on the lips, then pushed my head lightly beyond the jamb, and closed the door.

There was some pep in my step that morning. Why would there not be? Things were pretty good for old Brando…

Brando. I smirked at a vision of my old pirate crew and wondered where their mischief had led them to wake that morning. Likely bickering over the bill with someone who loved by the hour. Hungover, cold, stinking. They could have it.

With Sasha on my heels, we ventured across the landing to the children's room. They were indeed up, snuggled in their beds, but they sprung to life as soon as they heard me enter.

"Brandon?" Lilly chirped.

"How did you know it was me?" I growled playfully.

"I know 'cause you feet make a different sound than Teacher."

"Oh, they do, do they?"

"Yes!" Hans piped in. "They sound heavy. Like man feet."

"Yeah!" Gaby cheered. "They smell like man feet too!"

"Oh yeah? Well, maybe they smell because it isn't Brandon! Maybe they smell because I'm the tickle monster! *Grrrr.*" I made a round of poking ribs and grabbing little knees, causing them to scream and squirm with laughter. I even got Anna, who always led on that she was too mature for silly games.

I helped them all to their feet and Sasha aided me in rounding them up and over to our room. When Tatiana finally emerged from the shower, fresh and smiling, the children took their turns doing what they must. Anna liked to shower as well, but the rest just wanted to cover the absolute basics and get on with the day. But Tatiana wouldn't have it, and they were all strictly instructed to wash up properly. It was a special day and we should go out feeling our very best. There were groans and moans, but everyone did as told. I took my turn as a quick in-and-out, and the young ladies took their turn together, to help speed things up. Hans and I weren't convinced it worked.

Everyone scrambled with dressing. They tried to throw on whatever was readily available. Hans would've run out in his underpants, no doubt. But Tatiana already had their special outfits picked out, and made them all change.

Of course, we were left waiting for Teacher and Anna. As Anna yearned for adult, female guidance. The others whimpered and rolled around on the floor and furniture till Tatiana heard them and instructed them to stand patient and not wrinkle their outfits.

We had a hard time convincing any of them to stop in the cafeteria for a quick breakfast. But we had to stop anyway, to pick up the picnic basket Tessa had prepared.

The park was a few long blocks away, but as we were ready a little early, we took our time. It was a beautiful morning. The sky blue and unobstructed. The sun as radiant as the smile on all our faces.

I carried the basket for my girl, and we walked by what she mentioned to be one of her favourite coffee shops. She really liked a particular cappuccino they made, special. So, we went in and I bought a special cappuccino for my lady and a coffee for myself, then continued down the block. It was such an excellent way to be in that environment. Walking hand in hand with Tatiana. Our line of children walking out front, with Sasha leading. I couldn't stop marvelling at all the storefronts and cafés. I couldn't understand the many people who walked by and never seemed to take any notice of what an enchanting place they were in.

We made our way along, without incident. Clicking and clacking through the narrower of streets, where we took up the entire passage. People would smile and stand aside politely after taking notice.

It took just over an hour to reach our destination. We crossed the final street and passed by some bordering trees, and then a grand green space opened before us. I breathed in the summer day and raised my face to the warm sun.

"This is it, Westerpark," Tatiana announced.

The kids cheered. It was nice to have an open area to explore, without worry of passing traffic.

"What you think?" Tatiana squeezed my hand. "How is it? Many people?"

"Not bad, there's some people coming in. Looks like it's gonna get busy."

"There is many water parks, for children. Maybe if you look down this way, there is market? Many place for food and art."

"Hmm, well, there is a stage on the far side. There's some people setting things up there, but it doesn't look like anyone will be playing soon. Do you think we should go and explore the market for a bit?"

"Uh, yes, if you like do this. I try this some time, but is too busy for me alone. You think is okay for children?"

It doesn't look too bad yet. I think it'll be all right. If it's too much trouble, we'll come back to the park.

My lady was very excited and kissed me sweetly on the cheek and wrapped her arm tightly around mine.

"Okay, children. Brandon say he take us to market. We must all stay close. It may be very busy, okay?"

"Yeah!" was the response. So off we went.

As soon as we entered the narrow-paved streets of the market, I understood Tatiana's concern for navigation. The capacity was light compared to what I expected the afternoon crowd to be, but the little ones required a short leash in such an environment.

We didn't venture far. We stopped to listen to a man strumming a ukulele, accompanied by a woman on a tambourine. They stood next to little stands peddling an assortment of products from soaps and jewellery to fortune tellers and food—lots and lots of food. The little ones' noses were overwhelmed with the abundance of interesting flavours.

I whispered to Tatiana about the presence of an ice cream stand, but she said it was too early for such treats. I did manage to talk her into a round of freshly squeezed lemonade for the troops, turning some smiles to puckers and giving us all a laugh.

Strolling along, a certain stand caught my attention. A second-hand book stand. Though I felt it a long shot, I stopped in and asked. The shot turned out to be a lot shorter than anticipated, when the vendor produced three copies of the second book in the Harry Potter series. I picked the best of the lot and paid the man happily. Then I announced my find to everyone, and the kids lost their minds, all wanting to take their turns holding it and leafing the pages through their little fingers.

After some time, the crowd grew too dense for comfort. So we journeyed back to the green space. I described the landscape to Tatiana, and she picked a spot in the centre by the pond, where we laid out some blankets and brought out some bread and fruit for the children to pick at.

With everyone settled, we took a moment to orientate the children to the area. The pond had a cement beach of sorts, that tapered beneath shallow water, making it quite kid friendly. With a bit of foresight, we decided it a good idea to remove all little shoes.

The children remained in their line as they stood in the grass, squishing the fresh blades between their toes. Anna held onto Sasha in the front, who led them all directly into the pond. Little squeals of surprise echoed back as the cool wetness touched their feet, startling Tatiana.

I chuckled. "It's okay honey. Sasha took them all into the water. It's shallow. I'm watching them, you just relax." I rubbed her leg and leaned in to kiss her lips.

The sun grew hot as it peaked to high noon. The kids were so good; they stayed in view, wading in the water as far as they could, without soiling the bottom of little shorts and summer dresses.

It was good we'd found our spot when we did, because things began to pack up. Couples, young and old, had brought their own picnics; many were drinking beer and the smell of cannabis laced the air.

I talked to Tatiana about how strange it was for everyone to be drinking and smoking pot out in the open, how it wasn't allowed back home, but many still did it.

She told me about her life back in Ukraine, something she hadn't spoke of much. She'd lived with her parents, an older brother, and younger sister in a small city. On weekends and holidays, or when they didn't have a job, they would help their grandparents with the farm, which had been in the family for generations. It supplied much of the family's food.

It was easy to tell that she missed them all very much. She hadn't been back to see them since she left. They didn't have internet access there yet, so they corresponded through letters and by telephone, when they could.

She'd planned on returning at least once every year, but then she became involved with the children and… there she was. She thought it would be nice to take them back with her one time. But travelling over international borders with orphan children who didn't belong to her was a challenge, not to mention expensive. She was optimistic that an opportunity would come for her to return home to see her family sometime in the future.

I pulled her around to the front of my body and positioned her between my legs, letting her relax into me. I took time to spoil her with my attention, massaging and kissing her while she smiled and soaked up the energy from the day.

"Teacher?" Anna called from the pond, facing in the opposite direction.

"What, Anna? We here. You follow to my sound."

She reoriented herself, and the group made their way back. I could see there'd been some mischief, which made me smirk, but I wasn't going to say anything.

"Teacher Tatiana!" Anna exclaimed with disgust, as they approached. "Hans is all wet. He go all the way into the water. I tell him not to, but he not listen to me."

Hans brought up the tail end of the group, holding Sasha's leash, both of them soaked to the bone. Sasha looked as happy as a dog could be. I could see that Hans, on the other hand, was worried about facing what consequences may come and was trying to hold it together. First, his chin let loose with a quiver, and then he burst into tears.

"Hans! Why you do this?" Tatiana scolded.

"Easy sexy," I whispered with a kiss to her cheek. I leapt from my spot to help the little guy out. "He-e-ey, big guy, easy. It's fine, you're fine, it's just water."

"Sasha make me. I not want to go. I know Teacher will be mad." He burst into another round of tears and wrapped his arms around me as I kneeled beside him.

"It's really all right buddy, quit your crying. Teacher's not mad at you. No one is mad at you. Sasha's just so excited to be here. She just wanted someone to play in the water with her."

At that point, Sasha did the big shake right in the middle of everyone, spraying summer fun on us all.

All the girls squealed and turned away.

"Sasha!" Anna shouted.

"Yeah, Sasha! You make us all wet, this my favourite dress!"

"Hey!" I yelled, commanding everyone's attention. "No one's dress is ruined. All you ladies look absolutely beautiful, your dresses are fine. Just stay away from the water for a bit and the sun will dry your clothes. Everything is good. It's a beautiful day in the park, and what's a day in the park without getting a little water on you?"

What I discovered about little girls was, I knew that if I called them beautiful enough times, they would forget any wrongdoing. It left them all blushing in their shy poses.

"All right buddy, you're definitely wetter than the rest. But you're a guy, so there's a solution." I started unbuttoning his shirt. "Us guys, we can just take our shirts off and enjoy the day like that. We'll hang your shirt up to dry and everything will work out."

He grabbed my hands. "What? What my shirt?"

"Huh? It's all right dude. Half the guys in the park have their shirts off right now. Here"—I reached down to the bottom of my T-shirt and pulled it over my head. "See, my shirt is off."

He smirked curiously and ran his hands over my shoulders and down my chest.

"It's off man, no joke. Here." I handed him my shirt.

"Teacher! Brandon and Hans are taking they clothes off!"

Tatiana giggled. "Yes, Gaby, I hear this. Boys do this, they silly. Ladies keep clothes on. Boys is like dogs."

"Hey!" I called back in protest, then whispered to Hans, "She's right. We are kind of like dogs."

Hans giggled and finished unbuttoning his shirt, then threw it to the ground. He stood there for a second, face a little red around his big smile. But with no protesting from the public, he found some comfort with his new freedom.

We all settled on the blankets for a nice lunch. Shortly after, there was a chirp of feedback from the stage, before a voice echoed something I didn't understand. Most of the public responded with cheers. Then he said "Hello Amsterdam" in English, and the rest of the crowd erupted.

The afternoon passed with us all cuddled together, listening to the music and the cheering of the park dwellers. A band came on with a funky international beat. They used a wide array of instruments. But they put it together really well, and everyone got a little tap in their feet. The children started to fidget, then stood up, and one by one, little knees began to bend and bob and arms began to swing and sway.

"Tatiana," I whispered. "The children are dancing."

"What?" she whispered back. "Dancy? Really?" She smirked, and bit down on her lip. "I have not had them to dance. Do they dance good?"

I chuckled. "Yes, they dance good. They're very beautiful."

Sasha circled the flock happily, barking every now and then. People walking by took notice and some stopped to watch and clap to the beat, urging the children on. Then they busted a move too. There were some daring twirls by the girls, and

Hans was riding a thin line between shaking his booty and busting a hip.

Tatiana grabbed my hand. "What? What is happen?"

"Some people have stopped to watch the children and are clapping for them."

"Oh." She squeezed me a little harder. I looked at her and her eyes glistened with joyous tears.

I smiled. I wasn't ever a dancer, but I was taking that girl for a spin. I jumped to my feet and pulled her up. "C'mon, Teacher."

I don't know what dance we were dancing, and there was a lot of stepping on toes at first. But we laughed and settled into our own rhythm.

Sadly, every song has to end, and so did ours. But that girl of mine grabbed onto me like I'd never been grabbed before. She pressed her lips to mine with what felt like no intention of letting go, and I wasn't about to waste a moment of it.

"Brandon." I felt a pull on my shorts and looked down at a very sweaty little boy.

"I tirsty, Brandon. Did Teacher pack some water?"

Tatiana and I chuckled and I reached down to muss his hair. "She sure did, sport. Good dancing out there, little man."

So went the rest of the day. We managed to make it through a few more of the bands before the sun began its way down its western slope, and the children began to tire.

Deciding it was time to pack up, we walked to the street and hopped the next tram. Kids and dog flaked out in their seats, till we poured ourselves off at home.

Tired as we were, Tatiana insisted we all take time to shower all the festivities off before bed.

Fresh and clean, we gathered in the children's room, comfy and sleepy in warm pajamas.

That night I didn't even make it through half a chapter, when Sasha and I decided it was time to tuck everyone into bed.

When I got back to our room, Tatiana slept peacefully, her face bathed in still moonlight. I went to the window, looking out to the streets below and the stars above.

It had been a good day. Better than good, it was a great day. I hadn't been very taken by anyone since Katy, back home… way back home. I didn't think I'd ever find someone I'd feel that strongly for ever again. But Tatiana was no Katy, not even close. She was a big step up, and I was beginning to feel ready to take that step for her.

But, I'd also been making a healthy, six-figure salary back then. I'd likely never have that financial opportunity in Amsterdam. That bothered me, even though I knew this woman wasn't interested in keeping up with the Joneses. She couldn't even see the Joneses. She'd grown up with her large family in a small house. She even missed it. And she was happy living in an orphanage. She was in it for support, hand in hand, better or worse, till death.

I wouldn't have to worry about her leaving me for some douche in a Cadillac. 'Cause she didn't even know what one was, and she didn't care. But did that make me a bad person? It kinda felt like I was taking advantage of her, in some way.

I'd been ready to propose to Katy. So why could I not pull the trigger with someone more? Tatiana deserved it, but maybe she deserved better than me.

Maybe that was it? Not that I didn't have faith in her, or in us. Maybe it was in myself I'd lost trust in?

I watched as a couple passed below. Man and woman, arm in arm, laughing with each other beneath the streetlight.

Whatever the problem was, it had been enough thought for the night and it was time to crawl into bed with my woman.

38

It was a couple of gruelling weeks at work to get the hull completed, so we could set the boat back in the water before fall.

Rain had poured and sun had shone as Faas and I battled through to get it done, and the day had finally come to see her float.

This was no ski boat from back home, this thing sat tall on the trailer and setting it in the water was a big deal—for me anyway.

The yard man hooked up the trailer, while Faas and I cleaned up the scaffolding and tools set around it. Then we climbed aboard to take it down the launch.

Faas manned the wheel while I ran around frantically to execute every one of his orders. As big as the boat was, it pretty much worked like any other boat. And out we floated into the canal as Faas turned the key to fire the engine. She wined, coughed, and sputtered. Then, with a puff of black smoke, chugged to life.

We pulled away from the docks, and the warm morning sun beamed blindly off the deck. She was floating again, and she was beautiful. What a feeling of accomplishment.

Back on the oil rigs, you freeze your ass off, work ridiculous hours, and get covered in sweat, blood, and grime. And all you get is a hole in the ground. There was something a little more fulfilling with the end result in the boat industry.

As we rounded past the last boat between us and home at barely a crawl, there—waiting on the dock, was Helen, Tatiana, and the children.

"Wha'! What's going on? What are they doing here?"

Faas laughed. "I think because today so goot of day, we have everyone on boat and we go for ride. Is not much more nice weather now, we can treat our ladies I think, yes?"

I smiled at him. "Yes, I think it's a great idea Faas. Let's go get 'em." I waved ecstatically to everyone, but only Helen waved back, of course. I wasn't quite adapted to my special family. But it's the thought that counts.

We docked the boat and tied it off to load everyone up.

I jumped down to hugs from all.

"Helen come get us in morning," Tatiana said. "We pack food and drink and we have day with you, on boat. The children is very much excited. They not be ever on a boat."

"That's awesome!" I punctuated with a kiss. "I never thought to have a boat day. Helen and Faas are really good to us." I turned to the crew. "I think we all owe a big hug and thank-you to Helen and Faas, right guys?"

"Thank you!" everyone responded, followed by a round of grateful hugs for our hosts, who revelled in the attention.

We helped women, children, and dog aboard. Then set off into the channel, puttering along under engine power, until the water opened to a large reservoir.

"Okay, everyone!" Faas shut down the engine. "Now we put up sail and we be like real pirates.

"YEAH!" the kids roared.

As we hoisted the sails, I understood there was still a lot of work to do, even though the hull had been completed. The deck and interior were in need of some substantial TLC. The rigging for the sails was rusted, and nothing worked the way it should. But with my muscle and Faas's expertise, we got the old girl powered up.

The girls squealed as the sails inflated and the boat listed.

"Brandon? What is happen? The boat is okay?"

I snickered. "Yes, the boat's okay everyone. Best to sit down till you get used to it. The boat tips a little when you put the sails up, because the sails push on the top of the boat. When the wind is really strong, the boat can lean a lot. Then you have to sit down. But today the wind is light, so it won't tip any more than this."

Hans was the first to brave standing up again. He spread his legs wide at first, and knees bent. After a moment, his courage grew and he relaxed. "Look, Brandon. I stand now. I goot at this."

"Yeah, buddy, I see you. Looking good big man. I think you could be a sailor someday."

"Really! You think I can be sailor?"

"Yeah, for sure, why not?"

"I can't see. You should have to see to be a sailor."

"What? You do better than most people I know who can see fine. If you want to be a sailor, you can sail."

He beamed and came over to squish in between Tatiana and me on the bench. "Did you hear what Brandon say, Teacher? He say I can be a sailor."

"*Oh*, wow! You like be sailor?"

"Yes! I want to be this, like Brandon, he sail on boat. That is how he come to us, right?"

The girls were still struggling to find their footing, but their attention turned to us at the mention of my adventure to them, and they all came to sit with us.

"You sailed to here, Brandon?" Lilly asked.

I picked her up and placed her on my knee. "Yeah, that's how I got to Amsterdam."

"Really? On a big boat like this boat? A tippy boat?"

I smiled. "Yeah, a tippy boat like this one. I sailed a *long* way to get here. It wasn't just me though. I had friends who are a lot better at sailing than me. I'd never been on a sailboat before. Then I crossed the whole Atlantic ocean on one."

"Whoa!"

"I came from a little island in the Caribbean."

"A little island?" Gaby asked. "*C-a-r-i-p-p-e-a-n* island. I know this place. It is warm there, yes?"

"Yes, it is very warm there."

"Why you get on boat to sail to cold here? Why not stay in warm island?"

"Well…" I looked to Tatiana to help me out, as she knew most of the story. But she just sat with a cocky smirk on her face.

"He came here to be wit us! Right, Brandon?" Hans said.

"Uh, yeah. That's right Hans. I came here to be with all of you."

"Is fate, like Teacher Tatiana say."

"Oh, she does, does she?" I turned to her and saw that her cocky smirk had been replaced with a blush.

The children sat still as I told stories about my journey across the ocean. The vast majority of it was bullshit, because the real ones were not yet edited for their age group. But they held onto every word.

The reservoir was not very wide for sailing a boat of that size. So, even though the light wind played to our advantage, frequent turns required a lot of effort and attention on my part. I realized how much I'd actually learned on my drug-fuelled escapade across the ocean.

When I sat back down with the group, Lilly commented, "Maybe someday we get a tippy boat? All of us, and Sasha and Miss Helen and Faas. And we can go to somewhere so pretty and be a family."

…Kids. They can really just throw everything out on the table sometimes. There was an uncomfortable pause.

Tatiana wasn't a stupid woman, and I felt she had some idea of my internal struggles. Having me backed into a corner with such questions, seemed possibly even more uncomfortable for her than for me. I noticed it in her reaction. Her playfulness disappeared and her head bowed. But I reached down for her hand and gave it a comforting squeeze.

"Maybe someday" was as simple a response as I could give. It perhaps risked the hopes and dreams of little hearts, but how to avoid such a thing, when little hearts hold so many?

Midday arrived, and we let down the sails and threw anchor for some lunch. We gathered around the table on deck for some eats. Tatiana agreed I should join Faas for a beer, and she actually accepted a glass of white wine from Helen.

The day had been beautiful, but clouds accumulating in the western sky and a stiffening breeze suggested our sunny days were drawing to an end.

With lunch finished, we got the boat under sail to slowly make our way back to port.

Faas happily handed the wheel over to me, and I let the children take turns steering. The girls had fun on their turn, but their excitement seemed to fade quickly. Driving a sailboat was not really all that eventful, even if you can see. They were more interested in navigating the tippy deck, keeping Sasha busy with worry. But Hans, who patiently waited for his turn, had no intention of letting go, ever, once he got hand on the big wheel.

"Where are we going, Brandon?"

"Oh, well, we're just going across the reservoir, then we'll turn around."

"Am I good? Am I going to hit stuff?"

"No, buddy, you're doing just fine."

"Wow! You is right, Brandon. I can be sailor, is easy. I can drive boat all time."

"Yeah, no problem, right? I told you, you could do it."

"I can sail us all way across ocean, just like you. We be pirates togeter."

"Yeah, that'd be great." He sat so proud in my lap. He was such a good kid. They all were. I watched them wandering around the deck and wondered about their lives, their parents, and how they'd ended up in a little orphanage in Amsterdam. Part of me wanted to feel sorry for them, but… they were doing pretty good. It was hard to picture them doing much better, on a happiness scale, anyway. I could picture them doing a lot worse. But a lot of these happy times were happening because of the people who had come into their lives. Helen, Faas… and myself. What would life be for them without that influence?

I looked at my lady, the breeze blowing her golden hair as she sat and talked with Helen. Her smile could stop any man in his tracks. If only it could stop time.

She was the key to it all. No matter who the children belonged to biologically, they wouldn't be as happy in life if she weren't part of it. The way that it was, was the way it had to be.

"Is you go to marry Teacher, Brandon?" Hans asked.

I snapped out of my trance. "Huh?"

"You go to marry Teacher Tatiana? Lilly and Gaby say you and Teacher should be married. Lilly say, if you not marry teacher, then she will marry you. Girls whisper things at night, after sleep. They say you handsome."

"Oh really? That's nice of them to say. I don't think the law in Amsterdam's lenient enough to let me marry Lilly though. Maybe, they *are* pretty lax here, but I'm not sure I'd be comfortable with it."

He snorted a laugh. "Yeah, Lilly is silly. But we ask teacher sometime, when you gone to work, if you go to be married someday. She not answer very goot. But… I really like have you here, with us, and Teacher. Girls like you too. So, if you and teacher get married, we stay togeter always, yes?"

"Well, it's not just about me, you know. Teacher would have to want to marry me too."

"She marry you, yes. Girls say she marry you. Girls say to me that you must get a ring, then you go down on your knee and ask her if she marry you. You know this? I think maybe you not know. Maybe is different in Canata. In Amstertam, this is how to marry."

"Whoa!" I shouted as I jerked the wheel to the right. "Man! That was close. We just about hit a shark, I think."

"What!" he screamed. "A shark!"

"Or maybe an octopus, or a sea monster? I don't know what it was. But it was big!"

The girls heard and they lost their minds. They stood on point, their whole bodies tensed, then closed their little eyes, scrunched their faces, clenched their fists, and screamed at the very top of their little lungs.

Helen and Tatiana were quick to stifle the disruption.

There wasn't a shark, or a sea monster. What there was, was a need to switch topics. I had to get out of the sentimental marriage discussion with little Hans. It'd be great to be able to say that Tatiana and I were going to get married and we'd all sail off into the sunset together. But I just wasn't there yet, and wasn't sure I would ever be. As romantic as those types of conversations should've been, they grew really annoying, really fast. What was wrong with just spending a beautiful day together on a sailboat?

One by one, the children made their way over, feeling their way around the railing on the cabin. Drawn, I suspected, by their sea monster curiosity.

They squeezed in around me, squirming about till they found a position they preferred, and settled in. Then the questions began. Where is sun?... How big are waves?... What they look like?..."

Question period wasn't a bombardment. They were patient and sat in thought, absorbing my answers.

I made sure to raise my voice over the breeze and the sloshing of the hull through the chop. Because if one of them missed a word, they were prompt at asking me to repeat.

The physical description of the waves stumped me. They could sense my uncertainty and one detail bred countless sub-questions till I screamed "Sea monster!" again.

It was a handy play, the sea monster bit. I got to work calculating a land-based equivalent.

The sun hovered just above the horizon as we docked. A thick bank of cumulus threatened on either side, suggesting the sun may be going away for a while.

By that time, all passengers were plenty pooped. They huddled together on the bench with teacher and Miss Helen, wrapped tight with blankets.

With our mighty vessel secured, I brought Sasha down first, then sexy teacher and the rest, one by one. They were dragging their feet a little but were quick to get assembled for the walk home. I sensed they were anxious for a snack, warm showers, jammies, *Harry Potter*, and bedtime.

As we reached the end of the dock, Helen and Faas invited us up for some pie, but we politely declined. I could see they were also ready for quiet time.

The streetlights flickered to life as we crossed the street. It made me smile, but I was too tired to mention it.

I helped sleepy kids remove their shoes in the entry, then rounded them up the stairs while Tatiana visited the kitchen to grab whatever she could for snacks.

As tired as we were, Tatiana insisted we hit the shower, but make it quick.

Storytime went the same as always. After noticing everyone was out, I put the book down on my knee and rubbed my eyes, focusing on the distant view. I felt a little itch at the back of my mind. It was a great day with everyone. We'd had so much fun, I was happy.

I snuck out from beneath Tatiana, the same as the night before. I carried the children one by one to bed and tucked them in, the same. I picked up Tatiana and carried her across the hall to her room, with Sasha on my heels, the same. I tucked her into bed, the same.

Then I crossed the same room to the same window and looked out to the same street. The same… same… same…

Strange as it maybe is, same is what this was becoming. I'd had problems with same before, I remembered. It was a long time ago, and very far away, when I'd suffered from the same. It had driven me away before. Before I had gone so far and discovered so much about the world and life. Was that it for me? Had I completed my sewing of oats? Was I ready, then, for the same? Or would I continue to look out that window?

39

The next week came with new surprises.

As I rounded the corner to the boathouse, I noticed another large sailboat anchored to the dock. With no sign of Faas, I tried the knob on the house and found it unlocked, then poked my head in and yelled, to a quick response.

"Yes?" Helen called. "Brandon? You come for breakfast."

I made my way up to the kitchen and found Faas sitting before a healthy stack of pancakes and looking through a manual.

"Yes, Brandon, good morning!" Helen welcomed. "Please, sit now. I get you food."

Shortly after I found a chair, she placed a plate full of breakfast helpings in front of me. She seemed a little more chipper than usual.

"There's another boat parked down on your dock, do you know about it?"

I assumed that they were aware, as I could see it plain as day from the kitchen table.

"Yes," Faas grunted through a mouthful. "I know this. Is my boat, I buy last night."

"You… you bought that boat?"

"Yes, I buy this last night. Is from friend, he have dock down," he pointed his fork over his shoulder, "he have this boat. But this boat need much work. He have too much boat to work now. So, he say a goot price for this. He need it to be gone. It was goot price, so I buy boat."

"So, you have two boats now? Does this boat need much work?"

"Yes, boat need much work. But we get goot price. I think of price to fix and I think is goot to make money. But now, I must find someone to buy this boat. We must fix."

It looked like we were going to be head down, ass up for a while. That fact didn't overexcite me, but job security was nice.

We wrapped up breakfast and headed outside and down the dock, all the time Faas explaining to me about the new boat. We couldn't simply jump right into it. He preferred to find a buyer and then customize the boat to their liking. Until then, we could work on the more standard stuff—rigging, sails, and stripping and sanding the deck. All that was heavily weather dependent, so we would have to keep our eyes on the forecast.

For now, we would remain focused on our current project, as it already had a buyer and a deadline.

The day was dreary, with isolated sprinklings. We worked on prepping the deck for stain. It was painstaking labour, with much of it on my hands and knees as Faas took the more upright chores.

On that morning, you could say my life was focused, with more direction than I'd had, maybe ever. Then life brought back a touch of grey.

"Hey! *Chu* fuckers!" called a voice from the distance.

The familiarity of the sound caused Faas and I to instantly stop what we were doing.

I looked over the side of the boat to the end of the dock, where down, came three scraggly pirates. My heart skipped. Faas had said they would return. But after so much time passed, I wrote them off as having found something more interesting… or dead.

But there they were, resurrected.

I stood looking at them with a false smile. They looked… exactly how I left them. Ragged, unkempt, and most likely high and hungover. I felt the past like sandpaper against my skin. Heavy acid roiled in my stomach; my head started to spin.

"Brando!" Nick called. "Look at chu, motherfucker! Chu still alive! Chu still here? We know chu still here, Stephi say chu still here. You work now, with mean Faas?"

Faas grunted from behind me. "You shut you mouth! You come to have work here, you shut up."

"Ha, Faas! I only am joke with chu. We much love for chu, chu sexy man."

They climbed aboard, one after the other, and greeted me with a clasp of hands and a hug. Their resilience astonished me. I was certain those guys had not found a decent shower or good night's sleep since they'd left the boathouse, but you couldn't beat the smile from their faces or trip the swagger from their steps. They were wild and they were free because that's where they belonged. They wanted nothing more.

So, there they were, right in front of me. The time had come to catch up, and many, many things had changed for me, since we last saw each other. But Nick and Dong quickly took over the spotlight, telling about their great adventures with intoxicants and promiscuous women.

Adlar was pretty silent. He'd hung out with the others frequently, but he had relatives in the area, and had mostly stayed with them.

Nick had found a steady "freak" for a while, as he described her. She let him crash at her place. Until he got caught poking around with one of her friends, which killed one of the world's greatest love stories.

Dong ended up finding not just one lucky lady who liked the Dong but two at the same time. That was just a one-night thing. Since then, he'd been crashing wherever the party ended, or at local hostels.

I'd forgotten how infectious their childish energy was. It was easy to find comfort among them, likely because their standard for acquaintances was very low.

"So?" The three looked at me with excitement.

"What is the fuck with chu? Huh!" Nick said. "Chu go away? What chu do? Chu stay here with Faas and Helen? Chu go have some fun with the ladies?" He fluttered his eyebrows.

"I…" I smirked, then ran my hand through my hair and twisted my head, avoiding eye contact.

As fun as it was to see the guys and hear their stories, I wasn't sure how involved I wanted them to be in what I had going on. They weren't exactly the types you'd take home to introduce to your mom, let alone back to the orphanage to meet your hot, blind girlfriend, four blind children, and a dog.

As I raised my head back up to face them, Nick looked at me and cringed.

"Brando, what this?" He pointed. "What the fuck is 'round chu neck?" He leaned forward and looped a figure through my necklace.

I looked down. "Oh! Uh, yeah."

"Chu buy this? Chu pay money for this?" The other two joined him in staring. "Maybe the boat to here too much for chu? Chu mind fucked up now?"

The three comrades slapped each other and laughed, pointing to my neck.

I could see Faas in the background, clearly wondering if I was going to take shit from a bunch who'd never had something of such importance in their life.

"No, I didn't buy it. It was a present. It was made for me."

"What!" Dong responded. "They make this for you? They say is present? I no think this person like you, Brando." The laughter continued. "Or maybe they is have no fucking eyes, huh!" He slapped my chest and again they exploded.

My hands clenched. The guys had crossed a line, and it was time for me to put a stop to it. I looked at them all and the smile disappeared from my face.

"Yes, actually, they don't have eyes. Or use of them anyway. They're blind."

The laughter stopped and they all stood in shock.

"They're orphan children. They live in the orphanage, and they're blind. I'm in a relationship with their teacher. She's also blind, and I've been staying at the orphanage with them."

There was a long pause as it sank in. They blushed, a little and fidgeted. I knew they didn't mean any harm. They were just guys, being guys. They didn't know. So, I gave them the time.

Adlar ducked his head and walked off to talk to Faas. The other two continued to sit and blink at me.

Nick broke the silence. "Chu live in orphanage?"

"Yeah, it's just over there, not far."

"Chu… chu date a blind woman?"

"Yeah, she's a teacher. She teaches the blind children. They all live together in the orphanage."

He brought his hand up and began stroking his chin, perhaps expecting it all to be a big mistranslation. "So, there is teacher woman, and children? How many children?"

"There's four children." I clasped my necklace. "They made this for me. That's why it may not look that nice. But they made it for me and… I'm really proud of it."

That statement caused them to lean back a little, as their eyes widened.

There was another pause, before Dong eased the tension with the obvious question. "She is hot, teacher woman?"

The two smiled again, leaning in for the details I knew would be lacking.

"I know this woman, she have to be fucking hot. Chu live there with her, you have necklace from blind kids. She very hot, yes?" I got a taunting slap on my leg.

I grinned. "Yeah, she's hot. Really hot. She's from Ukraine."

"Oh yes!" They high-fived. "I know this, she fucking hot! Good for Brando, ha ha!"

We sat a little longer as I filled them in on everything that had happened since we last saw each other.

Adlar came back eventually and explained what he had discussed with Faas for work. They had a small celebration between themselves, happy to hear there was a lot of work to do on the two boats. They were also very excited to hear that the one we were on was in need of a good crew to deliver her to Peru in the spring. They included me in that celebration. None asked if I would be joining them; I sensed they felt it didn't need to be asked. Once a pirate…

With all sorted out, the guys shuffled around the deck, and without any questions or answers, they found some tooling and a project that needed attention, and went to work.

It didn't take more than a few minutes for me to remember why Faas continued to put up with the three. As dysfunctional and lax as they seemed, they knew their way around a boat, and they knew how to get shit done.

I learned a lot that day. Faas was a good teacher, but these guys had a knack for explaining things to me. Not just how to do it, but why to do it in that particular way. They also had some clever shortcuts.

As the day drew to an end and the sun began to fall, a little sooner every week. Nick, jumped off the boat and ran to shore, disappearing around the corner of the train station.

He returned a short time later, with a box of beer and a couple rolled joints.

Faas cussed a little under his breath, but how can you protest against such an all-star team?

The three huddled together on the bench, and Faas said goodbye and headed home.

I watched them pop the caps off their beers and Dong lit a joint, blowing out a perfect smoke ring, that turned and grew in the still evening air.

Adlar looked over at me. "Brando, you come, have beer and some smoke. You work much wit us today."

I hesitated and looked back to shore. I should go, I knew. Tatiana and the children would be waiting for me. But that day was somewhat of a special occasion. Spending the day with other semi-adult males made me realize how much I'd missed it. One beer and a joint wouldn't hurt. It'd been a long time.

So, I sat.

"Yeah!" the guys welcomed. Nick dug a beer out for me and Dong passed me the joint.

It didn't take long for me to get a bit of a buzz, and my mind relaxed like it hadn't in some time. I leaned back and watched the sun slowly sink into the ocean, listening to their stories and sharing in their laughter. It was a good thing I'd stayed, it was much needed. Selfish, maybe, but I'd let go of the stress of marriage. My shoulders felt light and I felt free.

Sounds of city nightlife carried from shore. Streetlights twinkled and the smell in the air was of sweet dew, with an exhaust of mischief.

I was expecting the guys to harass me about heading out for a wild night on the town. But they were playing it tame. For that week, anyway, as they were all broke. So, they planned on taking some time to work and catch up on rest.

I arrived at the orphanage a few hours later than normal. There was no one waiting in the entryway for me. They'd probably given up. So, I crept up the stairs and found everyone finishing up with bedtime preparations.

They all heard me coming, and the children welcomed me with big smiles when I entered.

"Brandon!" Hans yelled. "We are happy you make it back for story time. We think maybe we not get story tonight. You work late?"

"Yeah, buddy, I had to work a little late. Finish up getting ready for bed, and we'll read."

Tatiana stayed distant at first, busy fussing with the girls. Then she made her way over. She felt my face and kissed my lips, then recoiled.

"What?" I asked, holding her in my arms.

"You stink. You stink like booze, like this stuff they smoke everywhere. You work late, huh?"

"No, not really. We had a good day, got lots done. But… the guys came back."

"Guys? Who guys?"

"The guys, you know. The guys I came over on the boat with."

"Oh? Yes? The crazy boys?"

"Yeah, the crazy boys. We just stayed on the boat for a while after work. Had a few beers and smoked some of that stuff."

"I see," she responded, then did her smile check on me again. "Okay." She smiled and kissed me again. "You go have shower, brush teeth before story. Children will think Harry Potter is drunk. I will go to kitchen and get some food for you."

Her reaction was a pleasant surprise. "Okay, honey."

After my duties, we met in the children's room for story time. And that night finished like the one before.

The same.

40

For me, a new relationship can be like that new shirt, or that car—the one you really wanted and invested all your resources to make yours. You get it and flaunt it around for the first week, month, or longer even, for some.

Then you spill something on the shirt. Coffee, or a gooey chicken wing tumbles down the front. Or you come out of the supermarket one day to find a shopping cart has blown into the car's fender or that someone has squeezed into the impossibly tight space beside you, and then slammed open their door against yours.

The point is, nothing remains new forever. And no matter how small or insignificant the resulting defect may be, you know it's there. You can scrub it, wash it, wax and polish. Hide it away for a while and sometimes even forget about it. But once it's there, it will always be. And with a relationship, all parties can sense it, to some degree.

With the return of the Lost Boys to my life, what was once so pure and spotless got its first spot of tarnish. The next day was cold, the first day working on the boats when I was chilled to the bone. We worked on the deck between rain showers, retreating to duties in the cabin when it poured.

As that week went on, I found myself happy the guys had returned. It gave me a chance to be a guy again. Laugh it up, show some irresponsibility. Let my hair down—what was left. And I deserved it, right? I'd been a good man for Tatiana and the kids.

At lunchtime I noticed Tatiana walking toward us with a basket in her hand. She stopped at the dock and wouldn't come any farther, as she didn't like to be on it by herself.

She called softly to me. "Brandon?"

Everyone stopped work and looked over at her. The guys' jaws all dropped to their knees.

Dong slapped my shoulder. "Brando? This girl say you name? She know you? Is she you girl? Teacher-girl?"

I swallowed a hard lump, fearing the situation could take a turn for the worse.

"Yeah, that's her."

"She fucking hot, man!" A low whistle escaped his lips and he looked back at the others, who were agreeing.

I turned to them all with haste. "Guys! Please, just be good. Don't say anything nasty to her, she's… different from the girls you're used to."

Adlar gave me an earnest nod, and spoke for the lot. "We will be goot, Brando. You go."

"Brandon," she called again.

"Yes, I'm here. Just wait a second… honey." I knew the guys would give me a hard time for that comment, but anything less would be suspicious to her… rock and a hard place.

I jumped down to the dock and ran to greet her.

"Hey, sweetie, what are you doing here? Where are the children?" I kissed her lips.

"I bring lunch to you and other boys. I leave children in home, I do not know is good for them here. I know boys can be, maybe… rude some time. Bad language."

"Oh yeah, that's pretty accurate."

We paused. I had no clue what she expected.

"Well?" She nodded.

… "W-w-w-e-e-e-l-l-l…?"

"You will take me to boat? I meet guys and give to you lunch I make?" Her smile and the twinkle in her eye reminded me of a Cheshire cat.

There was nothing I could do. She had me in a corner and I was certain she was aware of it. Introducing her to them was something I'd hoped to avoid, forever. But it was unrealistic, given the circumstances. Especially when parties on either side of me wanted it.

"Okay," I said, and smiled to her touch. For any of you who think faking a smile for a blind woman is an easy thing to do, I promise you, it's much harder. I knew she could feel my hesitance.

I let her wrap her arm around mine and escorted her down the dock. I held my head up and wondered why I found it a challenge to do. She was possibly the sexiest woman these guys had ever seen, beyond faded, pasty pages of a *Penthouse* magazine.

I began to understand that it wasn't her, it was me. Whipped, chained to the ball with heavy shackles. One of their own, taken prisoner. I was certain I'd broken a pirate code, or several.

We reached the boat and called to the guys. Not that their attention needed fetching. They'd been glued to every step we took. I was doing my best to ignore the tent being pitched in Dong's shorts.

I helped her top the short ladder, and Adlar raced to help as well. Making sure to get there before the less cultured of the group.

"Here, please, miss. I help you." He reached his hand down to her.

"Oh, thank you much." She made her way up to the deck, with me immediately hopping up behind her and finding her arm again.

"Tatiana, this is Adlar. Adlar, Tatiana."

He accepted her hand like a gentleman and bowed. "It is pleasure to meet such beautiful lady. Welcome to boat."

She seemed caught off guard by his pleasantness. "Oh, hello, Adlar, is nice to meet you. Thank you for help."

The other two were more on track with what she'd had in mind.

Nick jumped between us, next to take her hand, and lowered his head to kiss it lightly. "I am Nick, I have travel all around world on boat and I have love many beautiful women… And they say they love me."

"Oh, I see, Nick. This good for you, they is lucky ladies."

Dong took a moment to fix his hair and tuck in his shirt , clearly forgetting she couldn't see him. He used his macho voice. "I am Dong. I travel with Nick and I have much women too. You like the D—"

We all waved him off frantically, before he finished his trademark introduction.

She stood for a second, holding the basket before her. "Well, is nice to meet you, finally. Brandon say so much of you. I like to come here and bring lunch. You work hard, is cold."

"Yeah, she brought us lunch," I said, accepting the basket from her. "Why don't we all go down below and eat?"

So, we did. I let Tatiana feel around the place for a moment to get her bearings, then she dug into the basket and set out lunch for us.

It was as awkward as expected. Adlar was good; he ate silently for the most part. Nick and Dong talked the most, speaking of their unethical worldly adventures. Their continual stuttering suggested most or all was highly exaggerated. But Tatiana sat through it and responded politely, faking interest and concealing what I'm sure at times was disgust.

I was confident the guys had done enough to ensure she had no desire to pursue any further interaction. Except Adlar; he did all right. But she understood they were a package deal.

The guys were all really impressed with Tatiana. Whenever she spoke, which she did very little, they all stopped everything to listen. They pitched in to help clean up and return everything to the basket, then helped her back up the stairs to the deck. I hopped down to the dock to help her down and walked her back to shore, as all the guys waved and said goodbye and thank you.

Arm in arm we stepped.

"So, those are the guys. What do you think?"

"Hmm," She rubbed my arm. "They is boys, I do not think I want to go on boat with them, to any place. But is nice to meet them. Now I know who you with. Is important for me."

"Ha ha. Oh really? And do you feel better about me spending time with the boys?"

We stepped off the dock, onto the street.

"Hello, Tatiana!" Helen called out from the top window of the boathouse. I looked up to see her wave.

"Oh. Hello, Miss Helen!" She took my hands in hers. "I do not know if I feel better. But I know you are much more a man than these boys." She popped up on her tiptoes and kissed me. "Stay warm, my honey. I see you when finish."

"Okay, my sweet."

We hugged and she turned toward the orphanage.

I waved up to Helen, then jogged my way back to what I knew would be waiting. Three stiff brains.

"Ooooh, my Brando!" Nick started right away. "This woman, this woman, she so… hot!" He placed his hand over his heart and lifted his dreamy eyes to the sky. "Like fucking hot! this girl. Chu know I say?"

"Yeah, I know."

"I mean she hot! yes." He stepped before me and placed his other hand on my shoulder. "She bring food to me. Uhhh! This girl, I tell chu, she make me felt special. Chu know, in my pants." He reached down and grabbed his crotch. "Right there."

We shared a smirk. "Yeah, a random hole in a wall makes you feel special in your pants."

"Oh yes!" His excitement grew. "I know this hole. I like this. Chu do no know what is on other side." He busted up and gave me a slap.

"Is best you not know is on other side," Adlar added. "Goot for you, Brando. You is fucking pirate." He turned.

Dong sat against the rail, tracing Tatiana's path. "Brando. Please tell this to me. She is such dirty woman in sex? Tell me she is so dirty, tell lie to me, please. She must be this in my head."

I looked back to the street. She was long gone, and she'd likely never know either way. The canvas was mine to paint however I wanted. My hand reached up to my necklace and rolled one of the large square beads between my fingers. What she'd done that day took real balls.

I stared blankly. "I don't know. We've never done it."

Did you know that you can hear a pirate's heart break? It sounds like a beer bottle smashing on the hull of a boat. Bottles were smashing all around me.

"Wha'!" Dong and Nick cried.

I shook my head. "No, we've never done it. She wants to save it for marriage. For her husband."

Nick was completely stunned. "I… uh? She do what?"

I looked at him bluntly. "We've never had sex. She won't have sex until she's married."

Dong clutched his chest and fell to his back on top of the cabin. "Brando… my friend. I tell you, lie to me. You kill me, you say this."

"NO… No!" Nick shook his finger at me. "This no right. Chu go… Chu live with this woman, chu look after children. Chu have necklace on chu neck.

Chu do this and she say she do no do sex with chu! This no right, Brando, chu do no let this woman do this. We do no let her do this to chu. Chu, Brando, fucking pirate!" He pounded his fist to his chest. "She play game with chu. I know this! The women do this! They try do this to me, always."

Adar and I rolled our eyes.

"Chu must have this." Nick pointed to the sky. "We help to chu. This girl, she like chu, she want this from chu. She just play game. Fuck in chu head, man! I know, we help." He placed a hand on my shoulders and looked into my eyes.

I really wasn't sure what he had planned. With Nick and Dong, it could range anywhere from serenading her through her window to letting Dong talk sexy to her.

I shrugged.

Everyone calmed down eventually and we slugged away the rest of the afternoon. Late in the day, Faas arrived to look over our work and hand out the week's pay. The guys were all very happy to have some money back in their pocket, and they were equally excited to spend it.

I knew it was coming. The invitation to join them for some beers after work. The responsible answer, of course, was no. And I said it, at first. But they kept taunting, and it was Friday night and the city would be bustling. And, being the man I was, I buckled.

"Only for one, though, guys," I said as we walked down the dock.

We immediately went to Stephi's and bought a round of joints and caught up on local gossip, that meant little to me. It was still cold out, so the guys took me to one of their favourite pubs down the street, passing a joint around as we walked.

The streetlights were on and the only thing left of daylight was a soft glow between the peaked rooftops. Nick slid up beside me, and put his arm around my shoulder. Then he began his devilish campaign in my ear.

"See, man, my friend. This woman, she play game with chu. Chu let this happening to chu. She think she have chu on her finger. Because chu go, go to work. Work and then chu go her when finish work. Feed children, chu be good man. Chu be too good man."

"Uh huh?" I said, humouring him.

"So, maybe chu do no go to home when finish work tonight. She start think maybe she no have chu on finger. She think maybe chu do no like her so much.

She know, then, maybe she must do some more for chu, huh?"

"Yeah, for sure." Nothing he said was revolutionary, like he thought it was. Just textbook male bullshit. I just wanted to get somewhere and have a quick beer. Then, while they got carried away, I'd slip out the back door and head home.

"Then, she give it to chu!" He clenched his teeth through parted lips and shook his fist in front of us. "Yes! Chu have all, my friend!" He slapped me on the back as he finished unveiling the master plan.

It wasn't my plan, at all. Smoke some grass, have a beer, then make it home in time for *Harry Potter*. It was new for us, Tatiana and I, to have me go out with the guys after work. But she'd been really understanding of me to that point. Nothing sinister was going to happen.

The pub of choice wasn't too far down the street. They pulled me over to a set of heavy old wooden doors dressed with two large-paned windows. The heavy wood decor continued inside. Its dark stain soaking up the dim light from the wall-mount lamps. The room was small and longer than it was fat. The bar at the back, was tended by a brunette with shoulder-length hair, dressed in Old World Goth. The doors to the bathroom facilities were just off the bar, painted a blood red. The tables were round and chest height, with just enough surface area to accommodate four patrons occupying four stilted chairs.

We found our spots about midway in, and no sooner had our weight rested on our chairs than a waitress appeared. Her dirty-blonde hair was more messed than curled, her eyes were dark, and her chin had a subtle dimple. She was small framed, except where it counted. And her attire looked to have been designed by the same architect as the bartender's, with a short skirt and just enough lace to keep the tip jar chinking.

"Ah! There is she!" Nick exclaimed.

All three guys were snickering. Adlar leaned over the table with his head down and the other two looked toward our server. I could see she was doing her best not to break a full smile.

Dong rubbed at her arm, and she slapped it away playfully. "You guys again, huh?" She looked around the table. "Except you, you're new."

I held out my hand. "I'm Brandon, it's nice to meet you."

"Whoa! You're definitely not from around here."

"I could say the same about you," I said, noting our similar accents.

"I'm Trisha, from Portland, Oregon."

"Canada."

"Oh, Canada-ian, eh?" She winked. "I've done some partyin' up there in my time. Left my mark, you could say." She smiled and scanned me up and down. "Interesting taste in jewellery, there, Brandon." She nodded toward my necklace.

"Hey!" Nick tugged lightly on her sleeve. "We guys here also"—he raised his hands, and tilted his head. "We work much today. We need drink."

"Yeah, all right!" She turned from me to face the others.

Nick and Dong rattled off something quick, which appeared to include us all. Then Dong spoke softly to her, something I couldn't hear. She slapped him on the arm and smiled wickedly, then took off to the bar.

"She is fucking sexy, yes!" Nick poked me. "She is fun girl. We party sometime with these girls. This and other girl, there." He pointed to the bartender. "They friends, from same home. America women! They fucking sexy!"

Dong cheered him on throughout his speech. "If you no married to other girl," he laughed, "this girls, they like you. I see this one like you. You talk all fucked like she." He punched my arm.

Trisha returned as a couple walked out the door, letting in a cool, damp swallow of air.

"Here, four beers and four shots."

"Whoa, what!" I held up my hands. "No shots for me. Take mine back, or someone else have it."

"Wha'!" Nick and Dong leaned toward me.

"Why chu say this? We no be together for so long. Now we here, we buy gift for chu and chu say no?"

"Yeah!" Trish spoke up, hand on her hip. "What's up, princess? I thought you Canada boys could drink. You're not gonna let these bums show you up, huh? Represent!" She snapped her fingers at me with a taunting grin.

A real man would step up to the challenge. A real man would turn it down… I shook my head, grabbed the tiny glass, tipped it back and swallowed it down with not the slightest flinch. Which was impressive, because I'm sure it was the cheapest shit behind the bar. Go Team Canada.

"There." She reached up and took the glass gently from my hand. "Not such a big deal, hey." Her eyes never strayed from mine.

The others chucked theirs down, and there was much squirming and making of awful faces as they slammed down the glasses.

"Blah! Is shit!"

But the commotion never fazed either of us.

The flirt in her gaze intensified. "So…" She rolled her tongue lightly inside her cheek. "You not much of a party guy? O-o-o-rrr… is there a special someone waiting for you somewhere?"

I broke the stare and looked at the table. I had a sip of beer, then turned back to her.

"*Hmph*." She smiled and walked past me, her hand sliding up my leg casually. Light enough to be a slip… Or maybe not?

"*See!*" The guys leaned in. "*Huh!*" Nick winked at me. "She like chu! Chu wait, this fun girls."

I feigned lack of interest. But there was the background, the beer, the sitting around a dark pub with a band of scrappy outlaws. The being served by flirty waitresses. I'd forgotten what it was like. I'd believe the part of me that would miss those times had shrunk into the background, but he was still very much there.

The booze warmed my body and lit a fire of confidence I hadn't felt since… I started working in a marina, and living in an orphanage.

The conversation at the table turned to work, and some of the Lost Boys' adventures. The language was complicated, and I found myself paying more attention to the two ladies conversing at the bar and looking over at us on occasion.

Trisha spoke English, real English. It wasn't till we'd spoken that I understood how much of my energy was being consumed flipping basic words around to translate a message. It was like I'd been looking at everything upside down for a really long time. When was the last time I could just sit back and let the words flow to me, no filtering required?

Trisha ran around tending to other tables, but before long, she was sliding up to the table and setting down another round between Nick and I. She turned her back to me and applied some obvious pressure to the side of my body while addressing the others. "Need anything else, boys?"

"Yes, we need titties!" Dong said with a laugh.

"Titties, hey? Looks like you got a couple of your own, right there." She held up her middle finger, stuck out her tongue, and stepped saucily away from the table. Patting my leg as she passed.

Beer two. I should've put up more resistance, but the first one went pretty quick, so there was time. Another wouldn't hurt.

The last two tables cleared out shortly after. The music got turned up a smidge more, and the bartender came to join her friend. They made their way over to us with another round in their hands.

Trisha made introductions. "Brandon, right?"

I nodded as she held up her hand. A delicate snake tattoo was wrapped around her forearm.

"Yeah, that's right."

"See!" Trisha poked her. "Canada-ian."

The girls giggled.

"Nice to meet you, Brandon, I'm Bobby. Trish tells me you're a fellow westerner?"

"You bet. North-northwest." I smirked.

"Well, it's not a state, but close enough." She smiled back. "It's nice to hear some familiarity around here."

"Oh? I didn't realize there was such a lack. Amsterdam is a pretty popular destination."

"Yeah, we run into some on party nights, but not in here," Bobby said. "This place is just a hole in the wall for locals, mostly… and these goons." She relaxed and leaned up against the table, with Trisha's head resting on her shoulder. The girls were not shy of each other, or me.

"You seem like a decent guy," she continued. "Could use some help dressing yourself." She nodded toward the necklace, "and your hair looks like it got in a fight with a weed trimmer."

I understood that they didn't know the background leading to my state, so I let it go. "Yeah, I've been living what you could call a rogue lifestyle the last few years. Just making due the best I can."

"We hear ya. Us to. we ran away from home a couple years back. Just wanted to do some travelling, see the world a bit, have some fun, you know? Trying to find ourselves—the old cliché."

They giggled again. Trisha wrapped her arms around Bobby and snuggled up closer. All mumbling from the guys stopped for a moment. I understood what attractions kept them loyal patrons of the place.

"We went to Paris first, worked odd jobs. But that place is definitely overrated, if you ask us. The novelty wore off after a week. But we stuck it out for about a year. Then we started looking around online. The internet stuff is really opening things up. We saw this place advertising for some help, so we wrote to them, and here we are. It ain't much, but the owners seem happy with what we're doing for business. We don't take no shit from anyone, run a tight ship. So, they pretty much let us be."

Time passed, along with the beer. After number two, three was already there for me. I got up to use the bathroom once, then twice. Outside had been black for hours.

"Hey, ladies!" Dong rapped his knuckles on the table. "Is more of us guy here, y'know. You do no have just Brando. *Hey*, baby, you like Dong?"

"Yeah, we like dong. Just not yours!" Trish tossed the response over her shoulder.

"Yeah, go jack in the alley, hot rod!" Bobby added.

"You party with these guys a lot?" I asked. The combination seemed more unlikely as time went on.

"*Pfft!*" Bobby rolled her eyes. "These guys? Hell no! They come around every now and then. A little creepy, but harmless. Trish and I are really close, and these clowns really take to it. They tip us well. We hung out with them one night, after hours, just pub hopping. Seems like they like it when pretty girls tell them to go suck each other's dicks. We've seen stranger shit."

The girls snuggled in closer to each other and giggled some more.

"So, how the fuck did you end up with these clowns, *Brandon?*" She emphasized my name and leaned in, placing a hand on my leg and taking a sip of her beer.

"Well, that's a bit of a story. And as incompetent as these clowns may seem, I wouldn't be here without them. In Amsterdam, or even alive."

The guys raised their beers. "Yeah! You tell this, Brando!"

I told the long story. Starting pretty much from the time I left Canada for Bonaire. The girls hung on every word, making me pause when they went for refills and clinging to my side as we went outside for another joint.

"So, that's it," I concluded. We all stood outside, doing our best to fit everyone under the shelter of a small awning.

"Holy shit!" Trisha laughed. "That's a fucked-up adventure. I'd call bullshit, but looking at the bunch of you, it's almost believable. You guys really are fucking pirates. To the extreme."

"Cheah!" Nick said in a burst. "Fucking pirates! We say to you girls this!"

"Yeah, but it's hard to believe the shit that comes out of your mouths," Bobby shot back.

The two ladies snuggled in around me, wrapping an arm around each of mine.

"Whew! The season is definitely changing," Bobby said. "It's fucking cold as shit out, 'bout time for us to close up and head someplace warmer."

My heart rate quickened. "Close up? What fucking time is it?"

"Midnight-ish, I'd guess. You boys coming with?"

"Yes!" Nick responded smoothly. "Chu know we come for chu girls, all time."

"How 'bout you, handsome?" Trish purred in my ear, while tracing a finger up my stomach. "You know, Bobby and I do a lot of things together. Sometimes, we do everything together." She giggled and slithered her finger around my necklace.

Necklace! I experienced an epiphany, one much needed—like a shot of pure fresh oxygen to a mind shoved deeply in one's ass.

I thought of Tatiana, and the children. Saw visions of them waiting for story time. Wondering where I was, and if I were ever going to return. Their worry and disappointment.

"Nope, I gotta go." I began to struggle free from her grasp.

"Wha'!" Nick called. "Brando? Chu go now? It just begin, we go have—"

"No, I gotta go!" I shouted back over my shoulder as I trotted out into the street. "Thanks for everything. Have fun!"

My trot soon turned into a jog. I was more intoxicated than I'd thought, and I cursed myself for letting time slip away. I felt like the biggest, most selfish piece of shit in existence.

It was damaging, what I'd done, and I knew it. Tatiana was a good woman, but not even a good woman should be expected to tolerate that. There would be dues to pay, if she'd let me.

I rounded the corner and saw the orphanage up ahead. I looked up to the windows of the children's room, and then to Tatiana's. All was dark. That raised an immediate question. How the fuck was I going to get in? And if I couldn't get in, where was I to go?"

My jog turned to a walk and my posture slumped. Things weren't looking good for a comfortable sleep. It was time for me to start optioning a plan B. Surely the front door to the orphanage would be locked. They couldn't risk the safety of everyone for me, especially due to me being a stupid asshole. I thought about the boathouse, but the wrath of Faas had potential to be even worse than Tatiana's at that time of night, and as intoxicated as I was.

The rain started to come down harder and I was chilled to the bone in my T-shirt and shorts. I stood before the door and looked up; there wasn't a flicker of light anywhere. I almost didn't even bother with checking the knob, but, I was there. I took a step up and placed a hand on the knob. It turned, fully. So, I pushed forward and, shockingly, it opened.

I entered slowly, cautiously, not wanting to disturb anyone from their rest. I may end up getting clubbed by Tessa, thinking I was an intruder. In my state, I surely felt the part.

I slid my hand softly along the wall, vaguely recalling the placement of a light switch. My fingers brushed over the fixture and I tipped it silently up, illuminating the landing.

I jumped immediately at the sight of a dark figure resting on the steps.

"Tatiana?"

She sniffled and looked toward me, her face heavily stained with trails of tears.

"Why are you sitting here in the dark?"

She pulled herself up with the railing. "I is blind, Brandon. You forget this?" Her tone was weighted with heavy sarcasm. "I no can leave this door without lock for you. Is not safe for children. So, I wait for you. I do not know where you go, or if you come back. I do not know what to do. So, I wait, many hours now."

"Oh… Tatiana. I'm really—"

"Sorry? I do not know what happen. I call to Helen on telephone, she say she do not know. She think you come home. So, I get worry. I know is possible you go with other boys, but I hear nothing from you. Time is late, and I worry maybe you hurt?"

"I'm so sorry. I'm not hurt, I was—"

"I know what you was. I know now! You stink, like booze and drugs, and other women!" Her chin quivered like a tuning fork, her face was heavy with disappointment. Maybe not at what I was, so much, but at my lack of respect for her.

"I just… I just went for some drinks with the guys. I got a little carried away. Nothing bad happened, we were just at a pub, not far. Time got away from me and I didn't realize how late it was. Then I came running home. I'm so sorry Tatiana."

She showed little patience for any explanation, turning and going up the stairs. "Lock door and turn off light when you come."

The atmosphere was so uncertain, and my mouth was dry and pasty. My stomach began to churn and I realized I'd had nothing to eat since she brought us lunch. Remembering that she'd gone through the trouble that afternoon made me feel even worse.

I heard the creaking of the staircase beneath Tatiana's feet as she made her way up. I locked the knob and turned the bolt, then switched off the light and followed the railing up the blackened stairwell.

I found my way to our…her room, and made my way over to the lamp and switched it on, filling the room with a dull glow.She was in bed, snuggled in the blanket, her back placed purposefully in my direction. She didn't say anything, didn't kick me out. Just… silent.

A deep wound had been cut, and it was in my hands to mend. I was grateful, to say the least.

The best first step I could take was to head to the bathroom and clean off the filth.

I turned the shower to just short of scalding and scrubbed my skin and massaged a thick lather in my hair. As inviting as it was to hide away in there till someone kicked down the door, I wanted to get to work on mending things. So, I stayed only till the shivering stopped, then towelled off and went to the sink to try to brush the disobedience from my breath. It was so embedded that time would be the only thing to wash it away completely.

Cleansed, I leaned over the sink for a moment and deliberated my strategy. But I was tired. Tired of the night, the booze, the drugs, and the stress of hurting the ones who cared for me. Who truly cared for me. The only plan I could cultivate was to throw myself at the mercy of the court, and so I did.

I exited the bathroom, stepped quietly across the room to the closet, and slipped on some pajama pants. Then I walked around to her side of the bed and sat on the edge with my back to her. She lay still, as if sleeping, but I knew it wasn't possible with such a heavy presence of tension.

"I'm sorry," I began. The simple statement drew a sob from beneath the blankets. "I know it's not enough for me to say that. But I want to work to make it right. It was really just me out with the guys for a couple beers at the pub. No… Naughty Hottie stuff."

Another sniffle. "But they is girls," she said. "I know this, I smell the perfume. I no stupid Brandon. Do not talk to me like I is stupid."

"Yes, there were girls, the waitresses. The guys knew them from before. They served us drinks and sat and talked with us."

"They are pretty girls? You like other girls? You like this because… because I do not give you the sex." She sputtered hard into the pillow.

"No!... Jesus, Tatiana!" Her comment frustrated me, but I reined it back. What was I to expect? For all she knew, I was out getting wasted and fucking everything that moved. It was maybe too soon, but I reached back and placed my hand lightly on her shoulder. She remained still, which was better than other possible reactions.

"They were just waitresses. We talked and drank some beers, in the pub. In public, all of us together. I was never alone with any of the girls. I had no desire to be. I just lost track of time. But I rushed home when I realized what I'd done.

"I was worried about hurting you. Scared you wouldn't let me back into the house, or back into your life. I thought I'd lost you and the children…. I was really scared. I know that doesn't make it right. I know I hurt you so much, Tatiana. I really didn't mean it. I didn't do this to hurt you. I just… fucked up, and I'm really, so sorry. I just really want to turn back the clock and make a better decision. But I can't do that. So, all I can do is work harder to make it right with us again… That's what I want."

There was silence for a moment. My hand caressed her shoulder, then slid down to her waist. I pulled lightly and she rolled to me, her damp cheeks shining.

"Yes, you want this? You work for this, for us?" A hint of relief glowed on her face.

I turned sideways and began massaging her arms with both my hands, deeply, caringly. "Yes, Tatiana, it's what I want. If I didn't want it, I wouldn't be here. It's late at night for us and the children. But those guys and the girls are still out partying. If I wanted to be with them, I'd still be with them. I knew you were going to be really mad at me, but I still came back here. Because I want to be here, with you and the children. I know it's easy for you to think about how mad you are and how much of an asshole I am. And that's accurate, for tonight. You have every right to be mad. But please understand that I'm here."

Her hands slid up my arms and I fell into her, kissing her tenderly on the lips. "Oh, thank you. I was so scared that I'd never be able to kiss you again. I'm so sorry Tatiana. Thank you so much."

"Honey." She smirked. "Is *honey* for you."

"Yes." I chuckled. "You are my honey, and you make me so happy."

She squirmed over to make room for me. I crawled into the bed and we kissed for a while, holding each other. My heart beat again, and my body warmed, and life was good. Very, very good.

41

I woke to a gloomy autumn sunrise and the sound of heavy bullets of rain pummelling the window panes.

I remembered the chill in my bones the night before, and it renewed how grateful I felt for Tatiana to be there, waiting for me. So many songs sung about shelter from the storm. She was that, for me. I moved quickly to find her beneath the covers. Her body smooth and warm to the touch. I curled my arms around her and pulled myself close to her beating heart. The smell of her next to me in the morning filled my soul with warmth and certainty. It was the kind of day when I wanted to pull the covers over our heads and never leave our sanctuary.

I pressed my lips firmly to the back of her neck and focused on showing her how much I appreciated her. She moaned lightly, and pushed back into me. I smiled to myself, so grateful for the opportunity to be there with her. As my fingers traced down her figure, I soaked up her every twitch and shiver.

Then I heard the pitter-patter of puppy feet come through the doorway, as Sasha returned from her morning check on the children. I could hear her heavy panting next to the bed, and knew then, that our time of solitude was limited. One move, one twitch, one breath, and Sasha would be on us like a dog lacking attention.

As motionless as I remained, there was no getting past the instinct of a dog. The still room echoed with the tickety-tack of canine nails on hardwood floors, as she came around the side of the bed to face us. She sat on her haunches, panting away, wondering why we weren't acknowledging her.

I slid my head ever so slowly down, behind Tatiana. In hopes of boring her till she left.

She snorted, then punctuated it with a slight whimper.

"Yes, good morning Sasha," Tatiana mumbled. And Eden was lost.

Sasha stood, and her eyes lit up.

"*No*," I groaned. "Why did you have to speak? I'm not ready to get out of bed yet."

Tatiana rolled onto her back and looked up to me. I had concerns about how her eyes would look after our troubled night. At first, they were dull and grey. But she blinked a couple of times, and I saw the caring twinkle return. Tarnished, maybe, but far from broken. I suppose, if nothing else, the night before was a test of our strength. And we were still there, in each other's arms.

I kissed her lips, over and over. "Why? *Why!*"

She lifted her arms around my neck, smiling sweetly. "Sasha know. She know when we wake. She is woman… and dog."

I chuckled. "Yes, she is that."

As we continued to snuggle, Sasha looked at us as if wondering why we were so hesitant to get up and start our day. A moment later, her ears perked and her head turned to the door. Then she took off out of in a trot. It was no secret to us what drew her attention; it was a common weekend morning routine for us. No sooner had she left the room, than we heard the quiet squeaks of sleepy children padding across the landing to our room.

Lilly was the first to enter. "Teacher?" she called. "Is you up yet?"

Tatiana smiled at me, biting on her bottom lip. "*Yes*, Lilly, good morning."

Hans was quick to pass Lilly. "Teacher Tatiana. Is Brandon come home?"

The comment made me blush, not in a good way, and I was quick to answer the call. "Yes, Hans, I made it back last night, buddy."

His face beamed. I realized, then, what a mess the place must've been with me missing. Not only would Tatiana have had to cope with her own worries, but the children would've been fuelling the fire. The debt to be paid had increased substantially, as did the size of ass I felt like.

"Oh, Brandon!" Hans found his way to the bed and crawled on up. "Is goot you come home. We worry for you. Teacher, she cry sometimes. Why you not come home?"

"Ah… well… I—"

"He is busy with work, Hans," Tatiana interrupted. "There is much to do on boat. Brandon work very late. No more questions please, children."

Again, she showed me the extreme quality of the woman I had. I leaned in for a kiss of gratitude and reached my hand down for a squeeze of her bum, before the bed was bombarded with children.

"You get up from bed now?" Gaby suggested… strongly. "What we going today?"

"I hear is rain on window." Tatiana turned to me.

"Yeah, it's pretty gloomy out there. I don't think it's good weather for outdoor stuff."

"Aw!" came the cries.

"I not like rain," Gaby remarked. "I think is stupit."

"Gaby!" Tatiana scolded. "Do not use this word. Rain is good, it help to grow plants and flowers, it clean the dirt."

"Well," I cut in, with a hint of suggestion, "I'm really sorry we missed story time last night. So why don't we have it today, after breakfast. *Then…*"

Little faces looked at me in suspense.

"Maybe we should go out for dinner?"

All was quiet, and I looked around to the many questioning faces. "Out for dinner, like to a restaurant?"

"Dinner!" Gaby repeated. "In restaurant! Like… like real people?"

I chuckled. "What do you mean, like real people? You're real people. Real people who come wake me up too early."

Tatiana squeezed my leg and whispered in my ear, "Brandon, you should not do this."

"Why not? I was thinking to just have me and you go to dinner. I'd really like to have a romantic night with just us. But, I know the children would be really upset. So… why don't we all go out?"

"Brandon, is nice for you. But is lot of work with children, I think."

I ran my finger down the side of her cheek. "We'll get through it, no problem. It'll be fun… honey."

She smiled, and the little dimples in her cheeks popped. She pulled me down for a kiss.

"So, do you have any place you'd like to go?"

"Oh." She stalled, and I assumed it was because the question was one she'd never been asked before.

After a minute of chewing her lip, a burst of light dawned on her face. "I know some place, is not far. All time when I walk by, it smell very tasty!" She grew excited. "I think maybe is Italian food place?"

"Okay, Italian sounds good. We have to figure out where it is, or the name of it. I'll call and try to get reservations."

"Yes, I ask Tessa. Maybe she know what is place?"

"Okay! Let's try to get it figured out. How does that sound, kids? You like Italian food?"

The girls all cheered. I don't think it mattered to them what the food was. They were going out to a restaurant. If it served hot dogs, they'd've been fine with it.

Hans, on the other hand, was a bit more skeptical. "It-a-lien?.. What is this?" He scrunched his face.

I smirked. "Italian, you know… lots of noodle stuff, with sauce and cheese."

"Sauce? What kind sauce?"

"Is just sauce, Hans," Tatiana intervened. "Is sauce, like spaghetti. You have this many times."

"Yes, I know this spaghetti, but I not have sauce."

The ladies started to whine. "Oh Hans, do not be trouble."

Tatiana whispered to me, clenching my hand even tighter. "See, I say this to you. Is not easy to do this."

I gave her a big wet kiss on the cheek. "It's okay!" I announced. "It's okay, everybody. Hans, we'll get something figured out for you, don't panic. What about pizza? You like pizza, right? That's man-food!"

"Man-food?" He smiled.

"Yeah." I pushed myself up and out from under the covers and jumped to the floor, making my way to the bathroom. "Me and you will order up some pizza, man-food, and the ladies can have saucy noodles. How's that sound?"

"Okay," he chirped, smiling like a boy who'd just got invited to a special club.

Everyone was happy again. The children found their way around to Tatiana and the women chatted giddily among themselves.

I brushed my teeth and freshened up. When I returned to the room, the little ladies were beyond carried away. Lilly and Gaby were starting to fuss about

260

who got to wear what to dinner. Hans was leaning against the foot of the bed, scratching Sasha behind the ears.

I stepped over to him and placed a hand on his head. He responded, looking up to me with his innocent blue eyes and a smile on his face.

"Girls are crazy, hey?" I said softly.

He nodded and chuckled.

"Let's go get your teeth brushed. I don't know about you, but I'm hungry for breakfast."

He nodded again and reached up for my hand.

I stood for a second, looking down at him holding his little hand in mine, The smile on his face and the twinkle in his eye. He was so little. I wondered how such a great little kid could end up in an orphanage.

I closed my hand around his and gave it a confident shake. Then I kneeled down beside him. "You gotta be my wingman tonight, and I'll be yours."

"Wingman? What is this?"

"Well, we're taking a group of women out for dinner. Things could get a little nuts. So, we gotta look out for each other, right? Make sure we're doing everything right."

"Yeah!" He smiled.

"Like if the zipper on my pants is down, you have to tell me. Or if I forget to put pants on at all, you gotta tell me that too. Sometimes I get pretty nervous on date night."

He snorted a laugh.

"All right, bump it!" I held out my fist and he bumped it. "You know what the best way to get to the bathroom is?"

He shrugged and raised his eyebrows.

"Shoulder ride!"

His little eyes popped. He didn't have a clue what was coming.

"C'mon big guy." I turned him around in front of me, counted to three, then lifted him over my head and placed him on my shoulders. He squealed and wrapped himself so tight around my head, I couldn't see, or breathe.

The girls stopped instantly at the sound. Tatiana sat up straight, in panic.

"It's hmkay! Hmkay!" I struggled to get free enough to speak a proper word. "It's okay, everything's fine. Hans is just getting a shoulder ride to the bathroom."

There was just silence and eye blinking. Except for Sasha, who was huffing and puffing and scurrying around my legs.

"Is this?... Hans?... What is he...?"

He relaxed a little and finally got out a yell. "It's me! I am up high, on Brandon shoulder!" He giggled.

As we found our rhythm together, I'd stepped around the ladies and Hans would call out to them. They'd look up and around, trying to locate him, until they finally started latching onto my legs and reaching up on tiptoes to find his little feet dangling.

What seemed like a really fun and "super good guy" thing to do, turned into shoulder rides for everyone. Even Anna wanted a round.

That went on till I knocked Lilly's head on the door frame. Then Tatiana, who was never comfortable with the idea to begin with, ordered fun time to stop.

The group took their turns in the bathroom while Tatiana tended to a lightly weeping Lilly, who was mostly concerned that the knock had left a mark and would ruin her first restaurant date.

With everyone cleaned up, we went down for a late breakfast. Tatiana spoke to Tessa about our planned adventure and asked if she knew of the place we wanted to go. Apparently, it was a prime choice in the neighbourhood. Very fancy, and she voiced concern that we may not be able to get in with such a large group, on such little notice. She called over for us and managed to secure a four o'clock table. She was very excited for us.

The rain was pouring outside, again. So, we went back to the children's room. The girls were just bananas about getting ready for the big dinner. They were feeling through the closets for what they wanted, and driving Tatiana to the edge of insanity with so many questions.

So, Hans and I went over to the piano to work on learning some Pearl Jam, but the chatter only increased until not even the all enforcing voice of Teacher could calm the mob. Clothes flew everywhere and ironing boards were out. So, we men escaped back to the adult room.

We found one of Sasha's balls and started tossing it back and forth. It was half a second before Sasha caught wind of what we were up to, and came running over to join the game.

It was a long, lazy afternoon. Sometimes Tatiana would come into the room in a huff and pull something from the closet, then head back over, yelling something or other.

I smirked at all the commotion. Maybe she was right, maybe it was too much to consider taking everyone for dinner. Hans and I, we were just chillin'. But what she was going through was not chill. Honestly, I felt kind of bad seeing it. Maybe I should've taken her away for a night, just her and I. She deserved it. But I bet if I'd suggested leaving the kids so we could go out for dinner, she would've said no. And the kids… they'd've burned it all down.

The room was quiet, other than the sound of the bouncing of the ball and Sasha scrambling across the floor, and the muffled cries of woman drama from across the hall.

"So…" I took a stab at starting some idle conversation with Hans. "What do you want to do when you grow up buddy?" Idle chit-chat was a complicated thing for me, with a blind kid, who lives in an orphanage. I felt a need to dance around some subjects. "You gonna have a girlfriend someday?"

He blushed and shrugged. "Sometime Gaby say I am boyfriend wit her. But sometime, she say my feet stink. So I not her boyfriend."

"Yes, foot odour. That's a big one. I'll show you some tricks for that later," I chuckled. "What do you want to do when you get older? For work?"

He smiled. "I want to work on boat, sailboat, like you."

"Oh? You want to work on boats, like me?"

His smile grew, as did the rose colour in his cheeks. "Yes, work on boats, wit you. Maybe we work together, when I finish school."

"Really? You want to work on boats, with me?"

He nodded.

"Well… I think that'd be really great. I think you'd be really good at working on boats. I already know you can sail them, hey!"

His face turned beet red and he looked toward the ground. Then he felt his way to me and pulled himself up into my lap. He curled into me, and sat silent.

I slowly wrapped my arms around him and then began to rock gently. I could feel the breath in his body, and the rooster tails in his hair rose up to tickle my nose.

We sat for a moment, just the guys, hanging out. I really didn't know what the next step was, what he wanted, or expected. It seemed to me that what he really wanted was to just sit there, quietly. So, we did.

Then, a tiny redhead appeared at the door, with an announcement.

"Hans," Gaby said. "You come in the room, here, if you like. But Brandon, you cannot come to room. You cannot see us before we ready." And when Gaby spoke, I knew it was written in stone. Then, as quickly as she had poked her head in, she disappeared.

"I don't want anything to do with what's going on over there. How 'bout you?"

He shook his head frantically, and giggled.

"Well, what are we going to do, huh? It's the big night. Italian restaurant night! We're gonna get us some man-food. What do you think? Maybe we should start getting ready, huh?"

He nodded.

"Okay buddy. I hate to do it to you, but why don't you go over and get Teacher to give you whatever she wants you to wear and bring it over here. I'll see what I can put together for me, and we'll have our own little get-ready party."

He nodded again, and hopped to his feet. Then went over to the other room. I heard screams and protests as soon as he entered, till they realized I wasn't with him.

"Is just Hans," little voices eased.

It didn't take long till he returned with teacher in tow.

"Here, please," she panted, handing me some garments on a hanger. "This for Hans, for to wear tonight. Thanks you for help. I sorry, I do not know what to have for you."

"Don't worry sexy, I'll figure something out." I gave her shoulders a quick rub and a kiss before sending her back into battle.

I held up Hans's attire to check it out. It wasn't bad. A little black suit jacket and grey pants. The tie, however, was "Grandma's Kitchen" yellow… and it looked like she was a heavy smoker. The outfit wasn't *GQ* cover quality, but it was pretty awesome that they had something like it for him to wear.

"Wow!"

"What?" Han's looked toward me with excitement.

"Teacher brought you a suit! Man, is it nice! I wish I had a suit like this one. I've never had a suit this nice."

"Really!" He reached up and felt around the ensemble.

"Yeah, dude. I've never had a suit this cool before. You're gonna to be one sharp-looking guy. This might even be Armani or something, *hmph*."

"Armana… is this?"

"Armani, it's the name of a high-end fashion design guy. This doesn't seem to have a tag on it, but I wouldn't be surprised."

"Oooh." He stroked the fabric. "It feel goot, nice."

"You bet buddy. Top-shelf stuff."

You couldn't have beaten the smile off his face, and he became just as excited as the girls about getting ready.

"You're gonna have to go all-out to wear this properly. Have to shower and brush your hair nice. I think I saw some hair gel somewhere, and maybe we could find some cologne? I can ask Teacher."

"Colo— huh?"

"Cologne, it's like perfume, but for men—man-smelling perfume."

"Okay, I go shower now."

"Well, let's give it a bit of time yet. It's pretty early still, and if you get duded up too early, you'll wrinkle your suit from sitting and rolling around like you do. So, we have to time it just right. I'm sure the ladies are going to be coming in to use the shower soon, then we have probably about two hours after they're done. Let's go see if we can find something for me to wear, eh?"

He nodded, and we went over to the wardrobe.

The pickings were slim. None of the dress pants fit properly, but I found a pair I could work with. Then I found a black sweater; nothing fancy, but it would get me in the door. I spread everything out on the bed.

"There, I think we have it covered."

Hans took a minute to feel around my selection. "You must have…" He *hmm*'d and *ha*'d for the word, then pointed to his neck, making a ring.

"Oh, a tie?"

"Yes, this."

"I don't know, buddy. I think I'm pretty lucky to have found what I got. But let me have another look." I flipped through the hangers again, and sure enough, there was a tie. It was bright green with wide, silver stripes running down its length. I paused and paused some more, contemplating whether to mention it, as it was a little flashy for my taste.

"Well… I… found one."

His face beamed. "Yes? Is goot for you? We both has tie?"

"Yeah. Yeah little buddy. Or should I say *wingman*." I mussed his hair. We're gonna be like Maverick and Goose out there tonight. Watch out for the kissy girls."

He smirked.

We played ball until the queen and all her princesses came chattering into the room. They didn't say much to us, as they passed straight into the bathroom. I heard the shower turn on and the door close.

So, we played ball some more.

What seemed like forever had passed, before they all filed out. One after the other, chattering away as they went back to the dressing room.

I looked at the clock, then turned to Hans. "All right buddy, I guess that's our cue. I'll go first, so you don't roll around in your duds, waiting for me. Can you hang out with Sasha for ten minutes?"

He nodded.

"Then here we go. Bump it."

I rose from the bed and made my way into the bathroom.

Warm water was limited, to say the least. So, I made the sacrifice and turned it as cold as I could take, hoping to save some for Hans.

I hopped out, brushed my teeth, flexed some muscle in the mirror, and went out to get the little man.

I did my best to use warm-water time as efficiently as possible. We washed him up, shampoo and all, and got him rinsed before he turned hypothermic.

All cleaned up, we went back to the bedroom and finished drying off. I got dressed first. The ensemble left much for me to desire. The waist on the pants was considerably oversized. I cinched it as tight as possible with a belt, but as I did the mirror twirl, I saw it still looked like I'd shit myself in the back. The sweater was a little short in the sleeves and at my waist, enough to heighten my self-consciousness. And the tie… what's left to say? Good thing it was a blind date, pun Intended.

With me set, I focused on making Hans look as stylish as possible. Once we got his shirt on, I found the gel and designed him a kickass 'do. Then I tested the cologne I'd found in the closet. It was… better than B.O.. So, we splashed some on, with only minutes to spare, before Gaby poked her head in the door and invited us over to the ladies area.

"I see you Gaby!" I called.

She squealed and blushed.

"Wow! You are so pretty!" I nudged Hans in the shoulder.

"Yes!" he responded.

I followed the two youngsters over to the closed door across the landing. Gaby knocked.

"Boys here," she announced.

I heard some shuffling in the room, and then they called, "Oka-a-ay… we ready!"

Gaby pushed the door open gently. All the lights were off and the curtains were drawn, so the room was dark, with slivers of gloomy autumn light.

"What's going on in here!" I barked. "How come it's so dark?"

Gaby shuffled across the room and then gave the signal. "Okay, now you turn lights up."

I fumbled along the wall for a switch, and with a click, the room became clear. And what a vision of beauty to see.

They were all in pretty dresses. Gaby's was a pale green that seemed to work really well with her curly, red hair, perked up nice and proper. Lilly wore a stunning deep-red dress that hung just below her knees, her dark hair drawn back into a perfect braid. Anna could easily pass for Tatiana's little sister. The strong influence the teacher had over her young apprentice, very apparent. Her dress was a deep blue and her eyes glowed like stars in the night. Her hair, like Tatiana's, fell like silk to her shoulders.

And about a one-foot step up from Anna was… I am so hot for teacher.

I was one lucky son of a bitch.

She wore a black gown, the oh-so-subtly-transparent material defining her every physical perfection. Her hair shone like pale gold, thin wisps trailing past her shoulders to hang just above her breasts. I was speechless. Looking up and down the aisle of beautiful, young ladies we would escort to dinner. I realized that Hans and I really got screwed over on our attire. Well, me mostly. Hans was in Armani.

"Wow!" I nudged Goose again.

"Yeah, wow!"

"Why Hans say *wow*? He cannot see."

"Lilly!" Tatiana scolded. "You must accept a man when he say nice things."

The ladies all blushed.

The children gathered round each other, exploring and giggling. Hans felt the girls' dresses and hair, as the girls did to him.

"Hans, you had this?" Lilly slid her fingers along his tie.

"Yes! Brandon say is Amanti."

"Ohhh!"

I went straight to Tatiana. "You…" I ran my hands gently down her arms. "I'm not educated enough to describe how beautiful you look, honey."

She sputtered and blushed. "Yes, you like?" She turned around for me, holding one side of her dress out.

"Where did you get this dress? It looks like it cost thousands of dollars."

"Yes? It not cost much money. My sister, she make for me."

"Your sister?"

"Yes, at home, Ukraine, my sister. She like to do this, make clothes."

"Tell your sister she does incredible work. I've never seen a woman look so beautiful in a dress."

She ran her hands along my sweater. I sucked in my stomach a little, so it fell all the way to my waist. She ran her fingers up to my tie.

"Oh, this is nice. Very handsome." She smiled and gave me a peck on the lips.

"Yeah? It's Armani." …Why not? Hans was wearing it, so could I.

The time drew near and the rain was still spattering the windows. So, we had some organizing to do before we headed out.

Tatiana took Sasha into the kitchen and found Tessa, who would look after her while we were away. But Tessa would not let us leave without taking a picture. Of course, everyone but me was super excited for that.

After a quick ten or twelve poses, we went down to the landing. Tatiana said it wasn't far, and not one person wanted anything to do with boots and slickers, so we searched through the bucket of umbrellas, looking for the ones with the fewest holes. I was beginning to grow tense, as time was ticking and we needed to get going.

Even with everyone happy, it was still difficult to form a proper line with all the commotion, so I had to herd them all along with Tatiana clicking and sniffing her way around the corner. The place was right there, just as she'd said, thankfully.

The exterior was made of full panes of glass bordered with dark-stained, roughly cut beams. A small patio sat out front, with the chairs tilted forward to lean against the round tables.

We walked into a tiny entry vestibule, barely big enough for the lot of us, which caused a log jam as the opposing door opened toward us. So, we had to back it up, scrunch in a bit, and get it figured out.

The inside was fancy. Fancier than we probably should've tries on our first run. But at least we were the only ones in there for the time being.

A hostess with a pleasant smile approached a small podium, and checked us in. Tessa had informed her of our background when she booked the table, and she was incredibly good at accommodating our needs.

I'd run over the drill of helping the ladies to their seats with Hans earlier, but as we approached the table, I wasn't sure how well he could handle it under pressure. I put him in front of me and made sure we were the first to get there. I walked around his side and got things started for him, pulling the chairs out from the table where he, Gaby, and Lilly would sit. I gave him quick directions, then scrambled around to the opposite side, where I would sit with Tatiana and Anna.

I pulled out my three chairs just as the ladies hit the end of the table. Hans was there to take Gaby's arm and show her to the middle seat. The two fumbled around each other for a moment, but Gaby was all for it. So, she eagerly met him half way in any effort. With her placed, he felt his way across the chair backs and helped Lilly into her seat.

For my part, I took Tatiana's hand and sat her down delicately in the middle chair, then I helped Anna and rushed to the other end of the table to sit across from Hans.

We were in! No one drowned on the way over. Nothing got broken and there were no known injuries. We were sitting down! That, in itself, was a titanic accomplishment.

Little fingers scurried lightly, feeling the edges of the red linen placemats, atop the white tablecloth. Not one clink or toppled glass between them.

The room was what you'd expect for an Italian restaurant. Dimly lit, the upper walls were painted a creamy clouded white that transitioned to dark wood panelling that met a faded, red-tiled floor.

The hostess came back with a round of ice water and took our drink orders. The kids ordered colas all around. I listened closely as Tatiana ordered, hoping she might go for a glass of wine so maybe I could indulge a little. But she ordered up a tea, so I followed suit.

I held her hand snuggly, as everyone spoke softly to each other. There were a few giggle outbursts from the other side. But they put in effort to muffle it, holding hands to their mouths. Other than that, everyone was well behaved.

The lady returned with our drinks. The glasses touched the table for only a split second before being snatched up by little hands. And all went quiet, while they sipped from the straws. A light switch clicked in my head as the menus were placed before us. No Braille option. That was another lack of foresight on my part. But to my rescue, our attendant suggested three of their signature dishes.

Tatiana ordered the alfredo and every single one of the other ladies followed with the same.

I flipped through the menu to find the pizza list and ordered up a tweaked version to fit Hans's liking.

With everything settled, I took time to sit back and relax, watching everyone enjoy themselves. I rested my hand on Tatiana's, as she answered questions. Soft, orchestrated music played in the background. It was turning out to be a pleasant evening.

It brought a humble understanding, watching the tiny fingers trace the placemats, the silverware, and the tall stemmed glasses. Their expressions and their tones told me it was all so special, so wondrous to them. It was as close to royalty as they had ever experienced.

I thought back to the crude, wooden picnic table at the orphanage. The mismatched cutlery and various plastic cups. It was home to them, and they were happy and grateful for it. But that night, as they sat back in their individual, comfortably cushioned chairs. There was a strong sense of pride.

I'd sat at restaurant tables my whole life, and I usually bitch about the service and the bill.

But they didn't care if the food took too long. And the bill? Seeing them sit so formal and even a little arrogant, it felt good to give that to them, whatever the cost.

The waitress returned, serving two baskets of warm, fresh-baked bread and topping up the colas. I thanked her and was about to relax again when a bout of laughter pierced from outside.

My eyes snapped to the window at the front of the building. The rain looked to have stopped, but the cloud remained and the daylight was murky. I made out the ghostly figures of a small group of young folks walking by, hunched over and laughing as they huddled together.

But they weren't young, they were my age. They weren't folks, they were people. Young people, out being young people.

I watched their every motion, till they passed from sight. Then, I looked back at the smiling faces at our royal table.

My hand reached for my tea. I faded into a mild hypnosis, as my thumb gently followed the contours of the handle.

It was okay… What happened outside without me, was okay. There'd always be something happening somewhere without me. It was okay, because something just as exciting was happening with us.

I picked up my cup and took a sip of my… tea.

I set the cup back down and looked to the window, and swallowed.

There was a very softly spoken message at the farthest reaches of the back of my mind. Asking whether I was making a statement, or trying to convince myself.

Was life simpler for some? Was I broken? Why did I always feel that constant pull from one side to the other?

I'd sunk so deep into my stupor that I must've forgotten to breathe. When my lungs inflated on auxiliary command, I snapped back to then and there.

The room was peaceful, Tatiana's hand delicate, yet strong and loyal, the children's faces alive and glamorous. It was okay. A smile eased in my mind.

The food service would be tricky, and I kept watch for delivery in order to be ready to help in whatever way I could. But when the food came out, I didn't even have to flinch a finger. The waitress was accompanied by a pleasant man, wearing a white apron and a humble smile. On my announcement, everyone lent as much room as possible, and everything found a peaceful resting place.

With everything settled, the room filled with wondrous chatter. Little fingers, fuelled by heavy doses of caffeine and sugar found the edge of their plates, and they leaned in their noses for further inspection.

As the ladies went over procedures, I grabbed hold of the pizza shovel. Hans's face was alight with expectation.

"All right buddy. First restaurant man-food. Ready, big guy?"

He nodded, his hands fidgeting in front of his face.

I scooped him a perfect-size slice, not too big and clumsy. Everything was freshly made by hand. From the lightly crisped crust, to the sauce, to the few vegetables and the pepperoni and salami straight from the… store, probably. The cheese was perfectly aged and held on by strings as I lifted it from the pan. I set it down in front of Hans and he leaned over it quickly, inhaling and fingering around the contours and edges.

"Is hot!" he exclaimed.

"Yeah! You bet it's hot, buddy. Fresh out of the oven!"

The girls stopped what they were doing and looked over to what was happening on the man side.

"What, Hans?" Gaby asked. "Is hot? You have pizza, for man?"

"Yes! Brandon say is man-food." His chest puffed out.

"Oooh! Is goot? I can smell, please?"

The two fumbled timidly to clear a path for Gaby to sample. It was a precarious project, but they managed.

"Mmm! Smell very nice, Hans."

I eyed the curiosity of the others. Before things could get out of hand, I stood and looked down the table. "Does everyone else want to smell?"

Anxious nods fell, one after the other.

I smirked. "Okay, no problem." I scooped a slice onto my plate, then did a round of the table, letting everyone have a sample. They all agreed it smelled wonderful. I admit, the alfredo was looking as equally delectable.

The ladies were busy with utensils, while Hans just sort of sat there. He picked up his knife and fork and then made a slight motion to the food, but he seemed really unsure of what the house rules were. At home, he'd just go for it. But this wasn't home, and I guessed he didn't want to be denied invitation for any future adventures, and be left at home with Sasha. It was cute to watch.

I leaned over the table and tapped his hand. "Just pick it up buddy. It's all right."

I caught Tatiana look sharply in my direction. Her lips pursed and her eyebrows curled into fighting position. I'd say we were right on the very verge of getting a talking-to. But then, she paused, and relaxed into a lighthearted smile, deciding to let the boys be boys on our special evening.

Even with my permission, Hans waited a moment for any repeal. Encouraged by the silence, he dug his fingers beneath the pie-shaped slab and lifted its gooey goodness to his mouth.

And I was right behind him. Move over Domino's, this shit was the real deal. It tasted like walking through the streets of old Tuscano. Even if such a place never existed in the world, I was there, right then. And it was beautiful.

"Mmm, hmm, hmm." I nodded, setting the piece down and pulling the stringy cheese from my lips, till it broke.

Hans was having some trouble—things were sliding, and he was slurping away, doing his best to keep everything on the plate and off his Armani. He sat his slice down and held his sloppy fingers in the air, as he chewed away, trying to separate the strings of cheese. His mouth was full and he chewed away for as long as it took, his face scrunched in approval.

I laughed, then leaned over and helped him out, showing him the ropes. "You liking that, dude?"

He nodded. Comfortable with the program going forward, he went after it like a caged animal.

The girls were quiet as well, everyone fully engrossed in their meals. I asked if it was good, and all I got back were polite "*mmm's*" and slurps.

It wasn't long into the feast when one soft-spoken request came from Gaby, to try a piece of the pizza.

I smiled. "Sure you can, sweetie."

Then, as I went to serve her up a slice, more requests came in.

I ended up sacrificing the better part of my rations, cutting a few of the bigger slices in half, to let everyone have an equal share.

Thankfully, the alfredo portions were large, and after filling up partially on the pizza, several children were unable to finish their pasta, and passed it down my way.

It was delicious. I've dabbled in alfredos before, but this would be the most memorable. The pasta was just the perfect bit of tender, and the texture of the creamy sauce had been practised to perfection over many generations in Grandmother's Tuscano kitchen.

As we reached the end of our meal, Tatiana and I allowed the children to order a small bowl of ice cream each, and we decided to split one between the two of us. The place was beginning to fill up, fast. So, it was perfect timing for us to soon make our exit.

Likely, we can blame the closing chapter of our experience on an overabundance of sugar. The ice cream was spectacular, and as beautifully handcrafted as the rest of the dinner's indulgences. Craving more endorphins, caution was thrown to the wind, and little hands went to work to capture every last creamy drop. Gaby got a little reckless, and her elbow bumped someone's cola glass, causing it to explode all over the table and onto Lilly's dress.

It was the beginning of the end. Lilly sat stunned, trying to understand what cold liquid had just splashed all over her exposed skin and, more importantly, her most-prized dress. As the reality set in, her eyes pooled with tears and her chin began to quiver.

At the sound of commotion, Tatiana placed her hand on my leg. "What is happen?"

"Oh," I patted the back of her hand. "Just a little accident. But I think it may be time to go."

Then came the waterworks, and our pleasant dinner came to a crashing end.

As Lilly began to wail, I jumped from my seat and ran to the scene of the accident. I tipped the glass back up, and reached for some napkins to soak up the deluge.

Gaby turned toward her friend. "Lilly… is happen?"

I could see that she understood her part in the tragedy, and that all hell was about to break loose.

"I… I am very sorry, Lilly. Is it get to you dress?" She reached over softly to her friend.

"No!" Lilly screamed between wails, slapping Gaby's hand away. "Ahhhhhhhhhahaa!" The emotional outburst took control.

At the ill-tempered response, Gaby began a fit of her own. Everyone else at the table froze, not absolutely sure what was happening.

I played what cards I could. "It's just a little spill, everyone, nothing to get upset about."

"Is not little!" Lilly spat. "She is spill, is all on me!" Her hands began to pluck around the moistened stains on her dress. "My dress! Gaby, you make it stain all over! Ahhhahhahahah!"

"*O-kay*." Tatiana set down her spoon and dabbed her mouth with her napkin. Then she rose from the table. "Is time for to go, everybody."

I watched as Hans realized the end had come. He began shovelling large scoops of ice cream in his mouth, as his forehead scrunched from what had to be a nasty bout of brain-freeze.

Tatiana came on the scene and I stepped aside to let her tend to Lilly. I moved one over, to try to comfort Gaby, who was also in full breakdown mode. Balling her eyes out and apologizing between wet snuffles.

I pulled her chair back and placed my hand on her shoulder. "It's okay Gaby,"

I whispered to her. "It's not your fault, it was just an accident. Everything's gonna be fine, but we have to get going now."

The hostess came to our rescue as much as anyone could. Clearly, we were disturbing the intended ambiance. So, we made our way to the door as quickly as possible, Lilly refusing to be next to Gaby. Tatiana continued outside with the children, while I paid the bill with a healthy tip, and said my thanks to everyone who'd helped us through. They were all very sad to see our night end as such.

Back out on the street, Tatiana held Lilly's hand in one of hers and Gaby's in the other. Trying to keep the two separated, as Gaby kept trying to console her friend and Lilly continued to bite at her every attempt.

Hans stood silent, holding onto Anna's hand to make sure he wasn't left behind.

"Okay," I said with a smile, looking down at the mess. Passersby couldn't help staring at us. I stepped over to Lilly and kneeled in front of her. "It's okay, Lilly, your dress will be fine. I can't even see anything anymore."

She didn't buy it. "Yes, you see it. My dress is no goot, is stain all over. I know this happen."

"Shshh." I picked up her hand in mine. "Whatever happened, it was an accident. I'm sure Teacher and Tessa can make it all better. If not," I leaned in closer to her ear, "we can go get you a new dress. Whatever colour you like."

She calmed down enough that the wailing stopped, but she wasn't ready to let go of the sobbing quite yet.

I stood up and ran my hand lightly on top of her head. She shook free of Tatiana's grip and wrapped her arms around my leg. So, I reached down and lifted her into my arms.

"All right! Everyone ready?" I looked around at the sombre faces. "What's everyone looking so sad for? We had a little accident, no big deal. I don't know about the rest of you, but I had a really good time. The food was really good, eh?"

Small smiles returned. Some more reluctantly than others.

"Do you think we should try it again sometime, maybe?"

The smiles grew a little more, and the heads nodded a little more.

I smiled. "I thought so." I patted Lilly gently on the back, and she rested her head on my shoulder.

"Let's go home. I'm feeling a little bit Potterish."

42

We made it home without further incident. Sasha waited anxiously at the door.

Gaby and Lilly had calmed, but there was still some healing to be done.

Up the stairs we went, to get changed into comfy clothes. Lilly insisted on a shower, so Tatiana took her to the bathroom and got her cleaned up. Everyone was silent for the most part. Not knowing how to cope with the disruption between the two who served as a solid foundation for harmony in the group.

After Lilly had returned from her shower and dressed for bed, we all assembled for story time. It was still decently early, but the effects of the tasty treats from our adventure were beginning to wear off, and little heads were growing heavy. They all lay in their usual spots while I read. As pages turned, I noticed the two girls breaking the crust from between them, with little touches and gestures of kindness. Before too long, they were snuggled together, restoring the bond.

Peace settled on us once again.

Storytime was extra-long, and we managed to finish off much of the book. Hans and Gaby were the only ones still awake, barely, when I decided it was time to shut it down for the night.

"*No,*" their sleepy voices protested.

"Now, you two, everyone else is asleep. If we read on without them, I'll have to read it all over again."

I lifted Tatiana's legs from my lap and pushed to my feet. Though Hans and Gaby were awake, they refused to get up on their own, and waited patiently for me to come and carry them to bed, like the others.

Gaby hung her head on my shoulder on our way to her bed. "Thank you to take us to restaurant, Brandon," she breathed into my ear.

"It's my pleasure, sweetie. I got to go out with so many beautiful young ladies." I laid her down gently. "I think I should be thanking all of you." I tapped the tip of her nose with my finger.

I turned back to the couch to see Tatiana sitting up and yawning. I stepped over to her and bent down to give her kiss on the lips. "It's late, honey. I want snuggle time."

She reached up and wrapped her arms around my neck. "Yes, you must carry me." She smirked.

I chuckled. "Carry you? But you're awake!"

"Yes, but I is tired, honey. Please carry me."

I straightened and pulled her to her feet. Then I reached down to her bum and took her weight. She wrapped her slender legs around me. I turned to check the children one last time, then carried my lady out the door.

We entered our room, and I kicked the door softly behind us to leave it open only a crack. Then I made my way to the bed, laid her down, and fell on top of her, kissing her neck.

She sighed, and pulled my face up so our lips met. "You such a good man. Thank you for do this tonight, for us. I sorry for trouble from girls."

I snuffed, still focusing on kissing every inch of her I could reach.

"They're children, you don't have to apologize for them. I just hope we can get Lilly's dress clean. I had a good time. Everything went really well… really."

Her lips found mine again. "Thank you," she whispered, with an extra hint of passion.

I pushed myself up and ran a finger down between her breasts. "Maybe Teacher has something special on for her man?"

A mischievous smile teased me. "Ma-a-aybe?"

My curiosity grew. "Yes?"

I pulled her up to sit, then reached behind her back to lift her shirt over her head.

Her bra was mostly transparent and left nothing to the imagination, her erect pink nipples threatening to puncture through.

"Oh, honey," I said as I exhaled. "You are so beautiful." I reached down to the waist of her pajama pants and she lifted her bum, allowing me to pull them down her porcelain-smooth legs.

The panties matched the bra. A string thong with a transparent triangle in the front. Her hair was perfectly trimmed to the border of the panties and tapered down to a point where the fabric formed to the contours of her untouchable. Held in trust, for the one who would pledge his eternal love to her.

Our advanced western culture has dispelled the myth of one "saving themselves" for marriage, or any type of commitment. We should be allowed to do whatever, with whomever, whenever. I'd be lying if I said the romance of her ideals wasn't just as intoxicating as her, spread naked before me. Perhaps it made her even more enticing. As I traced her body, her hands and legs bent and stretched with a subtle anxiousness. She was as much an animal as the rest. And when the time came to break the chains she had laid. That one man was going to be treated to something so special, something that would only be shared between them both. And the rest of us left to dream in wonder. Oh, to be the one allowed to pass. To experience her completely.

Love was a word with meaning to her. Marriage would be rewarded, and vows were eternal. The promise of marriage acted as fuel for her to be the best she could possibly be. To have a man want her to so badly, he would step up to the edge, take her hand, and throw himself into the unknown. Only for me, then, it was no longer unknown. I knew where I would land, straight into her arms, every time. With that thought, I lowered myself down to her again, kissing her lips and feeling her heart beat.

The way she responded to my touch—wrapping herself tight around me, thrusting her hips upward, rubbing her moist warmth against me—had the same effect as an injection of pure sexual ecstasy.

She attacked my neck like a hungry predator. Kissing and biting, purring insatiably. It seemed like she perhaps wanted it even more than I. And that maybe the time had come when I'd received enough of a passing grade to be rewarded.

I returned her desire, running my tongue down her neck to her abdomen. I placed my hands on her legs and pried them wide, and with little resistance, I continued my path down.

My lips travelled past her panty line, where I found her excreted excitement had all but melted away the visual barrier between us. My fingers dug into her hips and I buried my face deep in her, devouring everything attainable through the thin fabric. She let go a moan of urgency I'd never heard from her previous. My fingers slid up to pull aside the obstruction—

"No!" She panted heavily, pushing me from between her legs. "No, we no can do it!"

How she could muster the will to throw on the brakes in such a moment was beyond my comprehension. It wasn't so easy for me. She succeeded in pushing my face free, but I was quick to reposition myself on top of her, face to face.

I found myself grinding against her for every spec of satisfaction I could gather. It had been so long since I'd been anywhere near that level of passion, that I'd forgotten the pleasure. I was so full and I pushed myself harder against her, feeling the warmth through our thin layers of clothing.

"No, Brandon, we must not—"

"*Oh shit! Aaahhhahahah!*" I'd reached the point of no return, and exploded between us. I fell limp and heavy on top of her. There'd been no penetration, everyone's virtue was still intact. I'd just relieved a burden. A very large puddle of burden.

There was a pause before Tatiana said, "What happen? You is okay?" She kissed my shoulder.

"Yeah, yeah, I'm all right." I huffed. "Are you okay? I'm sorry, Tatiana, I really didn't want to push it this far but…"

I felt the warm mess below starting to sink through and spread across our midsections.

She pushed herself from underneath me. "What? What is it?" She felt her stomach. "Is this?… You do this? Is come from you?… All of this?"

"Yeah, I'm really sorry. But I mean, we didn't actually do… I mean, you're still good."

She traced her finger around in the pool. Then she reached across and slapped my crotch through my underwear, causing a sloppy splat of a noise.

"*Pfft,*" she snickered. "Is big mess, so big." She ran her hand up my stomach, wiping it off.

"Hey!" I looked at her. To my pleasant surprise, she wore a sexy little smile, not appearing offended in any way.

"What? I do not want on my hand. Is sticky. Is you mess."

I was still lost for breath, but my body felt loose and relaxed. It had been so long. I'd forgotten how beneficial the ritual could be.

We both lay on our backs, looking toward each other. I reached over and placed a hand on her cheek. "Thank you for not being mad."

She kissed my hand. "I not mad. I know is hard for you. Is hard for me too. Is okay, this. Is nice that you… have… excite by me." She smiled and kissed my hand again. "Now, I think we need shower." She laughed.

"Yeah, there's quite a bit."

She ran her hand across my stomach, then rolled on her side and kissed my lips. "Come, we go." She grabbed my hand and pulled me with her.

I scooped her up in my arms and carried her to the bathroom.

The shower was a nice finishing touch. She played coy, while removing what little clothing she had left. As the warm water fell over our bodies, we lathered each other up. It was the first time we were officially naked together, and we both found pleasure in exploring each other. Despite our newfound freedom, she gave me the impression that there were still boundaries. That this was a special treat, not to be often repeated. I wasn't sure if she was doing it to regain what she may have thought to be fading interest, due to my slip-up the other night. Or, if she was showing gratitude for my exceptional qualities.

Whatever the reasoning behind my sudden special privileges, I was soaking up every drop.

43

As the days grew short and cold over the fall season, I got up and went to work, then came home and tended to what needed tending. Rain was persistent, but I'd had yet to see any sign of snow.

It wasn't perfect. There were a few times when I stayed at the boat with the guys a little longer than I should have, or ventured into a pub. But I'd always mind the clock, and be home in time to read to the children. Sometimes Harry Potter sounded like a slurring drunk. But he was under a lot of stress, so it was accepted, on occasion.

Sexually, Tatiana and I never had a full repeat of that night. I think she felt that she'd gone a little too far, in the heat of the moment. And that to allow me such pleasures on a routine basis, would only prolong the fruition of her dream of becoming a wife to a good man.

My plays on her during evenings when I would return in a state of mild inebriation seemed only to annoy her. Over time, I think she grew tired of my insistence on getting into her pants, and my reluctance to commit to her for the rest of my life.

We'd settled into a routine that satisfied neither party completely. If it weren't for the children, I'm not sure I'd have stayed around, sometimes.

The monotony of our state solidified my doubts about marriage. So what if we were married? Then what? We'd still be there, doing the same things we were doing. Nothing would be different. Other than I'd hopefully get regular sex. But

I knew that wouldn't be enough. I mean, it would help. Really, really help. But I was experienced enough to understand there was more to it.

Before I knew it, Christmastime had arrived. Earlier than I was used to, as I found out that Christmas tradition in Amsterdam is much different from back home. Christmas had kind of become a thing from my past, something I'd pretty much left at home. I tried to think back to the previous Christmas I'd spent in Bonaire. But little reflection… reflected. It was likely I was out partying, or kiteboarding, or hungover, or… all of that. So, my first Christmas shopping safari with Tatiana began in mid-November. Much in advance of my traditional, December 24 ritual.

Tatiana made arrangements for us to have a Saturday to ourselves so we could get presents for the children. For the first time, she agreed to leave Anna in charge. Notifying Tessa of the situation, and asking her to check in on them every now and then.

Anna was very grateful, and I wondered how the experiment would pan out in the end. If the power would go to her head, and we would return to small children tending to her bidding, in prison attire.

The morning we stepped out, the air was cold and frosty. There was no snow, but a heavy fog overnight had cloaked the gingerbread town in ice. The sky was a blank, white canvass, the streets were slippery, and crystalline stalactites clung to anything lending support.

"Whoop!" Tatiana chirped, as her feet slid on the sidewalk, causing her to apply the death grip to my arm. "Is not good of a day for us. I think maybe we try another time?"

She looked so cute with her hair sticking out the bottom side of her white toque. When she slipped, her beautiful eyes widened and looked like giant blue Christmas balls. She was a girl for all seasons.

I smiled at her and realized how long it had been since we'd had a day together, by ourselves. "No, honey, you have it all set up for today and we don't have many weekends till Christmas. So let's go. I'm here for you. I won't let you fall." I leaned in and kissed her lips, which seemed to catch her a little by surprise. We'd both been neglecting our little investments of gratitude to each other. I really felt then, that we needed the time to ourselves. So, off we shuffled, arm in arm. There were already people out working to make the streets safer, spreading sand or ice melt. So, I led us around the corner and down to a point where we could get some traction. Once Tatiana found some sure footing, she was able to relax a little more and enjoy herself. I admit, there were some moments when I wasn't convinced I could keep us both vertical.

I thought it would be a good idea to give the rest of the city time to prepare the streets. I saw a small coffee shop up ahead and offered to buy Tatiana a light breakfast. She ordered a bagel and a hot chocolate, which was topped high, with a spiral of whipped cream.

She lifted the cup to her mouth and ended up burying her nose so deep in the topping that it cut off her air supply, causing her to sneeze it all over the table.

Her faced turned red. "Oh! I, I am sorry."

I leaned back in my chair and laughed. "It's fine. Nothing was damaged. I was wondering how that was going to go." I laid my hand over on hers.

"You know this! And you do not say to me!" She felt around the table for a napkin, then began dabbing at her face.

"Yeah, I knew. I didn't want to say anything. I was wondering if you were going to figure it out yourself. I didn't think you'd mind some whipped cream on your face in the morning."

She snorted a laugh, and I scraped a blob of cream off the tip of her nose.

As we ate our breakfast, I looked out the window and watched as the sun melted the frost from the air, and turned the ice to water. Causing it to stream down the sides of the buildings. With the sidewalks cleared, masses of Christmas shoppers began to flood the streets. We finished up, and headed back out. The conditions had improved substantially and Tatiana felt less endangered walking on her own. Though she still kept her arm joined with mine.

It had become a beautiful November morning, with a heavy presence of Christmas spirit. Boats passed down the canals and wreaths decorated the streetlights and buildings. Everything brought a peaceful smile to my face. It was one of those times when I wished Tatiana could see. One of those special days you were thankful to be a part of.

But her smile was equal to mine, and her head was turning side to side, taking it in her own way. I suppose she could hear the happy sounds of others' voices and the smell and spirit in the air. She could feel it, maybe even more than the rest of us.

"Do you think of what it looks like?" I asked her.

"What is this?"

"When we walk, or go anywhere. Do you paint a picture of it in your head? Do you try to imagine what it looks like? The city, and everything around us?"

"I see this place. I know where we is. I walk here many times. Is a picture in my mind." She stopped and began her clicking game, turning us slowly from side to side. Then she described the area to me in such detail that she pointed out things I'd honestly missed.

"This is building there, the top is flat, then many buildings beside but the roof is sharp. The rocks there, on this…" She cut squares in the air with her hands.

"Bricks."

"Yes, this. The bricks is big on this one and very much…"

"Rough."

"Yes, rough."

"There is canal, it is middle of streets." She clicked again, following the motion of a boat.

"There is big boat, for tour of people. There is part of the rock missing on the wall goes around canal." She turned to a light pole only a few steps from us. "They have Christmas hanging on the light, is not there last time I come. Is plant, with bow and bell."

And so that was enough of feeling sorry for the blind girl who couldn't see Christmas. It warmed me to know that we were both enjoying the day for everything it was.

We continued down the street, to a market she knew of, that opened especially for the Christmas season. When I first started working for Faas, she'd convinced me to let her take a small portion of my earnings so she could put it away for rainy days, or special occasions. She'd put it together with a portion of her earnings, and by the time Christmas rolled around, we were sitting pretty good. Still, she cautioned that there was no need to spend too much on the children. They were happy with simple presents, and the excitement of the season.

The market was a bustle, to say the least. Despite the lack of elbowroom, everyone in the crowd carried merry spirits. It was a condition that would usually cause me anxiety, but somehow, even I found spirit in that giving season.

The place was magically decorated with giant glistening snowflakes, mistletoe wreaths, candy canes, and crystal sculptures. Bells jingled and sidewalk performers strummed on strings, patted percussions, and whistled through brass contraptions.

I had my Christmas angel on my arm, searching out gifts for those wide-eyed special little people at home. She rolled out a list, and to my ignorant surprise, it included Tessa, Faas and Helen, my parents, and her family.

Tatiana was aglow with the giving spirit, chattering on and on about things she needed to find. Asking me about different colours, and reminding me to keep a look out for this and that. It was fun, yet mentally and physically draining at the same time. But the smile on her face and cheer in her eyes was a reward worth earning. By the time we were done, the baggage was plenty, and my angel had trouble finding any more hanging space on either of my arms. It made me think it would've been a good idea to bring along our trusted canine, with a saddlebag.

Exiting the market was much more challenging than our entrance had been. I found myself having to shift from side to side and shuffle forth and back to avoid disrupting another's path, or causing a catastrophe on one of the trinket stands lining our way.

It had been a long day, and the sun was already beginning to tire, as we made our way home. Despite the challenges, I found myself not wanting the moment to end. So, I lured Tatiana into another café, for some warm soup and another hot chocolate.

She sat across from me with her eyes wide and twinkling. Blabbering away about all the treasure we'd found, and how excited everyone would be. Her cheeks and nose were rosy red, and I found myself just staring at the beauty of her soul, and all that encased it.

When we stepped out into the streets, the light had faded even more, and the streetlights had just popped on. Tatiana was still nattering away, when I stopped her dead in her tracks. She turned to me with concern.

"What?"

"Over your head." I smirked.

She did her thing, and I wondered what the result would return. She looked at me shyly. "Is this plant for kiss?"

"Yes, a mistletoe."

"Mistle-o."

I dropped the load of bags from one arm, slid it around her waist, and pulled her hips toward mine. With enough dominance to assure her of my intentions. She welcomed me, wrapping her hands around my neck and meeting my lips with hers, warm and inviting. Her tongue tasted of sweet dessert topping. We held on long enough for the neighbourhood to know that she was my girl.

It was a perfect end to a perfect day. It was Christmastime like I'd never felt before. A time to be with the ones you love, and for the first time in a very long time, I was surrounded.

When we arrived back at the orphanage, I crept in the door and set the presents down softly. Then I ran up to the kitchen hall and checked to make sure the coast was clear. Tessa was there cleaning up, and she ran to me as soon as she saw me round the corner. We talked for a moment, then she rushed upstairs to make sure the children were distracted, and to instruct Anna that none were to come downstairs until further notice.

Tatiana and I scurried up to the dining room and began to wrap the presents. It was another thing she was especially and surprisingly talented at. All she needed was confirmation of which side of the wrapping paper was the print.

I dropped the ball for only a minute, it seemed, before she had completed two gifts in blank canvas, before I noticed. I received a swat to the arm and a gentle curse word for my slackness.

With everything complete, we found a suitable hiding spot in one of the pantries by displacing a lot of Tessa's supplies. But she waved it off, saying she could survive.

When we went upstairs, we were greeted with overexcited minds, and relentless questions. Asking what we did and why we'd been gone so long. It took some time to get them settled down. After cleanup and bedtime preparations, we settled in for story time. Anna must've done a good job keeping them busy in our absence, because none of them made it past a few pages. I was thankful, because we were coming to the end, and the next volume was wrapped up in the pantry. I would have to drag this book out until Christmas. Afraid that an absence of Harry Potter's adventures, would cause an all out revolution.

That night I squeezed Tatiana tight in my arms, kissing her shoulders and the back of her neck. She held my hand tightly and pulled my arm to rest between her breasts. The rain turned on and off, the drops at times hitting with more of an icy clack than a splash.

I'm not sure when Tatiana fell asleep, but I had trouble drifting off. My head stirred with the festivities to come, and the excitement of watching the children open their presents.

Tatiana had admitted to me earlier in the day, that this year they would be spoiled in comparison to the years before. Thanks to my contribution to the Christmas fund.

I was very happy to be where I was, and grateful to be included.

44

So… Christmastime in Amsterdam.

For those of you like myself, who by simple default, believe that Christmas is the same in every part of the world… hold onto your hats. I'll try to explain this in as politically correct a way as possible. Forgive any spelling mistakes.

The kids came crashing into the room and onto the bed.

"Teacher! Brandon!" Little hands shook our legs and pulled on the covers, as Sasha barked madly at the excitement. "Is time, time to see Sinter! He come today!"

"*Urrrrgh*." Tatiana pulled back at the covers. "Is too early, he no come now, is later."

I propped myself up on an elbow, blinking away the sleep from my eyes.. "What the heck is going on?"

Ilans crawled up and sat on my legs, bouncing up and down like he'd had jellybean ice cream for a morning snack. "Sinter coming today Brandon!"

"Who? What is a Sint— oh, you mean Santa Claus?"

"Santa? I say Sinter, not Santa. Sinterklaas!"

"Hmm, sounds familiar." I flopped back down, rolled over, and spooned my girl some more. "What the hell's happening? What's a Sinter whatever?" I grumbled in her ear.

"Is Sinterklaas, like you Santa. He come today."

"…He's coming today? It's fucking November!" I received an elbow to the ribs for language infraction.

"Yes, he come today. He come today and stay for many days."

"What! That's nuts, Christmas day is like, a month away. Why would he come now?"

"Ask children." She pulled the covers tighter around her shoulders.

"I can't believe no one told me about all of this. What in the heck is going on?"

"Why you not know this, Brandon?" Hans giggled. "You not have Christmas in Canata?"

"Yeah, we have Christmas. We have normal Christmas. With Santa Claus and reindeer, and he doesn't come until Christmas eve. Then he goes back to the North Pole."

Hans laughed. "Brandon, you is silly."

"I'm silly? I think it's you who is silly."

Lilly and Gaby climbed up beside Hans and the question/answer period began.

"You have Sinterklaas in Canata?"

"Well, it sounds kind of the same, but our guy is called Santa Claus."

"Was he look like?"

"Well, he's a big fat guy, with a long, white beard, in a red suit."

"Uh huh, is same."

"Yeah? That's the same as yours? Does yours live in the North Pole?"

"What is North Pole? Sinter live in Spain."

"Spain?" I decided to quit arguing, before I called bullshit on their Santa, and it ruined Christmas for them. "Really? That's… neat. Does your Santa—"

"Sinter," Gaby corrected.

"Right, Sinter. Does he have elf helpers too?"

"Is an elf? Huh? What is this?" Hans asked.

"You know, Christmas elves. Little elves, with pointy ears and green pointy shoes and little Santa hats."

"Sinter."

"Right, Gaby, thanks again, Sinter. Does he have elves to help him?"

"Is help for Sinter, is Black people."

I blinked a few times, in silence, then looked for a response from Tatiana. Finally, I asked, "What's that, buddy?"

Lilly stepped in, and, bouncing on the bed, repeated it a little louder. "They Black people! To help Sinter!"

Again, I looked for movement from Tatiana, but there wasn't a flinch.

I pressed my hands against my face and rubbed thoroughly, then scratched my head all around, before returning my focus to the children. Someone had obviously been led astray with the whole Santa/Sinter deal. I really needed help from an adult in a position of authority, and understanding of the whole ritual.

For the time being, I decided to continue with something else. "What about presents? Does Santa have presents?"

"Sinter!" Lilly corrected this time, with a huff and a roll of her eyes.

"Right, sorry, Sinter. Does he give presents?"

"Yes, Brandon." The three laughed at me. "Now, today, Sinter and Zwarte Piet stay and give presents to the next time… ummm… mont, is, Dee…"

"December?"

"Yes, is December." Hans held up five fingers.

"Fifth?"

"Yes!" They all bounced on the bed some more.

"Okay, well, that sounds like a lot of fun. We should maybe discuss this further, when Teacher is awake."

The children focused all of their attention on waking up Tatiana, who I think understood that her time of peace had come to an end anyway.

"Teacher Tatiana! Is time for get up. Sinter come today."

She rolled over with a groan and opened her eyes slowly. "Yes, children, I know is today for Sinter. But is not for long time, after breakfast."

"Awww!"

"What you want for me, huh? I do not make this happen."

"I don't think they're going away, honey." I rubbed her leg.

She sat up in bed to address the gathered crowd. "Okay, you like to see Sinter. You must go to you room and pick clothes and get teeth brush and all must shower."

"Awww!"

"Is no *awww*. You must do, or we no do go."

With the final command, the children scattered. Some back to their room and some to the washroom. Sasha spun around in circles, tail wagging, trying to figure out which child to follow for the most excitement.

With all little ears distracted, I turned to Tatiana. "Listen, sweetie. I'm not sure how much of our conversation you heard, but could you explain this whole Sinter thing to me? I don't think the children explained it right."

She yawned and lay back down, resting her head on the pillow. I leaned over her for a kiss.

"Is Sinterklaas."

"Yes, right, Sinter. What's his deal?"

"He deal?"

"Yeah, his deal… how does it all work?"

"He is Sinterklaas. He come today, now. He come from Spain, on boat. He stay now to next month, on five days. The children may get presents now. He go along on rooftops, he hide presents for children. He and Zwarte Piet."

"Zwarte piet? What's a zwarte piet?"

"Zwarte Piet… is help for him. I think in English is call Black Peter."

"What!" I said in hushed astonishment.

"*What*? They help Sinter to give presents."

"And they're… black?" I said it.

"Yes, is Black people. Zwarte Piet."

I watched her expression closely and carefully. But there was no sense of… guilt from her political slip.

"So, Santa—"

"Sinter."

I exhaled. "Yes, Sinter. He comes here, from Spain, on a boat… and he has black people helping him? Like elves?"

"Yes, is like elves. They dress same to this, but is Black people. Zwarte Piet, this Black Peters."

"…Is this real? Are you bullshitting me?"

"No, is no shit, is true. You see today. Why? What is problem with this?"

"What's wrong with it? You have a jolly white guy with black helpers. Are they, like, African?"

"Huh?" Her face scrunched, as if I were acting ridiculous. "Maybe they from Africa, I do not know this."

"So… everyone's okay with this?"

She shook her head and rolled onto her side, facing away. "Yes, everyone is fine. I do not understand you problem. Is like this all time here. Is Christmas,

Sinter and Zwarte Piet come to here. Is no problem, is happy time celebration. What is problem?"

"I can't believe you're asking me what the big deal is! Back home this would be a very big deal."

"Why? I know you Santa Claus, is not so different."

"*Pfft*! Uh yeah, of course it's different. Santa doesn't have"—I lowered my voice—"Black people, helping him."

"So, Santa have elf. This no problem in Canada?"

"Well, they're elves. They're fictional, made up."

"Yes, like this too. Is made up, is the same."

"It's not the same!"

"Why is not the same?"

"Because there are real Black people in the world. And I'm pretty sure a few of them are named Peter."

"Stop this, is silly. Is way of Christmas here. Is no same as Canada, is no the same as Ukraine. But is way for here. Do no break Christmas for children, please. You know?"

I huffed as I crossed my arms over my chest and leaned back against my pillow. "I know. I know Sinter'd be doing some hard time back home."

We took our time getting ready. Because the arrival of Sinterklaas and the parade wasn't supposed to happen until late morning, and the kids had us up super early.

As politically incorrect as the forthcoming celebration seemed to me, everyone was very excited, which eventually rubbed off. What the hell. Santa was coming to town, and if the whole country of Amsterdam was all right with the ritual, who was I to judge? The children were hopping and jumping and twirling, and when it was my turn in the bathroom, I remembered a little something in the form of half a brownie for just such a special occasion. Because, when you're a foreigner in Amsterdam, going to watch Father Christmas parade through the streets with a group of black helpers. You might as well be high.

After breakfast, we got ready and piled out onto the street. Much to my surprise, Faas and Helen were waiting with happy smiles… and a video camera. Which made me wish I could puke up the brownie.

The sky was overcast, but the air was still and mild. It was going to be an excellent day for welcoming Sinter and his merry band of homeboys. We walked across the street and down to the canal, where he was expected to arrive. Faas manned the video camera under Helen's very specific direction. He did his best to stay ahead of us and spread his time evenly, capturing every little joyous smile. The few times he pointed the camera at me, I did a quick look-away. Knowing old Faas the bloodhound would pick up on my less-than-sober state.

We were still early by my count. But when I saw the size of the crowd that had already gathered, I realized we were lucky to find a space along the canal that was large enough to give all the children a front-row spot. With children, it seems it doesn't matter whether they can see, they still want to be in the front row.

Hordes of elated families bustled around us. Bells were jingling and small choirs had gathered to sing words of welcome to Sinter. Asking him to bring his joy and promise to all.

Shortly after we settled, sounds of the official Sinterklaas band began to echo from upstream. The crowd fell silent; watching, waiting.

Then, in the distance, at the pace of a lazy drift, the tip of a boat peeked from around the corner.

I sucked in a breath of suspense, then reached down to the huddled children standing in front. "He's coming!"

Their little smiles were priceless, heavily laced with wondrous suspense. I was expecting them to lose their minds with screaming and trying to climb the barrier to get a piece of the Sinter man. But they fell silent, and kept their eyes trained in the direction of the approaching brigade.

The boat continued to creep around the corner. It was wide and low, like a barge that had been modified to usher tourists through the streets, with an enclosed cabin encasing the middle section and two large decks on the bow and aft. Band members were split between the two, dressed in festive garments that looked pretty much identical to what I was used to back home. Coats of white and candy cane red, pointed hats, and green accents. They rapped on drums, chimed on trinkets, and blew on an assortment of brass horns. The stable footing of the boat appeared to rock ever so slightly from side to side, under the jolly mass. For whatever reason, possibly the brownie, I related it all to a Dr Suess theme.

Ever so slowly, they drew closer, and more and more boats rounded the corner behind them. Just like street floats in the parades from back home. They were excessively adorned with Christmas spirit, and people dressed for the occasion cheered and waved to the onlookers.

It was at that moment, with the growing anticipation, that I felt the world turn a little dizzy. Just enough for me to figuratively kick back, put my feet up, and enjoy the show. I rocked back into my heels as a mellow grin blossomed on my face, and did just that.

It was sinking in just perfect. One of those beautiful, winter days. When you're out with the fam, taking in some Sinter, and you'd snuck half a pot brownie down in your morning shower. Everyone was occupied with other shit, and I was just chillin' back, sucking in that sweet, warm Amsterdamian air.

And then this big bright mass popped beside my head and shouted something right into my face in some strange language.

It was a guy dressed like an elf, only he wasn't an elf, because he was tall. Taller than me. That alone, is a pretty heavy challenge to a person who'd just been lying back in a moderate state of psychedelia. But there was even more to it.

He was black… and he was white. He was a white guy with black makeup splotched all over his face. When you've been aware of, and watching the program since your birth, you knew this was a Black Peter… no biggie. In fact, you're ecstatic for his attention. When you're me… well, there was nothing remotely common about it. This was a six-foot-tall, white man, dressed like an elf. His face painted for what I could only expect to be a coming battle, and he was screaming horrible noises at me.

Like a devil jack-in-the-box. Bang! There! Right now! One second life is great, and in the next instant… all that.

The merry smile on his face suggested that there was something very seriously wrong… with everything.

My mind decided it needed a time-out.

I took a step back toward the wall, forcing the kids to squish out to the side. Braveheart-the-black-and-white-Battle-Elf patted the children on the shoulder and placed some candy into each of their hands.

The children all smiled and yelled, "Zwarte Piet!" They reached out to touch his coat as he crouched down to greet them and pat their heads.

I took a deep breath, and things began to turn back on, one by one.

Zwarte Piet. Black Peter… Jesus Christ. I relaxed against my stoop, bowed my head, and ran a hand through my hair. Another moment later, I managed a smile and a chuckle to myself.

Tatiana's hand reached into the void where I'd stood. I pushed myself off the wall to find her touch.

Hands connected, she pulled herself to me and wrapped her arms around my waist. "Look, honey." She smiled and ran her gentle hand down my cheek. "Is Zwarte Piet."

I laughed and turned my head so I could kiss her palm, sweetly. As my arms found my way around her. I nodded, "Zwarte Piet."

45

I woke to yet another rainy Monday morning. A heavy, chill-to-the-bone kind of morning. A swarm of bulbous drops pummelled against the windows and made it torturous to leave my sexy, warm, half-naked girl in bed, alone.

By the time I'd crossed the street, I'd already all but given up on the day. It was Christmastime. Sure, it had started several weeks earlier than my normal, but what was the harm in having a month off for the season of giving?

I could tell the rest of the crew felt the same, as we all crowded inside the boat cabin, tripping and bumping into each other. The dreary weather made for dreary spirits, and the glazed look in all our eyes suggested we were mentally somewhere other than there.

We'd been making good progress on all the projects, and as the week passed by, I sensed that Faas had given up on trying to push production. He didn't seem like the type of man who liked to pay wages to ones lacking motivation. So, we'd cut things back to half days, till further notice. On Tuesday, Adlar simply stopped showing up, and by Wednesday, the rest had followed.

I continued to show up every day. Not so much because I wanted to, but because it was Christmas, and any spare bit of change I could muster counted.

I admit, it was me who was going a little overboard with the season. I took some time in the afternoons to sneak back to the market and visit some of the stands I'd taken special note of during our first visit. To buy up some decorative knickknacks for our room, along with scented candles and a round of snuggly plush pajamas for everyone. And there were always a few extra toys, here and there, that I couldn't *not* get. As the week passed, our little place was looking pretty Christmas cozy.

Tatiana always gave me shit for spending the money. Just a little bit, and it always ended with a super sexy smile and a juicy kiss. The kids were all in their glory.

Wednesday evening, I was told that the coming weekend was the Christmas party for all the children at the orphanage. A time when all the children, the blind and the others, would spend the evening together. They'd venture out into the streets, weather permitting, to take in all the Christmas lights and decorations. Then return home for a dance that would take place in the dining area.

That brought something heavy to weigh on my mind, in the form of Lilly's dress, which never did come as clean as we wanted. Even with all of Tatiana's and Tessa's old-family stain-removal techniques. Lilly had asked about it. She was concerned about wearing it to the party. Even though she couldn't see, many of the children at the dance would be able to. What stain remained, was obvious enough to be picked up by anyone who could see.

It took some convincing, but I managed to talk Tatiana into running out with me on Thursday to find a replacement. She insisted that it wasn't necessary. That what Lilly had would work just fine. But I laid the guilt trip on her, painting potentially horrible scenarios till she finally buckled.

She insisted on bringing Helen along, as she wasn't yet secure with my taste in little girls' clothing. So, we all went together, to her favourite second-hand store. As the women were shopping, I was quick to point out some things for the others, insisting it wouldn't be polite to return with something for just Lilly.

I dug in my pocket for the cash as we rang everything in at the counter. As I was handing it over, Helen touched my hand. I looked at her, and she smiled sweetly and held a roll of money out to me. She didn't say a word, just nodded. I picked up that she didn't want Tatiana to get involved, knowing she'd never let it happen. I was tempted to put up a fight, of course, but the look in her eyes told me resisting would break her heart. She had a special place in her heart for our little family, and she didn't have anyone to spoil, except Faas. I returned her smile, nodded, and accepted the money. After all was said and done, I returned her change with a big hug.

We invited her and Faas over for the Saturday night event, which she delightfully accepted. Then we said our thanks and goodbyes.

As soon as we shut the door to the orphanage, Tatiana turned to me. "I no can believe you let her pay for this!" she softly scolded.

"What! Are you kidding me! How'd you know?"

She returned a sly smirk. "You is slow learn." She patted my cheek. "I is blind, no stupid." She popped up for a kiss.

"Okay, I know. I felt bad about it. But I think I would've felt worse if I didn't let her."

"Yes, I understand this. This why I let you go, this time." She stepped past me and started her way up the stairs.

I followed, scratching my head yet again. Sometimes I wondered why she was even involved with a man such as myself.

The wonderment subsided as we approached our landing. We could hear the children in their room. Lilly was singing, while Hans played the piano. Which was a perfect cover for us to get around the corner to our room, and stash the gifts. Tatiana insisted on keeping it secret until the big day.

But there was a last-minute disruption, when some bells began to jangle from the children's room. Causing Tatiana and I to freeze on the stairs.

"What is this?" she whispered, reaching back for my hand.

I held my breath as the noise grew louder, then a furry head peered around the corner. It was Sasha, and she looked a little embarrassed. The children had dressed her in the seasonal attire I'd seen at the market, and couldn't resist purchasing for her.

A Christmas bell hung from her red velvet collar, and on her head sat a headband mounted with stuffed antlers. My hand shot to my mouth, to stop a bout of laughter. The look on her face was that of someone who had suffered a substantial demotion at work.

"It's Reindeer Sasha," I whispered. "Go! Go to the room, I'll distract the children."

She hurried the last couple steps to the top with me tight to her heels. When she banked right, I went left, straight into the children's room.

The music stopped and all the little heads turned as I passed through the door.

"Brandon!" Hans said, getting up from the piano bench and raising his arms for me to pick him up.

"Hey kids! How's it going? Looks like you've all been keeping busy, eh? We're all sure lucky to have that Anna girl around."

"Where did you and Teacher go?" Gaby shouted, as she and Lilly found their way to my legs.

"We went out, we had to go get some last-minute things for… stuff." I realized then that we'd never really come up with an explanation for what we were doing… and we should have.

"Last minute?... Things?... For stuff?" Hans relayed back.

"What stuff?" Lilly added.

Tatiana entered the room. "Is stuff for adult people, is no business for children," she said, coming to the rescue. "No more questions now. Do you all get you work done? Anna?"

"We practice music, Teacher."

"Okay, is good. Children, back to work, please."

We spent the rest of the day helping the children with their studies. It was nice for me to be able to spend the time with the kids. I'd been away working weekdays since the summer, and didn't realize how detached I'd become.

We did arts and crafts, some reading and math. I even found it challenging to keep up with some subjects. Had to dust off the old brain. I couldn't recall being as advanced as they were when I was that age. That teacher lady was sure doing a good job.

It rained off and on. I would escape to the window during the hard showers to watch the drops explode on the streets and the people below. Inside was nice and warm, and after dinner, we all got snuggled up in our comfy jammies, snacked on Christmas sweets, told stories, and of course, I read.

I was the only one to show for work on Friday. Faas welcomed me in for an early lunch and a couple beers before letting me go for the holidays. He said he wasn't sure yet when we would get back at it. But it wouldn't be before Sinter left, and that he knew where to find me. He handed me my final pay for the holidays, and I noticed it was a little thicker than usual. I looked down at the wad and then back at him. He blushed a little, and shot me a wink.

I smiled and turned to walk away, but looked back over my shoulder. "You and Helen are coming over tomorrow, for the party, right?"

"Yes, yes!" He smiled and waved me off. "We be there tomorrow."

"All right, see you then!"

I flipped through the bills on my way back and found the old bugger had slipped me an extra two hundred. From a guy like him, I was maybe expecting only an extra shiny nickel. He was all right, that Faas guy.

Saturday came, and the children woke us, yet again, way too early. Especially for the holidays. Sasha came jingling in with a happy smile. I saw that she'd managed to shed her antlers, but had grown accustomed to her collar. The children trotted in behind her and crawled onto the bed.

"Wake up, sleepy people!" they shouted. "Is special day for party, and Sinter come tonight also."

Tatiana and I groaned in unison. "No, is too early," she said. "Go back to bed."

They continued to prod at us to get up and start getting ready. Until, Tatiana finally snapped, got out of bed, and went to the doorway, where she shooed them back to their room and ordered them not to return for one hour. They instantly went silent, and obediently filed out the door, with a couple mild sniffles.

It was the first time I witnessed her lose it. I felt bad for them, at first. It was Christmastime after all. But they'd had many days of spoils up to then, and getting to spend an extra undisturbed hour in bed with my girl was an easy sell.

I pulled back the covers for her, as she returned and flopped down beside me. Then I threw the warm blanket back around her. She wrapped her arms around me and snuggled her head into my chest. I kissed her head and rubbed her back gently. There wasn't a peep from the other room.

I wasn't able to return to sleep. Looking out the window, the morning was brighter than it had been all week. Still overcast, but for the time, there was no rain falling. It looked like it'd be a good day for the coming festivities. I smiled as I held my woman. Everything was still and silent. Giving me time to feel the beating of her heart, the rhythm of her breath, the slight film of perspiration on her skin as we lay entangled.

It was a good time for reflection on the mad journey that had brought me to her. It had all seemed to happen so unbelievably quick, but that morning, I was able to give a great deal of thanks.

The dice could have rolled to the point where I was sipping champagne on a yacht with the rich and beautiful. But just as easily, I could be sleeping on a park bench under a pile of newspaper, wishing I were holed up in an orphanage somewhere.

Again, that morning, I felt like a very fortunate man. I even thought of my parents. We were planning to contact them the next day. Tatiana had transferred all of the video from the parade to the computer, and we were excited for them to see how much fun we were having. No doubt, Faas and Helen would be bringing the video camera again that day.

Half an hour had passed before Tatiana must've accepted she wouldn't get back to sleep. She responded to my gentle caressing by pressing her tender lips against my chest.

I smiled. "Mmm, you should be sleeping, sexy."

She tilted her head up to greet my lips. "Yes, I like to sleep. But the children, they make it no possible now." Her blue eyes fluttered.

"It's your own fault for making them love you so much. I bet they're over there in tears, missing you."

"Yes, this what you think? I bet lots of money they is listen at door."

I chuckled. "Oh yeah, I suppose that's a possibility."

"Is no possibility, is true. I know this, I hear them now."

"Well, I know enough now to never doubt your super-senses. Should we let them in?"

"No, I say one hour, we still have time." She kissed me again, fuller and longer. "Is Christmas for us also." She smiled and rolled on top of me. Her affection grew more intense as she ground herself against me, working her kisses down to my belly.

I always enjoyed her attention, but it was truly turning into a form of torture for me. We both knew it would only go so far, and it was never far enough. Enough to get me worked up into a frenzy, only to have her shut me down.

But being a man, I couldn't say no. So, we enjoyed ourselves. Crawling and rolling all over each other. Her breasts heaved and her panties were soaked and I was so hard I could've posed as a peg in a round of horseshoes.

Till there was a loud knock at the door and the children cried. "Okay, is been one hour now!"

I saw the doorknob begin to turn, and I jumped off Tatiana and ran to the bathroom. Doing what I could to conceal the enthusiasm in my fluffy, Christmas jammies.

I looked back to see Tatiana snarl toward me and scramble to get the covers back over herself. I closed the door behind me, just as the bedroom door opened.

I wasted no time turning on the shower and stripping down.

I finished up and opened the bathroom door. Hans turned instantly at the sound. "Brandon, you shower now? You ready for party?"

"Uh, yeah buddy. For sure, ready for the party." I made my way toward the closet, but couldn't make it before Tatiana cut off my path.

"You have shower already?" Her tone was condemning.

"Yeah, all showered up. Ready to go… honey."

"What you do in this shower?"

I laughed casually, through gritted teeth. There was no way I was going to try to get around it. God knows she'd probably heard it, or smelled it, or clicked her way through the wall and into the shower. "Well, *say* it was a Christmas present."

She gave me a look of disapproval, then reached up and patted her hand hard to my cheek. "You best to think of me when you do Christmas shower."

"Hehe, yes, of course, sweetie."

She turned off the interrogation lamp and continued on her way.

I helped Tatiana chase the children around and get them prepared. Then we went down for morning brunch, where all the children gathered. Tessa had brought in some of her friends for support during the day's events. After the dishes were cleaned up, she announced a one-hour window for everyone to finish getting prepared, before we all met back in the dining hall and headed out for the day.

We went back upstairs and Tatiana gave Helen and Faas a call to fill them in on the schedule. Then, in a rush, we revealed to the children the new clothes we'd bought them for the special day. Including Lilly's new dress. She was thrilled, and we both got big hugs and kisses. She put it on quickly, and twirled around the room.

Then there was the girls' hair to do. Gaby wanted this, Lilly wanted that, and they were both very insistent on having it done right then. Poor Anna was getting left out of the loop.

"Brandon!" Tatiana shouted to me.

I looked at her, being pulled in all directions.

"Please, Anna must have her hair brushed. Please, you do this."

"Oh, uh, okay. Yeah, sure." I'd never done it before, but I'd watched her do it several times. So, I grabbed a free chair and pulled it next to the bed, inviting Anna to take a seat. She handed me the brush with a sweet smile as I sat on the bed behind her.

I grabbed the brush and started chopping away, frantic-like.

"No!" she declared.

"What? No? I… What's wrong, Anna?"

"You must go slow. Please." She took the brush from my hand to demonstrate. "Start at top and go all way down to end. Please be slow." She handed the brush back to me.

"Oh, uh, all right." I did as instructed, and found a pattern satisfactory to her.

The way she sat, legs crossed femininely in her dress, her hands folded properly in her lap, her spine straight and shoulders back. There was a sense of pride to her. Special structure, engrained. A woman of morale and honour. Just like her teacher.

The rest of the gang were running around in madness, and then made their way across the hall to the children's room. Anna and I sat in an awkward silence as I pulled the brush through her silken hair. But it was nice to spend some attention on her. She was so proper all of the time. I honestly found her intimidating.

I cleared my throat. "So… big day today, huh?"

"Yes," she replied. "Will be fun, I think."

"Yeah, sounds like it. I'm really excited. And there's a dance tonight?"

"Yes, the dance. You think you dance wit Teacher?"

"Ha ha, I don't know. I'm really not much of a dancer. But Teacher is a very special woman. I think I'll probably end up taking her for a whirl. Should be an honour for a man to dance with such a special woman. How about you? Do you dance?"

"I… I would dance, if someone ask me. I have dance before, but only wit the others. Teacher and Lilly and Gaby."

"Oh, no boys ask you to dance?"

Her head sank. "No, no boys ask. The only boys who could ask are from downstairs. The ones who see."

"Yeah, well… do you know any of those boys?"

"Well…" She fidgeted a little. "There is one boy from downstairs."

"Oh?" I peered around to see her blush. "What is this boy's name?"

"He name is Fritz. He talk to me sometime, in dining room. One time he bring me a dessert. There was not enough, and I did not get one. So, he give his to me.”

“Hoho! Sounds like he likes you, eh?”

She smiled. “I do not think he like me. He do not talk to me much. He tell me his name one time, and he tell me he twelve years old. I think he has not been here long. I do not think he is here last Christmastime. If he was here, he did not talk to me then. Only he start to talk to me this year.”

“Well, I wouldn’t be surprised if he asked you to dance tonight, maybe.”

She blushed again. “I do not know. He do not talk much to me.”

“Yes, that doesn’t mean much. Sometimes guys are shy, you know.”

The conversation faulted for a moment as I continued brushing.

“Mr. Brandon?”

“Mister? What the hell you calling me mister for? Ooops! Don’t tell Teacher I said that.”

She snickered, then straightened her posture again. “You… you think that maybe, someday… I find nice man? A goot man, who can love me? Like you and Teacher?”

“What? Yes, of course, Anna. I have no doubt there’ll be many men. Lined up for miles and miles, wanting to marry you. Why would you ever think otherwise?”

She paused. “Because… because I am blind… and because, I am orphan.”

The brushing stopped as the seriousness of her interpretation settled into me. It was what she said, but also how she said it. There were none of the tears or breakdown one would expect with such a statement. It was something said by someone who some years ago had accepted it to be what it was. Truth of life.

I stood slowly and stepped around in front of her. Her eyes never strayed from staring at a point straight ahead. I thought about my words, carefully, as for a man such as myself, there were few to choose from. Finally, I knelt down and settled my hands gently on top of hers. I looked her in the eyes, her radiant blue eyes.

“Anna… please listen to me, okay?”

She nodded only once.

“I’m a man, and you say I’m a good man. You say you want to find a man like me someday. I can see really well, and very clear, with both of my eyes. And I can tell you, very honestly, that you are a young woman who is so incredibly beautiful. You have so much beauty. Men from all over the world will stop and watch you when you walk in a room. You’re so beautiful, that if I were a twelve-year-old man,

I'd be shy to talk to you. Not because you're blind, or an orphan. But because you are that beautiful."

Her hands fidgeted beneath mine, and I caught a small crack of a smile.

"I watch you here, with Teacher and the children. I know we haven't spent that much time together, but I see how you are. And as beautiful as you are on the outside, it doesn't even compare to how beautiful you are on the inside. You know, the more time I spend here with you and Teacher and the others, the more I'm beginning to understand that the best way to find the one. The right person, you should choose to spend the rest of your life with, is to keep your eyes closed."

I stared at her with intensity. I wanted her to get it, to understand everything that she was. How special and how beautiful, inside and out—and to never, ever, doubt herself. She was always so poised and seemed so confident, so unbreakable, that the whole conversation knocked me right out of the park. I was pissed off, to be honest. I wanted to grab her and shake all that shitty shit out of her. What or where had it come from? But I'd done some good. I could see it in the smile on her face, and the little extra glow that warmed her cheeks. I patted her hands, smiled, and stood from my perch.

Then she stood too… and we both stood there for a moment, and I didn't have a clue what the next step was. I'd gotten through the previous step, and it was a big one. So, I was pretty proud of myself.

Then she shot right at me, wrapping her arms around my waist and squeezing with everything she had. It felt *so* good. I squeezed her right back and planted a sweet kiss on top of her head.

I rubbed her back and spoke softly to her. "I guess I never really thought that you haven't really ever had a man, a dad, to talk to. You have Hans, but… he's not really there yet."

"His feet smell."

"Yeah, yeah, I've heard about the foot-odour thing. I'm gonna work with him on that." I broke our embrace and crouched down to her again, rubbing her shoulders. "I'm here now, okay? If you ever want to talk to a guy about something, I'm here for you. It's never a problem, so don't ever worry about it."

She nodded, and she looked as though her confidence had increased twentyfold. Something I'd never viewed as lacking in her.

"Okay, sweetie."

46

We managed to get everyone to the dining area on time. In her new dress, Lilly's chin was tipped up a little higher than usual, on our way down the stairs.

It was easy to tell that the children were a little nervous about spending the day with the children from downstairs. I could understand how they may feel a little inferior, for the obvious reasons, but I didn't know much about the sighted kids from below. There were at least a dozen of them, and they had their own teacher. I'd seen her a few times, but she didn't live there, and it was Tessa's duty to tend to them after hours.

Tatiana led the way down and into the dining hall, where the other children were already assembled with Tessa.

They were a decent-looking bunch, but I had to admit, our bunch looked a little more fortunate than theirs. So, maybe they could see. But they didn't have a Tatiana, and, I guess, they didn't have a me. They looked just as uncomfortable as our little ones. They stood still, lined up side by side on their end of the room as we lined up on the other. Like two battalions, one just as clueless as the next.

"All right, everyone!" Tessa said in her sing-song voice, as she walked around the room. "Is time for big Christmas day festival. Is everyone excited?"

There was some scuffling of feet on the hardwood, but not a peep otherwise.

"Oh, it does not sound like anyone is excited to go. Maybe then, we should not go this year. We can go back and have some studies, then, yes?"

"No!" That brave little voice belonged to our Hans. I reached down and gave him a pat on the back.

All it took was that one single child to say one single word. The tension had been broken and the group unionized instantly.

"Nooo!" the room erupted.

"Oh, well, all right, then. Maybe I try one more time. Is everyone excited for Christmas celebration day?"

"YEAH!" United they stood.

"Okay, this is much better." Tessa smiled at me.

Just then, in the doorway behind us, entered Faas and Helen. They found a place in our line and stood with pleasant smiles.

"Ah, and our other guests have arrived as well. This is Faas and Helen, they will be wit us today also, and can help if any children need. Everyone, please say hello."

"Hello," the group responded.

"Also, all of the children from downstairs, you understand that the children from upstairs are joining us today. They are very capable of doing all the same things we can, but they may need some help at times. So, it be nice if everyone makes friends and help everybody. Before we go, I like all children to introduce themselves so we know names."

After a round of introductions, we all headed downstairs, single file, with Tessa leading the way, and Faas and I bringing up the rear. It was a big group of kids, which had me concerned about how the day would roll out.

The landing at the doorway was a disaster. So Faas and I held back at the top of the stairs, till everyone managed their way out to the street. Outside, the air was mild. It would be a perfect day as long as the rain held off. And it looked like it would.

The ladies helped the children line up again, using the "buddy system." Which turned out to be an excellent idea, especially when they teamed up the seeing kids with ours. They'd meet some new friends and we wouldn't have to panic about them so much.

I watched curiously to see who Anna got teamed up with. I thought it might be Fritz, due to their being close in age. But it was another girl, maybe a year or two younger than her. Either way, everyone seemed to be happy with each other, and they all began chatting away.

"Okay everyone," Tessa walked up and down the line. "Because we a big group, I bring my whistle. One blow on whistle"—she demonstrated—"mean to stop. Two blow on whistle"—another demo—"mean to go. Everyone understand?"

"YEAH!" everyone called back.

"Okay." Tessa scurried back to the front of the line. *"Tweet-tweet!"*

The line moved forward, as designed.

The streets were alive with people doing the very same thing as us. Performers were in abundance, and there was no lack of stimulation for any of the children.

It was nice to see everyone work together. The sighted children were taking extra special care to inform their new friends of everything going on.

Then our kids started showing off their clicking skills and the tide changed from being told what was around them, to telling the others. The kids from downstairs were completely stunned by their ability, and it turned into a game of "guess what's over there." Our kids were hitting about a ninety percent accuracy. Not bad, considering they weren't nearly as fluent as their teacher yet.

It seemed we were heading in a specific direction. A direction I had yet to be informed of, but it wasn't long till I figured it out. It was a couple blocks down, a turn here and another there, till we hit the entrance of a giant Christmas tree market.

I was wondering about the Christmas tree tradition. I learned then that they do have them, and decorate them like we do back home. I was told that the tree decorating would happen at the party that night.

"So, children, here we at Christmas tree market. Today we help to pick tree, and we have two strong men to carry back for us." She smiled at Faas and I in the back row.

I looked over to see Faas's jaw drop. "Oh… shit," he muttered.

"Yeah, that goes for me too," I replied through clenched teeth. Smiling and waving to the ladies up front.

We followed the group around the market, while they weighed up the options and shortlisted some possibilities. Then, they let the children vote till one was finally selected. It wasn't the biggest of the bunch, but it was big enough to make me suddenly feel ill.

Tessa paid the merchant as they secured it with twine, and handed it over. It was at least ten feet tall by my calculations. To help prevent any excessive ranting from Faas on our journey back through the streets. I offered to take the heavy end, and let him lead the way. And so, we separated from the group. Tessa filled us in on their intended path, so we could catch up with them later.

It was mid-afternoon by that point, and the streets couldn't have been any more packed. As we maneuvered through town, shavings of bark and needles found their way inside my clothes, and into zones where one doesn't welcome prickly things.

There was a lot of shifting and chaffing, with one of us pulling while the other tried to stop or dodge. Pedestrians did their best to accommodate our blessed quest, but certain run-ins were unavoidable.

I felt like we'd crossed the checkered flag when we made it back to the orphanage and dropped the tree outside the front door. But maneuvering it up the stairs and around the corner into the kitchen was more of a task than the journey through the streets had been.

Finally, we got it seated in its base, which had been left out for us. It was bent over slightly, because the top skimmed the ceiling. But when we cut the twine and its branches fell to their natural state, she was a damn fine choice.

"C'mon man." I slapped Faas on the shoulder. "I'll buy you a beer."

We headed into to the first pub we saw and found a table by the entrance. The place wasn't that busy yet, as not everyone had just carried a Christmas tree five or so city blocks.

"Ahhh," Faas gasped after his first sip. He set his bottle down, took off his toque, and shook some plumage from it. "This needles is everywhere," he grunted, then raised his eyebrows at me. "So, we have this beer, then try to find them in all tis crazy?"

We both looked out the window, to the dense population.

"Yeah, I don't know. I might head off for a bit and do some shopping.'

"Shop? More of this shop? You always, too much shop. You should not spoil children so much."

"Yeah, it's not for the kids. Not for our kids. It's for the others, downstairs. I don't think they have anything for Christmas. Nothing much, anyway. I can't spend a lot on them, and I really don't know what to get. But it's beating my conscience a bit. We've never had much to do with them, but they're being really good with our kids today. I think… I just gotta go find some little things for them. Some treats at least."

"*Hmph.*" Faas smirked.

"You go ahead and find the others. Tell them I'll catch up in a bit. Don't tell

Tatiana, though, please. She'll give me shit."

Faas rolled his bottle around in his hands for a moment. "No, I will go wit you. Is right, what you say. I will like to help also." His grin flipped into a full smile. "Let us go. Is important for children to have Christmas."

So, we went to the market, and we had some fun. A couple of guys fighting through the stupendous chaos, gathering things we thought would be of interest to the kids. Some small toys, toques and mittens, bouncy balls, and what-nots. By the time we were done, we had a couple big bags, stuffed full. Then back to the orphanage we went, and stashed them on the top shelf in the pantry.

We hurried back out to the street, and there was no stopping for any beer this time, as it had been a couple hours since we'd parted from the group and the sun was beginning to set. Soon, the Christmas light show would begin, and we'd best be there. I knew I was going to receive a certain level of shit as it was.

It didn't take long to find them. They were sitting stationary on a bridge, overlooking the canal. Waiting for the spectacle to happen. Looking around the street, it seemed the rest of the crowd were taking the same approach.

I snuck up and wrapped my arms around Tatiana. "Hey sweetie."

She turned to me with a suspicious look. "Hmm, you be gone for long time. Was big tree, but should no have take you so long."

"Yeah, I know. Faas and I had some other things to take care of."

"Yes, I understand this. I smell on you breath."

"Oh, right, the beer. We did stop for a beer after we dropped off the tree. That thing was nasty to get back to the orphanage."

"Yes, I sure it is." She turned from me. Not cold, but definitely cool.

I let her think what she liked, she who knew all. What I knew was that after she found out what we'd really done, after she vented about spending the money of course, I'd definitely be getting some special dry humping that night. *Mmmmm, mmm! Love me some dry hump!*

"So," I looked around at what was going on, which was nothing much. "What's going on? What are we standing here for?"

She stepped back and leaned into me, the coldness melting away as she curled my arms around her. "Is for lights. Is get dark now, lights come on soon."

Church bells rang loudly and the streets grew silent. They played through a tune, which took several minutes. Then they began to count down the time. On the second *bong*, the city sprang to life. All the lights turned on instantly, and the crowd went nuts!

The bells then broke into a waterfall of notes. A shower of streamers, confetti, and fireworks exploded into the air.

The illuminations were like nothing I'd ever seen before. Rows of lights streamed from post to post. Windows aglow in fantastic design. Overhead, stretching from one building to another, across the entire expanse of the street, appeared to be a silken fabric woven from pixie light.

I turned around to see the famous Christmas tree of Dam Square, towering in beauty. I watched as the marvels of wonder twinkled in each child's wide and wondrous eyes.

Once the bells ceased, a choir began. Low and soft at first, and then building up to full volume. It was a beautiful night. The celebration went off without a hitch.

I turned to Tatiana. "It's beautiful, really, really beautiful." I leaned in and kissed her. She responded with lips pursed, firm and resistant. Similar to kissing someone who was upset with you because you'd gone for a beer after delivering a Christmas tree, rather than return immediately to her and the children.

"What?" I teased.

"Nothing, I is only no much happy with you. Of course, you have simple job to do, and you go for beer."

"*Pfft*, beer. We had one beer, and we earned it. That tree was a shitty thing to get through town."

"One beer. You say only one beer, but is gone many hours." She snubbed her nose in the air. "Is okay, you like beer better than to have time with children and I."

I grinned and pulled her closer. "But, honey…" I leaned in for another kiss and she turned her head, exposing her cheek. I took what I could get, and planted a big wet one. "Well, I'm not going to let it spoil our special evening. But you can, if you like."

We spent another hour walking around to view the displays. The children seemed to have become the best of friends. With the sighted children fighting over each other to explain the surroundings, and our group feeling flattered by all the attention. Then we began to slowly work our way back through the festive wonders of the holiday season, to the orphanage, as there were many things to get done that evening.

Back at the orphanage, groups of three children went into the landing at a time, in order to avoid the catastrophe encountered on the way out. Faas and I held up the back, as usual, and found a seat on a bench adjacent to the door.

My feet were killing me. It'd been a long, busy day, with a lot of miles put on by tree hauling, good-deed shopping, and light watching. I was looking forward to getting back inside.

Group by group, the sidewalk emptied. I gave it a minute after the last few disappeared inside, but no one apparently gave a shit about us. I supposed that Tatiana had spoken to Helen about the beer on my breath, and both had decided to write us off for the evening. Which actually would've worked for me, as I could've used another beer or two by then.

But we raised ourselves from the bench and made our way inside. The landing was all but black. The only light coming from the dining room, accompanied by sounds of delighted children getting ready to decorate the tree… the tree that we'd carried over.

Every shoulder in the room was cool to us men. I could say that Tatiana and Helen did it purposefully. The others simply had Christmas fever.

So, we pulled up a seat at one of the tables placed way to the back, out of the chaos. I didn't feel that Helen was as determined to make a point as my sweetie. She'd been married to Faas for many years, and if beer on the breath was a problem for her, their relationship would've failed a week into courtship.

Through the corner of my eye, I watched Tessa go into the pantry. Only a second after she'd entered, she returned and stood in the doorway, looking befuddled as she scratched her head. She looked back into the pantry, then back to the common area.

When Helen came close, Tessa pulled her aside. After a minute of dialogue, I watched Helen shake her head, then go and fetch Tatiana.

Faas was beside me, watching the whole thing unfold. We did a silent fist bump under the table, pretending not to notice.

The three women huddled together for a few moments, but there was no hint that any of them suspected it to be us. Which was a little disappointing.

Tatiana seemed to be in a bit of a huff as she went to the wall hanger, grabbed her coat, and exited through the door. I stood, but as soon as I did so, Helen was on me.

"No." She placed her hand on my chest and looked me sternly in the eye.

"Please, there is little problem, maybe she just need some time."

I leaned into her. "But—"

"No!" she insisted.

"But!?... You sure she's all right? She didn't look all right!"

"She just need some time. Sit now, she is fine."

I did as instructed, but I wasn't happy about it. This is how it was supposed to go: she would find the presents, to which I would announce myself and Faas as the heroes and saviours. Then she would sneak me upstairs, where she would proceed to strip naked and give me a private pole dance.

So far, nothing was going according to plan.

I watched the clock; five minutes passed, then ten. If Helen wasn't standing right in the doorway, I would've been gone after her. But I was blocked up. She really didn't want me going after Tatiana.

Fifteen minutes passed, then at seventeen minutes and forty-three seconds since her departure, she returned, and I gasped with relief.

She marched over to Faas and I and stopped right in front of us with her lips pursed tight… really tight. Then, from behind her back, she pulled out a six-pack of beer, with a little red Christmas bow stuck to it and set it down on the table.

Speechless, Faas and I looked at the beer, then up at the group of ladies, now encompassing the table.

"I sorry." Tatiana said. A smile had cracked somewhere just below the surface, but she was holding it back. "Please forgive to me, I was be a… bitch."

"Ahhh." I allowed myself to have some fun with it. "*Bitch*… that's a new English word for you."

Her cheeks began to glow, as she struggled to say anything further.

"The bags of gifts you found in the closet are for the children. The children from downstairs," I informed them. "We saw how good they were with our kids today, and I really didn't know if Santa—"

"Sinter." Faas nudged me with his elbow.

"Right, *Sinter*. We didn't know if Sinter would have any gifts to deliver them. So, we wanted to make sure that he did. After we dropped off the very heavy, and annoying Christmas tree, we went for one beer, then snuck over to the market to make sure all the children would have something."

All three ladies were standing in front of us with humble smiles. Their eyes glossed over and their jaws clenched tight to hold back a swell of emotion.

"Yes, this is what we think when we see this. I say, I is… sorry"

I pulled her around the table and down onto my lap, where I hugged her tight and gave her a big kiss. I noticed a stray tear on her cheek. She smiled and buried her face in my shoulder, with a huff.

A muffled question resonated through my collarbone. "Why you no tell me you do this?"

"Well, if I'd've told you earlier, Faas and I wouldn't have a free six-pack of beer in front of us."

My smartass comment earned me a playful slap on the cheek and a very grateful kiss. Helen wasted no time getting on her Faas, and then we all welcomed Tessa over to share in our thanks.

With all emotions settled, the women went back to help the children, while Faas and I popped a couple caps, and toasted to a great evening.

Tree decorating was quite the event. The bottom quarter of the tree was sagging under the decorative weight. While everything north of five feet was looking pretty desolate.

Again, the brood from down-under were being mindful of making sure our kids were included, handing them sparkling coloured balls and leading them to the tree to hang them. Gold and silver tinsel was everywhere, as if it had been shot out of a Silly String canister. A group of girls led by Gaby and Lilly had busied themselves decorating Hans. Everyone was laughing and chasing each other around the room.

It took some time for the ladies to relocate the tree's decorations a little more evenly, and then it was time for the main event. The mounting of the star. I sat back with Faas, chuckling and waiting to see their grand plan for getting it to the top.

"Brandon! Please come." Tatiana beckoned to me, and the mystery was solved.

I was expecting a bigger fight between the children over who would be the lucky assistant. But they all agreed fairly quickly that Hans would have his turn that year.

I unravelled him from the mess he'd found himself in, then handed him the star, which was really big and awkward. It had a cone on the bottom for mounting, but the tree was already scraping the roof enough to be hunched over. I lifted him onto my shoulders and had to push myself into the lower branches so he could get close enough to have a feel around for what he was doing. Of course, there was no lack of direction from the… everyone, causing my Christmas blood to boil.

There was a lot of commotion up there. Squirming around, raking of eyeballs, pulling of hair, and at least one breakage of wind. But it the end—I tip my hat to the little man—he got it done.

I stood back to have a look and brush the needles from my everywhere.

It was a miracle it managed to stay put. He'd gotten the cone over the tip of the tree, but there was no room for it to extend any higher. So, one of the points seemed to be carved into the ceiling to keep it in place.

Everyone paused for a study, then the cheers erupted.

"Okay, is time for lights." Tatiana rubbed my back.

"Nope"—I held up my hands—"I can't do lights here. The plugs don't even make sense to me. It's Dutch stuff. Way over my head. Faas is the man for this one."

I heard a complaint from the man table.

Helen was quick to intervene, scurrying over to her husband for a quiet discussion.

Her words you couldn't make out, but Faas's…

"But, Helen! Is bullshit!" He waved his bottle over in my general direction as she worked to calm him.

"But is not right. He know this plug. I see him. He plug in stuff all the time."

I couldn't help chuckling. "All right, you grumpy old Sinter!" My comment got a round of giggles from the children. "I'll help you out, c'mon." I waved him over.

Helen gave him a sweet kiss and thanked him. He grumped a little on his way over, finishing off the bottom of his bottle and setting it on a table as he passed.

The children cheered for him, and the grump-face cracked a grin, then a full-fledged smile.

There was a lot of lying on the floor and crawling through the branches. The children resisted at first, but after one broke the seal, they all took turns bouncing on Faas's belly.

There were several candid objections from Faas at first, then he exercised his tickling skills for defence. Which only added excitement to the game.

Lights took at least an hour. By the time we were done, the children had all found something more entertaining to do. Then, Tessa announced it was time to turn off the lights for the lighting of the tree, and all hands were back on deck. She lit a few candles around the room to give some light to the anxious dark, while Helen went over to the door and womanned the switch.

"Okay! Turn the lights off," Tessa directed.

The lights went off and we all stood in dim, flickering silence. Then Faas plugged the main cord into the wall and… It lit up!… Well, kind of; the bottom and the left side of the mid-section lit up.

"What!" Faas stood and scratched his head. "What in the f—"

"Faas!" Helen interrupted.

The ceiling lights were flicked back on and we went back to work, Faas crawling back underneath and me digging back into the branches. There was some yelling and slight obscenities. I found some connections I suspected to be wrong and made what I could only guess to be a correction. Then we were ready for round two.

Everyone went back to their positions, ceiling lights went out, and… number two was the charm.

The room was aglow with the warmth of Christmas.

I put my arm around my girl and gave her bum a little pat. She wrapped her arms around me. "Is work? I feel light."

I turned to her. She wore a little Santa hat, with the cotton ball tip flopped over the side of her face. The tree lights filled her eyes with a perfect reflection. It caught me in a trance as I stood and let her beauty consume me.

"Yes, it all worked. It's the most beautiful Christmas tree I've ever seen. And you… You're the most beautiful Christmas elf I've ever kissed." Then we had our most special Christmas kiss, in the warm Christmas light.

I took my elf back to the man table, where we met with Helen and Faas, who were snuggled together. Faas handed me a freshly cracked bottle as we sat down.

The children all sat on the floor at the base of the tree, then, to my surprise, Lilly stood in the centre of the room and announced she was singing a Christmas song.

It was just her, all by herself. Tatiana squeezed my hand.

"Watch now," she whispered.

Lilly stood in a single sliver of light, surrounded by complete darkness, and started singing. Low and soft at first, a little case of stage fright. But after the intro, she kicked it up and the room held its breath. She became so hypnotic that the room and everything in it just fell away.

It definitely wasn't Dutch "Jingle Bells." It was slow, tender, and enchanting. In the stillness of the night, in a room filled with candles and shimmering reflections of the season, it was impossible to focus on anything other than the angels reaching out to us through the voice of a little orphan girl.

There was a feeling of untarnished beauty and peace. The sound travelled unobstructed, directly to my heart. As if it were coming from somewhere within, beneath the darkness. I can guarantee there wasn't a dry eye in the place.

It was a moment I never wanted to end, and one I will remember, always. When she finished, the audience sat in silence for a second, before a light applause began. Then grew, one by one, into a standing ovation.

She lifted her dress and took a bow, then the lights came back on and we were all brought back to the present.

Tessa brought out some snacks she'd prepared earlier for everyone. We'd been so busy, I'd forgotten all about food till we dug in, and the room went silent again, besides the sounds of little mouths chewing. No one wasted anytime, as after the food was consumed and cleanup was complete, the Christmas dance would begin.

With everyone fed, the tables were relocated, then Tessa put out some treats and started some dance music.

The girls were into it right away, joining together in the middle of the room for a group dance. The boys moped around a bit, hands in the pockets, feigning a lack of interest and picking chocolates from the bowls. The adults all sat back and watched for a bit. Then, the beat hit the ladies' feet and they pulled on us to come out dancing with them. Faas and I resisted; we were pretty set on not getting involved with dancing. I had no skills past the honky-dork-dance, and I preferred to flaunt those skills never. But they laid on the guilt trip, suggesting that if we came out then the little guys would see it was all right to dance and they'd let loose.

But Faas and I had one and a quarter beers left a piece, and we were quite determined to sit there and enjoy them. We had hung the star, connected the lights, even gotten two big bags of toys for orphan kids. But instead of showing us some mercy, they expected stellar performances from us on an hourly basis. Really, forced dancing is very similar to assault, or at least harassment. *No* should mean no… right?

In the end, which came very quick, we lost. So, out to the dance floor we went for the honky shuffle.

DJ Tessa wasn't playing around with a little children's "Wheels On The Bus" soundtrack. She was playing the new hip dance tracks.

To that point, I'd never spent any time on the dance floor with Tatiana. It was yet another situation where her lack of vision worked in my favour. If she could see, I'm certain she would've considered other partners. I planned my routine to be evasive enough to stealth through any supersonic clicking that may be focused in my direction.

But as soon as we got out there, her attention focused on something other than my moves. That woman could dance! Stepping and gyrating. Twirling so her dress lifted just enough to make every man in the room pay attention. Hips wiggling as she wriggled down to the floor and back up. Raising her arms through her hair and letting it fall like she didn't care. She moved around me, running her hands around my body and grinding her hot sweetness all over me. She brought her lips close to mine and whispered the lyrics, the warm waft of her breath begging me to take a taste. But she spun around, denying me the pleasure. She pressed her back against me, reaching her hands back to hold me in position as she wiggled her hips hard against my groin and slid down my body.

I had no moves to match; the only sensible reaction I could muster was to increase my pace. Step left, right, left right, keep the arms moving, till I became short of breath and built a sweat. I wanted to give that time to her, as she was really enjoying herself. I didn't want her to stop. No one wanted her to stop.

All the young-ladies wished to be her. All the soon-to-be men wanted to be me. But with much, much better moves. I was a poster boy for instructional dance lessons for white males, on the "before" side. Someone with business sense should've been there handing out flyers.

Tatiana took a couple steps back, her long slender legs glowing like the most priceless of ivory. She grabbed the sides of her dress and shook back and forth, bobbing her head side to side, her hair swooping and spinning like silk ribbon.

Then the song ended. Everyone cheered and clapped, and her smile lit a fire in my heart.

She smiled to the room, a little shy from the attention, but soaking it up at the same time. She stepped toward me, and I reached out my hand to pull her in.

The energy had frisked her up some. She draped her arms around my shoulders and pulled herself tight to me, kissing me lustfully on the lips, then worked her subtle way down my cheek to my neck. "Did you like dance with me?" she breathed sensually.

"Did I like dancing with you?" I chuckled and kissed the top of her head. "Did I ever! You're a very, very sexy dancing woman. All the boys wish they were me right now. I'm thinking I may need some time alone in the bathroom."

She giggled through laboured breaths. "You think of me."

"I always think of you, sexy." I reached down and gave her bum a little pinch.

I took a break and returned to the table. I grabbed the remainder of my bottle and tipped back a healthy swig, then looked at Faas. He looked dumfounded, to say the least. His expression was mute, except for his wide eyes. "You fucking lucky man, hey."

My face turned hot as I looked across the table to Helen, who was smiling tenderly at me. She reached over and patted my hand. "You such beautiful togeter." She was tearing up.

"Hey!" Faas nudged me and lowered his voice as he pointed to Tatiana, who was waiting excitedly with the children for the next song to start. "I say now to you. You think of this time now. You not marry her, you is fucking stupit."

"Faas!" Helen reached over and slapped his hand. "Not be rude."

But he didn't waver, staring at me intensely. So focused, it was clear it was a complete fact to him that I would regret letting her get away. When you get locked into a conversation with someone that convinced, it stirs your mind. I felt the hairs on the back of my neck rise.

I turned from Faas and looked at her. Bent over and speaking to the children, her beautiful smile was like a magnet to everyone, young and old.

Was he right? Would I wake up one day, old and weathered, and go to the kitchen to pour a cup of coffee for one. Sit down at the table, and look out the window to reminisce of that time? Of the fork in the road that could have led to me happily pouring a cup for two and sharing a kiss with my love? If I let the opportunity slip past, would I ever find another as perfect? How far could I make it without her? As my story goes, I had proven caustic on my own.

Then the next song began, snapping me out of thought.

That time, all the children—boy and girl—went out on the dance floor. Tatiana was the centre of the commotion, helping everyone find some comfort in their performance and dazzling with her own.

But not everyone was out shaking it up. There was one single boy avoiding the mass. He was a downstairs kid. Bigger than the rest, then, I remembered.

I turned to Helen and pointed at him. "Do you know that boy?"

She looked. "This boy? Yes, I know this boy, he is Fritz, very nice boy."

"Yes, Fritz!"

I took another gulp of beer, then rose from the table and made my way toward him.

I took a seat at the table he was hanging around, picking from a bowl of treats. "Hey!" I smiled at him.

He was a bit taken back by my sudden attention.

"Do you speak English?"

He fidgeted. "Yes," he nodded, his tone very timid.

"Hey, right on." I smiled even bigger in hopes of helping him relax. "Do you know who I am? My name is Brandon. I help with the children upstairs."

"Yes, I know this." He managed a little smirk back.

"Your name is Fritz, right?"

He nodded again.

"You don't like to dance, Fritz?"

He considered the question, then nodded his head in a somewhat circular motion, which I took as a maybe.

"Do you know that girl over there?" I pointed to Anna, dancing close to her teacher.

When his face turned beet red and he lowered it to the floor, I knew I'd hit a sweet spot.

I couldn't help chuckling. "Hey!" I motioned toward her. "You think she's pretty?"

His face turned even redder, and if there was a hole somewhere convenient, I'm sure he would've shoved his head in it till I went away.

"Hey, it's all right to think a girl's pretty. I think she's really pretty. Her name's Anna, you know her? You've talked to her before, right?"

It took a bit, but he nodded again.

"You should ask her to dance."

He just stood there, stunned. I knew where he was mentally. A strong part of him wanted to run away, but an even stronger part of him wanted to dance with that pretty girl. It was going to take some solid convincing to crack his shell, so I had to lay it all on the line.

"Listen, you know why I came over to talk to you? You know how I know your name?"

He had resorted to shaking his head from side to side continually.

I pointed back out to Anna with added emphasis. "That pretty lady told me. She told me you've talked to her a few times, and she told me she thinks you're really nice and handsome. And she is hoping you'll ask her to dance tonight."

That got a smile out of him, but he still needed a push.

"So, you gotta ask her to dance, big guy. That's how it works. You're the man, you gotta make the first move. I know it's hard, but I'm telling you that she wants you to ask her to dance. She will one hundred percent say yes! That's my word to you. All you have to do is go up to her and ask her to dance, and boom! You're dancing with the prettiest girl in the room." I was certain I was talking too quickly for him to understand everything, but the main point was getting through.

"So, here's what I'd do. Fast songs are a little tough. You saw me dance with Tatiana, right?"

He nodded.

"Yeah, not very good, right? I mean, she's a great dancer, but me, not very good, right?"

He giggled.

"Slow songs are easier. So, when a slow song comes on, you gotta go ask her to dance. Can you do that, buddy?"

He shrugged.

"No, not this," I said, mocking his shrug. "Be the man, go out and ask her to dance. If you ask her to dance, she'll be really happy. I promise… Okay?"

He fidgeted a little and looked at Anna, then down to the floor to watch his foot scrape around.

"C'mon, big guy. I'll be right here watching, okay?"

He finally squeaked out a nod.

"All right!" I smiled, then held out my fist. "You know how to do this?"

He paused.

"Hold out your fist like this." I shook mine.

He followed my instruction and I bumped it, which produced a more confident smile.

I smiled back. "Okay man, next slow song!"

I sat up straight and looked around for DJ Tessa. Once located, I headed straight for her. Eyes wide with urgency, I caught her attention and stage-whispered, "Play a slow song! Play a slow song!"

She looked like she was beginning to panic, so when I reached her I explained the situation. She got very excited, and as soon as the current song ended, she found something slow, with a hint of romance. Then we stood back and watched.

As soon as the song came on, the dance crew broke up and went in separate directions. Leaving the dance space virtually empty.

Fritz looked at me, and didn't move.

I had to act fast and put something together to help him out. I ran over to Tatiana and pulled her by the arm.

She turned, startled. "What!"

"Go! You gotta go stand by Anna."

"Anna? Where is this?"

"Argh!" My frustration was building. So, I found Anna and dragged Tatiana over to her. "Okay, you two stay here. Don't move!"

With them in place, I ran back to Fritz. "Okay buddy, I'm gonna help you out here. You come with me. I'll ask Tatiana to dance and then you ask Anna, all right?"

I could see the reluctance was still there, but I was beating it down. He hesitated, then nodded.

"All right, c'mon."

I led the way and, thankfully, he followed on my heels.

I stepped up to Tatiana. "Tatiana," I began, then looked down at Fritz.

He didn't do anything, so I waved him on.

"A-Anna."

Anna flinched at the strange voice.

I leaned down to him and whispered, "Tell her who you are."

"Is me… Fritz."

Oh man, the smile on that little girl's face. Her cheeks turned rosy, and if I had a picture of her at that moment, we could start the bidding at priceless.

Tatiana's eyes widened. She clued in right away to what was happening and made sure to keep her focus on me, in order not to intimidate the youngster.

Ice broken, I continued. "Tatiana, could I please have this dance?" Then I turned to Fritz and gave a nod and a wink.

"Anna… c-could… you dance wit me… p-please."

Tatiana smiled and held out her hand, then whispered to Anna to do the same.

I accepted my lady's hand, and Fritz followed my lead.

The four of us made our way to the centre of the dance floor. I placed my hands on my lady's waist and gave Fritz the go-ahead to do the same. The girls placed their hands on our shoulders, and we began.

The song was already halfway through, but big steps had been taken. Tatiana pulled in closer and demanded I tell her everything that was happening.

Fritz watched me and followed my steps. There were a couple stumbles between the two at first, but they fell into a rhythm quickly. They kept a very respectful distance, until some toes got stepped on here and there. Which ignited some giggling, which led to talking and, slowly but surely, they relaxed and got a little closer to each other. Young love was in the air.

Happy tears streamed from Tatiana's eyes, which she repeatedly wiped on my shoulder, to the point it was damp. "Now I wish I can see," she whispered.

I kissed her neck tenderly as she laid her sobbing head against my shoulder. "They look very sweet together. He's being a real gentleman with her. And she's so happy, Tatiana, so beautiful. You've raised her into a very beautiful young lady." I tucked my finger under her chin and raised her head to kiss her lips.

Tessa followed that song up with another slow one. Many of the others had joined in, dancing with whoever was willing. I watched Gaby grab Hans by the hand, apparently frustrated by his not asking her to dance, and she dragged him out to the floor. After that song, DJ Tessa went back to mixing it up, some fast, some slow, and Fritz and Anna were inseparable.

Later on, Tatiana and I joined Faas and Helen, who were snuggled up at the table, and we all watched the children dance themselves out.

Tessa was winding things down with a slow song when a giggling girl from downstairs ran out to the young couple and held a small branch from the Christmas tree over their heads and announced it as mistletoe.

Everyone at our table held their breath. I thought things would blow up and the two would instantly part ways. Tatiana was pinching me violently in the arm for details.

Fritz and Anna stopped dancing but remained joined. It was obvious they were way beyond their comfort zone. But neither left. They looked at each other and remained perfectly still. Then Fritz leaned in with a stutter, and... it was quick! So quick you could almost doubt it had happened, but *man*, it had happened. And all the children exploded with little children taunting and giggles.

Tatiana and Helen burst into tears, holding each other.

Gaby wasn't gonna have nothing to do with Anna stealing the spotlight. She grabbed the branch and went after Hans, who dropped to the floor, covered his mouth, and turtled.

It was getting late and the kids were starting to tire and grow irritable. So, Tatiana stood and announced that everyone was to return to their floors and get ready for bed. If they did it quietly and quickly, they could all return to the dining area for one last special treat.

So, they all shut up and did as they were told.

We laid pillows and blankets around for all, and when they returned, I invited them all into my world of *Harry Potter*.

47

The rest of the Christmas season went on much the same.

On weekdays, I'd get up early and head down to the boathouse for breakfast with Faas and Helen. Then we'd consider variables, like the weather and our level of ambition, to determine whether we'd attempt to get any work done. Some days it was yes, others not so much.

It was nice to have time with Tatiana and the children, but after a while, I began to go stir-crazy. I confess that it was the first time in my young history when I wanted to go to work. For a break in the monotony, but also to fill back up the wallet, as Christmas had proved more taxing than planned. It was my own fault.

All the children were spending much more time together as a whole. Tatiana and Tessa would do what studies needed attention in the morning, then everyone would meet for lunch in the dining area and remain there, playing and helping the women with Christmas baking and cooking, till I would read them to sleep in the evening. It was good to see everyone expanding their horizons, but there were times when I missed our cozy little upstairs room. The times when it was just us. I was purposefully pacing the story out to finish by New Year. Then, perhaps leave Harry Potter to rest, so that maybe we could retreat back to the way we were, after the holidays.

Christmas Day and the New Year were celebrated around the tree. There was still one last celebration to go. The tree had dried to tinder, its branches bare and brittle. So, on the first weekend in January, I helped with a strange tradition. We tied the tree back up, as best we could and dragged the tree down the stairs and out into the street. Faas and Helen were there to meet us with a little dried up tree of their own.

Snow had fallen over the last few days. Thick, wet, heavy snow. The way it blanketed the city, over the old stone bridges right up to the waterways where boats still puttered by, gleamed a storybook setting. The streets were a bustle as always. Everyone dressed in their heavy, winter gear, sipping coffee or cocoa as they passed. What made the scene that much more extraordinary, was that every group was dragging at least one Christmas tree behind them, headed to a designated point in the centre of town, for the annual Christmas tree burning.

It was the most bizarre migration I'd ever witnessed. The streets were littered with branches and pine needles. The air was alive with anticipation. Many had their trees tied to the back of their bikes and were pulling them along the ground. The fresh snow making their attempts comical, to say the least. We had to pay extra attention to our flock, to ensure none got tangled up and carried away.

The thing I had a hard time wrapping my head around was that at the end of the line, all these trees would be thrown into one gigantic pile and set on fire. I didn't really believe it, but I'd already been proven wrong once that merry season.

Tessa derived an excellent plan of getting the children to help drag the tree to the event. So, they lined up on either side of it and each grabbed a branch. It kept everyone in line and prevented any straying. And best of all, Faas and I needed to put in minimal effort. Having only to drag their small tree.

We were the slowest group on the street, but it was early, and we were in no rush. It took a block for the barge of children to stop tripping and fall into rhythm. They were all determined to get it done together, without the help of the adults.

Anna and Fritz were side by side, and he was doing what he could to step up as a man and carry her share, along with his, so she wouldn't be burdened. Anna revelled in his care and attention to her. They had become very close, the best of friends. I'd noticed how Tatiana had been spending more time with Anna, talking to her about the ways of men, and she didn't hold anything back. Some of it made me uncomfortable, to the point I felt I should be somewhere else. But Anna absorbed every word. Guaranteed, any man hoping to get anywhere with her, best be packing the most honest of intentions.

It was good for the two of them, Anna and Fritz. The situation they were in wasn't favourable for them to find anyone similar to associate with. At that age, with all the changes soon to come, or already happening. Young curiosities, and a desire to be a part of something more than what they were. I wondered where those two would be in ten years' time.

We hobbled, grunted, and groaned for several blocks, holding up traffic at times and having a few near misses. But we made it to the centre.

The square was packed. We found a spot and set our trees down for the time being. I offered to get a round of coffees and hot chocolates, and Faas and Helen came along to assist. The lineups tested my fuse, but I seemed to be the only one in the area concerned with it. After we handed out the drinks, I managed to escape for a moment, to choke down half of a dry brownie I'd picked up on my way back from work one day. I'd decided it was always a good idea to keep one on hand. I was quick to rinse it down with a slosh of coffee, which I discovered was way too hot for gulping, only *after* I had gulped.

But my efforts to disguise it proved ineffective, as I returned to the group and found my Tatiana, who immediately detected an odour that had only become more familiar to her after meeting me. But she was in a good mood, and followed up with an innocent frown with a sweet kiss.

We waited patiently as the sun set, turning the sky a beautiful winter lavender. A healthy pile of trees had already been stacked inside a roped-off area in the middle of the square. The time to light it up was drawing near.

We organized the children again and they hefted the tree to start the final leg of the journey. Helen raced ahead to make sure the pile wasn't lit before they arrived.

We all crowded into the target area, and with a group effort, we managed to stack our trees with the rest, then retreated outside the ropes.

Two men inside the cordoned-off area prepared a couple of long torches, which looked like ones used to storm a castle. They sparked them up to flames that stretched high over their heads and danced with hunger. Then they made their way around the pile, igniting various points around the base. A slight breeze gave breath to the fuel and the carnivorous flames spread like… like a pile of dry trees on fire, on a breezy evening.

The heat was instant as the flames climbed high into the night sky. swirling to madness, hot enough to singe the feet of gods.

A brass band played a happy tune and we all stood back to watch. Tatiana was on my arm, Helen was on Faas's, and little Anna was on Fritz's. He was giving her a second-by-second playback of events.

My head tilted up to watch the highest tip of flame. It was crazy to me that they were making the bonfire right in the centre of the city.

I chuckled. "This is nuts, honey. Back home, this would be declared a natural disaster."

I put my arm around her and she snuggled in close. We shared a kiss, then sipped our drinks and relaxed in the warm glow.

People entered the ring, one after the other, hurling more trees onto the burning heap. Minding the flames, as they whipped from one direction to the next. The fire's savage roar grew and silenced the crowd, which fell into a trance as the fire stretched even higher into the darkness. I could feel its want, its need to spread, as it reached for anything out there to support its escape from its roped prison. Longing for more than what it had.

When the fire burned out, that would be it, and the season would end. Monday I would get up, grab my lunch, and head over to the dock.

My feeling of wonder became shadowed with concern. I felt a sinking in my chest, and I squeezed Tatiana a little tighter.

Would it be enough, day after day? What was the future? Or was I already living it? Could I settle for what it was?

A gust rushed between the buildings and the fire snarled, stretching to thin wisps, making a run for it, before dying back from exhaustion. All it wanted to do was run. To do as much with life as it could, before its time ran out and it was reduced to nothing more than a warm bed of ash.

Could anyone else feel it, the same as I?

48

Monday morning came, and I headed to the dock.

Snow crunched light beneath my feet, the air was cold and damp, and plumes of fog filled the air as I exhaled. With Christmas done, I was ready for springtime sooner than later.

I knocked on the boathouse door and went upstairs, where Helen had breakfast prepared. As I sat down, Faas started belting out a list of priorities that needed immediate tending. Things had returned to normal.

We'd made good progress on the boat destined for Peru in a few months' time. But we had to revisit ends that were left loose before the holidays. Although we could celebrate many things as completed, there was an equal amount left to tackle. There was no time left for backing down. Not for crappy weather or lack of interest. We were back into "head down, ass up" mode.

I was curious to see if and when the guys would return. It was Wednesday when Adlar arrived. He greeted me warmly and sat for a while as we exchanged some holiday stories. But he didn't stay long. He just stopped in to quiz Faas about whether there was enough work for all of them to help, and make some money.

Faas assured Adlar that there was lots of work left to do. Although the boat may have looked close to complete cosmetically, there was a lot of mechanical left to be done. And more times than not, that was the work that took the most time and patience.

Pleased with the news, Adlar shook our hands and went on his way. Never stating who would return, or when. Faas just shrugged it off, as always. It was their way, and he'd grown accustomed to it. Most of the rogues of the world were good people, they just lacked the concept of time or schedule.

The following Monday, all the guys returned, and again, we spent the better part of the morning talking Christmas. Of course, their tales were all of dizzy disorder. Booze, drugs, and women. All of it true in their minds. But knowing them enough, I guessed there to be a ten percent accuracy. Bullshit or not, they were always entertaining.

Life fell back into its routine. On the days we could get away a little early, we'd head out for a couple beers, but I never broke curfew—by much. Tatiana was never pleased with it, but she never got angry either. We had compromised, and found a middle ground. Christmastime had been so magical. Warm, full of love and self-discovery. Settled in it, I'd felt so full of love and giving. But as soon as it passed, the wonder faded. How quickly we can forget. It's disgusting, to be honest. But maybe it was just me who had the short-term memory.

Our heated encounters had even stopped. When, I couldn't recall. The ones where we would crawl all over each other till we were a sweaty pile of unsatisfied lust. I couldn't even remember the last time I'd seduced myself in the bathroom. It was possible my equipment was out of order. Was this to be my twenties?

The remainder of January flew past. In February, the sun began its return, and blessed us with random days of spring-like conditions.

One Friday the sun made an appearance from behind the clouds, for the first time in several days. There was a smell of blossoming flowers and days to come when we could shed our heavy coats and toques for shorts.

Springtime was a hard time for me to remain stagnant. I was one to suffer more than most from the fever I felt. It was the season for bloom and change.

After a long, hard day of stripping and sanding the railings, I cracked a beer and walked to the back of the boat, which was jutting out toward the canal. I took a swig and exhaled, then leaned against the railing, closed my eyes and breathed in the sweet, warm breeze.

I opened my eyes and looked at the glowing orange sun submersing into the water. My mind wandered to what adventures lay between me and it. I felt a strong urge to cast off the ropes, pull up anchor, and set off to find it. Back, into the unknown.

I took another sip, then shook off the urge. The truth was, that my anchor had been planted. And there was much more at stake than my own, selfish desires. The responsible thing to do was to turn away from such temptations. Convince myself that they were only temporary, and what I had was what I wanted. Perhaps the word was *needed*, more than *wanted*.

I turned away from what might be, and focused on the present.

I didn't know it then, but I wouldn't have to look to the far horizon for change. Go or stay, it always found me.

49

That night, when I got home, things didn't seem right.

Tatiana was being very short with me. There was beer on my breath, so obviously I attributed it to that. She'd been good with me in the New Year, as I mentioned earlier. But maybe there was a limit. Like, say, twenty. Twenty beers, either in one night or over a couple weeks. Once I hit the designated number, there was going to be some trouble. I made a mental note to keep track of my beers, so I could identify the breaking point. Maybe bring home some flowers or something.

I didn't say anything at first, nor did she. I just took the cold-shoulder treatment at dinner, which continued throughout the evening. Then she cancelled story time. We were working through the next book in the Harry Potter series. The children lived for story time. She'd never cancelled it before, and the smugness with which she denied the children's pleading, gave me notice that something beyond the smell on my breath was on her mind.

She'd left me to do the nightly rituals of tucking the children in, and I couldn't help noticing they'd also lost some of their normal liveliness. I started to ask about it, but then thought it better if I didn't. My mind started to race with possibilities. The biggest of them being that my bags would be packed and waiting for me in the other room.

I stood at the door, bid them a good night, then stepped across the landing and entered the bedroom, with caution.

Tatiana was already in her pajamas and tidying up some. I wouldn't describe her as angry, more like festering. Thankfully, I didn't find a pile of bags anywhere.

I knew she was aware of my presence, but she didn't give any acknowledgement. I sensed it was one of those times when I should make the first move.

I stepped toward her, just loud enough so as to not startle her. I stayed a couple of feet back; having no clue what was in store for me, if she might take a swing at me.

"Tatiana… Honey. I know something's wrong. Is it me? Did I do something to make you mad? Can you please talk to me?"

She didn't swing. She didn't turn and yell. She just continued on, mussing with the bedding.

So, I reached out and gently laid my hand on her shoulder. "Honey, please. I really don't know what's wrong. You're scaring me."

She turned to me, and her eyes looked mildly swollen. And although faint, the streaks on her face told me some tears had been shed.

"Sweetie," I placed my other hand on her shoulder. "What is it? Is it something I did? Please talk to me!"

"No, is nothing you do." She wiped at her eyes.

I felt a little relieved. But nothing I could think of outside of myself would set her off like that. So, I still wasn't convinced I was off the hook. I waited for her to follow up with some snide comment like *Is everything you do!…* But that wasn't what she said.

"Is people." She sniffled, sat down on the bed, and wiped at her eyes again.

I plucked a couple of tissues from the box on the nightstand and handed them to her. I crouched down in front of her and massaged her shoulder. She trembled.

"Okay… people. What people, honey? What did they do to you? Did they do something bad to you? Something to the children?" My muscles tensed.

She shrugged and huffed. "Bad, maybe good, I do not know this." She shook her head.

"Tatiana, you gotta tell me what's up, all right?" My voice grew loud. "If someone has done something bad to you, or the children, you have to tell me so I can fix it. Okay?!"

"People, they come back today. They no suppose to come on Friday, only on Wednesday. They have come here now two Wednesdays. Now they come today also."

People… Wednesdays?

My mind began to race. Some time ago, I remembered filing away something about Wednesdays. Something I thought to be insignificant, so I'd stacked in the mental "junk drawer." I'd absorbed a lot of junk since then…and burned some.

I dug deep and rifled through everything, throwing scraps left and right over my shoulders. Then I found it in a crumpled ball. I straightened it out, and my heart picked up, sending a hot, tense wave through my body.

"People, on Wednesdays?" I had a strong suspicion, but I didn't want to say it. As if saying it myself would make it true.

"Yes, people, for adoption. They come to here Wednesday in January. They spend time here with children. They come back then on this week, Wednesday. Now they come again today," she sputtered, tears coming more fluidly. "They come to speak at Tessa. I see them here. She say to me, 'The people, they liking to Lilly.'"

I know many would think for a guy like me, at my age, feeling so tied down, my thoughts may be *Woo-Hoo! One down, three to go!* But it actually hit me really hard. A sucker punch to the heart… Our Lilly.

I fell back onto my ass. I reached out and rubbed her leg and took a moment to myself. Watching her sob, as I considered the news.

I was lost for words. It wasn't supposed to be anything that could happen. She'd even said it wouldn't happen. But now it seemed possible.

"Well… I mean, it's not for sure, right? This doesn't just happen, right? It takes time. There's gotta be some sort of… process."

She nodded. "Yes, is no to happen now. But I meet them, when they come. They look nice, married people. Look like have good money. I think if they like, it is possible."

"Well… does Lilly know? Does she… like these people?"

"She no know now, what they thinking to do. I do not know if to tell her. She meet them, yes. They come to spend time with all children. But I see they like Lilly, she sing for them. They like her, yes. All people like to her."

I thought for a while longer—thought of Lilly, her pretty smile, and what a sweetheart she was. Of course, people who gave her a chance and saw her ability and her beauty would be crazy to not want her.

"I guess…" I felt my chest tighten. "That's what this is, right? That's why they're here. It's what's supposed to happen. So… so we should be happy… right? We should support her with this. As long as they're good people, and they're good for her, we should support her… them."

Tatiana held her breath and gave a courageous nod. Then she burst into her tissue.

I scrambled to my knees and held her tight. She shivered, and I squeezed tighter. I had no idea what to do from there. For her, for Lilly. Surely the others were going to be equally affected. No matter what, I had to play my part and get us all through it.

50

Not a cloud was to be seen in the bright sky, and the sun was warm, with a complementing breeze. I was back out at sea, and boy did it feel good.

The guys were all there. Not the pirates, the boys from back home. We were cheering and hollering at each other, each of us tucked into our own little, wooden rowboats. We were formed in a circle in the middle of the ocean, not a spec of land in sight. We were bouncing and bubbling on a behemoth geyser. Burbling to the surface, from somewhere fathoms below. It wasn't a geyser of water though. It was a gurgling dome of oil.

Our boats tipped and tilted, forth and right, back and side, like a mechanical bull. Every one of us was hooting and hollering at each other. We were high on life, with a confident attitude that life was really good and we were untouchable. It felt great! Everything, so great. We sat back, rode the bull, and got off on it.

Then the black boil receded, and set us adrift on the open ocean. Slowly, the good feeling eroded, and we all sat up and looked at each other in wonder. What had happened?

We began to drift apart, farther and farther. There was no tool for propulsion in my boat, or any of the others.

"Hey! Hey, guys!" I called out, but all I got back was a lonely echo, as they all retreated to small specks on the horizon. Then… gone.

I felt so alone. So helpless. Abandoned. What now?

I felt a coolness on my feet and looked down to see a pool of water building in the bottom of my boat. Inch by inch, it grew deeper. The boards began to creak and moan, then splinter. I was going down.

"Guys!... Hey!... What the fuck!? Somebody!" I screamed, but there was nothing, no one.

Sinking and sinking, to my waist, then up to my chest. I never had the urge to swim a stroke, just stood on the floor of the drowning vessel, to my neck, my nose. I breathed one last, final gulp of air, then—

I blasted upright in bed, sucking for breath and grabbing my chest.

I was in our room, in our bed, with Tatiana sleeping soundly beside me. I took a few more breaths and brought my heart rate back to living.

Thunderous drops of rain spattered against the windows. I welcomed the sound as soothing. All was dark and still in the room. But I wasn't going back to sleep, not after all that.

I crept softly from bed and stepped over to the window. Nothing moved beneath the streetlight. My mind was still spinning. Working on separating dream from reality. Going over events and bringing me back to what was real. To the events that had unfolded that night, the ones that had likely sent me to sea in my slumber.

What did it mean? Something?... Nothing?

I stood there, leaning against the sill, listening to the rain and looking over Tatiana's painting again. Funny, it hadn't changed a stroke since I arrived.

My mind relaxed back to reality, and the news of possibly losing our Lilly. And from there, my mind trailed down the branch of having referred to her as *our* Lilly.

But... she was ours. Ours from the day I stepped into that orphanage. I remembered meeting her. Remembered watching her sing, and grow. Remembered the time at the restaurant, when her dress was ruined. Remembered the beautiful performance at Christmas.

She was our Lilly. Each one had their own special light, and she definitely had hers. How dark would the place be without her? How much more lonely would the rain sound on the window, when she was not around? How much of us would leave with her?

The rain thundered down harder, or maybe it was only in my mind. How did we stop it from happening? Could we?... Should we?

Maybe Lilly would say no. But I remembered her saying she wanted to be part of a family, that day the kids made the cupcakes. So, what were we? I felt tears swell, and my sinus began to clog, as I swallowed a lump in my throat. I looked over at the bed, at her golden hair, which sparkled even in the dim light.

What were we?

It would be a long shot to convince a social worker that Lilly would be better off in an orphanage, with us. People with no future, and a man unwilling to commit. A man who comes home drunk and stoned.

If these people were as Tatiana described, we really didn't have a chance.

Of course, there was the "M-word." But it would take more than even that.

Really, we were just a couple of kids. Stowaways, in a small orphanage, taking advantage of government funding to play house. No education, in my case anyway. My only profitable experience came from the drill rigs, and I'd yet to see one of those around. Who'd want to plunk one of those ugly beasts down in the middle of the storybook village? Sneezy, Bashful, and Rig-Pig... kind of kills the romance.

I was in a land of prosper, for the educated. Outside of that, your options included tending bar, selling pot, waiting on tables, or scraping barnacles from boats... Billy.

I'd reached a point where I decided it best for me not to be alone with my thoughts. I slid softly around the room and got dressed, then gave Tatiana a tender kiss on her cheek and headed off to work.

The rain was heavy when I stepped into the street. A cold breeze was blowing in off the water, and it had no trouble biting through the light fleece I'd thought to be adequate. It went straight to my bones. So much, as to almost turn me around, running back to the warm shelter beneath our blankets. I pulled the hood over my head and watched the drops pound through the glow of the lights. I took a step off the curb with a splash, the icy water flooding into my shoe like a tsunami. A great start to the day.

I was exceptionally early to the boathouse. But, as I rounded the corner, I looked up to see the light on in the kitchen.

I knocked and entered, calling up the stairs.

Faas was sitting at the table and Helen was brewing a pot of coffee. They both raised their eyebrows when they saw me climb the last step.

"I, uh, couldn't sleep," I said with an innocent smirk. "Must be all the rain. Still not used to it."

They both grinned, and went back to their business.

I wanted to tell them… I'd planned to tell them, just to have someone to talk to. Maybe they could share some words of wisdom. Maybe, somehow, they could make it all better? But when I sat down and looked at them in their silent, sleepy state, I decided against it. I guessed it wasn't their concern. Besides, so far it was nothing, really. Just a slight chance… a small glimmer of interest. There was a better chance it would all pass by, rather than result in anything. So I convinced myself.

I remained quiet, and I waited for time to tell the tale.

All systems were full steam ahead at work. I kept myself busy and noticed my own lack of socialization with the others. I caught some of their curious glances, and was waiting for someone to ask. But they just let me be.

There were no beers after work, it was straight home to Tatiana and the children. Waiting for the next batch of news, hoping things would dissipate. A few days passed with nothing, then a week, then…

I returned home one evening and the tension hit me as soon as I entered the room. The children lacked their youthful energy, and were overly obedient. As if they'd been scolded all day. Even Sasha had her head down and her tail between her legs.

I found Tatiana alone in our room, fussing around.

"Hey!" I walked over to her. "How was your day, honey?" She stood straight and sighed. "The people come today."

I placed my hand on her shoulder. "What people, honey? The people who are interested in Lilly?"

"No… No those people. The people from government, who do adoption for children." She sniffled as her chin trembled.

"Okay, okay… and?" I sat down on the bed in front of her and held her hand between mine.

"They sit with I and Tessa. They say about people who like Lilly. The people, they contact this government. They say they like Lilly." She was barely holding on enough to finish the story. Her free arm wrapped around her chest and her hand lay over her mouth as the quiver from her chin began to echo through her body.

"Shshh." I stood, and pulled her closer.

She wrapped her arms around my neck and clutched me with an unfamiliar urgency. As if looking for something, or someone, to pick her up and carry her away.

"Now they start papers. I come get Lilly for them, and they sit with her and speak to her."

"Speak to her about what?"

"Just ask questions, try to understand her. Is nothing bad, but Lilly… they tell me to say nothing to her now. Wait until later, when they is more certain." More sniffling and the tear taps were turned on high. "But I know Lilly, she look like she do know what is happen. I think she must know something, because many people pay her attention. But we no can say… I just… I just… I want talk to my Lilly." Her tiny frame convulsed and she passed into a state I had yet to see. A state past the simple sob. Tatiana was breaking down in my arms.

The worst part for myself was that she needed someone to help her, and other than standing there with her silently, I had nothing more to offer.

I caught movement in my peripheral vision. I looked over at the door and saw a sad Sasha, her head just barely peeking past the frame. Sasha had no filter for disrupting private conversation, had no reason to not enter a room, other than tiny little hands holding her by the collar. They were there… listening with super-natural ears. They could hear the snot dripping from their teacher's nose, and the sound of her heart struggling. Common sense told me to go close the door, but there was no distraction on earth that could've moved me from my post.

So, I stood there, and I held her.

51

Over the next few weeks, the mood in our little home steadily soured. The adoption process was proceeding. From the outside I'm sure it seemed slow, but from our perspective, it was all way too fast.

I hadn't seen Tatiana smile for weeks and couldn't remember the last cheerful day we'd all spent together. Story time had become bland. My reading had become monotone. The children's excitement had all but dissolved.

What made it worse was that she knew. Tatiana knew she was dragging everyone down with her, but she couldn't help herself.

I wanted to talk to her, to try to help lift her up, but she had turned cold to me. Like she had to everyone else.

Work had become my escape. I still hadn't mentioned anything to anyone. The guys wouldn't give a shit anyway, and Faas and Helen… I really didn't know what their reaction would be. What should it be? Lilly was going to be adopted into what seemed to be a very happy and fortunate family. She would probably have every advantage available in order to live a prosperous life. So, were we being the bad guys?

I knew that on the family's next visit, they were scheduled to take Lilly for an afternoon. The government representatives had been working with them for some time. Teaching them about the responsibilities of caring for a child such as Lilly.

That day had finally arrived.

They had set a pick-up time for just before noon. I told Faas I had to run some errands, and took off a little before then, to catch a glimpse of these parents-to-be for myself. I grabbed a coffee to help with my innocent-bystander façade. And found a bench across the street and down a bit from the orphanage.

I timed it perfectly. Or, you could say they were very punctual. It wasn't hard to pick them out. It was the only large series Mercedes I could recall seeing in the area. Stretched out, long and black. Polished to a mirror finish, and costing in excess of a hundred thousand Amsterbucks, I figured.

I'd noticed it coming from down the block. A part of me suspected it immediately, and a bigger part wanted it to continue past.

But it stopped, and a man got out of the driver's seat, then walked around to get the passenger door for his wife. He was tall and slender, in a long black coat. His dominantly blond hair was becoming infested with grey, but he wore it well. He was very clean-cut, with proper posture and a smile that gleamed all the way across the street and down the block.

His wife looked cut from the same cloth. People of wealth. She was blonde also (it was the trend in these parts), and she was hot. Why wouldn't she be?

He helped her out of the car and stood beside her, smiling. He placed his hand on her back and rubbed lightly, then leaned down to her for a kiss. They both looked very excited.

I wanted to slash their tires.

Fucking rich people!... Who do they think they are? Do they have any fucking idea how many lives they're ripping apart with their gotta-have-it bullshit? Why don't they just go fuck and make their own kid?... Maybe big shot doesn't have a dick? I took a sip of my coffee, then grinned a grin that quickly faded. *He's probably got the biggest dick money can buy.*

They went inside and I stewed on the bench, elbows resting on my knees as I turned the cup in my hands. Maybe Lilly wouldn't want to go. Maybe she'd put up a fight, kicking and screaming.

But it was only a few minutes later when the door opened, and they exited. The man first, then the lady, then, trailing behind with her hands clasped came Lilly. Smiling sweetly, as always.

As they stepped out onto the street, Tessa and Tatiana walked out and stood on the step. They watched with humble smiles as they all loaded into the car, the lady choosing a spot in the back seat with Lilly.

I looked at Tatiana. Most would see a beautiful young lady with a pleasant smile, but I could see her pain. She remained composed. I honestly never expected for her to make an appearance, but of course she would do it for Lilly. She'd do anything for any of them, even sacrifice herself. No matter how proper and professional she came across, that woman loved those children as if they were her own. And whether it be right or wrong, she didn't want anything to tear them apart.

And there I sat, on my bench, letting it happen.

I knew what that feeling was. That burning emotion, jealousy. It wasn't my first trip down the green carpet.

I returned to work, a little more distant than before. The guys all stopped what they were doing as I walked by. I was pissed off, and anybody with a beating heart could sense it.

It had been drizzling in the morning, but by the time the end of the workday arrived, the clouds had parted some. The guys broke out some beer and a couple joints to enjoy the spring-like weather on the deck of the boat. They asked me to stay, but I responded with a short, simple no.

With a slight sense of urgency, I climbed down from the deck and began my way home. Anxious to find out what had happened that day, and if Lilly had been returned safely.

As I passed the boathouse, Helen was out front shaking off the welcome mat. She smiled. "Hello, Brandon."

"Hey." I managed a quick smile, and continued on my path.

"You like some tea before you go?"

"No, thanks, I'm fine."

"Brandon, darling, you should come. Please."

I really wanted nothing to do with tea or anything else. I just wanted to head home. But it wasn't common for Helen to invite me in after work or to bother me at all. I sensed there was something more to the invitation.

"Uh, all right, but I can't stay long."

In the door and up the stairs we went. The view from the big bay window was beautiful that afternoon. The days were growing longer and the sun was moving back to the north. It was one of those days when you could really feel the power of springtime. I would've enjoyed it more if it hadn't been for the other concerns. But still, when I took in the view and a deep breath, I'd found some sense of relief.

No sooner did I take a seat, than Faas walked up the stairs. He was never one to beat around the bush.

"Hey, you come! Goot." He nodded and set down a satchel of tools, then wiped a thin film of sweat from his forehead and approached the table. "So, what the fuck is wrong, huh?" He placed his hands on his hips and looked directly at me.

I immediately bowed my head to the table and began fidgeting with a napkin.

"Huh? You gonna say this? The guys, they ask is something wrong. Helen, she see it also when you come in the morning. I see it too." He paused for a moment, waiting. "Well, you gonna say this? You must say this… is no goot to not say this."

Helen busied herself in the kitchen, rubbing away at a clean coffee mug. One she'd been rubbing since we'd come upstairs.

"Is something at home? We know is possible. You and Tatiana, you have problems?"

I finally broke from my shell. "No…Well, yes, but it's not me and Tatiana, it's Lilly. Some people maybe want to adopt her."

Faas's demeanour changed instantly. His shoulders arched back and his look of concern turned to one of enlightenment. Helen gently placed the mug and dishtowel on the counter. They both slowly made their way to the table and took a seat.

Faas rested his elbows on the table and clasped his hands. Helen placed her hands softly in her lap, her jaw tightening with an obvious sense of grief. I could see my information had been something neither expected.

"*Hmph.*" Faas nodded. "So, this is what is happen."

Helen reached out and rested a hand on mine. "How is Tatiana?"

I looked at her, then sighed. "She's a mess, honestly. I don't think she thought she'd ever have to deal with this. She said that the people who visited for adoption were never really interested in blind children."

"*Hmph.*" Faas nodded again. "You meet these people, the one who like Lilly for adoption?"

"No, I haven't met them, officially. According to Tessa, who's been dealing with it mostly, they're good people. Wealthy, educated. I did see them just today, at lunch. I snuck across the street and watched for them. They came to pick Lilly up and take her for the afternoon."

"How Lilly think of it?" Helen asked.

"I don't know. We were instructed not to say anything to her about it for now. I think because they don't want to get her concerned about it yet. In case maybe they change their mind, or something doesn't work out legally. But, I mean, they picked her up today, so I would think they'll have to say something to her soon. She probably already has a good idea about what's happening. The others too… I'm pretty sure they were listening at the door one night while Tatiana was talking to me about it."

"Yes, how is all the children?"

"It… It's not a nice place to be, everyone's pretty depressed. Tatiana has a lot of power over those kids, and when she's in a bad mood, everyone's in a bad mood. Plus, if they think they're losing Lilly… It can't be nice for them, and we can't talk to them about it."

Helen patted my hand and went to the counter and pulled a couple tissues from the box. I noticed Faas following her with his gaze.

He huffed and sat back in his chair. "Well, is goot, yes?" He held his hands up and shrugged. "I know is not goot for us. Everybody, they love Lilly. I know Lilly, she is beautiful young girl, very goot wit singing, she very goot girl. So, this is how is to go. Is orphanage, children there, they like to get mom and dad… family. So, is goot for her. We maybe not too happy wit this, but is what is best for Lilly. So, we can be happy and have thanks."

"Yeah, I know that's how it's supposed to work. It's just really hard. I know Tatiana doesn't want her to go. But she knows there's nothing she can do, and I can't do anything."

"What, huh?" He waved his hand casually. "You say no to this, you stop Lilly from maybe be very happy life. You will be even bigger asshole."

"Faas!" Helen reprimanded.

"What!" He looked at me. "You must have what is right for girl. Is not about you."

That's how the conversation went. I was hoping, somehow, that they'd be able to make it all better. That Faas would go to the closet and grab his Rambo-sized machine gun, and then we'd cross the street and seize the building, taking a heroic stance and protect all the women and children. And shoot that black Merc up like Swiss cheese. Or maybe that Faas would break out the fat wad of cash I knew he had buried somewhere, and pay whatever it took to make everything okay.

But he was right, like I already knew. It had to be about what was best for Lilly. But… would it be better for her? Maybe someone else could love her, but no one could love her more than us. There was no fancy car or house, but she never went without. We had fun… Well, we used to have fun, and we could again.

I got a hug from both Helen and Faas on my way out. It was good to have them there to talk to, even if they didn't always say what I wanted to hear.

When I stepped out of the boathouse, the last rays of daylight hit me in the face. It was warm, warmer than I'd felt in what seemed like a really long time. It felt good. Good on the face, good on the shoulders. The light breeze hit me in with the smell of everything enjoying being warm and happy. Through the turmoil, it bloomed a modest smile. Then I turned and headed for home.

52

I arrived home to Tatiana working with the children in their room. Hans and Gaby ran to me with a cheer and clung to a leg when I entered. Anna simply turned and smiled. Tatiana didn't even give me that.

Gaby would ask about Lilly every now and then. To which her teacher would reply "At seven o'clock" with a stern tone. No one else seemed willing to stir the pot. Anna was being great, doing extra bits to help out in the time of need. She carried an aura of pride and sensibility, more so than the adults.

Lilly arrived back at the orphanage at 7:00 p.m. sharp, as scheduled.

Tatiana never officially declared that she was mad at me, but she made it impossible for me to think otherwise. I wasn't really sure why it seemed like she was blaming me for everything. Maybe I was just the person who needed to be that for her. All stories need a villain.

At night, in our bed, I held her and she snuggled in like she appreciated my presence… she just didn't like it.

When I got home the next day, Tatiana was waiting for me. She told me that Lilly's parents-to-be were ready to start the adoption process, and that she had been instructed to talk to Lilly that night, officially, to let her know what was happening.

I followed her over to the children's room, and we asked for Lilly to come visit us for a bit. As we exited the room, I spoke softly to Anna as I pulled the door closed behind us. "Anna, please make sure the children stay here."

She smiled and nodded.

We took Lilly over to our room, where Tatiana had her sit down on the bed next to her. I pulled over the painting chair and sat across from them. Lilly looked concerned, while Tatiana took a moment, before beginning.

"So, Lilly," she said pleasantly, "the other day, when you go with this people—"

"The Van de Bergs?" Lilly corrected.

"Oh, yes, of course. This is the name of people, you know this." Tatiana managed an uncertain smile.

Van de Berg, pfft… Even their name sounds snobby, I thought. *Probably Van de Berg the third, or some fucking shit.*

"You know why this people, Van de Bergs, come see you?"

"I think, "Lilly seemed to be crawling into a shell, and I got the feeling she was just as uncomfortable with the conversation as we were, "because they like me?"

"Yes," Tatiana sighed. She snatched Lilly's hand and held it in her lap. "They like you, is right. They like you, very much. They say…" She was choking up, pausing frequently for air. "They say, maybe they like for you to… to live with them."

There was a long pause, and Lilly's head dipped. It wasn't the enthusiastic response I was expecting.

She fidgeted. "You mean they like to… adoption wit me?" She raised her head and tears rolled slowly from her eyes. She was scared.

Tatiana squeezed the little girl's hand tighter as tears ran down her face as well. She sniffled, then continued on with a happy ambiance. "Yes, for adoption. You can be part of family. No more to live in orphanage."

Lilly's face was stained by that point. She let go a soft sob, and her body trembled. "But… I… What can happen to Gaby, or Hans… Anna?"

It was the last that Tatiana could bear. There was no way for her to continue a sensible conversation. I reached over and rubbed her leg gently, then took it upon myself.

"Hey, Lilly." I reached over and squeezed her shoulder. "Gaby and Hans and Anna, they'll stay here, with us. They'll be fine, nothing for them would be any different, except…" I shouldn't have added the "except" at the end, so I just trailed off to incompletion.

The conversation was having the opposite effect on me. I was fuelled by Lilly's lack of interest. So, I pushed on. Giving her an honest chance, to choose her path.

"But these people, the Van de Bergs, I hear they're very nice people. They're successful. They probably have a nice big house. Enough money to give you anything you need. You could go to a really good school."

"I have school here, wit Teacher. I have family, is here, wit you and Teacher and Hans and Anna and Gaby." Her little face grew tense. She'd gone from sad and scared to very defensive. Her lips pursed tight, her lower jaw jutted out, and she clenched a little fist.

Tatiana had stopped sobbing and was paying close attention to the little girl's insistence.

"So… you don't want to be adop—"

"No! The people is nice people, but I have family here." She stood. "I do not like to talk more. I will go back to room now."

I looked over at Tatiana and placed my hand on her knee. She nodded lightly.

"Okay sweetie, it's all right. You can go back to your room. Thank you for talking with us." I smiled and patted her arm as she turned and marched from the room.

I waited till I heard the door across the hall open, before I all but jumped from my chair and clapped my hands together with victory.

Tatiana returned a look of confusion.

"What?" I asked. I crouched down in front of her and held her hands. "Don't you get it? She doesn't want to go! She loves it here. She wants to stay here, with her family. Where she should be."

Tatiana started to take interest, and her tears subsided.

"They can't force her to go if she doesn't want to… right?" I clenched her hands tighter and gave them a reassuring shake. Then I stood up and gave her a hard smooch on the lips. "So, we have to go talk to Tessa now?"

She nodded.

"All right, c'mon, you can stop crying, and stop worrying, honey. Everything's going to be fine."

I pulled her to her feet and led her out of the room to go find Tessa.

She was in the kitchen, cleaning anxiously as she waited for us to report back after our conversation with Lilly. She threw down her washcloth as soon as we entered the room.

"So, what she say?" she asked, as we sat at a table.

"No!" I slapped the table with the same smile I'd held all the way down the stairs. "We talked to her. We talked up the people, the Van de Bergs. Said it would be a good opportunity for her and yadda, yadda. She said no. She doesn't want to go live with anyone else, she wants to live here. With her family! Where she belongs!" I know my smile was cocky, but so what, let me have it.

Thing was, no one else was smiling. Tessa went as far as to lower her head to avoid eye contact.

"What?" I looked at each lady, who showed no sign of celebration. "She doesn't want to go. Done deal."

"Yes," Tessa said, "I understand now, she may not like to go. But is not how this will work."

There was a moment of silence. She raised her eyes to me, and I stared her down like a dog.

"What do you mean, it's not how it works? She said no, she doesn't want to go… She said no!"

Tessa sighed. "Is not so simple. This people, the Van de Bergs, they is goot people for adoption purpose. Very goot. Almost we never have people this goot." She sat a little straighter in her chair. "Of course, we all think she will say no, right now. She has live here almost all her life. But… the system, if it find these people are goot family for her, she will go. They can provide a goot life for her. Here, she live off government money. It is in their interest to have the children adopted to goot families, if become possible."

My voice raised. I never had expected to raise my voice in such a manner, to such a good woman as Tessa, with everything she had done for me, for us.

"She said no!"

"Yes, is what we expect for now. Please understand, this will not happen in one day. The Van de Bergs will now be allowed time to spent with Lilly. They have more time togeter, maybe a day or more. Lilly will go to stay wit them at they house sometime. There is still much for process. So, Lilly will have time to have familiar wit the people. So, maybe in six monts, she will feel better about this. But if the people are accept by government, Lilly must go."

I clenched up tight, trying to hold back, looking for a sense of sensibility, trying to be rational about it all. Then I slammed my fist down on the table and I let it fly. "That's fucking bullshit!"

Both ladies startled.

My body fumed. "You can't MAKE her go!... Against her will? She said no! How could any place be better than here for her? No one can love her as much as she's loved here! It's… it's enslavement! Entrapment! What kind of… communist bullshit is this place!"

"Brandon, please," Tessa said. "Is not communist. Is how the system works."

"Oh, it's how the system works? Selling children? Forcing them to go with people when they say no!"

"I know, Brandon, is not seem fair, but—"

I stood and looked to Tatiana, who did nothing. Just sat there with tears rolling down her face.

"It's fucking bullshit, Tessa! You know it's bullshit! She's just… She's just a little girl!"

I turned and stormed out of the room.

53

Things were bad before that night. They really went to shit after.

There was no conversation after that conversation. I stopped chasing her around in her depression. I stopped waiting for the time when that dazzling smile would return.

It was I who turned cold. Cold to her, cold to the children. Somewhere, somehow, the switch had been flipped. There was a time in my selfishness when a ray of clarity dawned, but only for a moment. I thought about how Tatiana's mood reflected in the children, and realized, as I looked around the room, that she wasn't the only one with direct influence over the ones around her.

She was more, sad. For my turn, I'd chosen anger… and it spread, so fast and so strong. But whenever I tried to lift my foot off the pedal, a wave of guilt spread through my gut like a wrenching virus. So, I kept the hammer down.

Work… Work was where I wanted to be. I even smiled at work, laughed it up and managed to push the other to the side. The more I neglected, the easier it became.

I even started staying after work when the weather was nice. The guys and I would hang out on deck and slog back a couple beer. After I did that a few times, I'd stay for a couple more.

On the nights when I stayed past curfew and returned a little tipsy, I slept on the couch in the children's room. Not that Tatiana ever gave me shit for the booze on my breath, I just knew it disappointed her, and I didn't want to deal with it anymore.

At that point in a relationship, can you ever really turn it around?

But, you see, there was more to it than that.

That time was coming when the boat would set sail for Peru. Soon, like the following week soon.

She knew it. She paid attention, and I knew that date was etched deeply in her mind.

Those days when the sun was strong, I'd lean over the side of the railing and feel the reflection off the water hit my face. Huge shot of good ol' vitamin D to charge the battery. Wind would shoot the smell of new adventure up my nostrils, with a cleansing flush of everything that had turned sour.

It was a symbol for me, that boat. That day when it would set off. I didn't realize how powerful it was. There were countless ways to get out of Amsterdam. There must be a thousand flights a day, a thousand train departures, but the idea of that boat leaving without me created a stranded feeling that left me empty. She was holding the door open for me… *Why?* Did she simply want to give me the option to choose? Or was she, herself, tired of it all? Tired of us?

Was it what she wanted? Me… gone? But, maybe out of respect, she refrained from kicking my wasted ass out on the street and was just letting nature run its course? Was she patiently counting down the days?

The more the questions stirred in my head, the more plausible it all became. Not that any further evidence ever surfaced. I was just talking myself into it.

That last week, time flew. The day before launch arrived in the blink of an eye. There was some chaos in the morning, as we did final touch-ups and went through checklists.

By noon, it was complete. Faas did one final walk around, and on his declaration, cheers erupted.

The sun was out in full force, and everything was alive beneath its blessing. It was the first time in the year I'd been able to wear shorts and a T-shirt, and it was somewhat liberating. The ladies on the street had also welcomed the change, getting all their bits and pieces out as a gift to the sun.

Dong broke some beers out of the cooler and slapped a bag of green down on the table.

Adlar hit the tunes. "Yes," he grinned like he was cruising down Main Street. "Is time for some celebration."

Faas didn't look happy with the development, but "Not wreck boat, fucking kids" was the only warning given, with the shake of a finger. Except for me. I got a very hard, disapproving glare. Which he held for a second, before turning to leave the boat.

It stalled me for a moment. Those times flashed through my memory. The way she blew my mind when we first met. The look on the children's faces as they spread out below me in their jammies at story time.

I shook it off, tipped the bottle to my lips, let the music dilute the guilt, and stepped back hard on the pedal.

We spent the rest of the day getting sloshed and catcalling to the ladies on the street.

The guys couldn't stop talking about their next adventure. They described the route they were going to take and which places they would stop at along the way, hoping to hit some local festivals. Of course, all of their expectations included naked women.

They were ready to go. Amsterdam had run its course. There was a respectable chance they'd return. Faas would find a boat somewhere, sometime, for them. But they were happy for change.

That night, they were going to give'er one last go. One last mark on the town, till that maybe-day when they'd return.

Of course, I was invited. I didn't accept, although I wasn't sure why. In my condition, there was nothing but trouble back at the orphanage. I think I thought it was something that needed to be done. Like grabbing the corner of the band-aid.I walked up the stairs quietly and peeked into the children's room. Gaby and Hans were sitting around the crafts table, busy working on something. Sasha was lying beside the table. She lifted her head to me and perked her ears, but she had no other reaction beyond that. Anna was walking around, tidying up. She stopped and looked toward the doorway, blankly. She knew I was there; it was entirely possible they all knew. The welcome-home celebrations had ended a long while back.

Lilly was nowhere to be seen.

I decided to let them be. I wasn't anywhere near proper father-figure condition.

I stepped cautiously across the floor to our bedroom.

The room was dark. I'd expected Tatiana to be busy with end-of-day chores, as always, but she was sitting in front of the easel. Her forearm rested in her lap and a paintbrush hung from her limp hand. Her other hand covered her face. I heard a soft sob.

A wave passed through my body, tingling to the surface of my skin. Whatever was going to happen wasn't going to be easy, and there was no playbook on how to begin.

"Hey." My voice echoed through the dimly lit room.

She sniffled, then dabbed at her nose with a tissue. She pushed back from her station, stood and straightened her dress.

"Hello." She turned to me. "Is hard day for work?" she asked with heavy sarcasm.

"Uh, not really. We finished up around lunchtime, actually."

"Yes, at lunch?"

"Yeah, we… we finished the boat up." I did my best to keep my approach positive.

"So, you finish for lunchtime? You do no like to come home?" She reached down to the shelf on her easel and began cleaning up her brushes.

"Well, I… I stuck my head in the kid's room. Where's Lilly?"

"Lilly? Yes, she go. She go for weekend to have time with new family."

"What! I didn't… You didn't say anything about that to me."

"No, of course, you busy man. I do not like to bother you for this. Is no you problem, hmm?"

The hurt was on. The corner of the Band-Aid had been picked back enough to grab hold, and we were pulling, slowly, tearing at the skin.

I had no immediate response, still deciding which angle I was playing. Cinch up the gloves for a fight, or double knot the laces for a flight?

"Is beautiful day, hmm? What you do after lunch?' Paint bottles and wooden brushes began to rattle and slam as tension grew.

"I... uh, we—"

"You stay on boat, you drink beer, smoke you marijuana, hmm? The sun, it feel nice, yes?"

She stared me down. For a woman with dysfunctional eyes, she could sure stare you into a small state of self. I held her stare as she crossed the room toward me.

"You no have to say it, I know. This whole room, it stink. It stink like you.

I know this before you come. I know it in morning, when I wake. I know it... I know it from..."

She stood within a foot of me. Her blue eyes cut like razor-sharp shards of ice. Tears began to cascade and she did nothing to disguise it, she welcomed it. Welcomed me to see what had become of her... what I had done.

Any playbook ever written on male-female negotiations would state strongly that pushing back was not a good idea in such a situation. So... I pushed back.

My breathing deepened, my jaw clenched, and my heart pounded. "Listen! I don't need this shit from you! What the fuck are you coming down on me for? Huh!" All the alcohol in my body was tossed into the fire, and holding back was off the table. My voice was strong. Stronger than I'd ever been in resistance to her.

It was her, then, who was caught without speech. She wanted it, wanted to hear what I had to say, wanted the cut, deep and searing. We both knew what this was about, and where it would end. We were just reading the script.

"I didn't do any of this! None of this is my fault! But night after night, I come home to you being so fucking cold to me! For what? What the fuck did I ever do wrong to you?" I leaned in closer so she could feel the stink of my intoxication blow on her face. "So why the fuck should I rush home after work? So you can be a bitch to me, for no fucking reason?"

We were both right, in the end. Right or wrong, hard blows were being dealt. The things you can't take back were being screamed.

She was breaking; her shoulders shuddered and her expression turned from aggression to acceptance. As much as it dug into me, it was better that way.

The bigger an asshole she knew I was, the less she would feel like she was losing something special. That was the way it had to be.

"I come here, I come and live with you here, and there's no... no sex. You're holding all of this back from me. Then all this shit with Lilly, and you turn to me as if I should be able to fix it all? How the fuck am I supposed to fix anything? I have nothing! Nothing!... I scrape shit off boats, and if it wasn't for staying here, I'd be on the fucking street! I have nothing! There's nothing here for me! But I stay, and I do my best to show you that I'm a good man, but in the end, you still shit on me! It's like this is all some... some big fucking trap!"

That stirred a reaction.

"Oh *yes!*" She waved her arms madly. "Is trap, big trap for Brandon. He such a perfect man! All women in whole world love have such man. He drink, and smoke drugs, he no come home! He no give shit about nothing, about no one… but himself! *Yes*, Brandon! Is trap for you! Is big plan I make!" She was screaming at me so hard, she could hardly keep her breath. Her face was fire red, and she looked like she wanted to rip open her chest and throw her heart in my face.

"You know this? Huh? Is trap! So big trap!" She fanned her hands around her body. "Is bigger trap that you ever have!" She leaned into me, eyes wide and wild. She was blind, but I could swear to God that woman saw me then.

"So, Mr. Big Guy! Think! You think much in you mind before you step in this!" She held her finger in front of my face, breathing heavily through her nostrils.

I decided it had been enough. "Fuck it! I'm done with this shit!" I screamed back, then turned.

Standing in the doorway across the landing were Sasha and the remaining children. Every one of them sniffling, with tear-streaked faces. Gaby had her hands over her ears.

It was the straw that broke. Tears swam from my eyes and I muffled a sob. I took one last look at them, mentally wishing them all the best. Then I ran down the stairs and out to the front walk. The Band-Aid swirled in the turbulent wash behind me, then, slowly floated to rest on the ground. Forgotten.

54

The streetlights were on by the time I made it out of the orphanage. I sucked in a deep breath of fresh air. I needed every bit of cleansing I could grab to erase the apocalyptic visions I'd left in my wake. Crying Tatiana, on the verge of complete collapse, left to console children whose whole world was falling apart. It wasn't easy. Don't ever think it was. But it had only become more clear, over time, that our parting was inevitable.

The damage had been done, and now the cleanup could begin, but not if I turned back. *Never* if I turned back. Best thing I could do, was go get completely shit-faced.

I had a pretty good hunch where the guys had headed, and I jogged over to the pub.

Dong was the first to see me walk in the door "What the fu— Hey!" He held his hands out to the side. "Guys! Hey, guys, look… Look!" He pointed to me, and the other two sitting at the table turned.

I marched up and greeted them with a round of brotherly handshakes, then pulled up a chair.

"Hey, Brandon, look at chu man!" Nick smiled. "Chu come. Come party? See us to leave?"

I smiled, and huffed. I pushed down an uncertain swallow. "No, I… I'm coming. I'm going with you. Let's go to Peru."

Adlar looked at me with a curious smirk. "Oh yes? You go to come wit us?"

"Y-yeah." I nodded. "Absolutely."

Dong cheered and held up his beer. "Brandon come with us! Fucking yes! He back, fucking pirate."

Nick joined in the celebration, but Adlar raised his brow while twirling his bottle between his hands on the tabletop.

"You come to Peru? What is this wit the girl, Tatiana? What about this girl, the children?"

"Oh, yeah… *That* isn't working anymore."

"No? It no work no more?"

"Yeah." I chuckled and lowered my head. "It hasn't been working there… y'know, for a while now, I guess." I waved it off.

"Oh." He dropped his guard, pushed back from the table and straightened, then took a swig of his beer. "I'm sorry to hear that, my friend. She seem like she is nice lady."

"Yeah, she is nice, really nice. It was just… just a lot of things, y'know?"

He smiled. "Yes, I know this. Is not easy." He held his bottle toward me. "Is goot, goot to have you back to us." He handed me a beer.

"Thanks man, it's good to be back." I tapped his bottle with mine. Suddenly they were bombarded with bottles from all around the table, violent and splashing.

Dong mussed the shit out of my hair. "*Yes!* Fucking Brandon is back with pirates. We get smashed now!"

He yelled to the women behind the bar. "Hey, pretty ladies! You hear that shit? Brando back, he fucking pirate with us! He like the Dong!"

I scrunched my face and shook my head. Then we all shared a laugh, clanked bottles again, and chugged them back.

The girls paraded over to join us in a round of shots. They slid up on either side of me, and Trisha looked at me seductively and whispered. "Shook off the chains, huh? Now you're leaving us already, tomorrow? Would've been nice to get to know each other a little better." She ran her tongue between her lips. "I guess we still got tonight." She winked and giggled, then ran her finger down my cheek to my neck and tugged lightly at my necklace.

The necklace… I'd completely forgotten about it. As she headed back to the bar, I reached up slowly, found one of the beads, and rolled it between my fingers. It was a trigger to memories. The day the children made it for me, the pride in their eyes. Then, Tatiana and the children huddled on the floor, crying endlessly.

I let go. Then I reached up and released the necklace, quickly stuffing it in my pocket. There was no need to look at it.

The future was set, and I plowed on with my mission of purging purity with poison. The girls happily agreed to join us for our send-off night.

After closing down the pub, we headed out into the streets to discover a heavy fog had rolled in. Drugs in all shapes and forms were passed around the group. Some were familiar and some I wasn't sure about, but it wasn't a night for questions.

Before long, the fog grabbed the lights of the street and threw them in every direction, like a soiled kaleidoscope lens. Laughter was constant, as the variety of ingested toxins took their turns pulling the strings of our minds. The wave would lift us up to hysterics, pause, hunched over in the streets, and then drop us down, like being handed a cannonball before taking that step over the edge. The fog closed in, cloaking insecurity. Voices would call, maybe screaming… crying. Swift visions of people pacing, talking to ghosts, losing control. Then back up we'd go, shooting like rockets through waves of dementia.

So much going on, from every angle. Those guys could make more money with a clinic for forgetting the past. In that state, I thought of Tatiana and the children not once.

I fell into zombie mode. Being pulled one way, then the other. Sometimes I was sitting, sometimes not.

Sometimes there was a naked ass right in my face. Other times, it was Dong, yelling something about Dong.

There were soft whispers, touching, warm wisps of breath.

Lights dazzled while small portions of bizarre scenes played out before me, leaving my mind to run wild to construct motivations and conclusions.

Sometime during all the craziness, I guess I shut down.

Then I woke. There was an alarm, or maybe a phone chime? I was on a couch, dark brown, velvet of sorts. The way it sucked me down in the middle suggested it had had some heavy miles.

My mind was still right sideways. But I could form a simple sentence, at least in my mind. There was no girl present in the room, which felt like the waiting room in another brothel. With multiple doors branching off.After focusing my senses as much as possible, I heard some rhythmic groaning, with someone playing a bedspring in the background.

I rolled myself to the floor. I managed on all fours for a bit, but things were spinning viciously, and my mouth was choking dry. The room was dark, and I had no idea what time it was. I wasn't sure what the outcome would be, but I pressed myself clumsily to my feet to find out. I held the position for a time, waiting, hoping for muscle memory to reboot and take over the ship.

There were voices, soft voices, sometimes from one way, other times from another. I couldn't make out what they were saying or locate the source, but they were there, saying something.

I suffered a look around and located the only logical option for an exit. Trusting only in my logical state of mind. I turned a knob and pushed out to a concrete landing, with stairs going up. A bright light on the wall stung my dry eyes. It was shrouded in a protective metal cage and emitted a low hum.

At the top was a plain white door with a window covered by a plastic shade. I placed my hand on the knob, then paused and let my forehead brace against the glass.

I was pretty roughed up. Getting up the stairs was decent, but pushing out to the open wilderness, where there'd probably be other people, that was big. I'd learned from many great adventures before that when you step out of a door, you'd better be ready for it to lock behind you.

But it was time to go. I couldn't miss my ride, so I pushed out.

The fog was still there, thick and moist, but there was the faintest of a blue hue to the east. There was no one blocking my way this time.

The streets were quiet, except for the voices hidden somewhere in the surrounding fog. Sometimes it sounded like a man, sometimes a woman. I could only guess at what was being said. My best guess was always something about me:

"Just another wasted tourist, wandering the streets."

"Another pig from the West, unable to control himself in a world where the illicit is licit."

"Look at him… what is he doing?… How messed up is he?"

Let them talk… It wasn't the first time I'd been alone with the voices. I'd just keep to myself and maintain course.

The problem with maintaining course was that I had no idea where I was and couldn't see more than three feet in front of my face. There was a credible chance I was walking in circles, which was better than walking farther away. Although I'd been in Amsterdam for almost a year, I wasn't that familiar with anything outside of my neighbourhood. The next problem was that I had no coat. It took only minutes for my T-shirt and shorts to hang off me like a well-soaked chamois—soaked in ice water. There was little I hated more in the world than being smashed in every way possible and cold on top of it. As if my mind didn't have enough to deal with.

So, I walked… and walked. I wrapped my arms tightly around me for warmth, but it wasn't enough to stop the convulsions.

Between the voices, all I could hear was the thrum of my heart, the rush of my breath, and the soft whump of rubber soles on concrete.

Slowly but surely, the morning began to brighten and the fog started to lift. The dirty deeds of the night had been done. It was time to lift the veil and let the sunshine dwellers come out. Oblivious to any sinful happenings while they slept.

Up the lather crept, like bubbles in a lager settling to the surface, giving clarity to my surroundings.

Voices again, but no matter which way or how fast I turned. I still couldn't find them.

I stopped at a couple intersections and scanned the streets, up and down, locating a little piece of familiarity here and there. Finding my resting place was becoming critical, as I was beginning to fear hypothermia. Something equally troubling, was the sobering effect.

Somewhere, sometime, I crossed the path of the route we'd taken that morning, and as the fog lifted further, the day began to resemble the one of almost one year previous.

Sasha's shadow would appear before me, now and then, tail wagging, huffing and puffing.

The thought stirred a smile. How beautiful she was…

Then the thought of Tatiana, warm and snuggled in bed, and how good it would be to have that, to be there with her.

Laughing and exploring beneath the covers… the way it used to be.

But that time had passed. She was likely curled up somewhere in the children's room. They'd probably had a tough night. Maybe she didn't even sleep at all. Was she thinking of me, right there, right then, like I was thinking about her?

I came to the corner near the station, where I had to take an indirect line past the orphanage. I picked up my pace. Somewhere between the streets, a church bell began its countdown, bouncing between the brick labyrinth, lonely, searching for someone, anyone.

I designed a path around the boathouse for the best chance of avoiding detection. If Helen were to catch me, the whole thing would be blown. I suspected it was still too early, even for them, but there was no room for careless risk.

Down the block and around the corner. I hugged the building, sped past the windows. Down the dock I picked up my pace even more, shuffling my feet and stepping lightly to minimize the noise.

At the end of the dock, shivering and on the verge of collapsing, I looked back at the city of Amsterdam. I gave one last thought to the times I'd spent there. A well of emotion finally caught up and slapped me right in the face, sending icicles flowing down my cheeks.

Then I climbed up the ladder onto the deck. I found the hidden key, opened the door to the cabin, and slipped below. I piled every blanket I could find and anything with insulative qualities onto a bunk and slipped beneath them. I curled into a ball, hugged myself tightly, and waited for relief from the cold.

My mind twirled with flashes from the previous night. Pieces of what may have transpired. I would never really know. Some things should be forgotten.

It didn't take long for thoughts of the orphanage to surface, and once I let one in, the rest followed.

Laughter, little smiling faces…Beautiful Tatiana. The warmth of Christmastime with… our family.

The thought of me then and there, messed right up, with not a one to stand beside me and give a shit.

Then back to Tatiana, at the end… the things I'd said. She'd kind of fell apart then. But I knew she really didn't expect me to fix anything. She just needed to have that someone who would be there for her. There, during her worst of times.

I knew it, and I'd used it as a door for my own selfishness. Shit rolls downhill. It's best you jump out of the way and let it hit the next person. A good motto to live by… if you're a complete asshole.

With no one around, I let it buck. The sobbing, the crying, the moaning, the self-loathing. My body tensed until my ribs hurt, but I kept going. I needed the cleanse so that if and when I survived that morning, I could begin the repair. It was one of the loneliest times in my life. Being that alone, with those demons… a guy's gotta be careful.

55

I was hot, hot as hell! My breathing was laboured and my mouth, my lungs, everything felt deathly polluted.

I could feel the weight of the nest I'd piled upon myself and wondered what would happen when I tried to move. Anything? For the first bit, I kept everything exactly where it was and just focused on my breathing, on getting that up and mastered before taking the next step. Then I twitched a leg. It was stiff as hell, and weak, but there was no pain and it felt nice to change position. I remembered back to however many hours ago, to being so cold.

Then I remembered more. Then more… What had been said, what had been done, what could not be taken back. Not then, not ever. It was one of those nasty, dirty hangovers, with flashes of regret between the throbs of the migraine.

But I gave thanks that morning. Thanks to the powers-that-be for helping me survive once more. I remembered the last time I was at a similar point in life, almost one year ago. A one-year stretch between waking up with the urge to give thanks for surviving another night of drunken chaos, was a pretty big personal triumph.

Now the healing could begin, for everyone. I definitely had some work to do, once I could get my feet back underneath me.

With confirmation of all components functioning, I opened my eyes. The cabin was bright. The sun's rays busting through any open window and crevice. It, combined with the lack of air movement, was to thank for the suffocating temperature.

I blinked once, then strained my eye muscles for focus. It was so challenging, there could've been something broken. Then I blinked again, and again, till things started coming together. I closed my eyes and let my body relax, heavy, into the bed, taking some last-minute relaxation and some time to think of my next move.

I had to get up top and find the nearest source of fresh water.

I sighed. None of it would be easy. I'd have to learn to walk again, basically, and every step would hurt my everything.

So, I opened my eyes again and scanned the room, flagging obstacles and anything sturdy enough to brace me as I transitioned from the bunk to the door.

I found it. Just off the corner of the foot of the bed, right beside the chair where Tatiana was sitting, staring at me.

I froze solid.

She cleared her throat. "Is okay, I know you is wake up now. I hear you."

I smiled, then rolled slowly to my back and stretched. "Yes, you can hear I'm awake, and probably smell it too."

Her eyes were dry. She was dressed very nicely, everything pure Tatiana. She looked many things, hurt, concerned, curious, and pissed off. But I didn't think there'd be any tears from her, not anymore.

"You get on wrong boat, huh?"

I snickered and rubbed at my eyes. "No…"

She paused and brushed at her lap as if it were wrinkled. "This boat, we still here, at boathouse. The different boat… it has—"

"I know what boat I'm on, thanks." My tone was maybe a little on the rude side from how I'd envisioned the conversation going.

"—gone," she finished.

I choked down what was available for moisture in my mouth, causing me to cough and sputter because it was disgusting.

I saw her reach down to a bottle beside her chair. She lifted it and made a tossing motion. "Here." She threw it a little wildly.

I cracked it open and all but polished it off in one go. I set down the bottle and lay back in bed, blinking and churning saliva in my mouth, as awful as it tasted.

"I know which boat I'm on. I'm glad the other boat's gone. I don't want anything to do with it, or travelling all the way to Peru with those guys. I barely survived last night."

"So, you stay here… Why?"

Her tone was smug as she emphasized the "Why". As in *Why, because there is nothing here for you now. Not after what you put me and the children through last night… fucking asshole.*

I rubbed my forehead and tensed my face. It wasn't the conversation I wanted to have first thing when I woke up, as sick as I was. But I wasn't in a spot to have a say. I was just very happy to see her there.

"Why stay here, in the boat?" I repeated. "What other option did I have? How'd you know I was here?"

"Helen, she call, say she see you pass window. She see you get on boat, then other boat leave. She call and say it to me. So, why you stay?"

I rolled onto my side and looked at her. "Because I realized where I'm supposed to be. I stayed for you… you and the children… and for me."

"*Pfft,*" she spat. "I do no know why you do this. Is too much now, is nothing here for you no more."

As brash as she was being with me, I had no fear of handing it right back to her. With my head pounding, the room spinning, and my guts churning, it gave me the "no bullshit" edge I needed.

"Really? Why are you here then?"

That question threw her off-track. "I… is…"

"You wanted to make sure I was here? That I was all right?... Because you care?"

She gave her lap another couple strokes. I could tell she didn't like being backed into a corner, but I knew that the reason she was there, with me, was the same reason I'd stayed.

She thought for a moment, probably trying to come up with something to wriggle herself free. But she just responded with blush-faced frustration. "I have to be sure you no die, cause you fucking stupid! Huh! Why do you stay? Huh? Why you no be gone on boat with you boys? Get drunk, do drugs, and sleep with many oth—"

"AhhhhHHHHHH!" I screamed as my hands shot to my head and my legs slammed down on the mattress, demanding it all to stop. It was all such bullshit. "Because I love you!" I sat up straight, legs hanging over the side of the bed. I looked at her again and spoke with as much sincerity as I could in my current state.

"I love you, Tatiana. I love you, and I love the children." I took a breath and sighed before I continued. "I don't want to wake up tomorrow, or the next day, hungover, with some strange woman beside me. I want to wake up with a clear mind and a clear conscience, with the woman I know… the woman I love."

"*Pfft*, yes. You say to this now, when you sick."

I nodded and pursed my lips at how stubborn she was being, but I expected nothing less. "Yeah, you're right, I'm sick, I get it. You think I'll only admit to it when I'm down and out. So… ask me again tomorrow, and the day after, and the week after, then month after. Because I'll still be here, whether you like it or not."

She sat silent. "I am sorry, Brandon, there is too many things speak of last night. It hurt me, hurt the children. Is no possible to make it okay."

"That's bullshit, Tatiana!" I shook my head. "I know a lot of bad things were said, a lot of mean things. But… I'm new to all this, really new. This is the first relationship I've been in with so much at stake. Things were really good there, for the first bit. Then the Lilly thing started, and things turned around. I know… I know *now* how I should've reacted. You just needed support, and I let you down. I let you down big. But I didn't see it then. All I saw was you blaming everything on me. But I know now, I get it. But as much as you needed help from me, I could've used some support from you. I'm not stupid, Tatiana. I'm just new, and I get scared. I know you get scared, and that I'm the man, I'm supposed to be strong, yadda, yadda. Thing is, I'm really not scared of being with you and the children. I'm scared of failing you and the children. I feel like I'm stuck… in the work, career, financial sort of way. I don't see how I can work toward doing better? I wanna… I wanna be that guy for you, support you and all that. Give you the things you deserve… right." My tone slumped and my head sank to the floor. I had such a fucking headache.

We sat still and silent in the stuffy bunk. I felt as if I were beginning to suffocate in a pressure cooker. A heavy trickle of sweat ran down my back and then into my crevice.

"Well," she finally responded, "is too bad, we maybe could have this… talk, many days ago. Maybe we could make something work?" She stood.

I looked over at her, about to walk out on me. "Where do you think you're going?"

She paused, "I must go back to the orphanage. Children will begin to wonder."

"I'm sorry, Tatiana. I'm sorry for everything that I said and did last night, to you, and to the children. It was awful, and I feel like a complete piece of shit. But… we had a rough patch. Things went bad, and I'd say we both could've handled it better… Both of us." I stood and stepped closer to her.

"But that's a relationship," I continued." It can't always be good. But that's how we build it stronger. We work together, and we get through it… right?" I reached up slowly and placed a gentle hand on her shoulder. "I stayed here for you and the children. I love you, Tatiana. I get that those words may not mean much to you right now. I get that you're still mad. But I mean it, and I'm going to prove it to you. I'm here, and you're here, so it's not over. Go back to the orphanage, see the children, get some rest and… try to let go of the anger. I'm gonna stay here till I get my head pried out of my ass and back on my shoulders. Then I'm gonna come see you. We're going to work at making this right again, everything. You, me, the children… all of us, together."

She didn't say yes, but she didn't say no either. She listened to the speech, then took a slow step forward, sliding out from beneath my hand.

I let her go.

I took a moment to make sure I'd done all that I could with what I had at the time. There was no point to push it further then. I stunk like someone who really doesn't have any respect for themselves.

I left the room and climbed the stairs to the deck. The crisp air swirled around my body, and every pore sipped at the freshness. It was another key ingredient on the road to recovery.

I saw Helen walking with Tatiana at the end of the dock. Then the two turned to each other, had some dialogue, then parted ways. Helen looked back at me, and though the distance was considerable, I could see a slight smile form on her face, and it gave me hope.

I stood on the deck and felt the sun on my face, the breeze through my hair. A moment later I saw Helen making her way down the dock with a basket hanging from her arm. A basket full of much needed food, no doubt.

She dropped it off, but didn't stay to chat. I sat in peace and reflection as I enjoyed the nutritious, home cooking, freshly squeezed juice, and water. After, I ventured up to the boathouse for a shower.

Once again, I was on the mend from my own self-destruction. I held a cup of tea and turned to watch the big orange ball of light sink into its waterbed for the night.

I'd told myself last time that it would be the last time. Yet there I stood, another time. But it felt different. The guys were gone, that was a big plus. It's hard to settle down to a domestic environment. Wife, kids. When you have jokers like that tugging at you every day.

I stared at the horizon, wondering where they'd made it to, before their first night back on the high sea. One thing I knew for sure was that they were right fucked out of their minds. The previous night was the end for me, but only another beginning for them. I lifted my cup and smiled to myself. *Godspeed… fucking pirates!*

I lowered my cup again, then rested my other hand in my pocket. There I felt something unusual. I rolled it around in my fingers for but a quick second, before I remembered.

I set my mug on top of the cabin, then pulled the necklace from my pocket and held it up in front of my face.

I was quickly overwhelmed by emotion. My jaw locked and I felt tears begin to well and almost burst. But I drew in hard through my nose and managed to hold everything in place. How could I ever have taken that necklace off? What kind of man would do such a thing?

He wasn't a man, he was an asshole—an asshole from last night. And tick by tock, he was going away.

I secured the necklace back in its rightful place. I vowed to never, ever, remove it again.

I picked up the mug and turned back to the last slivers of light.

Time is distance.

56

The next morning, I was up at the crack of dawn.

I walked along the dock toward the boathouse, breathing in the crisp morning air and listening to the pleasant sounds of the birds and the soft *thunk* of my soles on the wooden slats.

I gave a quick knock before entering, then went to the old bunkroom on the bottom floor, where the pirates and I first stayed when we arrived. Helen had laid out a clean change of clothes for me, and on the other bed was a large heap I recognized. There was a note attached to the top, with *Brando* written in bold letters. Below it was a poorly scribed message*: For our friend, you fucking pirate!* It was a board, harness, and kite assembly. I smiled and chuckled.

I set down the letter and hopped in the bathroom for a good shower, then changed and headed up to the kitchen.

Normally, I'd feel a little self-conscious about using someone's boat as a flophouse for a couple nights after a dirty bender. Especially one belonging to people who probably knew I was being an asshole to their loved ones. But, in order to press into the future, I had to kick the past behind. Man up, and get on with it. No matter the situation, I got a welcoming smile from Helen, who was ready with a plateful of breakfast as I sat down. Faas never lifted his head from whatever he was reading. My mind was focused on one thing, and one thing only, that morning. It was all business for me, and if certain people didn't approve, fuck 'em. So, I just got on with it.

I cleared my throat to grab Faas's attention, but he didn't flinch. "Hey, Faas."

He finally stopped chewing his food and looked up at me; not fully, just enough so I knew he was listening.

"I'm gonna need the da— Wait, what day is it?"

He grunted, "Is Monday."

Helen pulled up a chair between us.

"Right, so, I'm gonna need the day off. Maybe tomorrow too."

He stopped his munching again and looked back at me. Then he continued eating and lowered his face back down to his article. "Yes, we have time now."

Helen looked very sunny and happy that morning. I was curious as to what her reaction to me would be, because I knew she and Tatiana talked more than they ever let on. So, I believed her happiness meant there was some hope left for us. I decided to use that leverage for my next question.

"I… I'm maybe going to need an advance too. Some money."

"What! You get drunk and make a mess in boat. You tell me you need time off from work, and now you need more money?"

"I don't know for sure that I'll need the money. I'll hopefully know later today."

His face scrunched and he pointed his fork at me. "What? You don't know now, you know later?"

"I'll pay you back Faas. You know I'm good for it."

"*Hmph!*" He wiped his fingers on a napkin, then threw it down on the table. "What? Why you need so much fucking money for?"

I cleared my throat again and looked him in the eye. "A ring."

Helen let a slight squeak go as she sucked in a breath and held a napkin over her smile.

"I need it for a ring, I hope… when I get my family back."

That was the one time I beat Faas down in a staring contest.

The whole kitchen paused. I couldn't tell which direction Faas was leaning toward. But as it turned out, it didn't matter.

Helen patted my hand softly. She was still smiling behind her napkin, wet trails town her cheeks. She nodded to me, then pulled her napkin down. "Yes, we have this for you."

There was a clang as Faas's fork fell onto his plate. He looked like he was about to have a struggle for power. But all Helen had to do was hold up one finger to him. That finger had some special kind of power, because Faas bit down on that tongue of his so hard, I thought he was going to pop. Like when Bugs Bunny plugs the end of Elmer's rifle with his finger.

I decided then, having gotten the answers I wanted, to get the hell out while the getting was still good. I grabbed a couple items to munch on, then leaned over and whispered thanks to Helen and followed up with a kiss on her cheek. The walk across the road to the orphanage was one of the longest in my life. It was a walk of shame. If there was a time for it to be raining for dramatic effect, it was then. But it was a beautiful, spring morning. The only storm was in my thoughts. The children, the yelling, the crying, my drunken stupidity. Helen's positive response at breakfast had given me some hope, but it was fading with my every step.

I thought about going to find some flowers as a peace offering. But nothing would be open at that time, and I didn't want to imply that it was all right if I fucked up because I'd bring flowers in the morning. Or that that was all I really had to offer to make things right. This was beyond flowers.

Maybe… maybe she'd have my shit packed and waiting at the door for me. Maybe she'd throw it in my face when I knocked. Maybe she wouldn't even answer, leaving it all in Tessa's hands.

Maybe… maybe she'd be waiting with a pleasant smile and a loving kiss. Maybe she'd say she forgave me completely and we could start over.

Maybe she wasn't even there. Maybe she'd packed up her broken heart and headed back to her family in Ukraine.

I stood on the walk directly across the street from the orphanage. I looked up at the top windows and saw no movement. It was early Monday morning, possibly not the best time for me to be riding in on my Velcro sandals. But it was what it was. I really just wanted the question answered.

A cool morning breeze lifted the hair from my face and delivered the soft scraping of a crumpled sheet of paper as it tumbled to its next point of rest around the corner, where the wind would eddy and drop all the other travelling artifacts. I appreciated that moment. The freshness in the air, the silence, the calm before the shit. I would've liked to stay there a while longer, even a long while longer. But the suspense was a killer. So, off across the street I went.

I reached the door and stalled. Should I use my key and just go in, like I always had. Or should I be knocking? If I knocked, who would come? It was too many questions, and my head was beginning to hurt. So, I stuck my key in the lock, turned the handle, and crept… No, I didn't want to creep. That would insinuate guilt, and I wasn't completely guilty. But I didn't want to disturb anyone I didn't need to. So, I stepped in, really, really careful and quiet-like.

But the door was squeaking and the floors were croaking. It really was an impossible place to do anything privately. I looked up to my path. There were a lot of tattletale stairs to climb and doors to pass. I was waiting for people to begin poking their heads out, but no one did. I could hear footsteps in the kitchen and water running, off and on.

One step at a time, I made the climb. Doing my best to prepare for any obstacle that may pop out.

But… no one did.

I'd made it all the way to the first landing and stopped to look up at the next landing, where I wanted to end up. Waiting for a familiar face to pass. My heart transitioned from pumping to pounding, my hands grew clammy, I was perspiring a little more than I liked, and my mouth was beginning to paste.

I could hear them. It sounded like they were all in the children's room, getting busy with the day. I wished at that point that I was back across the street, standing on the curb. I would've used that time a little more wisely, maybe come up with an opening speech or something. But I wasn't there, and it was only a matter of seconds before one of the Incredibles picked up the sound of my breath or the smell of my whatever.

Then I saw the one I'd forgotten. The one who was always there, for any of us, when we needed. Little Sasha poked her head around the corner of the children's room. She stopped her panting when she saw me, her head tilting and her floppy ears lifting as if to say *What the fuck you down there for?* Then her head righted, her happy panting returned, and she smiled.

I smiled back as a rush of heat passed through me; it was fight or flight time. Sasha wasn't going to let it continu—

She let go a soft snort.

I felt my face crunch and sweat run everywhere. I held my hand up to her slowly; I just needed one more minu—

She let go a full-on bark, her claws tapping loudly on the floor as she did her little nervous twitch.

The gig was up, so I jumped up the last couple stairs to give her a pet before she lost her mind.

She lifted herself onto her hind legs and pawed at me for as much attention as I could spare. I did my best to satisfy her while I looked into the room, at all the tiny heads stationed sporadically around the space. Everyone was looking in my direction. Tatiana stood in the middle of the room, and I watched as she slowly crossed her arms over her chest, her expression mute.

"Brandon?" Hans squeaked. "Brandon, is you? You back?"

My every word, every move was with extreme caution. We'd never been here before, at this stage. I didn't have a clue how she would react to my seeing the children again. So, I kept my eyes trained on her, waiting for any sign that I was crossing a line.

"H-hey, buddy."

She didn't flinch.

"Brandon!" Hans pushed back his chair from the table, then crossed the floor as fast as he could. Once the others heard his scramble with no scolding from the boss, their faces all lit up and they followed his lead.

"Brandon!" cried all their tiny voices.

It was sweet music to my ears.

All the little ones clutched onto a leg, including Lilly. It was really good to see her back. I crouched down and gave each of them a big hug.

"Brandon, you is back! We miss you! You back to stay wit us? Forever?" Their little arms squeezed me so tightly. I squeezed them back to the point of almost crushing them, till they made a little "blah!" noise. It felt so good to hold them close again. Something I'd taken for granted. Their little bones and tiny muscles so innocent, so special.

When I stood, Anna was also there to greet me. Her smile was beautiful and sincere. There was even a hint of a tear in her eye, though she'd never let it fall. But she wouldn't cross the room to hug just anyone, and it was an honour to hold a place in her heart.

Kids, they really are miracles on their own. At a time when I felt I'd dropped the ball on the whole world and expected nothing less than all of it to turn its back to me, their forgiveness was instant. Instant, and complete. Hugs from little children. That shit'll change the world. For the first time that day, I felt like I had something solid to boost me on up the next step. That next step was still standing in the middle of the room, with her arms crossed over her chest. She looked completely neutral. She didn't appear to be excited for my return, but I didn't feel like she was going to kick me out on my ass either.

"Okay children. Is enough time for Brandon, now all must go back to study."

No matter how strong my power of seduction was over the kids, no spoken word was more powerful than Teacher's. It drew a smile from me, the way they all broke off without so much as a complaint, and headed off to their workstations.

There I stood, awkward and alone again, except for Sasha. My loyal friend stood tight to my side. I stood there and kinda swung my arms a bit, wiping my sweaty hands on my shorts and watching Tatiana. She was answering some questions from the children and was not really paying any attention to me. But she wasn't running away either.

I had to refocus. The warm welcome from the children had tossed me off to the side a little. I was there to make things right again, for all parties, and that meant stepping up to the plate.

So, I stepped up to her, respectably.

She turned to me, as I approached.

"Hey," I said. Which wasn't as powerful of an opening as I'd imagined, but I was at the plate.

She raised her brow, as if she were also expecting something a little more heart fluttering. "Hello." She managed a polite and strictly professional smile.

"Is…" My follow-up wasn't going any better than my opening. "Is it all right… for me to be here, now? I really didn't want to walk in on all of this." I cleared my throat. "But I couldn't wait any longer."

"Mmm." She held her pose. "Is fine, I think. The children like to see you." She paused. "You smell better."

I let out a small snort and smiled. "Yeah, thanks. I've really been working on that."

"You do no have work today?"

"Yeah… I mean, I'm supposed to be working, it's Monday. But I asked Faas for the day off… Maybe, maybe a couple days off."

"Oh? Is nice for him to do this. Now you is here, now you must help with lesson today."

"Oh. Uh, yeah, for sure."

That was it for the opening conversation, and we broke from our huddle.

It was a good day. It wasn't what I was hoping for, in my most spectacular of expectations. But it could've gone a hell of a lot worse.

The sun was warm and bright through the windows, with that specific springtime hue. I worked my way around the stations, taking my time with each of the children. I'd never really felt like I was much help during lessons, but I was good with encouragement, and we always had a lot of fun. It felt good, really good, to be back. I'd known that I'd missed it, but sitting there, I really understood the meaning of *Home, sweet home.*

I could breathe again, and colour began to return to my vision. To things that I'd never realized had slowly faded over my time of uncertainty.

In the afternoon, the day had grown so beautiful, I couldn't take it anymore. I rounded up the troops to help persuade Teacher to let us go to the park. She put up just enough resistance to make it understood that she was doing us a "special favour."

Down the street we walked. New beginnings were all around. Plants and flowers were in full bloom, and the breeze was just enough for a constant refresh.

The children were lit right up, as they should be on such a day. I was enjoying it for the most part, but there were times when I found it hard to fit in. Normally I'd be beside Tatiana, holding her hand or with her arm wrapped around mine. It was always that special final touch that made everything perfect. That day, Tatiana walked out front with Sasha and Anna, so I herded the sheep from the rear. As I watched them converse, I grew a slight suspicion that Tatiana was maybe giving Anna a lesson on how to treat your man, after he did something really dumb.

All the remaining, unanswered questions were eating at me. What was really happening? How far were we going with this? Would I be sleeping in the boat again that night? Had I been permanently downgraded to "friend" status, with visitation rights for the children? I understood that it wasn't the right time. Not the time to risk screaming obscenities, layered over fits of crying.

So as much as I was focused on enjoying the day, there was still that big elephant in my brain. It was one of those situations where I really, truly hoped we could go back to how it was before, because I missed it that much.

We spent the rest of the day outside. We found a park with swings and spinners and jungle gyms. Keeping them all from killing themselves was a full-time job for me. When I say "for me," I mean exactly that. As all Tatiana did was find a comfortable spot in the sun, swirl her hair around, pitch her head back, and soak up the rays. She lifted a finger not once.

It was tough work, chasing everyone around, pushing on this and pulling on that. Sasha was doing what she could, keeping track of what I couldn't and barking when there was a concern. The only way I could convince them all to take a break was to bribe them with ice cream. I corralled them all beside Tatiana, then recruited Hans to come and give me a hand with the refreshments.

When dinnertime drew near, we worked our way back to the orphanage. It was a long walk, with everyone tuckered out, but we made it back in time. Tessa flashed me a sweet smile when she saw me, and I got a hug when a sorta-private opportunity presented itself. But there were no words spoken, which again, sent a lot of mixed signals.

After dinner, the children took turns playing on the piano and singing. Then it was story time. The little ones crowded around the couch, seeming too insistent on keeping a hand on me. As they lay curled in their pillows and blankets, some played with my toes and marvelled in my leg hair. I got the feeling that they were wondering where I would be in the morning, and that we were all hoping it would be right there.

Tatiana had done what she always had before, fallen asleep with her head in my lap. One by one, I watched all the pairs of tiny eyes grow heavy. I announced bedtime to lazy protests. Their little voices laid over the background of the quiet room, brought warmth to my heart. I gently slid from beneath Tatiana, my legs strong and stable. My body felt good. I felt good, as I picked up the children one by one and carried them to bed.

"You be here for us in morning, Brandon?" Gaby asked, refusing to release her arms from around my neck.

I smiled. "I don— Yeah… yeah, I'm gonna be here for you, no matter what. I'll be here." I leaned in and gave her a big kiss on the cheek, and she squeezed my neck with everything she had, till her little arms gassed out.

With all the minors in their sacks, I turned back for my next project, only to find the couch vacant.

I stood for a moment, in the middle of the room and looked around at all the sleeping children, unsure what to do. Sasha, down by my side and panting happily, had no direction for me.

It was time to take that next step and find out. Maybe the future I thought lay in my hands, was not as much in my control as I'd felt. It now felt like those times when a slow, lonely song plays in your mind. That feeling when you realize you may have fucked it up beyond repair. And there's a high probability you'll be dry humping the blankets in the boat until you can figure out another direction for you, yourself, and no one else.

I thought back to the morning. When I was full of gusto, or maybe it was full of shit? When I was going to walk in there and grab that bull by the balls, even if it kicked me in the head. I wondered where that no-bullshit guy had gone? Maybe I was just tired from the day. Maybe having that time with the children had reminded me how much was at stake when I acted like an asshole. Maybe I realized how big of a risk I really was, and that it was possible I had proven a risk not worth taking.

Knowing Tatiana the way I did, she had made up her mind, either way. All I could do was walk through and accept the sentence handed to me.

So, I took that lonely walk. I stopped at the door of the children's room and took some time to look back over each one, in case it was my last chance. Then, I switched off the light.

I stepped into our— Tatiana's room to find it all but dark. The small light on the nightstand shedding the only light. She was nowhere to be seen, but I could hear the sound of running water coming from the bathroom.

After a moment, the tap shut off.

She walked toward the bed, dressed in her silk jammies, giving me no acknowledgement.

The suspense was exhausting. I wished she'd just kiss me on the lips, or kick me in the balls already.

I cleared my throat. "I… have all the kids in bed."

"Oh." She stopped in her tracks, acting surprised by my presence.

It was bullshit. I knew the whole act was bullshit. She knew I was there, she always knew.

"Yeah… I got them all tucked in." I stuffed my hands in my pockets and waited for her to respond.

But she didn't say anything, just stood there in the dim light, looking toward me.

"So, I guess… Can we talk now?"

"Talk?" She acted as if she'd forgotten all about… everything. "Yes, I guess is good time for this."

She ended her speech there and left me hanging once again. It was getting late, and frustration was gaining weight. I reached up and vigorously ran my fingers through my hair, digging at my scalp, wishing she would contribute in some way, any way.

"Listen, Tatiana. I'm really sorry and—"

Motion tugged at my eye. I looked up to see her take a step toward me, gently, quietly. Then another.

"And I—"

She took another step closer, one more, and again, till she was right in front of me. Her face inches from my own. She reached her hand out carefully, touching it to my chest. Then she slid it slowly up to my cheek and felt, the way she always did, like she belonged in a time so far away.

"I is sorry," she breathed. She continued to rub my cheek as her other arm slid up my chest again and then draped around my neck. "Much of these things you say about me, you is right. I want… I think you know now, how to be with me. But how can this be possible when I no do speak to you my feelings?"

She pulled herself closer, till I could feel the warmth of her body press to mine. My entire body flushed with emotion. I slid my hands around her waist, my fingers clawing for purchase.

I leaned in and looked her in the eyes, for what it was worth. "Yesterday, in the boat, when I told you… when I said… I meant it, Tatiana. I really meant it… I love you. I really honestly… I love you."

She smiled and patted me softly on the cheek. "I know this. Is why I let you live still." She gave me a super-sexy wink. Then sealed the deal with a kiss so sweet, it was like none I've tasted before. My tension eased, and I melted into her.

She broke from me and looked up, feeling for what was now my most honest of smiles. "Next time," she said, "you bring flowers. Then I not make you wait so much."

She got a hearty chuckle from me, and I nodded. "Yeah, flowers."

Her hands slid down to mine. "So, now we have the first fight. We see, we get through this, together." She kissed me lightly, then whispered, "I love you too, honey."

She turned and pulled me over to the bed with her.

There was no crawling all over each other to try to get in our pants. We just lay beneath the covers, as I stared into her sparkling blue eyes, giving thanks for the second chance. I told myself over and over again to never fuck it up, because

I would never get another.
    Then we kissed, over and over, till sleep overcame us.

Marc Gregory

57

The next morning, I was up with the sun and life for me was amazing. You couldn't have beaten the smile off my face even if you'd beaten me to death.

The first thing I saw when I opened my eyes was my lady. Somehow, she'd gotten away from me during the night. So, I wrapped every limb granted to me around her and pulled her back in, nice and snug. She gave a satisfied moan, reached back, and rubbed my leg.

The day was clear and the sun was bright, flooding the room with a sense of anything being possible. As much as I wanted to stay in bed, I had to get to work.

I smothered my love with kisses, then forced myself away from her, resisting her lazy protests and her sexy-as-hell morning smile. Even with her hair scattered across her face, it was literally impossible for her to look unattractive.

I got ready for the day, and before I headed down the stairs, I popped into the children's room and went around to every sleepy-headed one of them, giving them a kiss and wishing them a good day. Their precious smiles were another healthy boost to the start of a wonderful day.

Out the door and across the street I bounded. I wasn't really going to work that day. I was going to the boathouse for breakfast, but afterward, I was taking Helen shopping.

I walked up the stairs to the kitchen, two at a time. When I hit the top, I clapped my hands and pumped them victoriously in the air.

Faas remained in his usual position, and Helen turned to me from behind the counter. When she saw the smile on my face, she clasped her hands in front of her breast and happy tears danced in her eyes. "Oh," she whimpered.

"That's right!" I cheered, giving Faas a healthy slap on the back as I passed, resulting in a healthy burp, which didn't really surprise me.

I hurried around the counter and grabbed Helen by her hands. I grinned and looked her dead in the eyes. "You have to come with me today. We have to go pick out a ring."

"Oh!" She wrapped her arms around me. "Yes! I am so happy for you!" She started to ball on my shoulder. "Is so excitement! Yes, we will go. First, we have some breakfast. Then I must get ready, and then we go. Be there just in time for store to open. I know!" She clapped her hands and bounced on the balls of her feet. "I know perfect place, yes!"

I smiled and nodded.

"Oh!" She broke down again and pulled me in for another generous hug.

I pulled up my usual chair while Helen finished making breakfast. I looked across the table at Faas.

After I sat down, he finally lifted his head and looked at me, still chewing on his mouthful, his eyes squinted. "So," he said, among his chewing, "she let you back?"

I smiled and gave a sigh. "Yeah, she let me back. I'm a very thankful guy today, I'll tell you that." I looked at him with sincerity. "Thanks Faas... Really. Thank you to you, and Helen, for everything. I can't say it enough. I'm really sorry for being such a pain in the ass sometimes, and I'm going to pay you back for the ring. For everything, no matter what the cost. So, don't worry about it. Just... thank you."

He stuffed another forkful in his mouth and continued with his chewing, looking me over. "So, now you ask this girl to marry?"

"Yep, no more fucking around. I got my second chance, and I'm not letting her slip away. I'm in love with her, and the children. We're a family."

He continued to chew for a second longer, then lifted his fork and pointed it toward me. "Maybe I wrong on you. Maybe you not so much stupit." He gave me a wink, but kept the fork pointed. "You have today, for what you need, tomorrow we must go back to work."

"Yes." I nodded. "I know, it's no problem. Thank you for all of this. I'll be back at work this afternoon, actually. I'll have nothing to do after we're done. I don't want to go back to the orphanage too early. She'll know something's up, she's really quick like that. I want this to be a total secret. So please"—I looked at him and over at Helen, who was watching me with a daydream smile—"please don't say anything."

Helen nodded, dabbing at her eyes with her towel. "I no tell anything. When you go to do this?"

"I have no idea, yet. As soon as possible. But I'd like it to be romantic. I don't know if I should do it with the kids around. I'm not sure it's right to put that kind of pressure on her, maybe it's not fair? I don't know…" My palms began to sweat and my nerves began to tingle. "I've never done this before. I… I don't even know if she'll say yes."

I caught Faas and Helen sharing a smile between each other, a jog down memory lane perhaps.

I drifted off for a bit, while they returned to what they'd been doing. I'm not sure if my having a moment to dwell on things was good or bad, but as I sat there going over what exactly I was planning, the more nervous I became. Maybe I was going too fast? Wasn't marriage one of those things a young man should at least talk over with his parents? Sit on the fence and chew on some straw with the old man? What would they say?… Married!… I could be getting married.

Any time I stopped to reflect, my feet grew cold… real fast. So, the only responsible approach was to not think anymore. Think about the happy children, think about happy Tatiana, think about the sex coming my way—anything. Was it normal to be that nervous?

After breakfast, we sat for a few cups of coffee, as it was still too early for the shops to be open. Then, Faas went out to do whatever Faas does, and I helped Helen clean up the kitchen. Then I paced the floor in the living room while she got ready.

Back and forth, again and again. Alone wasn't a good place for me. I watched the time tick by on the wall clock. I would've thought that each back and forth would eat up at least a minute, but it was more like a second. I tried to identify the different sounds coming from Helen and Faas's bedroom, estimating what stage of preparation she was at.Gruelling! It was like an endurance competition in there. I felt as though I was being ground down, worn out like a bull in the fight. Piece by piece, being picked apart. I'd been working off a heavy adrenaline dump for at least an hour. If Helen didn't hurry the hell up, she might find me dead on the floor.

Finally, she emerged from the bedroom humming a tune. Then she walked by the table and around the counter toward the coffee pot. She poured a cup, then looked up at me, and her jaw fell.

I was a complete mess. I knew it, and the look on her face confirmed it.

"Oh… Brandon, sweet boy, you not look well."

Sweat… everywhere sweat. I turned and caught a brief look at myself in a mirror. Sweat down my chest, armpits, face, and hair. I looked on the verge of a seizure.

"I guess I'm a little nervous."

She smiled sweetly and placed her hand over her heart. "My poor boy. Is okay for you to have this." She laughed softly, then slid out from behind the counter and came toward me. "Come, you must relax. Go have shower, make it cold shower, yes. I go to find you more clothes." She placed her hands on my shoulders and looked me in the eyes. "Is okay… She is goot woman. You is goot man. I think I know, in my heart, she will say yes."

Honestly, I think that's what scared me the most.

I did as told, and hopped in the shower. I started it warm at first, then bit by bit, I cooled it down. Normally, I'm not the type of guy to do cold showers, but I really needed to get my core temp down. I just couldn't be alone anymore. I turned the shower down another notch, to the point where it was pretty much unbearable. I stood in it till it sunk into my bones a little, then shut it down and wrapped myself tight in a towel.

I crossed the hall to the bunkroom and found that Helen had laid out yet another set of loose-fitting clothes. A button-up Hawaiian-print shirt and grey shorts. The style, I guessed, dated back to Faas's more slender days. It wasn't the high-roller image I wanted for ring shopping, but it was accurate for rummaging through the discount bin.

I met up with Helen upstairs. We checked the time, and although she wasn't certain the store would be open yet, we decided to make our way there. We could find a café and have a tea as we waited, if necessary.

Helen led me past the train station. Farther east than I'd yet to be, to a small hole in the wall, with a modest, wooden sign hanging over the door from a decorative iron rail. She tried the door handle and found it locked. Then she cupped her hands around her face and peered into the window. There were some lights on and some figures moving around in the back. They froze when she gave a weighted knock on the glass, as did I.

Turns out it was a mom-and-pop shop, and everyone knew Helen and greeted us at the door with warm hugs. They invited us to come in early for a private showing, locking the door again behind us.

They had coffee on, and brought us out a cup. As Helen spoke to them in their language, the couple looked over at me and smiled. While Helen chatted it up, I perused the display cases. There were rings, and more rings. I realized I didn't really know what was required in an engagement ring. I knew Tatiana was blind and would likely never be able to tell the difference between a real diamond and a fake, but that clicky thing she did—that scared the shit out of me. No matter, it was the thought that counted, and even though the diamond wouldn't be the biggest in the store, I wanted to get one that was real.

"So— Brandon, yes?"

The man had broken away from the ladies' chatter and slid up behind me. He was a slender gent, dressed tastefully in neat, and well-fitted clothes. He had his own bling on. A watch and a ring here and there, and a gold necklace. He held out his hand.

I accepted with a smile and a firm shake. "Yeah, I'm Brandon."

"Yes, Helen say you are very big help for her and Faas. We know each other for many years, since we are children. You call me Henry, please. For English, I am Henry."

"Oh, okay, Henry, it's very nice to meet you. Thank you for letting us in early, you really didn't have to—"

"Yes, of course, this is no problem." He gently cupped my elbow and steered me around beside him. "Helen, she say you have met a special lady. You are now ready to take this step for making proposal to her?"

"Yeah, well, I hope I'm ready. I hope she's ready. I'm pretty nervous, really."

He smiled and wrung his hands together. He seemed like a very warm and genuine guy.

"Yes, I think I not know any young man who come here, over all of my years, that is not nervous. I know a little about this lady of you. My wife and I, we know Tessa from orphanage. We have never yet to meet this lady for you, uhh…"

"Tatiana."

"Yes, yes, Tatiana. Is beautiful name, for beautiful young lady. We see her many times, walking wit the children. Many people here, they talk of her and we hear so many nice things, how she work wit the children. Is very special lady."

"Yes, she is very special."

He gave me a joyous smile and patted me on the back. "You very lucky man! I think all is going to go well for you. But please, Brandon, I would like to help you to pick this special ring for this lady, please."

"Yeah!" I nodded. "Absolutely! I really have no clue about any of this stuff."

"Yes, yes!" He smiled and placed his hand on my back, lightly pressing me to the case across the room.

As soon as the ladies noticed us, they excitedly joined in. There were fingers pointing in every direction, and conversations about things I couldn't understand. Several examples were brought out for closer inspection, and after a bit, I began to take a liking to a smooth band with a sort of ying-yang swirl at the top, cradling a single diamond. Simple and elegant.

Everyone agreed. The problem came when I looked at the price tag. I had an idea of what I wanted to spend, and this was a little higher than I was comfortable with. Especially with Faas and Helen fronting the cost.

The others watched me for a while as I continued my search, then got back to their chattering. I think I looked at every ring in the store, but nothing in there was cheap and nothing caught my eye as strongly as my first pick.

After a moment, Helen tapped me on the shoulder and held my favourite ring up to me.

"You like this, yes?"

I gave a shrug and a nod and lowered my voice a little. Doing my best to relay what the problem was. "Yes, I like it, Helen, but." I flipped the little price tag with my finger. "It's more than I'd like to spend."

"Yes, yes, I understand this. We talk and they will make some change for you. They say this price for you." She held up a slip of paper, with a dollar amount hand scribed on it. It was about a thirty percent discount.

My eyes popped and I looked at all three of their smiling faces. Henry and his wife were hand in hand, nodding enthusiastically.

"Oh… well, okay, I guess." I smiled. "Thank you." I nodded to them. "Thank you very much!"

"Yes, yes," they happily responded. They came around the counter and Henry's wife gave me a very big hug, then Henry took my hand in both of his, congratulating me.

That was the ring-shopping experience.

Helen and I headed back to the boathouse around noon, arm in arm. She was on top of the world, and I felt much better, surprisingly, having it sorted out and in my pocket.

Faas wasn't anywhere to be found when we returned. Helen said he was out running errands. So, I walked over to the boat and climbed on deck.

I sat there for the rest of the afternoon, opening and closing the little velvet box.

I had it. A complete circle that would symbolize us being together for the rest of our lives. We both had a lot of life left… and we would be together for the rest of all of it. Just me and her, and the children would be there, too, forever… till death did us part. What was the big deal, people do it every day… *Right?*

As the butterflies fluttered, I took myself back to a few nights past, and the following morning. To how much I'd missed her and how much I would've given to be back in her arms. I thought about the morning when I woke up snug and smiling with her beside me. Clear-headed, healthy, happy, and madly in love. I remembered…

Around my usual quitting time, I slammed the little box closed and headed home, proud and happy with the path I was on. But there was one more thing still weighing on my mind.

That night, after I'd put the children to bed and Tatiana and I were getting ready for our bedtime, in between kissing and groping sessions, I asked the question that was bothering me.

"Honey, have you talked to Lilly at all, lately?"

I sensed the question unnerved her some, but she handled it.

"No, I do no talk to her much about it. I ask how she like the time when she went for weekend. She say the same. Is nice people, but she no do like when I say too much about possible they be her family."

"She still wants to stay here, with us?"

"Yes, but you know, here is no what is best for her. Is best to have her with a family."

"I… I get that, but if she really doesn't want to go, isn't there something we can do? Can they really force her?"

Tatiana breathed in deeply, then she put her arms around my neck and looked up at me. "I do no think there is something we can do. I think is just going to happen. I think is best we help Lilly with this. Is all we can do."

I could feel that the conversation wasn't one I should be pushing right then. But if we were married, maybe, just maybe, we could do something more? Maybe we could keep Lilly around? It wasn't the reason I was going to propose to Tatiana. But, what if it would allow us to keep Lilly with us? Even if we had to move out of the orphanage and get our own place. Maybe we could take them all, adopt them all and be a real family?

I knew it was a long shot. But I was going to be the man of the house, or I was planning to be, anyway. It was my family. What kind of man would let someone fuck with it?

58

The next day it was back to work as normal, and I welcomed it as it gave my mind something else to focus on. Still, every break I got, I sat down and had a look at the ring. I'd decided to keep it stashed in the boat with no one's knowledge, beyond my own. I didn't know if Tatiana had any suspicion about what I was planning, but I knew that woman's-intuition thing they speak of can be scary accurate. Although she kept herself all calm and professional-like, I could see her throwing that to the side to search for a ring. She wasn't *that* professional. So, I played it better-safe-than-sorry.

The next obstacle I was scratching my head over was how to get it done. Every time I thought about it and how it may go down, I felt sick to my stomach. I again, found myself in one of those anxious situations.

The next evening, what could be the perfect opportunity was dumped in my lap. While we were settling down for story time, Tatiana announced that the something-or-other festival was on the coming weekend.

Apparently, it was something the children had been to before, because they cheered at the mention. It was an annual thing, from what I could gather. It took place in some park, or farm on the outskirts of town. It sounded like a bit of a haul on the train, but the children loved train rides. And the festival was focused particularly on children, with rides, things to climb on, and animals. There would also be some stuff to keep the adults entertained, some bands would come and play, and a pretty kickass fireworks display would go off at night. If we could make it that long.

That was it! That's where I would propose to her. It almost seemed a little too easy, like maybe she was handing it to me because she knew. I gave her the squinty eye, but she never wavered.

Saturday was the day, I only had a few more to kill, and then I would know. Know for sure, if she would become *Miss Tatiana Baker.* It did have kind of a nice ring to it. Then my knees began to buckle. It was another obstacle to overcome, and one step closer. One step closer to *What the fuck am I doing?*

I couldn't sleep, and was a complete wreck for the rest of the week. I was tempted to call either of my parents, but I really wasn't sure what they'd say. Maybe they'd try to talk me out of it? Convince me to wait? Maybe that was good advice, maybe it wasn't? But as I sat by the window at night and looked over at her sleeping, I felt a very strong loyalty to her and our little family. As scared as I was to go through with it, what sense would it make for any man to postpone what I had in front of me? How does a young man aspire to succeed in life with no support, no inspiration?

Then… that day came.

I was up at the slightest crack of light—if I even slept. I rolled over to her, squeezed my arm beneath her neck, then pulled myself tight to her. I took a slow, deep inhale of the smell of her skin, then gave her shoulder a soft kiss and pulled her a little tighter. She gave a low groan and I eased off and lay there, holding her, keeping the butterflies at bay. Watching silently, as the reflection in the room turned from a deep blue, to violet, then transitioned to citrus, as the crest of the sun peeked over the horizon.

I crawled out of bed and stepped softly over to the window for a sentimental look at what could be my last sunrise as a bachelor. I might return that day a very changed man. If it turned out that way, somehow, I knew It was all gonna be okay. We were all going to be just fine, as long as we were together. If I had to get up at the crack of dawn every day for the rest of my life and cross the road to the boatyard, it would be all right, as long as I had her. It was a very comforting feeling.

I looked over at my angel sleeping peacefully, with that sexy little smirk on her face. She was such a beauty, everything about her. That night when we returned, we could be engaged to each other. *My fiancée…*

I wondered, then—very, very quietly, to myself—if she was really serious about holding off on the sex until we were officially married? Or, if maybe, we could call it close enough that evening?"

I'd look out the window for a while, then I'd pace the floor and stop to look out the adjacent one. My gaze following any lonely, early morning straggler I could latch onto, in order to keep my mind occupied.

I'd grow cold and snuggle back into bed for a bit. But I found I disturbed her too much with all of my groping affection. I didn't want to wake her up on the wrong side of the bed. I couldn't have anything interfering with her "yes" reflex.

I was back in bed and just beginning to dose off, my eyes finally growing heavy, then… cue the children, enter stage left.

They walked in quietly, with their scout dog, looking, sniffing, and listening for any sign of life. I closed my eyes tight, regulated my breathing, and didn't twitch a muscle.

I could hear Sasha's nails slowly tapping toward the bed, along with the scuffling of stocking feet and muffled breaths.

I was really hoping they'd do a lap and then retreat back to their room, until we woke peacefully on our own. But I knew that was never going to happen on a festival Saturday.

I took a risk and opened one eyelid. They were all around us, searching ever so lightly with their investigative fingers. It was like an eerie scene from a close-encounters documentary. They traced their way around Tatiana some, but they were a little more frightened of waking her up than me. So, eventually they all migrated to my side of the bed. The opportunity they were looking for appeared when they found my bare feet sticking out from beneath the covers, and the games began. They were so sweet and so diabolical at the same time.

When the first unsuspected tiny appendage crossed my arch, I instantly twitched, then cringed at my giveaway. The twitch startled them as well, then I heard giggles and felt a full-on assault of little fingers poking my soles and toes till I was jerking and jumping constantly, while the giggles grew louder.

The dominoes began to fall, as the children's master plan unfolded. All the tussling stirred Tatiana, and she unconsciously gave a snort and rolled over to me, slopping her arm over to try to shut me the hell up.

Her motion threw caution to the tyrants for a moment, but only for a moment. Then I felt Tatiana's legs begin to shimmy. The little buggers had gone into a mindless, tickle frenzy.

Finally, she let a lonesome groan out, and the giggles got louder, then muffled by little hands over mouths.

"What?... Why is this now?" she growled. "Is no school today, go to you bed, sleep."

"Is morning, Teacher Tatiana, is time for wake up!" Gaby yelled.

One by one, the children crawled onto the bed, wedging themselves between us and settling into the warm spots.

I couldn't help chuckling at them all. They were quite the team, our little hooligans. I was happy to have them all, so I stretched my arms out and grabbed all of them in one big circle and squeezed them with a big bear hug. To which the girls, and possibly Hans, let out ear-piercing shrieks.

Tatiana rolled off her side of the bed, barely catching herself on her feet. She stood, waved her arms in the air, and grumbled something foreign and nasty-sounding as she headed straight to the bathroom.

The children and I paused for a moment, and then, after the bathroom door closed, we let the giggles fly.

After we were done having our fun, I explained how it was way too early to be up, and they should apologize to Teacher when she got out of the bathroom. Then I ran down to the kitchen and grabbed her a cup of coffee as a peace offering.

We took our time getting ready. I lay back in bed and watched them all running this way and the other. Looking for their clothes and asking Tatiana for help.

I was happy, genuinely happy. When I could break away from admiring my life, I would contemplate on how I was going to pop the question. Should I do it in front of the children? Should I plan it all out, or should I just wing it and act on pure instinct? I knew the latter would likely result in me doing it maybe the next day, or the day after, so I decided it was probably best to employ a little strategy, and that would be easier once I got a look at the surroundings. Should I do it right away? But then I realized that if she said no, it would be a pretty long, rest of the day. I really didn't feel like she was going to say no... but then again, she might... what more reason did she have to say yes?"

My thoughts rambled me into a trance and I had to forcibly shake it off to snap out of it. Back to morning madness in the orphanage.

Out the window, I saw the sun was fully up and the sky spotless. I checked the forecast and it was gonna be a beauty. Nothing but sun and a light breeze till

Monday. It would be our first full, beautiful weekend of the year, together in the park.

We had some breakfast, packed up a basket lunch, and finished our preparations. As usual, it was Hans and I in one room and the ladies in the other. The smile on his face was constant and his eyes sparkled with that innocence of his.

"So, you ready for the festival, buddy?" I was working on getting his hair styled up just right.

He nodded. "I is happy you are here today, Brandon."

The comment caused me to pause and I looked at him. "Yeah, thanks little man. I'm happy to be here with you too."

"Gaby and Lilly and Anna, they is all happy you here also."

"Oh? Well, I'm really happy to be here with all of you, everyone."

I lifted the brush to continue, then was cut off once again.

"The night, when you and teacher, you have to fight togeter. We was very scared… maybe you not be back…"

He was trying. Trying really hard to hold it together, but I could see the worry and sadness creeping in for an emotional breakdown. So, I placed my hand firmly on his shoulder and looked him dead in the eyes.

"Hey! I know… I know. That night, what happened… it never should've happened. It definitely never should've happened in front of you children. I know that if me or Teacher could take it all back, we would. But just because we're adults doesn't mean we're right. This, us, all of us being together—it's new for everyone, even Teacher and I, and there's some things we're all gonna have to learn. That whole thing that happened, we should've handled it different. I'm mostly to blame for all of that, and I'm really, really sorry, Hans. To all of you. But Teacher and I have talked, and we still want to be together, and I really want to be here. I just have to work a little harder at… being better. I promise you, I'm going to, okay?"

He sniffled back a tear and nodded.

I stood up, smiled, and gave his shoulder a friendly shake.

That set him loose and he lunged at me, wrapping his arms around my legs, squeezing them with everything he had and holding it for as long as he could.

I rubbed his back and soaked it all up, fighting back a little tear of my own. I felt more ready than ever to take the plunge and make things right.

When everyone was ready, we stepped out into the warm spring air. The sun felt fantastic. We assembled in our lines, with Anna in front with Sasha, Tatiana and I in the back.

I remember how she looked that day, in this sky-blue, summer dress I'd never seen her wear before that hugged her so perfectly. I remember that firm, sexy little bum of hers swaying side to side as she walked. Her hair flowing like a veil around her shoulders.

I remember how she looked.

I remember how they smiled that day. As if it were their first time walking through the world, all dressed in their summer best, laughing, playing, growing.

I remember how they smiled.

That morning, I followed along, admiring them all with my hands in my pockets, one on the velvet box, and a shit-eating smile on my face. I was the proudest man in Amsterdam that day—fuck, I'd put myself up against anyone on the planet.

Beautiful! My family was the sexiest sonofabitch out there, and it was all mine. I was so fucking excited for the walk back, with that ring in its rightful place. With everything so right that morning, it was impossible to imagine it ending any other way.

We crossed the street to the station and got our tickets, then headed down the stairs and walked along the corridor and up to the proper platform.

After we'd found a spot to stand and wait, Gaby and Lilly began poking at each other over something, then Lilly reached up to her hair and her jaw dropped.

"Teacher! Teacher!"

She'd forgotten to put on some butterfly barrette she'd been really excited about wearing that day. I recalled her mentioning it several times. It must've gotten missed during the rush.

Normally I would've let Tatiana calm her down and given it time to pass, but… it was Lilly. As soon as the proposal was over, Lilly would be my next focus, so going the extra distance for her was in my best interest. I was competing with big-shot Mercedes boy. *Fucking asshole.*

We still had some time before the train came. More than enough for me to make a round trip. And I could use a few minutes to myself; the butterflies were beginning to flutter again. Just a few more hours and it would be decided, hopefully in my favour.

"Okay, okay." I smiled and placed a hand on each girl's shoulders. "Do either of you know where it is? The barrette?"

Lilly beamed a big smile up to me and clapped her hands. "Uh huh! Is in the stand, where I keep all things for my hair. You know this?"

"Yeah, I know where that is. You sure it's there?"

She nodded. "Uh huh."

Tatiana placed a hand on my shoulder. "No, Brandon, you should no—"

I wrapped my arm around her waist and pulled her in for a kiss. I looked into those beautiful blues and kissed her passionately. Longer than any man would before running back for a barrette.

"It's okay honey, if I don't make it back in time, just let it pass and we'll catch the next. But I'll be back in time, with the barrette." I reached down and tapped Lilly on the tip of her nose, earning a sweet little smile.

Tatiana smiled at me too, biting softly on her lip the way I loved. I maybe should've taken it down a notch with the kiss. I may have given something away, just a little bit. She placed her hand on my cheek and returned my smile, then popped up to her toes for one last peck before I turned and left.

Once I got down the stairs, I picked up the pace to a power walk, but not fast enough to draw too much attention. Out on the street, the crowd in front of the station had begun to build. I broke into a full-on-jog when I hit some clear straightaways, but things were tight.

Despite being away from Tatiana and the children, the thoughts in my mind began to get a little crazy. Last-minute things that probably shouldn't have been last minute, like kids… Would she want to have kids? Ones of our own? She'd never mentioned wanting to have children of her own. So, what if she did?

Thoughts of everything bombarded my mind at once. A pregnant Tatiana walking around a kitchen, waving a wooden spoon and cursing me while a food-splattered infant cried in a high chair.

My legs weakened. My head grew fuzzy, disturbed only by the throb of my heart. I knew I was on the verge of passing out. I'd never been there before—not sober. I stumbled my sorry ass to the nearest trash can and I held for a second, not convinced of what was going to happen, before it happened. I got sick in the trash can. Not a dry heave or a little spittle, I let 'er buck in one big heave. Passing pedestrians formed a big arch around me, looking at me with hands over their mouths.

I straightened slowly, the pounding static in my head fading as sound slowly returned to the world. That was a lot of serious shit to take on, all in one blast like that.

I looked back at the station. My mind was running away from me. I had to get it under control. Then I remembered the time and panic set in, giving me new focus. *Get the barrette and get back to the platform.*

I took the stairs to the children's room two at a time. I looked in the drawer where Lilly said it would be, but I didn't see it and I panicked again and turned the whole drawer inside out. By some bit of luck, I caught a familiar colour out of the corner of my eye. It was on one of the beds.

I grabbed it and headed straight for the door. Back on the street, I looked at the tracks leading into the station. It didn't look like ours had arrived yet, and even if it had, they usually wait for several minutes before leaving. I had time, so I slowed down to a brisk walk. I breathed deeply and took time to feel the warm sun on my face, then stretched my neck side to side and let myself relax. Breathe the happy thoughts back. I remembered how completely happy I was walking over with them only a short time earlier. I was a happy, happy man; from there on out, I would always be happy, because it was right.

The shit-eating smile had returned to my face and the excitement had renewed. I reached into my pocket and rubbed the little box. I couldn't wait to see the look on her face!

Everything was turning out perfect, how many times does that happen in life?

The weather was perfect, everyone who needed to be there was present, and all were happy. It was all playing in my favour. It was a sign, a sign that everything was going to work out, that it was meant to be.

I'd just crossed the street to the sidewalk in front of the station and was smiling at a couple coming toward me, when everything swayed, very, very subtly, like the station itself had heaved in a giant breath.

A split second later, the whole thing exploded.

I didn't have a clue what had happened. I just remember being on the ground, trying to push myself up. I felt sharp pains in places, my head was spinning, my ears were flooded with loud ringing. Everything else had grown silent.

The air was saturated with thick grey dust, so much I could see nothing. I tried taking a breath, but the dry air choked me, my lungs burned, my balance…

nothing worked.

It seemed like forever had passed before sound began to return. Sounds of crying… a little girl, somewhere… then a woman, bursting out in a terrible scream from somewhere very deep.

I struggled to gain my footing, but I fell.

What the hell had happened? Tatiana… the children…

Fear grabbed hold of my heart and squeezed. I tried to move again, blind in the thick cloud, but I fell again, hard, and my head spun. That's the last I remember.

59

I could hear voices. I couldn't understand much, but there was some English, some with a sense of urgency, some with a sense of direction.

Someone started to sob softly. Someone else grunted and hissed, as if they were holding back screams of anguish.

I parted my eyelids slowly, then blinked several times to clear my vision. I stared up at a ceiling. I was in a hospital. I didn't know how I knew, but I did. There were fragments somewhere, quick flashes of past happenings, a broken path to the present.

I took a breath, then wiggled my toes, then my fingers, reaching down and reconnecting with all my bits and pieces. Everything seemed to be in place and functional—all but a heavy pain when I inhaled.

I carefully lifted my head from the pillow and began to direct my vision away from the ceiling. I was definitely in a hospital. Doctors and nurses scurried in every direction, beds were set up side by side along the entire length of the room. The beds' occupants were in various states of repair or despair.

There was Helen, dozing in a chair next to my bed, her head dropped off to the side in the most uncomfortable of positions. I wasn't sure what I looked like, but she looked like she'd been beaten with a brown paper bag of shit.

Why?... Why was she there, beside my bed, in a hospital?

"Oh, Mr. Baker!" said a cheerful voice from the other direction.

I looked away from Helen and faced a nurse hurrying toward me. I managed a weak smile, but I had nothing to say for the moment, still coming to from wherever I'd gone.

She was a very pleasant lady, with lovely dark hair and a promising smile. She made idle chitchat with me while she shone a flashlight in my eyes, then placed a hand on my wrist and monitored her watch.

To the left of the nice lady was a small table. As the items on top of it came into focus, I found them familiar. My shirt and shorts, nicely folded and stacked. The necklace that… that… ignited my recollection. Continuing on beside it was a beautiful blue barrette. It was a butterfly. I knew it was. Fear clutched my chest. Beside that was a small velvet box.

The day… the street… the warm sun… their beautiful, innocent smiles moved in slow motion through my mind.

Right when I began to lose it, I felt hands on my face, turning me from the table till I was looking deep into Helen's tear-swollen, bloodshot eyes.

The nurse sensed the tension, and went straight into a very practised speech. "Mr. Baker!"

I felt her hands clamp down on my wrist and shoulder, pinning me to the bed.

I never broke eye contact with Helen and got a very strong grip on her hand.

"Mr. Baker!" The nurse commanded again, but I paid little attention. "You've been in an accident. There was an explosion…"

I opened my mouth to speak. My throat burned, but I choked through it. "Where?!" I said, my eyes burning with terror.

Helen's face said everything, as she shook her head and began to melt in my grip.

"Where?!" I clawed at her, pulling her closer. I was beyond control of myself, feeling my soul being ripped from my body. How could everything have changed so fast? "Where are they?!" My voice turned to a squeak as reality tightened.

Several staff rushed over when I began to fight my way free. Hands grabbed every part of my body. Voices instructed me to calm down. Pinned down at every angle, I jerked and flexed, my ribs burning with stabbing pain. I kept my focus on Helen as she was torn from my grip, and her face crushed in despair.

Then I felt the sharp piercing of a needle into my arm, and very quickly my body fell limp, and my voice trailed off. I watched as Helen sank down in her chair, leaned forward, and cupped her face in her trembling hands. Things went black again.

60

"Good morning honey." She blinked at me with her smiling blue eyes as her head rested on her pillow. She raised her hand to my cheek.

I returned her smile and tilted my head to kiss her palm. "Good morning beautiful."

The room was full of peace. Soft laughter periodically echoed through the stillness. Her laughter, mixed with the children's. I reached up and ran my fingers through her hair, and my smile flickered.

"Oh." Her look turned to one of playful concern as she gently wrapped her hand around mine and pulled it to her lips. "What is this? You smile, it is no certain."

I smirked, maintaining my gaze on her beauty. "I… had a terrible dream."

"Aw," she mocked. "My poor, strong darling. You have bad dream?" She pouted her lips. "What is it dream? You tell it to me. Maybe I make this better for you."

Our hands played between us. I let the radiance of her touch warm my body.

"No, I don't want to talk about it. It was just a dream. Let's just lie here. Can we do that? Just lie here, forever… will you do that with me?"

She giggled and tapped the tip of her finger to the point of my nose. "Yes, stay here for always. Only me and you."

"Me and you and the children and Sasha. That's it, no one else."

She giggled again. "Yes, is nice to think this. But how can we do this, my silly boy?"

"We'll just do it. Stay here, and never leave."

She snuggled into my arms, so close I could smell her and feel her breath on my face, so sweet. "But we must leave sometime. We need food, and sun. We need to breathe air, is good for us."

"No, it's not good. We have everything we need right here, us."

I felt tiny fingers poking at my feet as the mischievous snickers of children grew.

"It would be nice, but is no real. Is no life only in here, is life outside."

I ducked and shook my head. She placed a finger beneath my chin and raised my face back to her, just as lonely tears rolled from my eyes.

"You is sad?" She traced a tear down my cheek with her finger.

"I... I don't wanna..."

"Shshh." She placed her finger to my lips.

"I... I can't... tell me how... please..."

"You know this, you is my big strong man." She ran her fingers through my hair. "I see... I can see now. You such handsome man... My prince."

"I love you!"

"Yes, I know this, with all my heart. I love you also, always."

"I don't wanna..."

"You must. You can no stay here. Is no real."

"But... you... the children..."

"Yes, the children is here, we are together. Is going to be okay."

"I... I gotta... will you, will you marry me, Tatiana? Please!"

She smiled and a tear strayed from her eye. "What you say?"

"I, I have a ring, I just... I left it... but I have a ring. It's really nice, it's beautiful. I know you'll love it."

She bit down on her lip. "Yes, I know it is beautiful. I know this, Brandon, my handsome man. I love you, I will marry you... Yes." She smiled with such warmth, melting the cold, the way she always could. "Yes... yes... yes, my love..."

My eyes opened. I was back in the hospital. I knew then that was the last time I would ever lie with her in our bed. In that little hideaway room, in a small orphanage in the middle of Amsterdam. At that point, everything—inside of me and out—turned to grey.

Shock, is that the medical term? Was "not giving a shit for nothing anymore" a legitimate diagnosis?

Poor, sweet Helen was still there, wiping at her eyes with a tissue, when she noticed I had come to again. She smiled, then slid her chair over and cradled my hand in hers.

She took a second to collect herself, then spoke. "We are so happy to have you okay. You have some cracking in you," she patted my torso, "you rib. Doctors say you be goot, in time. You have some cut, but is all to be okay. I see Tessa, we call to you mom and dad right away. I call and tell them you is okay. They try to come here, fast as possible. But is much hard for all people now. Many travel is not goot here now." She bowed her head and took another moment. "Is… is terrorist. The train station, is gone. There is bomb…"

She broke down, unable to finish, but I got the drift.

I didn't say anything, didn't have any response, really, other than to blink and breathe. What difference did it make? It was done. Terrorists had come, put a bomb in the train station, and blown up our special day… everything special in my life.

One moment I had my feet planted on solid ground, so solid. Focused, directed, and happy. Happier than I'd ever been. Then, from out of my blind spot, I got pushed off the side of the cliff, and there was nothing… nothing. Nothing to grab, nothing to swim against, no way to brace or escape. Just falling, into nothing, for probably the rest of time. Empty… nothing.

The nurse noticed I was up and hurried over, starting to read off her cue card again. *Blah, blah, blah.*

I stared at her. I considered smacking her in the face, maybe putting my hands around her neck and seeing how close to death I could choke her before someone shot me full of some more of that good stuff. That stuff that had sent me back there, back to her… back to them.

But she wasn't there anymore. They weren't there anymore. "There" wasn't a place anymore, and would never be again. No matter how hard I fought.

If there'd been even the slightest chance it would bring them back, I'd have done it. I'd have done 'em all. Burned it down. All of it, all of them, everyone. No mercy, no prisoners, no exceptions.

Bring them back. Line them up, Tatiana, Gaby, Lilly, Anna, little Hans, and Sasha. All their smiles, their laughter, the fucking brilliance they brought to the world. All these people, none of them knew them like I did. If they took a second out of their fucking lives to stop and give a shit, maybe none of it would've happened! Maybe they'd all still be here?

The hospital was overcrowded. So, they were as anxious to get rid of me as I was to get rid of them. They monitored me for a few more hours, made sure I wasn't gonna be a threat to Helen. Then they basically kicked us out the door.

I don't know what the fuck Helen was made out of. My only guess was everything that is sweet in the world. How—or why—she ever stood beside me through all the shit was beyond my comprehension. Looking back now, I know I'd never have made it out alive without her.

She kept her arm around me and carried some of my weight out to the street. I still hadn't said a word, but she never pushed for one.

We waited for a tram, then hopped on-board and found a seat. The sun was starting to go down. People on the bus were doing their best to appear preoccupied with something other than staring at me, because I looked like I'd been blown up.

The whole ambiance of Amsterdam had changed. No more "It's a small world after all" display. Parents held their loved ones close, looking at others with raised suspicion.

I don't know how long it took us to get back to the boathouse. I just remember a tram and some walking. But, when we finally did arrive, the sun was nothing more than a blue sliver on the horizon.

We stepped off the bus just down the road from what used to be Central Station.

It was gone. It had been larger than life. An elegant centrepiece to a city once filled with magic and wonder… and then it was gone.

People had gathered, hundreds, thousands. Stretching down the main streets as far as the eye could see. Everyone held a light of one form or another—lighters, candles, some with torches—and they were all softly singing together, some song I didn't understand.

I pushed myself away from Helen. I felt her protest softly, but she never tried to stop me. I slid through the crowd. Some who saw me coming stepped aside.

I stood there, at the base of the devastation. People with flashlights on hardhats and some heavy equipment were working very meticulously to lift rubble, without causing a landslide.

It was massive, a massive pile of what once was a grand station. Totally deconstructed to a tightly packed grave. It wasn't a good place, not for my family.

It was too dirty, too cold.

Then I had that feeling. Like, what if they were still alive, buried, dying slowly, starving, calling, *"Brandon… Brandon, help us, why can't you help us? Why did you leave? If you didn't leave, we would still be togeter. Please help us, Brandon!"*

"No!" I sputtered. Tears sprayed from my lips as I reached critical breakdown. "NO!" For some reason, I reached down and picked up a piece of rock and threw it into the pile. "NO!" I shouted.

I ran up to the edge of the rubble and started pulling at the pieces. "You fucking… huh! You want some of this!" I screamed with furious rage. "You want some of this! Huh! You fucking! *Fuck*!" I kicked and pulled, unable to create even the slightest of effects. Nothing would budge.

"Nooo!" I collapsed to the ground.

Tender hands began to settle on me. On my head, my shoulders, my back, anywhere exposed. As people gathered around to soothe me, singing and humming and smothering me with kindness, drowning out the madness inside.

61

I woke in the bunkroom of the boathouse the next morning.

It was quiet, for the most part. too quiet for my liking. But it was the new way of my reality. Quiet, but for the voices in my mind.

The floor croaked softly overhead and I heard the muffled voices of Helen and Faas. Despite the barriers, I could sense suffering.

After some time, I managed to get myself out of bed and up the stairs. For the first time I could remember, possibly ever, Faas was not shovelling down food in his chair, ignorant to everyone around him while reading his precious papers.

He was behind the counter, holding his wife in his arms while she sobbed quietly on his shoulder.

I waited for a moment, for them to realize I was there. Then cleared my throat as a subtle hint.

Faas startled a little and looked over at me standing at the top of the stairway. It was the first time we'd seen each other since…

I don't imagine I looked any better for wear. I was still bandaged up pretty good. It was my first experience with damaged ribs, and it's not one I would recommend. Movement of any kind was a struggle. I felt exhausted, but Helen had dosed me up pretty heavily on painkillers from the hospital before I'd gone to bed. So, I felt like I'd gotten some sleep.

He held the same stern expression he always had at first, but after a second, his shoulders relaxed and the hardness in his eyes softened to the point where he broke and let his gaze fall to the floor. Then he looked back at me with a sympathetic smile and nodded, oh-so-slightly.

Helen turned to me and pushed herself back from Faas. "Oh, Brandon, you is up." She wiped at her eyes and straightened her morning attire. "Did you get some sleep okay, in the night?"

I managed as much of a smile as would ever be expected in such a case and nodded. "Yeah, I think I did all right, thanks."

Faas came around to his side of the table, pulled out his chair, and sat down.

With that, I proceeded to my end of the table and did the same. The same thing I did every morning I visited.

That was it. Four days ago, the bomb had exploded. It had easily placed as the worst act of terrorism ever in Amsterdam. The final death toll was expected to be in the high hundreds. Possibly surpassing a thousand.

That morning, Faas sat in his chair and I in mine while Helen prepared breakfast. The push was on for things to return to normality. For them, normal again was something that lay in the past. What would be my future normal be?

Helen served us our plates, then took a seat. Faas had assumed his usual position, eating and looking down at his paper. Then he spoke. "Now, I am thinking of new idea for boat."

"Faas!" Helen slammed her fist down on the table and everything stopped as we both looked up at her. She held stern focus on Faas.

"What?" he finally responded.

"Is no time for talk of boat!"

He took a minute to extinguish his mouthful. "No! It is goot time to talk of boat and to go back to work." He poked his fork toward me. "He must have something different to think of! What happen is shit! But is done! We must go back to life!... He! He must go back to life!"

It was yet another brilliant dictum by Dr. Faas Freudian. Though what he was saying made sense, I wasn't ready yet. I wasn't ready to forget. I wasn't sure I would ever be ready.

I had a sudden loss of appetite. Or maybe I'd never had one to start.

I managed down a few mouthfuls. The food tasted bland and dry, maybe due to the meds. Either way, I wasn't feeling the morning breakfast cheer. So, I excused myself from the table and went down for a shower.

Sometimes, when I closed my eyes, she would be there. As I leaned against the wall and let the warm spray wash over my body, I could hear her laughter and her voice speaking to me. Feel her gentle arms wrap around me, and the soft touch of her palm against my cheek. I stood there for as long as she remained, watching her laugh, dance, and twirl in the sun as I listened to the water fall and swirl down the drain. Then the warmth left, the water turned cold, and she disappeared. I turned off the taps, alone again, listening to the final streams gargle down the drain.

I got dressed. The process was slow and laboured with my range of movement limited. I pulled on some shorts, although the sky suggested that rain would be coming, I had limited options. I threw on a raincoat as I walked out the door.

The sidewalk was dry, but the air was cool and damp and I could smell the swell coming. I knew where I was going, or at least I knew where I wanted to go, but I was undecided why I wanted to.

It was a short walk down the block, then up to the road. To the left was what remained of the station, but I forced myself to never look in that direction. Instead, I kept my focus straight ahead until I came to the street where what was once our little home sat.

I stood across the street from it and tilted my head up to look at the rooms on the top. At the windows I used to look through to the streets below. The lamp was on in our room. I was curious about who or what may be happening in there, but not enough to take the next step.

I just needed some time, that's all. So, I walked a little ways down to the bench where I'd sat waiting for the Van de Fucks to arrive. I took a second to wonder what had happened to them in all of it, then decided I didn't give a shit. They were probably sipping martinis on a yacht somewhere, catalogue shopping for a replacement.

So, I sat, and I waited. What I was waiting for, your guess is as good as any. I would sit back and look up toward our room, then I would lean over and look at the ground with fidgety hands.

With the flip of a switch, the rain started. It was more of a drizzle, really, by Amsterdam standards. As I sat in the wet, the chill began to sink in and my mind began to wander. Though I refused to look, I couldn't deny the voices, and the voices spawned images.

Cold rainwater splashed down on top of the twisted pile. Seeping, running, gathering, and washing down every slope and crevice, deep, deep into the ruin, undoubtedly locating every precious treasure lost.

My body began to tremble, my mind churned in anguish, and my eyes ran uncontrollably.

"Why, Brandon?... Can you help us, Brandon? Please help us. Is so cold."

I sat there, terrified of myself, as the rain mixed with the dirt and dust and washed it all down, burying them deeper.

Hours past unnoticed. I slipped into some detached state, rocking softly and sobbing to myself. Wanting the pain to leave, yet begging for it to stay.

My cold body had turned numb. It was late in the afternoon and I'd put in at least and eight-hour shift.

I heard a slam. The familiar slam of the front door to the orphanage. I looked up.

It was Tessa. She was dressed up in her heavy rain gear and her hood concealed her face completely in shadow, but I knew it was her.

As soon as we made eye contact, she rushed across the street.

I stood up as soon as she arrived. Both of us were crying hysterically as she thrust herself into my arms and we wrapped ourselves around each other, like two lost souls.

It felt so good to have someone, someone who understood.

She parted from me, but kept her hands on my shoulders. I guess I looked as cold as I was.

"Brandon, how long have you been out here? You must not have this. You look like you are dying."

"I… I w-wanted t-to come to the o-orphanage." My shivering had triggered an intense stutter. My gaze rolled to the upper floor, then fell back down to her. "I can't, Tessa… n-not now."

Her lips tightened and she nodded. "It is not a nice place to be, for now. I understand. But, Brandon, please, you can no stay out here, in this. Here…" She opened her coat, where she had stashed a thermos of hot tea in an inside cubby. She quickly twirled off the lid and filled it, then handed it to me. Half the liquid instantly jumped the side at my massive tremors, and what did make it to my lips scalded instantly.

She shook her head at me. "Brandon, you must come in… Please. You can no be out here anymore."

I considered it, then shook my head. "I… I can't."

"Then come!" She grabbed my arm firmly. "We must take you to Helen and Faas." She gave a gentle tug.

But I didn't move, not a budge, other than turning my head back to the window. The lamp was still on in the bedroom. I could feel the warmth up there, beneath the covers.

"Brandon!" Her tone grew more commanding. "You must come!" She pulled harder, but I stayed strong as a post. Looking up to the warm glow.

"Brandon!" She came back in front of me and leaned her face into me. "Brandon!" she yelled.

I turned my head slowly back to her. I think I'd forgotten she was even there, because her presence confused me a little. "I... I just had to come and check... y'know? I had to make sure they're all right."

My statement visually troubled her, as she stood there with a blank expression. She turned her gaze up to the window, held it for a moment, then returned to me.

She reached both of her hands down to mine. Mine had become so stiff and numb that her touch caused a sharp, tingling sensation.

"They is all right."

Her assurance caused my chest to heave. I smiled through the deluge of tears. I nodded.

"Look," she motioned her head toward the window. "The light is on. They is warm, they is safe. They maybe read a story... huh?" She smiled. "You know, they like to have story."

I managed a little smile back because I knew she was right, they did like stories. I read to them all the time.

"So... is no goot for you to be here now. They would not like if you freeze here, in the street. So, please, we must go back to Helen and Faas. Please, Brandon." She pulled on my hands.

I looked up one more time, then turned back to her and nodded.

The first motions were so awkward. I'd had no idea how cold I'd become. Every muscle and joint in my body had grown impossibly stiff.

62

Tessa kept her arm around me, assisting me in my weakened state. Once we got within respectable eyeshot of the boathouse, Helen came scurrying out the door to meet us. Undoubtedly, she'd been looking out the window for hours.

They escorted me inside to the dry warmth and began stripping the wet clothing off me. Helen had a couple blankets waiting by the door and wrapped them snuggly around me. Then both ladies helped me up to the kitchen.

Faas was nowhere to be found, and I was thankful for that. I knew he sympathized with me, as much as Faas could sympathize for anything. But even with such a tragedy, his sympathy would only stretch so far.

They laid me down on the couch and smothered me with blankets, and Helen brought a fresh cup of warm tea to me. She brushed back my hair, smiled sweetly, and kissed me lightly on the forehead.

Then, the two ladies left me be while they took up a seat at the table and got to some chatting and serious sharing of emotions. They spoke in their native language, and I'm sure it was on purpose. There was a full box of tissue set in the centre of the table and they both clearly had the need for it.

I looked toward my cup of tea and saw Helen had left me a couple of my painkillers. So, I popped them back and washed them down. Whatever they were, they packed a punch, and a punch was exactly what I needed. During my bout with hypothermia, I'd actually somehow forgotten about my ribs.

I lay my head back on the pillow. The ice slowly melted from my veins and my blood began to circulate once again. As the warm blood flooded back to my brain, it flushed away any happy mirage in which I could submerge my thoughts.

My mind slowly faded out the words of sorrow from the kitchen and dialled up the hypnotic deluge of raindrops on the exterior.

They weren't up in the room, enjoying warm story time.

My mind began to drift, back down into the cold, hard, twisted darkness. The pain returned. It hurt so much. Like a merciless carnivore with razor-sharp teeth, ripping and tearing at me. Bite by bite, eating me alive. It was taking its time, shredding me piece by piece and chewing slowly. Making sure that my death would be, without a doubt, the shittiest experience of my life. It wasn't just eating my flesh, it was feasting on my soul. That was really what it wanted. My laughter and my tears. My past, my present, and my future. My hate, my fear, my jealousy… and my love.

I steadied my breathing and closed my eyes, praying to God for the painkillers to take me where nothing could find me…

I woke in the night. Startled at first, not immediately recognizing my surroundings. As my eyes found focus in the darkness, I recalled enough to piece together the puzzle.

I lay my head back down. It was quiet, but for the tiny clack of the wall clock. The rain had stopped, so had the chatter. The cloaked moonlight did little to light the room.

I was alone… I really was alone… Really detached from anything to give me a sense of purpose. I used to have purpose. I had purpose every day. From the second I got up, till I went to bed. I loved my purpose, and I missed it.

I really didn't know what to do. But I knew I didn't want to lie on that couch anymore. So, I carefully picked my way out of the avalanche of blankets I'd been buried under and swung my feet quietly to the floor. The instant flex of my core as I sat upright caused my injured ribs to throb painfully.

I sat for a minute, and looked out the large bay window. To the boat drifting on the shimmering water of the canal.

I remember how beautiful it was. I remembered. The images were there again, in my head. And the voices were back. Nasty, terrible things they were. Tears were filtering through my eyelashes. There were always tears. Tears and rain. Lots of tears, and lots of rain… all the time.

It was a struggle to get myself to my feet. I felt very old and very beaten. One more knock might have done 'er. *One more knock and I could've been with them,* I thought, as I stood and admired the view. It really was, really beautiful.

Things were different, I could feel it. I felt that the things prescribed to heal my pain were throwing fuel on an already-burning depression… but I didn't let it bother me. I took soft steps to the kitchen, avoiding as many squeaky boards as I could. Then I quietly rummaged through a couple drawers. I looked up, and spotted my meds on the kitchen table. I hobbled my way around and took enough to help my mind relax, then painfully made my way down the stairwell.

The lower level was dark and desolate. A little bit of light filtered in through the window. I could probably see a lot of things out those windows, back up the street, to places I used to go.

But I didn't want to.

I felt my way along the wall to the bunkroom, then turned on the light with a hollow click of the switch.

The room was empty, and everything was made up proper, just like every time I'd stayed there. And I'd stayed there a lot in the last year.

I was drowsy and tired, but I wasn't ready to lie down. I looked across the hall to the bathroom, then took a step over and flicked on that light. I went over to the tub and flopped down on the edge. The drugs had kicked in to the point where my whole body sagged.

I turned on the hot tap. The sound of the sudden burst of water splashing on the porcelain was shockingly loud at first. But once the flow and rhythm became established, it was kind of soothing.

I pushed myself carefully to my feet. Thankfully the pain had softened. I undressed, then stood in front of the vanity and looked at my body, all wrapped up in tensor bandages. I felt around for an end and began to peel them off, another challenging task. But once they fell to the floor, my skin took a deep breath.

I slid myself down to the floor beside the tub and turned on the cold water, swishing it around with my hand, watching it swirl and bubble.

Once the temperature felt good enough, I struggled back to my feet, a little tipsy. I placed both hands on the edge of the tub and slopped myself into the bowl. It was hot. Hot enough to make me almost jump right back out. But I'd been there before, in hot water. The initial sensation faded and I was able to relax. It was still fucking hot though. No sane person would risk being submerged for more than ten minutes, but I didn't have a watch.

AE II - Blow Me

I filled the tub until the water ran cold, which was deep enough to comfortably support my weight. I leaned forward and turned off the taps, then drifted back and looked up at the cloud of fog that had filled the room.

I let my arms rise and float in front of me, swaying them slowly back and forth, just enough to feel the pain in my ribs. I thought I might've already taken some painkillers, but I couldn't recall. So, I reached down to my heap of clothes beside the tub and popped two, plus one more, because it was bath time.

Heavy sweat drained out every pore, the blood pulsed through my ears and my lungs had to work to take in the thick atmosphere. Voices filled my head, winding their way between my laboured breaths. They grew louder and crisper. In my mind, in the room, bouncing between the walls just out of sight… somewhere in that fog… Fog again… What was up with that fucking fog?

They were speaking to me, calling to me, so crisp, so clear, right there. But I couldn't make out what they were saying. I felt stuck, drifting between two dimensions like a revolving door. Out, then in, round and round.

My breathing grew shallow in my ears, replaced with the static beat of my heart. They were getting closer… soon they'd be with me… soon I could feel the soft brush of her lips against mine.

I could hear the knock on the door, but I wasn't listening. I heard the banging soon to follow, and then a thunderous bang. The fog began to swirl as a sweet, cool tang quenched my nostrils.

There was a hoarse grunt as I felt a heavy force slam down on top of my head, fingers dug into my scalp as a giant claw clenched around my hair and pulled my torso up and over the side of the tub like I was nothing. Faas pulled me down so that my head was face down in the toilet. Then he shoved something very long and slender down my throat, forcing me to heave the contents of my guts. Stuff I'd eaten weeks ago came out, all while I was supported by my battered torso.

When there was nothing left to choke out, he hauled me completely out of the bathtub. Again by the hair. He drug me across the floor, toward the open door. Then he stood me on my feet in the corner and finally let go of my hair. Then he backhanded me something nasty, holding back nothing. As if he'd been waiting for that chance for years, and I'd just drawn the short straw. I slammed hard against the wall and crashed to a heap on the floor. You wouldn't think that anything, after all the pills I'd popped, would be able to snap me out of it. But I was suddenly very aware. Aware of my surroundings. Aware of Faas standing over me, fuelling up for another assault. Aware of the intense pain pulsing through every part of my body.

"You not have this," he growled, his eyes focused with rage as spit sprayed out from between his clenched teeth. He reached down and grabbed me by the hair again and lifted me up to his level. Then he shoved his other hand beneath my jaw and squeezed till I was paralyzed, then lifted me up to the very tips of my toes.

"You have this?!"

His eyes bore into me as I held onto his forearm with both hands, trying to relieve some weight off my face and catch a breath.

"You want this? You want this? I can no stop this. But you"—he leaned in, nostrils flaring and hissing. "Not this in my house!" He slammed his free fist against his chest.

He had put the fear in me. He was like some dark-alley mafia thug, and I believed he would do whatever he had to. But as I struggled and panicked for air, I realized his anger toward me wasn't making much sense.

Breathing through my nose, I did my best to speak through my crushed jaw. "But… but I was just having a bath, what…?"

"You shut up! You talk at me like I am stupit!"

He tilted my head to the side and toward the floor, where my pile of clothes lay, along with the bandages, the spilt prescription bottle, and… the glint off the blade of a large carving knife.

At that sight, I stopped my struggle. Where did it come from? In my mind, I traced back… Then I remembered, vaguely, that when I'd searched the drawers upstairs looking for my meds, I'd found something interesting about the knife and taken it in my hand. Maybe I wasn't even looking for my meds.

What was I doing? How close had I come?

I started to sob, and my body went limp in his grasp.

He released me. I kept my eyes trained on the accessories. Each complementing the next, for a person who was about to do themselves in… in Helen and Faas's bathroom. Two people who were part of my family. Two people I loved…Helen more-so.

Had I really reached that point? I wrapped my arms around myself and started to blubber. Tears rolled heavy with beads of sweat.

I closed my eyes and she popped into my mind, beautiful as always. But her expression wasn't playful—more disappointed. She reached up and slapped my cheek, gently. My eyes opened. I blinked a couple times as I gained control.

I felt Faas's shadow leave, as he stepped away and lowered the seat on the toilet to have a seat. He sighed, then looked into the tub, reached in, and released the plug.

He shook his arm and dried himself with a towel. Then he sighed again, and slouched, rubbing his hands across his face.

I'd stopped my weeping and I looked at him, doing my best to show him I'd gained at least some control.

I shook my head, slowly. "I… I don't know…" The floor was beginning to cool, so I curled up. "I'm… I'm really sorry, Faas. I don't know! I don't know how, how it all happened." I looked down and shook my head again. "All this shit…" I broke out in tears, unable to hold it together, even though I wanted to, for him. "The fucking pills! I don't know, how the fuck…" I sobbed into my hands.

He sighed again and tossed me the towel, then leaned toward me, resting his elbows on his knees. "You cannot have this." His voice was soft and calm. The anger had subsided. "They is gone… dead. You must know this now," he whispered.

I stopped sobbing and stared blankly at a spot on the vanity. I wondered what kind of an asshole could sit there and say something like that to me? But… he was right. As big a piece of shit as he was being by saying it, he was right. They were gone. I was left there, and they were gone.

"She not like this for you," he said. "I know Tatiana. Not like you to know her, but I know her. Helen and Tatiana is been goot friends, they speak all time. She not like this for you." He continued shaking his head, keeping it low. I knew he was fighting back tears of his own. "She think always, things in life, they is for reason. She think you and her meet for purpose. She know this. Her heart know this. She love you, Brandon."

The statement drew my attention, and our eyes met. He nodded.

"She love you. Children love you also… very much. They gone from here now. You must know, you must know this. But they still there, wit you." He placed his hand over his heart. "You must know this, all time. They gone now, you is here. This happen because for something. She know this, you must now know this also." He tapped his heart.

I just kept my focus on the vanity. I was hearing and listening to his words.

The way he spoke of her, of her strong belief. I knew he was right.

"I'm sorry Faas," I finally spoke, rocking gently side to side. "I'm sorry for all of this. I don't know how… how it got this far. I honestly didn't even know about the knife till you showed it to me. I… I'm pretty fucked up right now, Faas. More than I thought… Everything happened so fast. So much…" I wiped at my eyes. "You and Helen, you've both been so good to me, so good to all of us. I'd never want to do this to you guys. I'm really sorry… Thanks, thanks for coming in."

I was there, and they were all gone. It hurt like nothing else. But, if she were there beside me, she would shrug her shoulders and tell me to get on with it.

Maybe that was all so? Maybe it was right? The truth was, no matter what the special purpose of anything was, no matter how much it hurt, I wasn't ready to let them go. If I couldn't have the pleasure, I'd take the pain. Whatever it was, just to have whatever was left of them. I wanted it, all of it. So, if I had to sit there and think of them, let their memories haunt me until I almost slit my wrist in the bathtub, so be it. But I knew, in my heart, she wouldn't approve. And, if I found my way to where they were, I could expect a swift kick in the nuts. No matter how romantic I meant for it to be, she wouldn't put up with it.

We sat there until I grew too cold to sit there any longer.

Faas stood up and helped me to my feet. He grabbed my clothes and shovelled the pills back into the bottle and handed them back to me. I looked at the container, then popped the cap, tossed the contents into the toilet, and pushed the handle. I'd be looking at a lot of sleepless nights to come. But I couldn't have them. Not then.

Confident that I had enough of my head back on my shoulders for him to not have to pull me out of the tub again that night, Faas helped me to the room and laid me into bed.

We said our goodnights, then he turned off the light and pulled the door to only a crack, and I listened for his footsteps to clear the stairs.

As I closed my eyes, the voices in my head showed me some mercy and turned down the volume. I managed to get some sleep.

63

I woke suddenly, in the morning. Bone dry and feeling like a bag of shit. My throat burned and my ribs and everything attached to them were stiff and ached with every attempt at movement. I was weak, beaten, felt like I'd aged thirty years.

I lay back in the bed, collecting my mind and building motivation for the big move to get water. The previous night played out in my mind. It was another one of those times that made me want to never leave bed again. Faas had taken some caution to not disturb Helen after our bout. But, she must of known, or at least heard something. Getting out of bed was a fight. I ended up rolling onto my stomach, then sliding my legs over the side till I was on my knees. Once in that position, I paused for a breath, then squirmed my way up to my feet.

Standing was no celebration either. It was bad before, it was even worse without my tensor bandages. I thought about wrapping myself back up. I really should have. But it was too much hassle, and I felt the whole process would cause more pain than it was worth.

No bandages, no pills, and lots of pain. Yes, the voices were still there, and the images. It was an all-around shit start to the day. But I knew I had to get control. There was no escaping that thing I was going through. If I'd've actually done it that night, would they be there, waiting for me? The only thing my suicide would guarantee, was my death.

Of course, Helen had washed my clothes and folded them nicely on the chair. So, I bent over, slowly. Every motion was slow. New limits had been set as far as my ability, and it would take some time to discover them all.

With many whimpers and several cringing groans, I managed to dress myself. Then I hobbled to the bathroom.

I was shocked at first, then a little pissed to see the bruise Faas had left on the side of my face. When I saw it, it instantly began to hurt. There would be no hiding it from Helen. So, on top of all my other shit emotions, you could add, "ashamed for being an asshole" to the top of the pile.

I could've decided to not go upstairs, ever, again. But, I needed that—to be part of something. They were going through it too. And Tessa, and a lot of people.

I can't really describe my mood accurately that morning. I was sad, that hadn't changed. But I wasn't fighting it anymore, and somehow it felt better to work with it. There was still a long-ways to go, and there would be times I couldn't be that tough. The combination of it all was a shitty thing to wake up to, and I'd be waking up to it for a long, long time. So, I needed those special people in my life.

I brushed my teeth, and as I grabbed for the towel to wipe up, I heard the telltale creak of someone coming down the stairs.

Helen rounded the corner.

I turned to her and saw her eyes bulge as she looked directly at my cheek. It was quick, but her reaction was definite. She immediately shifted her focus to my eyes and reached for my hands.

"You mother, she is wit the phone." She gestured down the hall.

Ah, shit! Not that I didn't want to talk to my mother, or didn't understand that I definitely should. It just really wasn't what I needed at that specific time. I was working hard to keep myself together. Any more drama could send me back over the edge.

Helen stood aside to let me pass. She followed my sloth-like mass till I hit the bottom of the stairs, then she tapped me on the shoulder and pointed to a counter where another phone sat. She picked up the receiver and spoke to make sure my mother was still there.

"Yes, Miss Baker, he is here now… Yes." She smiled and handed the phone to me and rubbed my shoulder gently, before heading up the stairs.

I took a fresh breath, then placed the phone to my ear.

"Hey, Mom."

She let go a large gasp. She was crying, and as soon as I heard it, I couldn't help bursting a little myself.

"Oh, Brandon. I… I've been so worried. How are you?"

"I'm good, Mom. Sorry I haven't called you yet. I've been pretty drugged up the last few days. Painkillers."

"Oh, Brandon. You, you're all right though? Helen, she said you're going to be all right. She's such a wonderful lady. We're all so lucky they can be there for you."

"Yeah, they're really great. I don't know what would happen if they weren't here. I'm gonna be fine. Some cracked ribs are the biggest thing. They hurt like hell, but nothing that won't heal, hundred percent."

"Thank God! You… I can't believe what happened. Those awful people who did this. Have you heard anything?"

"No, nothing. I haven't really been paying attention."

"Brandon." I could hear her sorrow grow. "I… I'm so sorry… for, for… I don't know what to…"

"I know… I know, Mom." My small foothold began to crumble. "I… Thank you, but I, I can't talk about it, can we just talk about something else, please?"

"Yes, yes, I'm sorry. So, your father and I were going to fly there and see you, but it hasn't been easy. They have travel to there restricted right now. But I've been looking every day, and there's usually some open seats. There's one leaving there at eleven tonight. It won't get you all the way home, but it'll get you back to Canada. We can get you a flight home as soon as you land."

"I… Mom…" I leaned on the counter and began to massage my forehead. I didn't want to have that fight, not then. "I can't Mom, not yet."

She huffed, and her voice grew tense. "Brandon, son. I really don't want to go through this with you right now. I, I can't believe you're going to fight me on this! You want to know what's happening over there? There are terrorists, Brandon! Running around that city… terrorists! That's who blew up the train station, that's who almost killed you and… and you know! It is time to come home Brandon! Don't you give me that shit attit—"

"I'M NOT LEAVING! NOT YET!" Spit flew from between my lips as I lost it. I squeezed so hard on the receiver, I could feel the whiteness in my knuckles. "I AM NOT LEAVING HERE UNTIL… UNTIL THEY GET THEM OUT! I WILL BE HERE WHEN THEY GET THEM OUT! DO YOU GET IT?" My ribs throbbed with every word, but nothing held me back.

When my screaming ended, I heard a defeated sob on the other end. I hated doing it, but she would never've laid off if I didn't. "I love you Mom. I'm fine, everything's going to be fine. But I can't come home, not now. If you or Dad want to come here, I'll be happy to see you. But I'm not coming home. I love you, tell Dad I love him too. I'm fine, bye." I set the receiver down softly.

I took a breath and stood. Taking a minute to settle down. Through the window, I could see Faas moving around on the deck of the boat.

I turned and took the stairs one at a time. At the top, Helen came from around the counter and held me in her arms. It hurt, but it was a good pain, a very good pain. I did what I could to wrap my arms around her, and I rested my head on her shoulder.

She patted the back of my head, then pushed me back. She placed a finger beneath my chin and turned my head to the side to give my bruise a closer look.

Then she smiled. "He is man, Faas. He is man."

I raised an eyebrow, a little put off by her reaction. "Yeah, he's a man. I got that."

She maintained her smirkiness. "Sometime life need this… man."

I looked back out the window to watch him working away, getting on with it. She was right. "Yeah, I guess you're right. Sometimes we need a Faas." He'd covered all twelve steps of therapy in one encounter… and I'd probably get a bill.

She helped me to a seat and served me some breakfast.

After I ate, I helped her clean up a bit, then let her know I was going for a walk. I hobbled down the stairs to the bedroom. I opened the top drawer of the dresser and found the stuff returned to me from the hospital. I picked up my necklace and wrapped it back around my neck, and then I stood for a second with my eyes closed, massaging the little beads between my fingers. I remembered their happy faces the day they gave it to me. It was a good day, that day.

I reached back into the drawer and grabbed the velvet box. I held it up and thought about opening it, but I decided to take one step at a time.

I shoved the box in my pocket and headed out the door, into the fresh, mid-morning air.

It wasn't raining, but the sky was heavily overcast. I breathed in and pulled my shoulders back, then began my walk across the street and into the main hub. I kept my stride steady and my head down while passing between the orphanage and the disaster zone. The area around the station was crowded with people mourning. I maneuvered my way through the mass, but never looked back.

I was just going. I wasn't sure what I needed to get done, but I couldn't sit around anymore. I'd just have to figure it out as I went.

The streets were bustling, just like any other morning. The majority of the flow was toward the station, people looking on, gasping and pointing. The atmosphere had changed. Once happy and carefree, there was now a wonder of why, or how? As shitty and devastating as it was, I didn't sense fear. There was sadness, but the most prominent feeling was unity, and it was very strong.

I came upon a gathering crowd in front of a café, which had its windows open. People had stopped to watch something happening on a television.

Curious, I tried to catch a glimpse of what had captured their interest. I found a space where heads were parted just enough to view limited portions of the screen. It was a news channel, with cameras focused on the doorway of a building. Eventually, a man, my age maybe, stepped out, looking nervous. He wore a white hat and robe-style clothing, something I would place as Middle Eastern. As he stepped out, he raised his hands and placed them behind his head, then dropped to his knees. At that moment, heavily armed military types raced over and pinned him to the ground.

The crowd erupted into cheers. Everyone turned to each other and celebrated with hugs, handshakes, and applause. I even got drawn in by a nice lady standing beside me with a group of her friends. They all smiled with tears in their eyes, taking turns coming over to hug me and anyone else within arm's reach. I winced with every touch, but I wanted to be there, I wanted to be a part of it… I was part of it. There was power there, and it helped me see that I wasn't the only one whose whole world had changed that day. There were others, many others.

After things died down, I walked the street again and found my next stop. I went inside and purchased the six most beautiful floral bouquets I could find.

When I exited the store, I turned and looked directly at the station. Where it once towered, there was open sky. I took a breath, then walked straight toward it, preparing myself for the confrontation I'd been avoiding.

As I drew closer, the mob grew thicker. I managed my way through, till I stood at its base and I looked upon its mass with sober eyes.

There was a constant low murmur in the congregation, and lone sounds of industrial equipment picking meticulously.

Down the length of the block, laid out before the mess, was a row of pictures, flowers, candles, and personal tokens of remembrance. I felt like an ass. While all those people had been up there every day, paying respect to the ones lost, I'd been down in the boathouse crying over myself. They deserved better than that. They deserved everything everyone else had gotten. Even more.

My tears began to pour again as I walked the line of memorabilia. So many happy faces. Young, old, innocent. I'd known there were many, I'd heard the numbers. But it doesn't sink in till you get there and you see it laid out in front of you. One smiling face after another. People from all over the world. They weren't alone; no one on either side of this thing, living or dead, was in it alone. Only by choice.

I walked with my flowers, feeling kind of stupid for not setting up some kind of shrine. But I wasn't sure I could handle looking at pictures…

With that thought, I came upon a display of pictures set up a little higher than the others. On top of a wooden box, sat a half-dozen framed photos. Every face in them had a very deep, personal place in my heart. The sight of them dropped me to my knees. They were our photos, the ones we'd made together. Someone had made a shrine for them, and I was very thankful for it. Because all these people should know that they were there, too. Just like the rest. Just as precious, just as beautiful.

As I sat there balling my guts out, I felt gentle hands come to me again. My reaction was to let it go even harder. I felt the presence grow thicker, with soothing words of encouragement. After a minute, they began to pull at me softly, urging me back to my feet.

Instantly arms were wrapped around me from every side. Then arms were wrapped around them, and so on, until we had formed a giant circle.

A lady directed the crowd to part enough to open it to their shrine. She leaned down and placed the flowers nicely for me, then she straightened and looked at me, speaking loud enough for all to hear.

"This is you, yes? In the photos? This is you family?"

"Y-yeah," I replied, sobbing.

She nodded, and she radiated a sense of strength and security. She beckoned me with her hand. "Come! Say it! Tell you story! Come!" She nodded.

"I…" I cleared my throat and looked around at all the supporting faces, to all the people holding onto each other. "They were…" Unsure how to start, I pointed to the pictures. "Tatiana. She's from Ukraine. She's blind, she worked there." I pointed across the street. "She lived and worked there, in the orphanage. She was a teacher and, and a mother to the blind children there." I turned my hand back to the pictures. "That's Anna, and Lilly, and Gaby, and the boy is Hans, and their puppy, Sasha, who always looked out for them. I met Tatiana a year ago, and we were together, we were a couple. I was staying at the orphanage with them. They were my family. I used to read *Harry Potter* to them every night."

Smiles and soft laughter came from the crowd.

"That… the day, when the bomb went, I was going to propose to her." I pulled the little velvet box from my pocket and opened it slowly. They all nodded and smiled at me. "We were going to a festival with the children, and I was going to ask her to marry me. I was right here when the explosion happened. I was injured." I held my arms to my ribs, while the lady pointed to the bruise on my face. "I wanted to marry her, and I wanted to adopt the children. We were very happy together."

"Yes, goot." The lady paced with purpose, looking over the crowd. "And you? Where are you from? What is your name? Come, share this wit us."

"I, I'm Brandon. Brandon Baker. I'm from Canada."

"Yes, Brandon." She smiled and clapped her hands together. "Now, you lose you family. We here, we all feel this for you." She walked back over to the box and pointed beside it, to another group of pictures. "You see here. This my husband, and our son and daughter. They were also go to this festival." Tears began to stream down her face, but she never broke.

"They are goot, my husband is a goot man! Strong! And the children, they are very goot. They help wit everyone, always, very smart." She stepped back over to me and placed a hand on my shoulder, looking me in the eyes. "You family is not alone. My family is there also. They togeter, helping each other. And this man, over here," she stepped over to a husky guy in a fleece jacket, and his hand instantly shot to the bridge of his nose as his tears began to flow. "His family, they are there also, togeter." She waved her hand down the long row of mementos. "All these people, is all goot people, and they is all togeter, for each other!" She held a finger up before her and rocked it back and forth like a wiper blade. "No one we love is alone. No one we love there, and all that we love here!" She turned back to me. "They are not alone, Brandon, and you are not alone. We are here, we always be here! No one will take our love! No one will take our heart! No one… no one will break us!"

She held up her hand and the people erupted in cheers. Then they all closed in for another group hug, singing a song of promise.

It managed to give me some comfort. We hugged it out for a while, then everyone parted, and went on with their grievance. I turned back to the shrine, to the pictures of us happy, together. The breeze ruffled the petals on the flowers. I told myself I needed a break, a break from it all, if only for a moment. No booze, no drugs, no sulking.

I said goodbye, looked over the pile of rubble, then headed back to the boathouse.

Somehow, I felt strengthened. My determination renewed. I stepped into my room and placed the velvet box back in the drawer, then went out to the main room, grabbed my gear, and headed out.

I wasn't sure exactly where I was going, I only knew west. So west it was. Some people I stopped and asked pointed me in a direction. Bus, tram, foot, bit by bit I made my way. People looked at me with curiosity, and I was sure I didn't care.

Toward the later part of the afternoon, I found what I was looking for. The white sand beach stretched as far as I could see in either direction. The wind blowing in off the Atlantic was stiff and cold. Several people were out already.

I didn't have a wetsuit. My kite sported a few holes, and no doctor would ever give me the green light in my current state. But I remembered that long-ago feeling. That one thing that could take me away from everything, complete, if only for a short time.

Every move was painful as I laid out the kite, hooked up the pump, and started inflating. Nothing was in prime condition, including myself, so the process took longer than the norm. Set up, I stripped down to my shorts, launched the kite, then picked up my board and stepped into the frigid water.

Some looks were shot in my direction, as if I was fucking crazy. And for that time, I absolutely was. It'd been a long time. I wondered if it was like riding a bike.

I threw the board down in the shallows, stepped in, dove the kite, and took off from the beach. Struggling to find that point where I could manage the pain. The wind was a little too much for the size of the kite, and the cold spray had a vicious bite . I leaned back and felt the pull, the power. I'll admit, what I was doing was dangerous as fuck. But I'd found it. That mindless place, weaving and cutting through the chop. That feeling that all things bad had no choice but to let me go till I returned. People on shore, no doubt, wondered if I would ever make it back.

But I knew I'd be back. No matter where we were, no matter what side of that fence we were on, we were together. All of us, and I would return for them.

I sheeted in and felt the cold and pain rip through my body as the wind beckoned me to come, run with it. It hurt like shit, and it was going to, for a long time. But there was nowhere to run. I had no idea what would happen in my tomorrow. Maybe I'd make it to the next sunrise, or maybe I'd pull the trigger on my misery. But right then, there was only that day, that time.

The wind pulled harder, I leaned farther. I sunk into a rhythm and unleashed a primal scream as I raced out to sea.

So…was it all for a reason?

A beautiful young lady I once knew, would swear to it.

END

www.ingramcontent.com/pod-product-compliance
Lightning Source LLC
Chambersburg PA
CBHW061345190726
48288CB00005B/1606